The fun never ends

"The house of mirrors?" I hissed, pointing the gyrapistol into the dim hole.

"He likes to hang out in here," Rasputin whispered. "He's waiting. Waiting for *you*."

I reworked my sweaty grip on the pistol. "All right, I'm right behind you," I said, grabbing his shoulder and shoving him into the Clown's maw.

"Listen!" Rasputin said. "Did you hear that? *Giggling.* He's laughing at us. He'll rip out our throats and we'll all die like dogs!"

A small rustle of noise came from behind me. I froze in place and held my breath. Slowly, quietly, the small patter of movement came closer and closer. It could have been anything, I thought, a curious rat, a stray cat...or maybe even a serial killer.

I spun around wildly and fired, shouting gibberish designed to freeze Cain in his tracks. In the light of the muzzle flash I saw a blurred vision of the devil himself, staring out of the abyss, surrounded by a halo of blackness, looking me straight in the eye.

Also available in this series:

AVENGING ANGEL
THE DEVIL KNOCKS
DAY OF JUDGMENT

JAKE STRAIT

BOGEYMAN

TWIST OF CAIN

FRANK RICH

A GOLD EAGLE BOOK FROM
WORLDWIDE®

TORONTO • NEW YORK • LONDON
AMSTERDAM • PARIS • SYDNEY • HAMBURG
STOCKHOLM • ATHENS • TOKYO • MILAN
MADRID • WARSAW • BUDAPEST • AUCKLAND

First edition February 1994

ISBN 0-373-63610-5

TWIST OF CAIN

TWIST OF CAIN

1

"Help me!" the man screamed, lurching down the subway platform, his face a bloody mask from a gash on his forehead. "They took my wallet! They have my wife! Somebody help me!"

The crowd of commuters on the platform kept silent, recoiling when the bleeding tourist pawed at their clothing. They looked away or right through him, mouths clenched tight, their hostile indifference wound around them like prickly armor. The bleeding man caught sight of a group of armed militiamen and lurched toward them.

"Are you SPF troopers?" he cried.

They enjoyed a cruel laugh. "There ain't a spif within a kilometer of here, you stupid burb," the bearded leader said.

"Will you help me? There are four of them. They have my wife. Hurry!"

"How much you gonna pay us?"

"I can't pay you! They took my wallet."

"Then why should we risk our necks for you?" The leader raised his assault rifle menacingly, and the tourist drew back.

To hell with this, I thought, stepping out of the crowd. From the hatred I immediately sensed around me, I knew I might as well have shouted them all down as cowards.

"Show me where they're at," I told the bleeding man.

He blinked at me as hope rose anew in his eyes. "Oh, thank God!" he cried, seizing my arm and pointing down the platform. "They're down there. Are you a plain-clothes trooper?"

"No, I'm a private enforcer."

He let go of my arm and flinched back. "Bogey-man?" he shrieked, eyes brimming with fresh horror. *"Bogeyman?"*

"It's all right," I said, reaching for his arm. "Just come with me and ID your assailants."

"Don't touch me!" he wailed, scuttling away.

I started down the platform in the direction he'd pointed. Low talk from the militiamen followed me, but I already knew they didn't have the guts for a lynching. I passed the hulk of a long-abandoned newsstand and moved onto a dim and deserted stretch of platform. A woman's scream was answered by male laughter, and I started to run, drawing my gyrapistol.

They had her pinned against the concrete wall—four young Russians with spiked neon red hair, flotsam from the endless waves of Slavic refugees who had swept across North America since the beginning of the twenty-first century. Two held the woman's wrists, one held a flick-blade to her chest, and one merely watched, arms folded, his chubby face twisted into a lecherous grin. The woman's shredded blouse lay on the floor, and the man with the blade sawed at the front of her bra, giggling.

"Stop that," I said, coming up behind them.

They froze. The Russian with the blade turned around to stare at the gyrapistol. I immediately took in the small black skull tattoo on the side of his neck, the mark of an endliner, a death-loving nihilist.

"You know her, *chaka?*" he asked.

"Never seen her before."

"I knew that burgher was holding out. How much did he pay you?"

"He didn't pay me anything."

"Oh, I understand," he said, his frown spreading into a crude grin. "You want in." His pale blue eyes flashed to the woman. "A piece of this burgh pie."

I glanced at the woman. Her eyes were crazy with fear, her neck muscles taut as steel cables. "Naw," I said, "she's not my type."

"What the fuck do you want, then? Are you some kind of nut?"

"Maybe I'm a Good Samaritan."

"Of course!" he howled. "Exactly my luck. Probably the last Good Samaritan the whole fucking City, and he has to crush *our* groove."

"I'm not a Good Samaritan," I said.

"Then what the..." he said, then it clicked. "Hold on now, handchopper," he said, holding up his hands. "We're not free-lancing here. We've a Pleasure Syndicate charter to work this tube. Full rights—robbery, assaults, rape, the whole bit. Even a murder clause if they resist." He dropped the flickblade to distract me as he reached into his jacket. "Here, let me show you our charter."

I shoved the gyrapistol against his chest and pulled the trigger. A gyrajet punctured his rib cage and exploded, rupturing his heart. He staggered into one of his comrades, who lunged at me with a short steel-tipped whip. The first jet stopped him dead in his tracks, the second slammed him against the platform wall, the third sent him to hell. I turned the pistol to the Russian still holding the woman. He jerked her in front of him, gleaming razor at her throat.

"Shoot, and I'll open her up!" he snarled over her shoulder.

"Faster than a speeding gyrajet?" I asked doubtfully, aiming at his exposed right eye. "Are you sure, Superman?"

The eye went out of focus then completely blank. A giggle deep in his throat grew into insane laughter. "Life, death," he whispered, "I wouldn't know the difference."

The razor wavered, and I touched the trigger. A gyrajet whooshed into his eye, blowing his brains out the back of his skull. The Russian and the woman collapsed in a heap as I turned the pistol to the last Russian, the chubby voyeur. His arms were no longer folded; both hands were busy in the pockets of his greatcoat. He stared at the pistol and stopped digging.

"I was just watching," he said.

"Apathy is the henchman of malice," I countered.

"What?"

"How fast can you reach the stairs?"

He looked slowly over his shoulder at the concrete steps thirty meters down the platform. "I don't know."

"Take a guess."

"I don't know, fifteen seconds."

"You're underestimating yourself. I think you can make it in ten."

"I don't think so."

"What if your life depended on it?"

He eyed me. "Does it?"

"One," I said.

He tried on a smile. "Hold on now. Let's—"

"Two."

"Cheater!" he cried. "I'm not ready yet!"

"Three."

He spun around and broke into a wild sprint down the dim platform, screaming as he went.

"Six!" I called after him.

He nearly slipped in a puddle of water but caught himself, pumping his arms comically high.

"Eight!"

He skidded to a stop in front of the stairs, glancing back at me.

"Ten!" I yelled, and he cleared the steps in two great bounds.

The woman wailed and sprang up like a deranged jack-in-the-box, thrashing out of the grasp of the dead Russian. She threw her arms around my neck, smearing my face with blood and gore.

"Thank the Lord," she sobbed, shoving her breasts into my chest. "Oh, thank you!"

"It's all right," I said, uncomfortable with the intimacy of the embrace. I patted her back awkwardly, and she hooked her ankles around my calves, grinding her pelvis against mine.

"Take your reward!" she moaned. "Take it now, you great valiant beast!"

"No, really, it's all right," I croaked, trying to break the stranglehold. "A heartfelt thanks will do!"

"Margaret!"

Marge and I both turned to face her husband, crouched three meters away. Marge sighed with disappointment and dropped to her feet. I holstered the gyrapistol and picked up her blouse. I handed it to her, and she more or less put it back on.

"I was only thanking him, Howie," Marge said. "It was the least I could do."

Howie dashed forward and grabbed her arm. "Let's go!" he hissed.

"Hold on a goddamn minute," she said angrily, holding her ground. "At least tell the nice man thank you."

"He's not a nice man," Howie snarled, "he's a *bogeyman.*"

"Oh, Lord!" Marge shrieked, backing away. "Manhandled by a handchopper!" With a final wail of despair, they stumbled away, leaving me alone with the dead.

I took a palm-sized handscanner out of my jacket and passed the humming machine over the right hand of each corpse. The scanner read the embedded microchips, cross-referenced their IDs with the files stored in its memory, then told me their tragic stories in a squeaky voice. Two of the men had Party death warrants for criminal offenses. The would-be Superman only had an apprehension warrant for political crimes, but that's what he got for running with a bad crowd. I traded the scanner for a miniature power saw and went to work.

Minutes later I was back among the commuters, two small plastic bags dangling in my left hand. The commuters gave me plenty of room, and I could feel their eyes watching me, hear the dry rustle of their mean whispers. The air became thick with them, making it hard to breathe properly. An ugly, brooding moment passed, and the train did not arrive. I crept upstairs to the street and caught a cab.

2

The cab dropped me off at SPF Central, the last inner-city bastion of World Party's law-enforcement arm, the Security and Protection Force, or SPF. My private-enforcer license earned me ugly looks and passage through the heavy security and I walked the halls to the bounty-reward office. I passed the bagged hands to the clerk manning the aluminum counter, and he placed them under an industrial-sized scanner.

"So tell me, bogeyman," he said, tapping at a keyboard, "what's it like not having a soul?"

"It means not having to waste any time at church," I said. "Inspector Degas around?"

The clerk glanced up from the monitor he was staring at. "He don't wanna talk to you."

"I don't wanna talk to him. I wanna take a swing at him."

"He ain't around," he said. He finished typing, a drawer popped open, and he counted out a small pile of credits on the counter. "Two C-4 death warrants equals four hundred and twenty-three creds."

I stared at the plastic squares. "Is that it?"

"What else you want?"

"How about a slap on the back and a hearty 'atta-boy'?"

"How about you taking your plastic and beatin' it?"

"Gee," I said, stuffing the plastic into my nearly empty wallet, "I kill another five thousand like those two and I'll be a goddamn millionaire."

"It's something to shoot for."

"You dirty bastard," I sneered, and left.

It was much too early in the afternoon for a civilized man to drink in a bar, so I had the cabbie drop me off in front of a liquor store a block from my office. I picked up a liter of vitamin-fortified rum and started for my office.

"I got somethin' better than that, Jones," a slim, bushy-haired mop of a man said, falling in step beside me. "Shit that'll take you hunnerd times higher than juice. And you won't have no hangover in the morning, neither."

"But that's what I like about it," I said. "That certain balance, the give and take, the pleasure and penance."

"Shit, I don't see no reason for no penance. Why there gotta be bad times?"

"Because a man who hasn't lain in the gutter cannot appreciate the mountaintop," I said sagely, cutting into the lobby of my office building. I waved to the junkies and winos sprawled on the sagging furniture and bypassed the elevator for the stairs, taking them two at a time.

Two flights and a short hall put me in my office. There was a water glass on my desk, which I loaded with rum. I took a good, hard hit, the liquor burning a path to my belly like mean medicine. I walked the glass to the bay window and looked down at Hayward Avenue, an ambitious contender for the most decadent and criminal street in the civilized world. It also happened to be the source of most of my income.

There's really no reason to get drunk at all, I thought, swallowing rum. Those Russian bastards had it coming in a big way. They were all endliners, just waiting to die. Hell, I probably did them a favor. My real worry was whether the Pleasure Syndicate would want to talk to me about it.

I picked out a single ripple of human meanness in the river of iniquity below. Five hooligans in gang colors harried a squat bag lady, tipping over her shopping cart and kicking her possessions into the street. Whores, pimps and hustlers took time out from their daily hustle to watch, mildly amused. The bag lady barked at her tormentors, stooping to gather the treasured trash they kicked out of her hands. She could be somebody's mother, I thought.

My office door banged open, and six hundred pounds of muscle squeezed into two expensive suits took up station at either corner of my desk. A large silver-haired man followed in their wake. He wore his tweed suit like a uniform and his mustache like a walrus. He came to a brusque halt before my desk, jabbed the floor with his wolfs-head cane and menaced me with a monocle-enhanced squint. A foppish boy just out of his teens brought up the rear, closing the door behind them. Unless the Pleasure Syndicate had recently taken on extreme airs, I appeared to have a client.

"I'm Sir Henry Bowlan," the man in the tweed suit said. "Commandant of the Hillsdale Defense Society." He jerked a thumb back to the young man. "This is Christopher Pennings, son of Hiram Pennings and sole heir to the Pennings fortune."

"And I'm Prince Jacob of Hayward," I announced regally from the window, not to be outdone. "Slayer of subway thugs and sole renter of all you see."

Sir Henry looked down his nose for a moment, then stabbed an accusing finger at me. "You've heard of a serial killer called Cain, *haven't you,* Mr. Strait?"

I turned back to the window. Not content with scattering her things, the fun-loving gang was now shoving the old woman between them. "Isn't he the masked mutilator working Riverside?" I asked.

"No, that is the Iceman."

"That's right," I said. "You must mean the caped sniper with the big fan club."

Bowlan frowned. "That, Mr. Strait, is the Rooftop Sniper."

"Don't tell me," I said, turning to hold up a hand. I thought for a moment, then snapped my fingers. "I got it. Cain's that rather rude chap butchering millionaires on the Hill."

Bowlan nodded curtly. "I would have hoped a man of your profession wouldn't need three guesses."

"Well, you know how these tabloid killers are, Mr. Bowlan. They come and go like teenage pop stars." I looked out the window to find the old woman laid out on the sidewalk and the hooligans putting the boot in.

"Right, then," Bowlan said. "We would—"

"Excuse me," I said. I crossed the room to the file cabinet and picked up the speed rifle leaning behind it, making the muscle men flinch. I went back to the window, threw it open and, aiming carefully, squeezed off an 8-round burst.

The high-velocity bullets ripped over the heads of the gang, thunking into the wall of St. Christopher's Lounge. They stopped kicking the bag lady and ducked, peering around wildly. After a moment they spotted me pointing the speed rifle at them.

"What's the freaking idea?" the apparent leader of the five yelled up.

"Leave her alone," I shouted back, "or I'll send the lot of you to the protein vats."

They eyed each other for a moment, polling their group courage. They seemed to fall a few points short of suicidal defiance.

"She's just a bag lady, for crissakes," the leader complained.

"Watch it," I warned, "that's my *mother* you're talking about."

They stared down at the bag lady, suddenly embarrassed.

"Christ," the leader said morosely. "We didn't know she was nobody's *mother*. Why'nt you take better care of her, for crissakes?"

"Just move along," I said. They took another poll, then shuffled off down the sidewalk, shoulders hunched, muttering to themselves.

The bag lady got up, stared after them, then squinted up at me.

"How's it going, Mom?" I called down.

"Who are you?" she barked.

"It's me, Mammy! Your long-lost sonny-boy!"

"You're not my son!"

"Good God! You mean I'm adopted?"

"You're no son of mine, period!"

"You don't love me anymore?"

"I never loved you!"

"How grim," I sighed, closing the window. I leaned the rifle against the wall and sat behind my desk. Bowlan crouched in front, his startled eyes peering over the top of the desktop computer. The kid lingered near the door as if nothing had happened, and the muscle boys were in their attack position, knees bent, hands inside their coats, eyes crazy with blood lust.

I smiled at Bowlan. "Cain, you say?"

Bowlan continued to stare.

"I thought I saw a guy who owed me money," I explained.

He rose out of his crouch with the eyes of a man who, despite his best judgment, was about to jump into a pit knee-deep with hissing vipers. He cocked his head back, reset his shoulders and forged ahead courageously. "We would like him dead!" he blurted.

"Me, too, but then I'd never get my money."

"No! We want *Cain* dead."

"So would a lot of other people."

"Yes, but we're prepared to pay you to kill him."

"How much?"

"Five hundred per day and a fifty-thousand-credit bonus if you bag the bugger. How does that sound?"

"Sounds like I'm on the case. Have a seat, and we'll talk it over."

Bowlan looked around, took in the plaid sofa next to the door, searched the room for something more dignified, found none, made an indignant harrumph sound, marched to the sofa and sat down efficiently. He rested his hands on the silver head of the cane and gave me a good view of the underside of his chin. The two muscle boys backed up and took positions on either side of him. The kid continued to fidget near the door, glancing incessantly at his chrono, jumpy with the suspicion that, even as he stood there, life was passing him by.

"What's Hiram Pennings's personal interest in Cain?" I asked.

Bowlan lowered his eyelids a little, suggesting he wanted to be coy. "What makes you think Mr. Pennings has a personal interest in Cain?"

I cupped a hand to my mouth and whispered, "That's his son standing over there by the door."

Bowlan glanced at the boy without moving his head. "That doesn't mean Mr. Pennings is in any way involved. And if he was, what makes you think his motives are personal?"

"I've heard about Mr. Pennings," I said. "He doesn't strike me as the Good Samaritan type."

He made that harrumphing sound again and restiffened his spine. "Cain killed a lady friend of Mr. Pennings."

"As opposed to his wife?"

"Yes."

"I see."

"It's not what you think."

"It doesn't matter what I think. My employer's infidelity doesn't interest me. What interests me is my retainer."

"Retainer? Are you questioning Mr. Pennings's integrity?"

I shrugged. "I've worked for millionaires before. Some think they're so rich and important they don't have to bother paying anyone."

He made that sound again then lifted a checkbook from his coat.

"I'd prefer plastic," I said. "A week's worth."

He dead-eyed me, replaced the checkbook and came out with a fat satchel like a paymaster's pouch. He carefully laid out thirty-five hundred-cred squares in two rows, bridging them with a business card. I was polite enough to read the card before scooping up the plastic.

Beneath Bowlan's name and position was a phone number. Below the number was a regal crest depicting a mean-eyed unicorn and snarling lion at odds over some manner of hideous flower. I transferred card and credit to my pocket. Now that I had his money, I felt I could ask some stupid questions.

"Why are you hiring *me?*" I asked, my self-esteem as secure as the wad of credits in my pocket. "I thought the SPF was hot after Cain."

"That is thoroughly correct, but it so happens Mr. Pennings believes in the old adage that it takes a killer to find a killer. He feels you bogeymen lack, shall we say, the constraint of morality that hinders civilized men in such grisly business."

"I *am* house-trained," I said. "He knows that, doesn't he?"

Bowlan eyed me for a moment. "I believe Mr. Pennings is less interested in your sanitary achievements than your knowledge of the inner city. We have reason to believe Cain hails from the ghetto, an area in which the SPF has little presence."

"What makes you think Cain hails from the ghetto?"

"Why, because he kills rich people."

"So what? It's not unusual to prey upon your own class. The poor do it all the time."

"That's not what Mr. Pennings believes."

"Are you the security chief of Hillsdale or Mr. Pennings?"

He harrumphed, and I thought his monocle was going to pop out. Before he could work himself into an indignant rage, Christopher Pennings spoke up.

"It's the same thing. My father practically owns the Hill."

"Christopher!" Bowlan exclaimed.

"Well, it's true."

I nodded, then addressed Bowlan. "What information do you have about Cain?"

"No more than the SPF does at this point, I'm afraid. Although I have some of my own people working on the City side of it. You can get the details through your SPF contacts."

"What makes you think I have SPF contacts?"

"I thought you all did."

"You've watched too many old movies. Private enforcers and spifs don't pal around like the PIs and cops of yesteryear. Hell, we don't even wear snap-brim fedoras anymore."

His eyes flickered to the bottle on my desk. "I see you've kept some traditions alive."

"I'm not completely unsentimental."

He harrumphed, pushed himself up with the cane and came out with another card. "Here's the number of the SPF man heading the investigation."

I took the card. "Inspector Truman Degas," I read aloud.

"Yes," Bowlan said. "I'll have him put at your disposal."

"He'll love you for that."

"Oh? Have you and the inspector worked together before?"

"You might say that."

"Good. We'll be on our way, then." He came forward to shake my hand. "Good hunting, as they say."

"Tallyho," I replied.

They exited and I went to the window. A minute later the two heavies appeared on the sidewalk, both barking into wristcoms. An armored limo screeched up to the curb, and two more thick suits jumped out, hands in jackets, making a good effort at scowling in every direction at once. One of them waved, and Bowlan barreled out, running the gauntlet between the four guards and disappearing into the limo. Christopher followed at a slower pace, appearing almost embarrassed. The heavies jumped in after them, and the limo roared away.

I remained at the window to watch the creatures below stream down the street and sidewalks, an army on the march, dull eyed and numb from the journey, like ants frantically searching out crumbs and enemies. Somewhere in the anarchy and chaos was Cain, invisible and protected.

Yet as chaotic as the street appeared, I knew there was a grim subcurrent of order, a rushing underground river of information accessible only to those who knew how to tap it. I knew the street. That's why they came to me. The street would tell me more about Cain than all the SPF contacts in the world.

I opened the window, put my hands on the sill and leaned into the brisk spring air.

"Hey, buddy!" I yelled at a passerby.

A young guido suited in neon baggies looked up. "You talkin' to me?"

"Yeah. You seen Cain around?"

"Fuck off, ya drunk," he shouted, and continued down the sidewalk.

I shut the window and wrestled mightily with the notion of going straight across the street to St. Christopher's Lounge and digging for clues there. Hell, Cain could be over there right now, knocking back Mai-Tais and bragging to the whores. But how would I recognize him? How did serial killers dress? What were their habits, the quirks that made them stand out in a city crowded with criminals?

"Computer on," I said, sitting down at the desk. The monitor flashed to life, and I said, "Encyclopedia." The encyclopedia menu popped onto the screen. "Look up serial killer," I told it.

The computer told me that serial killers were repeat murderers whose motives were often psychological, with strong sado-sexual overtones and evidence of impulsive behavior.

A long, general article followed, which I skimmed through, getting a feel for the animal. The archetypal serial killer was a lower-income white male of above-average intelligence. A loner who thought he was doing society a favor, eliminating those he considered evil or without human value. He had a history of cruelty to animals, fire starting and bed-wetting, and was probably a victim of child abuse. He often took a piece of his victims with him as a form of trophy or souvenir and sometimes practiced cannibalism. Psychologically speaking, most recreational killers were amoral sociopaths, incapable of rehabilitation after they tasted first blood. After capture and conviction, few displayed true remorse, unable to see the wrongness of their grisly deeds.

"News file search," I said. "A serial killer named Cain." I spelled it out and told it to start with the most recent article.

While the *Hillsdale Journal* and the suburban rags had nothing nice to say about Cain, the City's underground dailies splashed his slayings across their front pages like the exploits of a local boy done good. Cain Nails Another Hiller! the *Riverside Rebel* said of the latest mutilation-murder. Cain Sticks It To Them Again, exclaimed the *Barridales Vindicator,* topped only by the *Colfax Outcry's* Idiot Investigators Baffled By Daring Mutilator!

With the SPF keeping a tight lid on the investigation, the papers had to rely on lifelike drawings instead of photos, each depicting Cain's work in glorious detail, based solely upon eyewitness accounts provided by "reliable and confidential sources." What they lacked in hard facts they more than made up for in gushing enthusiasm. Each rumored stab, slash and gouge was described in such lush prose I suspected they'd turned the story over to their gourmet-foods editor instead of the crime beat.

The yellow press not only shared Bowlan's conviction that Cain hailed from the ghetto, they revelled in the notion. Glowing editorials equated Cain to the ever-elusive poor man's redemption, a latter-day Robin Hood, the frustrated common man driven over the edge by ruthless oppression.

I went back to the main news file menu and indexed all the serial killings in the City for the past year. If Cain was as fine a killer as the papers claimed, I figured he might have warmed up in the City before moving his act to the Hill.

Since Cain's meteoric rise, the City's vast roster of serial killers had been quietly exiled to the back pages to compete with the obituaries and classifieds. From the coarse Beast of Barridales to the flashy Rooftop Sniper, I read through graphic descriptions of their work, looking for similarities to Cain's style. Among the many snipers, snippers, hammer fiends and stranglers were an elite inner corps of mutilators. The closest match to Cain was also the most prolific, the Iceman, a hack-and-slash man working Riverside. He got his name from the ice pick he used to disable his prey before going to work on them with a razor. He remained a local favorite; the *Riverside Rebel* reported an enterprising Riverside council member had the idea of placing a holo-plaque at the sight of every Iceman slaying, a direct appeal to the suburban tourist's morbid fascination with graphic violence.

A comparison of dates however, revealed the Iceman was busy killing an elderly couple in Riverside at roughly the same time Cain was cutting up his first victim.

I cleared the screen and used my private-enforcer code to access ART, the SPF's monstrous crime computer. I went to its warrant file, the SPF's vast roster of all the wanted criminals in the City, the wellspring of fiends I selected targets from when I wasn't killing for a client. I spelled out Cain's name, and the monitor blinked to a nearly blank screen. No rotating 3-D picture, no sound bite, no name, no known haunts, no wealth of personal data. Just the tag Cain, brief mention of his two victims, and the death warrant and bounty code. The code was the highest possible, an $A-1$ with a triple bonus modifier, equating about twenty thousand credits. There were those in the warrant file with five times more kills than Cain and lucky to have a C-1 rating. Which proved the old adage, it's not how many you kill, it's *whom* you kill, at least as far as the SPF was concerned.

An idea struck me. I went back to the news file and called up the morning's edition of the *Rebel*. I scrolled to the ad section to find a dozen Cain fan clubs had sprouted in the personals like gore-loving toadstools. From the patriotic Sons of Cain to the generic Cain Support Committee to the forthright Butcher the Bourgeois Bastards, claims of support rang out from every segment of the City's vast political spectrum.

"Commo mode," I told the computer, then read the number of the Cain Support Committee. "No outgoing image," I added.

A snappy logo of crossed knives under a ski mask popped on the screen. "Cain Support Committee," an earnest voice chirped.

"I want to join your club," I said.

"Pardon me, but I'm not getting a picture."

"I can't afford a comcam," I snarled defensively. "Is my physical appearance requisite to donating credit to your organization?"

"No, sir, not at all. Just how much of a donation did you have in mind?"

"I don't know, maybe a hundred creds."

"Fine, sir. A hundred-credit donation gets you an official Cain Support Committee ID card, an I'm Insane About Cain four-color T-shirt and bumper sticker and a one-year subscription to our monthly newsletter, *Friends of Cain*. Now, what is your Party Bank account number? Do you have a handscanner attached to your com?"

"Not so fast, chum. Does any of my donation actually go to Cain?"

"Well, not directly. Cain's greatest weapon, after all, is his anonymity, and we must protect that at all costs."

"How do you plan to support him if you don't know who he is?"

"Moral support, through ads and our Friends of Cain Cosupport Group meetings. Believe me," he added smugly, "Cain knows of our work and applauds us daily. What did you say your account number was?"

I tapped the disconnect button, then buzzed the Cain-Sappho Connection.

This time the screen stayed blank. "What do you want?" a female voice snapped.

"Tell me about your organization," I said.

"Why should I?"

"I want to give you plastic."

"How much?"

"A whole bunch."

"How much is that?"

"How does five grand sound?"

"We're an activist cell dedicated to aiding and abetting Cain in her attack on the entrenched male bourgeois establishment. And if you don't like it, you can stuff it."

"*Her* attack?"

"That's right."

"You think Cain is a woman?"

"We happen to know that Cain is in fact an upright woman of color, probably a lesbian."

"How do you figure?"

"Well, it's obvious, isn't it? Consider her choice of victims, the way in which the symbolic nature of her mutilations cry out against oppressive white male clitism."

"Wasn't Cain's last victim a woman?"

"A traitor who sold out to the he-pigs! The lapdog quislings will be cut down with their fascist masters! They'll drown in pools of their own blood!"

"Why does she call herself *Cain,* then? Why a male name?"

She laughed at my obviously hopeless ignorance. "*Of course* she chose a male name! Can't you understand her sly feminine irony? Oh, but of course you don't. You're a *male.*"

"I can't help it."

"That's *your* problem."

"One more question."

"What?"

"Didn't we go on a blind date once?"

The line went dead, and I rung up the next club on the list.

"Sons of Cain," a well-groomed young man said. He reached out and adjusted his monitor. "I'm sorry, but I'm not getting an image."

"Of course not," I snapped. "Do you think I want the whole world to know who I am? My anonymity is my greatest weapon. I mean, just whose side are you on?"

"I don't know," he said carefully. "Whose side are *you* on?"

"*My* side, that's whose. How much money have you raised so far?"

He smiled tolerantly. "That is a private matter, sir."

"Forget it, then. When can I pick it up?"

"Pick what up?"

"My goddamn money."

"*Your* money, sir? May I ask who you pretend to be?"

"A trifle slow, aren't you? I'm Cain, for crissakes, the goddamn ghetto avenger. The dashing and daring mutilator. You've been using my name to pad your pockets, and now I want my goddamn cut."

He folded his hands and gave me a smile that said, *you're an even bigger cretin than I imagined.* "I'm sorry, sir, but to receive any support from the Sons of Cain, you'll have to prove beyond a reasonable doubt that you are in fact the perpetrator called Cain, responsible—"

"All right, all right," I interrupted. "What's the criteria?"

"Well, you'd have to present, in person, conclusive evidence to a panel of experts of our choosing that you are in fact—"

"Why don't I just turn myself in to the SPF? Wouldn't that be easier for everyone?"

"It just so happens that, if the unfortunate happenstance of Cain's capture comes to pass, we are setting up a legal-defense fund to rent an excellent defense computer for his trial."

"Trial? You really think I'd make it to trial? They'd shoot me on sight, then turn my corpse over to a rabid mob of burbanites. You're not really interested in helping me, are you?"

"Sir, you must understand that since we began soliciting contributions we have received over three hundred calls from individuals purporting to be Cain."

"And none have passed the criteria of proof?"

"No, they certainly have not."

"Could you call me when one does?"

"Certainly not."

"Swell," I said, and disconnected. I continued down the list, getting much the same line: everyone was willing to adopt Cain to their cause but no one knew a thing about him beyond the fact he dissected rich people. It wasn't until my last call that I hit pay dirt.

"Butcher the Bourgeois Bastards!" a middle-aged man howled, his long hair and beard as wild as his wide-set eyes. "How much you gonna give us?"

"Plenty," I said. "But only if the money goes directly to Cain."

"Zing-a-ding-ding!" he shouted, and went into his Rasputin routine, hopping up and down, shaking his fists and bulging his eyes. "You can join our Cain murder marathon! Every time our man Cain executes a Hiller, you pay us the amount of your pledge!"

"*Your* man Cain?"

"Right," he said, then gazed around to make sure no one was sneaking up on him. "The lovely bastard works for us. He's on the payroll. And baby, his salary is high, high, high! So you gotta gimme, gimme, gimme!''

"Hot damn," I said, getting worked up. "I want to give you *all* my plastic."

"Click, click and *click!* Man, I click that! Grab a pen! Send the cash to Box 34—"

"No," I interrupted. "I don't trust the mail. I want to give it to you in person."

He blinked at me. "How much were you going to pledge?"

"Fifty thousand credits."

"Fifty thou—" He leaned toward the screen. "Honestly?"

"Honest to God. I have it right here in a big fat satchel. You see, I'm a very rich man. But I'm not bourgeois, mind you."

"No! Of course not! I knew that from the start!"

"Good. Tell me your address, and I'll bring the cash right over."

"Can't tell you that. Top secret." He rubbed his beard. "We'll have to meet somewhere. There's an empty lot on the corner of Marshall and Ball, do you know it?"

"I can find it."

"Good. It's one after three. Let's meet there at four."

"Super. See you then."

"Hold on. How will I recognize you?"

"I'll have a big fat satchel of cash in my left hand."

"Right. Good. See you there! And don't forget the cash."

3

I arrived forty minutes early and parked in front of Mockingbird Manor, a three-story plastiboard-and-concrete apartment building next to the empty lot. I sank low in the seat and waited.

A primer gray van parked across the street from the lot twenty minutes later. Rasputin and a gangly man with a guitar case got out and spoke briefly on the sidewalk. Rasputin pointed at the roof of Mockingbird Manor, and the gangly man nodded and started across the street. Rasputin got back in the van.

I took a lead-pellet sap from the glove box and palmed it. I waited until the gangly man had disappeared into the lobby of the Mockingbird, then slipped out of the Olds and followed him in. I stayed a flight behind him on the stairs, then hurried to catch up when he came out on the roof.

"You gonna play that thing?" I asked affably.

He spun around in the gravel, hugging the guitar case to his chest. "What? What do you want?"

"I live downstairs," I explained. "I saw the guitar case and, being a musician myself, I was wondering if you wanted to have a rooftop jam session."

"No, no," he said, glancing around the empty roof. "I don't need any jam sessions."

"Oh, come on," I said, moving closer. "At least let me hear you play. I'll accompany you."

He stared at me a moment, then smiled meanly. "Okay. You wanna hear me play? A little jam session? Okay. I'll play for you." He put his back to me and laid the case down. "I'll play for you, all right."

"This is great," I said. "Guess what I play?"

"What?" he asked, opening and reaching inside the case.

"The gong," I said, gonging the back of his skull with the sap. He dropped the rifle in his hands and collapsed atop the guitar case, out cold.

I pocketed the sap and picked up the rifle. It was a 7.62 mm Mitsubishi rotor rifle with videoscope and suppressor attachment, a professional's choice of weaponry. I walked it to the edge of the parapet overlooking the vacant lot and peeked down. Rasputin was out of the van and crossing the street. He looked up, spotted me and gave a little wave. I waved back, then backed away from the parapet. On the way to the stairs I leaned the rifle against a steel vent pipe and broke it in half with the heel of my boot, spilling small parts and bullets from the rotor. I left it there and started down the stairs.

I exited the Mockingbird to find Rasputin standing in the center of the lot, facing the street. I came up on his right flank, crossing the lot with my head down, as if I were a local taking a shortcut. He heard me coming, glanced down at my left hand, then resumed his vigil of the street.

When I stopped beside him, he said, "Where's it at?"

I jabbed the gyrapistol into his ribs. "Right here."

"I don't have any money, brother," he said, shooting a meaningful look at the rooftop of the Mockingbird.

"I need a ride," I said. "Who are you waving at?"

"No one," he said, dropping his frantic hand to scratch at his head.

"C'mon," I said, "we'll take your van."

He spent most of the walk to the van glaring over his shoulder at the Mockingbird. I guided him to the passenger door and patted him down, finding a small Killtech .380 automatic in the pocket of his overcoat. I put it in my pocket, and he unlocked the door. I shoved him inside, pushing him into the driver's seat. I took the passenger seat, resting the gyrapistol on my thigh.

"Where we going?" he groaned.

"Cain's house," I said.

He goggled at me. "Cain? You set me up!"

"Naw. I just want to hand over the cash to him personally." I gestured significantly with the gyrapistol. "You know, eliminate the middleman."

"I knew it," he whined. "Never trust a man with fifty grand."

"I don't really have fifty grand."

"You poor bastards are even worse."

"We sure are. Now get going."

"You can't trust anyone these days," he said, starting the engine. He wheeled onto the street, shaking his fist and cursing the Mockingbird as we passed. "No one!"

We drove in circles for the next fifteen minutes. "You're driving in circles," I said.

"I'm lost," he said, sweating badly. "I don't know where we are."

"What's Cain's address?"

"I don't know."

"You said he was on your payroll."

"He is."

"How does he collect his excellent salary?"

"We mail it to his secret P.O. box."

"Who is Cain?"

"Don't know. He keeps his identity secret."

"All right, pull over."

"You're going to let me go?"

"No, I just don't want the van to crash when I shoot you."

"No!" he moaned. "I'll take you to one of his hideouts, okay?"

"Swell," I said.

He drove as if he were driving to his own execution, and twenty minutes later we reached the desolate southern end of Hayward. He parked in front of a long-abandoned amusement park surrounded by a three-meter chain-link fence.

"This is it," Rasputin said.

"Binky's Fun Park?"

"Yes," he said solemnly, looking over the group of dusty plastiboard shacks and rusted amusement rides. "He hides here sometimes." He turned his solemn look to me. "Good luck, brother."

"Thanks," I said, opening the glove box. I dug around in the clutter of junk until I discovered a disposable flashlight. I made sure it worked, then poked Rasputin in the ribs with the gyra. "All right," I said, "let's go."

"I have to go with you?"

"You have to introduce me."

He shook his head morosely and got out. I followed him out the driver's side door, pulling the keys from the ignition, and we stopped at the padlocked gate.

"Oh, too bad," Rasputin said.

"Stand back," I said, and shot off the padlock. I threw open the fence and shoved Rasputin through. I closed the gate behind me and looked to Rasputin. "After you."

He wandered down the rotting boardwalk between the sagging concessions, then stopped in front a large tin building. The gaping mouth of a sinisterly smiling clown formed the cavelike entrance.

"He's in there," Rasputin said.

"The house of mirrors?" I hissed, pointing the gyra-pistol into the dim hole.

"He likes to hang out in there," Rasputin whispered. "He's *waiting*. Waiting for *you*."

"For me?" I whispered, reworking my sweaty grip on the pistol. "All right, I'm right behind you."

"I'm not going in there!" Rasputin said. "You don't know him like I do. He'll claw open my stomach and gnaw on my entrails if he finds out I fingered him."

"Enough of that kind of talk," I said, grabbing his shoulder and shoving him into the clown's maw. I turned on the flashlight and aimed it over Rasputin's hunched shoulders, and together we crept through a short corridor that doglegged past a ticket booth into a dark narrow hall of warped mirrors. My back muscles stiffened with each step, and I could feel sweat beading on my forehead. As I glanced into a mirror to my left, a grossly elongated face peered back, eyes deranged with fear. We reached the first intersection of halls and stopped.

"Listen!" Rasputin whispered hoarsely. "Did you hear that?"

"Hear what?"

"*Giggling!* He's laughing at us! He knows we're here! He'll rip out our throats, and we'll die like dogs!"

"Be quiet," I ordered, "he'll hear you."

"You be quiet!" he wailed, chopping at the flashlight. It clattered to the floor and died, and absolute darkness swallowed us whole. Rasputin let out a shriek and scurried down the left hall. I got on my knees and felt around in the dust and rat droppings until my hand closed on the flashlight. I flipped the power switch repeatedly without effect, then dropped the flashlight and took out my cigarette lighter. I sparked it aflame and peered in each direction. Rasputin was nowhere in sight; the maze of mirrors had swallowed him up.

The lighter became too hot to hold, so I let it go out. I stopped breathing and stood perfectly still, straining my ears in the the total darkness for the slightest whisper of sound. I heard the echo of footsteps, but they could have been Rasputin's. I thought hard about doing a quick about-face and leaving the place at once. Find a bar, have a beer, tell the whores how smart I was.

I breathed deep and walked deeper into the maze, sparking the lighter every third step to show the way. The corridor veered right, and I stopped to peer around the corner. I sparked light down the long corridor and saw only my own distant and horribly distorted face gawking back at me. I slipped around the corner, and halfway down the corridor I heard it.

A small rustle of noise behind me. I froze in place and held my breath. Slowly, quietly the small patter of movement came closer and closer. It could have been anything, I thought, a curious rat, a stray cat or maybe even a creeping serial killer.

I spun wildly and fired, shouting gibberish designed to freeze Cain in his tracks. In the light of the muzzle-flash I saw a blurred vision of the devil himself, staring out of the abyss, surrounded by a halo of blackness, looking me straight in the eye. I fired again and again, screaming until I ran out of ammunition and the beast had exploded into dust.

The hall filled with enraged squeals, and many terrible, hairy, clawing things ran up my legs, racing for my eyes. I screamed and ran forward, whipping at the monsters hanging from my limbs, flicking the lighter to see the floor around me alive with huge, pink-eyed rats. I crushed them under my boots as I ran, turning left at the pane of trick glass shattered by gyrajet explosions. I sprinted toward the dim haze of sunlight far down the hall, my ears filled with the angry squeals of an army of pursuing rats.

Rasputin wheeled out of a side corridor in front of me, his eyes huge in the flash of the lighter. He took off down the hall, and I passed him as we hit the dogleg, bouncing off the grille of the ticket booth and lunging down the short entrance hall into the sunlight. I hit the gravel and rolled, squashing and shaking off biting rats. When I'd rolled off the last rat, I jumped to my feet and slapped a fresh magazine in the gyra, pointing it into the clown's mouth.

Hundreds of pairs of pink eyes stared out from the shadows of the entrance, watching me with territorial malice. I backed toward the gate, looking over my shoulder to find Rasputin hustling toward the van. When I caught up with him, he was clawing and cursing at the door latch.

"You'll need these," I said, jangling the van's keys.

"Don't kill me," he whined, sagging against the side of the van.

"Cain doesn't hide out there," I said. "The rats would eat him."

"Yes, yes, yes," he moaned.

"The truth is you don't know where Cain is. You don't know a thing about him."

"Yes," he wailed, his voice breaking. "The BBB is a terrible sham. We're swindlers. We live in the suburbs. We don't even kill rich people. Oh, we mail the odd letter bomb, but that's just for publicity purposes. We're frauds! Terrible evil frauds!" He broke down and began weeping.

"Don't take it too hard," I said, holstering the pistol and helping him back to his feet. I unlocked the door and pushed him to the passenger seat. I got behind the wheel and drove up Hayward to my office. When I got out, Rasputin crawled behind the wheel.

"I swear to change," Rasputin said, rolling down the window.

"Sure you will," I said, and Rasputin raced away.

Instead of going up to my office, I ducked into St. Christopher's Lounge. The St. Chris was a free house, meaning no single pimp or syndicate exercised control of the premises. Which meant a lot of free-lance miscreants gathered there, whether that meant whores, hustlers, pushers or shooters. If you wanted to screw someone cheaply, in any sense of the word, the St. Chris wasn't a bad place to go.

I took a bar stool and ordered a shot of vodka and a draft beer from Amal, the one-eared bartender. I used a napkin to apply half the vodka to the bites and scratches up and down my body, wondering if I could look forward to a bout with rabies. I swallowed the rest of the shot, chased it with beer, then leaned my back against the bar to appraise the night's players.

They lurked around the dim and hazy room like sullen vampires waiting out the sunset. Some held quiet conversations, but theirs was the conditional camaraderie of outcast hyenas who just happened to be staking out the same water hole.

None of them are innocent, I thought, of anything. Devils and deserts inside them all.

"Jake, honey," said a familiar-looking redheaded prostitute, sidling up next to me. "Kill anyone lately?"

"Just the odd wrongdoer," I said. "Slept with any serial killers lately?"

"Depends."

"Depends on what?"

"On if you have enough money."

I laughed sparely. "I don't mean me."

"Oh. Any serial killer in particular?"

"Cain."

"The ghetto avenger? I wish I had. Why you want to hassle him for?"

"Oh, I don't know. There's a rumor going around that he likes to murder and mutilate people."

"Yeah, but look at *who* he's murdering. It's about time a street kid went to their part of town and gave them what they've been giving us for so long. You know what I mean?"

A trio of nervous-looking burb teenagers walked in the door, and Red slipped off her seat and pounced with the speed of an alley cat.

I ordered another beer and collared Amal. "Who's the chumps in monkey suits?" I asked, gesturing to a collection of cheap suits sitting quietly in the corner beyond the end of the bar.

"I don't know what their day jobs are," Amal said, "but they told me to put out the word that anyone wanting anyone croaked should come talk to them. They even slipped me a fiver for the favor."

"Wow," I said, looking them over. All five sat backward in their chairs, backs to the wall. They smoked cigarettes, chewed toothpicks and fairly reeked of unbridled machismo and misdirected impotence. "They don't look like shooters," I observed. "They look like a burb bowling team playing dress up. I better have a word with them."

Amal seized my arm before I could detach myself from the bar. "No trouble," he warned.

I smiled. "Have I ever?"

"Yes. Every time you come in here."

"Don't worry," I soothed. "I'm working a case. I'm here on business."

His look intensified and his grip tightened. "No shooting!"

"Take it easy. I'm just going to talk with them."

"That's what I'm afraid of."

"Relax. I'll be as civil as a doorman at Christmastime." I pulled my arm away and carried my beer to the end of the bar.

I took a drink, looked them over and said, "So, you're a bunch of goddamn sissy boys, are you?"

An affronted jolt went through the group, and they shed their bored looks like flimsy masks. "I think you have us confused with somebody else," a fat, sloppy, middle-aged man with a low-canted fedora said.

"You mean you're not sissy boys?"

"Hell no, we're not," Fedora said. "Hell no! Just goddamn he-men here."

"Good," I said. "Because I don't want to drink next to a bunch of sissies." I took a drink. "He-men, you say?"

"That's *right*."

"Huh. By your getups and the way you're sitting so cozy, I mistook you for a gang of male harlots."

"Gimme some goddamn room here," Fedora said, throwing out his elbows. Chairs scraped and scooted as the group spread out.

"What's wrong with the way we're dressed?" an acne-tormented young man asked.

"You kidding me?" I said. "You're suited up like Hayward yoo-hoo boys. I figured the first sod swishing in here waving a fiver would have the lot of you scratching and kicking to see who'd get to play patty cake with him in the back of his cruiser."

"Say, you better watch it, friend," Fedora warned. "You don't seem to know who you're messing with."

"Why don't you tell me so I can be scared."

"We're goddamn *shooters,* that's what we are!" Fedora said in a low and menacing. "Now do you see?"

"Shooters, huh? Granny shooters or big-time?"

"Big-time," Fedora assured. "We do a lotta jobs for the big syndies, it just so happens."

"The Big Cindys?" I sneered. "Isn't that the transvestite act down at the Night Owl?"

"Syndicates! Syndicates!" he clarified, then peered around slyly. "We even do some capping for the gangs sometimes."

"Which gangs?"

"Well, it just so happens I worked with Tiny 'the Torpedo' Tokorov of the Red Horde coupla times."

"Tiny the Torpedo?" I sneered. "Only thing he's good for is keeping the adult-diaper industry in the black. Where do you think he got the nickname Torpedo, for crissakes?"

"Yeah, well how about Herman 'Golden Boy' Gorman? I used to work big-time syndie contracts with him."

"You mean Girlie-Boy Gorman, don't ya?"

"Say, you better watch it," Fedora said, narrowing his beady eyes. "Herman'll flip if he hears you're dogging him."

"Yeah, he'll probably write me a nasty letter and everything. So, you really dig working with those syndie sissy boys."

"Who says they're sissy boys?"

"I say they're sissy boys. Everyone in the business knows it. That's all they let work for them. It's in their goddamn charter, for crissakes."

"I'm no sissy boy," Fedora complained. "Ask any of the guys. None of us are. Am I right or am I right?"

"That's right," they bellowed, their voices dropping an octave.

"The only he-men in the killer business are free-lancers," I stated unequivocally.

"Right. That's what *we* are," Fedora assured me, "free-lancers right to the bone."

"Yeah?" I said doubtfully. "What big-time free-lancers you know?"

"I know Jake Strait," Fedora said.

"The handchopper? I wouldn't admit knowing that scumbag if you had my balls in a clamp."

"Now you've done it!" Fedora bristled. "Strait's a close personal friend of mine. I tell him you said that, and he might just take a mind to crush your balls *personally.*"

"You can tell him I said he has a bad haircut and dates ugly women while you're at it. When I say big-time free-lancers, I'm talking free-lancers like the goddamn Iceman."

"He's not a free-lancer," the acned boy objected. "He's a psycho killer."

"Don't know him, huh?" I said. "Naw, he wouldn't be caught dead hanging with rubes like you."

"I know him," Fedora said fiercely, his voice tight. "Had a coupla beers with him once."

His compatriots eyed him doubtfully.

"It's God's own truth!" Fedora said, the weight of the lie hunching his back. "Early on he came to me for some advice on monikers, and I gave it to him."

"You suggested 'Iceman'?" the acned kid asked.

"No," Fedora said modestly, "I said 'Icer,' and he took it from there." He gulped his beer and shook his head. "I still like 'Icer' better."

"Yeah," I said, "but the Iceman's kind of low tier anyway."

"Who's bigger than the Iceman?" Fedora said, leaping to the defense of his sometime drinking buddy.

"Cain," I said gravely, "that's who."

Fedora's face drained, and his mouth clamped shut.

"Don't suppose you rubes know anything about *him,*" I said.

A reverent silence fell over the group. Even Fedora didn't claim private knowledge. "Cain," they whispered to each other. They might have been talking about God.

"Not even a squeak of a rumor," I said. "That's how much in the know you guys are."

"I heard plenty," Fedora assured.

"Like what? You don't even know what neighborhood he's working out of."

"The hell I don't. He works out of Riverside, sure as shit."

"I heard he worked out of Colfax," another said.

"Cain wouldn't be caught dead in Colfax," Fedora said, shouting the interloper down. "Cain's a class act."

"If he's from the City," I said, "how's he get past the Hill's security?"

"Secret underground tunnel," someone piped up.

"Stealth skimmer," another contended.

"Catapult," said another, nodding solemnly. "God-damn catapult. I know a guy whose brother *saw* the goddamn thing."

"Are you guys shitting me?" Fedora said, looking around the group. "He goes right through the gate like everyone else."

"How?" I said. "How's he get past the guards?"

"Shit, man, he just *bluffs* them, that's all. Cain can do that. He just waltzes right through whenever he likes."

"He has all kinds of special abilities," the acned boy confirmed.

"You're damn right he does," Fedora agreed. "He ain't even a normal human being like you and me. He's something else entirely."

"He's like a phantom," the kid agreed a little wildly. "He can walk through doors and walls like a ghost!"

"Wouldn't surprise me if he could," Fedora said, "wouldn't surprise me one bit. You know, sometimes I swear Cain's some sort of, you know, *supernatural formulation* of all the hate and anger in the City. That's why he goes after them Hillers. Whenever things reach the boiling point in the ghettos, he appears out of the air and sacrifices a slimy Hiller to God.

"C'mon," he said, lifting his beer, "let's have a toast. Here's to good ol' Cain." Glasses went up and Fedora glared at me. "Ain't you gonna raise a glass with us?"

I leaned against the bar and sneered. "Cain ain't no ghost and he ain't no supernatural formulation. He's a first-rate, class-act sissy boy and a bed-wetter besides. And you can tell him I said so."

As one they heaved out of their chairs. "You just went too goddamn far," Fedora said, his voice low. "You can say what you want about anyone else, but shoot your mouth off about Cain and you better be ready to receive a good ass whipping."

I put my beer down and separated my feet. "And who's gonna give it to me?"

They remained motionless for a moment, eyeing each other. "I don't know," Fedora finally huffed as they retook their seats. "But someone will, you better believe it."

"Sure," I said, finishing my beer. "Well, you just pass the word around that Jake Strait's gunning for that pansy Cain and if he has anything to say about it, my number's in the directory."

"I'll do better than that," Fedora said. "I'll tell Jake Strait you're going around using his name. Just wait and see what happens then."

"You do that," I said. "And tell him to get a goddamn soul while you're at it."

I went to three other bars on Hayward, employing the same time-tested stratagem. Most heavy criminals spent a lot of time grooming their reputations, and I'd found if you insulted them enough they'd eventually break cover and try to kill you. I didn't know if serial killers lugged around the kind of ego syndicate hit men did, but I was willing to find out. It was a cheap trick, but I liked cheap tricks.

I abandoned the ruse around midnight when I became certain that if I heard one more solemn lie about Cain I'd throttle someone. I went back to my office and consulted the bottle. In its amber depths there was a murky truth I could understand. I knew the bottle. It was my friend. It fed me giddiness and escape, then mercifully hammered me unconscious before I realized it was all a monstrous lie.

4

A buzzing woke me. I jumped up from the floor and lunged around the dark office for a moment, totally out of my head with fear and panic. I finally slapped at the keyboard, and the monitor lit up with a gray lump of static shaped vaguely like a human head.

"What?" I barked at it.

"Strait?"

"Yeah."

"This is Inspector Degas. You still working out of the same dump?"

"Yeah."

"I'll pick you up in front in fifteen minutes."

"What for?"

There was a moment of silence. When he finally spoke, there was hardly any contempt in his voice at all. "I was told to take you along."

"Along to where?"

"The Hill. Cain left you a welcome present."

The screen went blank, and I stared at it dumbly for a moment, groping at fragments of nightmares about butchered bodies and phantom serial killers. I crept to the bathroom and stripped off my shirt, every movement a prelude to pain. I splashed water in my face, then looked in the mirror. I looked to be the sure-money favorite in the Ugliest Bastard in the World Contest. I averted my eyes, toweled off, put my shirt back on, added a leather motorcycle jacket and, hung over and unshaven, went out to confront the forces of evil.

I waited on the sidewalk, thinking the frigid downpour would somehow make me feel human again. A heavy mist dimmed the streetlights, and black clouds buried the dawn. A derelict Chevy reeled out of the light traffic and braked in front of me, splashing my legs with gutter water.

"I see you're still not on the take," I said, climbing in the battered machine.

"I see you're still a drunk," Degas said, pulling away from the curb.

"I have no soul," I explained. "I have no soul, no one loves me, and I can't seem to kill enough people to pay the rent. I'm utterly wrecked. I'm wrecked and I can drink as much as I goddamn want."

Degas ignored my cry for help, his fleshless head cocked toward the garbled static buzzing from his wristcom. Rain whipped against the windshield, and the wipers did a poor job of slapping it away.

"What sort of present did Cain leave me?" I asked, massaging my aching temples.

"The maid discovered the body an hour ago." His sunken death-camp eyes flickered my way. "Where were you tonight, by the way?"

"That's no way to start a working relationship, Inspector. I was sleeping in my office."

"Any witnesses?"

"No, I usually sleep alone."

"Don't cry on my shoulder."

"Let's get something straight right from the start," I said, jabbing a finger at him. "*I* deliver the snappy one-liners. That's *my* job. I'm flippant and clever, and you seethe beneath the smothering weight of your hopelessly dull wit."

"It looked like your act could use some help."

"Let *me* worry about that. Once I lose this headache, I'll have you cringing like a whipped dog."

Degas nodded and turned off Hayward onto a speedway ramp. The sedan shook and groaned as it got up to speed, and the City faded behind us. We drifted through thick rings of suburban development, each newer and tackier than the last, until the road began to climb in earnest and the cottages and lawns ballooned into mansions and estates.

"What about this Cain guy?" I said conversationally.

"What about him?"

"Have you worked up a profile yet? Do you have any clues?"

"ART has him figured as a low-income white male sociopathic sadist."

"Sounds like ART subscribes to the same data bank I do," I deduced. "In other words you don't know a thing about him."

"We know he likes to kill rich people and makes quite a sport of it. He has free access to the Hill, is handy with a nail gun and likes collecting certain body parts."

"Huh," I said, looking out the window. "I heard he was a supernatural entity with the power to move through walls and hypnotize."

"Who told you that?"

"A friend."

"I didn't know you had any friends."

"A less hostile enemy, then. I also heard Cain was an irony-loving lesbian of color out to stick it to you white male bourgeois elitists."

Degas shrugged. "Who knows, maybe he is."

"You know that little?"

He shrugged.

I looked out the window at the trappings of the rich. "You're not going to be a big help to me on this, are you?"

He didn't say anything.

"You resent the fact they brought me in," I continued. "You think I'm way out of my league."

"I think you're a major pain in the ass."

"All right, that's a start. We can build from there."

Degas braked in front of the heavily fortified security gate connected to the necklace of electric fences and mine fields ringing the Hill. An extra allotment of SPF troopers milled around the gatehouse, wild-eyed and heavily armed. Degas passed one of the guards two plastic cards, and the guard used a long-necked scanner to check them against our handchips. The guard returned the cards, the gate went up, and we powered through. Degas handed me one of the cards.

"What's this?" I asked.

"Your Hill pass."

"Christ, I never thought I'd see the day."

"I warned Bowlan against it."

"What do you know about Bowlan?"

"He's Pennings's lapdog. What else is there to know?"

"What do you know about Pennings?"

Degas's eyes shifted. "Why do you ask?"

I shrugged. "Isn't he one of the corporate vampires that slipped under the rug when the World Party made the big grab and nationalized everything?" I said, stabbing at Degas's strong socialist sympathies. "Maybe the biggest bump in the rug. I wonder why they let him keep so much."

"They owed him a lot," Degas said bitterly. "Hiram saw which way the wind was blowing early on, when the Party was a third-rate militia dwarfed by the corporate armies that had weathered the corporate wars. His factories and banks secretly provided the Party with desperately needed weapons and cash, his private army trained the Party's ragtag force. When the Party finally came out on top, Hiram was not only allowed to keep his empire, they awarded him the title of Revolutionary Hero."

"But you figure he wasn't so much interested in revolutions as he was in wiping out the competition."

"I don't figure anything," Degas said. "If you're smart, you won't fuck around with Pennings. I know you think you're some kind of heroic smart-ass, but if you dick around with Pennings he'll cut it off with a dull ax."

"Ouch," I said, making a face. "Threats of castration are never wasted on me."

I gazed out the window at the big houses rolling by. Aesthetically speaking, Hillsdale was to the City what chilled Dom Pérignon served in crystal was to warm ripple served in a bedpan. But I'd had enough dealings with Hillsdale to know that behind all the wealth and glitter was as much human depravity and corruption as you'd find in the poorest ghetto, maybe more.

Degas wheeled off the main road onto a short drive. It ended in a cul-de-sac crowded by mobile crime labs and a half-dozen SPF vehicles, each growling with radio traffic. Silhouettes leered from neighboring windows, curious but too snooty to actually mingle with the working-class troopers. The manifestation of Degas's wreck in their neighborhood probably outraged them as much as the visit by Cain.

We got out and Degas opened the trunk. He pulled out two disposable clear-plastic bodysuits with hood and mouth mask. He handed one to me. "Put this on," he said.

I eyed him. "Not on our first crime scene I'm not, you kinky bastard."

"You can wait out here, then," Degas said, pulling on his suit.

"All right," I said, climbing into the plastic. "But you tell me I have to wear a leather jock and heels, and I'm calling a cab."

Degas paused to glare, then moved off briskly. I followed him through the sea of armor-bloated SPF troopers gathered on the lawn, their submachine guns at the ready in case Cain had an idea for a follow-up visit. Degas spoke briefly with a plastic-suited SPF sergeant, then followed him inside. We climbed two flights of magnificently sculpted staircase to a hall guarded by quarantine curtains and plastic-suited troopers. The sergeant pointed to a door at the end of the hall, and Degas and I walked in on the scene of the crime.

Red flood lamps lit the bedroom, making everything appear splashed with blood. Space-suited, bubble-helmeted forensic techs scurried around in a ritualistic dance around something in the middle of the room I could not see. Each tech held some manner of electronic device: whirring cameras, humming DNA scanners and molecule-crunching environment analyzers that sucked and squawked like vacuum cleaners with mouthy parrots caught in their nozzles.

A tall florid man, his fat ass a powerful testament to the resilience of his red rubber suit, strutted among the techs. He possessed the manner and diction of a man who'd spent his formative years in strict private school where they stressed discipline, bearing and, judging by the stiff-backed way he stalked around the room, in-

serted a broomstick up his posterior. He marched to
where Degas and I stood and gave Degas a snappy salute
while rocking back on his heels.

"What've we got here, Burt?" Degas asked.

"A discotheque in Martian hell by the looks of it," I
said.

Burt stopped smiling at Degas and began staring at me.
I noticed that, unlike the rest of the forensic spooks, his
clip-on ID tag bore his full name, Burt Swinburne, and
the regal HDS crest instead of the SPF acronym. "Who's
he?" Burt snapped.

"I'm a drama critic," I said. "The haunted-house effect is really neat, but why don't we turn on some lights
so us professionals can do some goddamn detecting?"

His head turned to Degas, but his eyes stayed on me.
"Who *is* this terrible man?"

"This is Jake Strait," Degas said.

"Oh," Burt said, putting on a patronizing smile that
bothered the hell out of me. "*Him.* Well, since he's obviously completely ignorant of modern forensic methodology, I'll explain it so even an especially dull
Mongoloid could understand. The lighting is essential to
the spectrum analyzers. The other devices you see de-
ployed extract data from every possible arena of physical evidence, the sum of which will be fed into powerful
computers that will analyze and assemble the data
into—"

"A big stack of printout that doesn't mean a thing," I
finished for him. "No wonder this investigation isn't
getting anywhere."

Burt's face gorged with blood, and his teeth ground.
"Says who?"

"The newspapers, for one. Now I know who the idiot
was they were talking about. Three bodies and all your

data suckers and mainframes have come up with is an encyclopedia entry. Now I see why they brought me in on this gig.''

Burt blustered and huffed until he had to paw at a helmet valve to let in more air. "It just so happens," he shrilled, "we brought you in solely to provide the insider's point of view. Though, in my opinion, enlisting you to find Cain is akin to hiring the neighborhood wino to find Jack the Ripper."

"Is that how they're billing me?"

"In politer quarters."

"Fine," I said. "Step aside and I'll tell you how I would have done it."

"Certainly," Burt screeched, moving aside. "Have a look!"

I had a look. "Jesus fucking Christ," I said, drawing back and wishing I was in some faraway bar, stinking drunk. "We have to *grease* this bastard."

The nude dead man lay on his side, his crushed face pointing up from a huge pool of coagulating blood. His torso bowed toward his remaining leg, and his remaining arm stretched out behind his back. The severed arm lay nearby, missing a square patch of flesh from the biceps. The severed leg wasn't in sight. Three large stainless steel nails pierced the body, one each through the wrist and ankle of the attached limbs, and one through the forehead, caving in the skull. The stomach was sliced open, and intestines spilled out onto the carpet.

Worst of all was the face. Mashed lips framing broken teeth were painted with blood into a leering ear-to-ear clown smile. The nose and eyes were mostly not there, and the scalp was peeled back six inches from a horizontal slash across the forehead, exposing bare skull.

"I thought you bogeymen thrived on this sort of thing," Burt taunted.

"There's too much blood," I said. "He doesn't kill them immediately. He nails them to the floor, slices them up, and they die later, after the heart has pumped for a while."

"Well, you're not quite the dullard I suspected," Burt said. "To be more specific, Cain stuns them with an electric shock, strips them bare, nails them to the floor, removes the tongue and eyes, does his various dissection and dismemberment, then puts a nail through the skull. He's followed the same m.o. every time."

"How long does it take him from start to finish?" Degas asked.

"Just a matter of minutes," Burt said. "He uses some sort of portable pneumatic nail gun to drive the nails and a portable power saw to do the cutting."

I took the minisaw out of my coat pocket. "Something like this?"

Burt and nearby spooks all took a look at it. "Yes. What are you carrying that for?"

"Take a wild guess."

Burt's jaw dropped. "May I see it?" I passed it to him, and he caressed it. "Something similar, but larger. You'd never get through a thigh bone with this." After he took some pictures, he passed it back.

"Where's the rest of him?" Degas asked.

"The leg was in the closet," a petite, cat-eyed blonde holding a small whirring device said. "The tongue and eyes were under a pillow on the bed. The right hand is missing, of course."

I glanced at her. "What do you mean, 'of course'?"

"Cain takes the scanhand with him," Degas said, moving forward to squat beside the body. "Just like a bogeyman. DNA scan pick up anything, Burt?"

Burt shook his head and frowned at the footprints Degas's plastic-encased shoes left in the tacky blood. "The only recent traces are from the maid, the houseboy, the deceased and the first troopers to arrive."

"Fibrometer?"

"Nothing nonindigenous. He's still wearing a nonporous bodysuit, the clever bastard."

"So he walks in here wearing a space suit and a bunch of power tools and no one notices him?" I asked.

"The night maid was downstairs the entire time," Burt said. "She said the deceased came in at 1:00 a.m. and went straight to bed. She heard the thumps around three."

"Thumps?" Degas said.

"Probably the nails going into the floor. She went upstairs to investigate and apparently surprised our killer."

Degas's head jerked up. "She see anything?"

"No, she just heard someone jumping out the back." Burt gestured to a pair of french doors opening onto a balcony at the rear of the room. I moved around the body to the balcony and gazed down at the marble patio two stories below. A forensic team had laid out a search grid, and large vacuum devices sucked at the stone.

"Just flew off like a bat?" I said over my shoulder.

"Apparently," Burt said from inside.

I ran my hand along the balcony's gilded rail. Near the center the paint was chipped raw all the way around.

"How'd he get in?" I asked over my shoulder.

"We don't know," Burt said. "The maid said no one could have come in downstairs without her noticing.

There's no sign whatsoever of forced entry. I guess he flew in like a bat, too."

"Either that or he used a grappling hook to climb this balcony," I said, turning to point at the chipped paint of the rail. "Probably got down the same way."

Burt hustled onto the balcony, detaching a cylindrical instrument from his belt. He pointed the buzzing device at the rail. "Are you certain?" he said, frowning. "How can you tell?"

"Use your hand," I advised, demonstrating. "See?"

He reached out tentatively with a rubber-encased hand and touched the chipped paint.

"Do you feel it, Burt?" I asked. "Do you know what that is?"

"What?"

"A *clue.*"

"Infrared spectrometer!" Burt shrilled angrily and the cat-eyed blonde sprang forward, camera whirring. "We would have found it sooner or later," Burt muttered, then went back inside. I lingered on the balcony, watching the blonde take pictures. "Like your work?" I asked.

"Yes," she said flatly, crouching to get a shot of the underside of the rail.

"You find killers interesting?"

"As a matter of fact, I do."

I folded my arms and gazed into the rain-misted night. "I'm a killer, you know."

Her eyes flickered my way. "I heard."

"Don't you want to study my habits?"

"I don't take my work home with me."

I nodded and went back inside. It's this goddamn plastic clown suit, I assured myself. Johnny Humungo would get braced in this getup.

Degas still crouched in front of the body, like a child watching an anthill. "There's something in his mouth," he said.

Burt peered over his shoulder. "How can you tell?"

Degas took a penlight out of his pocket and tapped it against the dead man's sightly bulging cheek.

"Give me some tongs," Degas said.

Burt hesitated. "Actually as head forensic pathologist—"

Degas looked at him sharply, and Burt came up with a pair of gleaming steel tongs. Using them in cooperation with the penlight, Degas forced open the stiff jaw. The tongs went into the dark hole, fished around for a moment, then clamped on to something.

"Who is this poor bastard anyway?" I asked.

"Jordan A. Lindquist, pharmacist," Burt said.

The tongs pulled at a cylindrical vial that was larger than the space between the broken teeth. Degas tugged, and with each tug the blind head nodded, as if agreeing with Burt.

"Pharmacist?" I said. "I didn't think they let that kind of riffraff on the Hill."

"This kind they do," the blonde said, appearing beside me. "Lindquist was a *recreational* pharmacist. He designed and distributed most of the fun drugs the Hillers eat. And made quite a bit of money doing it."

With a final tug, the clear plastic container slipped from between Lindquist's teeth. Though caked with blood, I could make out blue fluid inside.

"Looks like Newlife," the blonde said, holding up a plastic bag to receive the vial.

"Newlife?" I said. "What's Newlife?"

"A new kind of superpsychedelic," she explained, sealing and marking the bag. "Hit the streets maybe a month ago. Almost impossible to get hold of, from what I hear. There's more vials in the closets."

"Did Lindquist design it?" I asked.

She started to reply, and Degas shot her a look that didn't leave much to interpretation. The blonde shrugged, averting her eyes.

Degas shined the penlight into the mouth, then handed the tongs back to Burt. He stood up and looked at me with eyes that showed a horror his face did not. "Seen enough, bogeyman?" he asked.

"Plenty," I said. We left the room, and the techs fell on Lindquist like yapping jackals. "I thought the SPF was running the show," I said as we descended the stairs.

"We are."

"Someone should tell Burt that."

"We're on the Hill. The HDS has a right to participate."

We crossed the living room and went outside. "I need you to modem over everything you know about Cain tonight," I said.

"I'm too busy right now. Maybe later in the week."

"I was told you were at my disposal. I thought we could become chums, maybe pal around off duty." I shrugged. "You know, have a few beers, talk about broads, really get to know each other."

"Listen, Strait," Degas snarled, suddenly rounding on me. We were on the lawn now, and the rain pitter-pattered on our plastic suits. "I've a psycho killer to catch. I've a strong suspicion my job depends on catching him quick. I'm averaging two hours' sleep a night and I don't have the time to pander to some cheap ghetto handchopper."

"Don't mince words with me, Degas," I retorted. "Just what exactly are you trying to say?"

His eyes shot full of rage, and he leaned into my face. "I'm saying you better stay the fuck out of my way."

Degas turned to go, and a luxurious patrol car screeched to a dramatic halt in front of him. The two front doors flew open, and Bowlan and another man bounded out, splendid in swanky blue uniforms brazen with flashing brass and waving tassels.

"Oh, fucking great," Degas muttered as Bowlan marched up to us.

"What's the status, gentlemen?" Bowlan bellowed.

"Pretty much the same as the others," Degas said dryly. "I'll send you ART's report in the morning."

Bowlan nodded, then turned to me. "Well, it looks as if you've a fresh trail to follow into the ghetto, Mr. Strait. I trust Inspector Degas is aiding you any way he can."

"You bet he is," I said. "He'd just volunteered to send me over all the data he has on Cain the instant you pulled up. Right, Degas?"

Degas's dead gray eyes drilled into me. "Yeah, that's right. I'll get right on it." He nodded stiffly to Bowlan, then stalked back to his car and drove away without me.

"This is my second in command, Deputy Chief Roger Eliot," Bowlan said, nodding to the young man on his left.

"Pleased to meet you," he said, extending his hand. His haircut was fresh, his teeth capped, his nails manicured, his eyebrows shaped, and during his thirty or so years of life he had yet to acquire a single line on his face. His exterior was vain and polished, yet his manner was humble; he probably kissed the mirror only once after shaving.

"I'm your biggest fan," he announced as we shook hands.

"Always glad to meet a fan," I said. "Who are you confusing me with?"

He laughed. "No, there's only one Jake Strait. I've read your SPF bounty sheet a dozen times. Your body counts are shocking."

"Thanks, I guess." I turned to Bowlan. "You said you had some of your own people working the City angle."

"That's right," Bowlan agreed.

"Have they turned anything up?"

"I'll have Carlos brief you tomorrow morning."

"Carlos who?"

"Carlos Melendez. A man of your profession. Do you know him?"

"Yes. I'll stop by his office tonight."

Both saluted, then drove away without going inside to view the carnage. I lingered outside the Lindquist mansion until the forensic teams came out. I tried to solicit a ride from the blonde, but she slapped the lock and sped away before I could get the passenger door open. I ended up riding down with Burt.

"I figured you lived on the Hill," I said after we cleared the gate.

"I do. I'm going down to SPF Central to make sure those dullards don't misconstrue the data."

"How does a pathologist get a place on the Hill?"

"Criminal pathology is not my job, it's my hobby. Some men of means collect stamps or paintings. I myself find the criminal field much more naturally exhilarating. But don't think me unqualified. I've five advanced degrees in the field."

"With such a fine education you must have a strong opinion about Cain."

"Indeed I do," Burt said, demonstrating his natural exhilaration for the subject. "To begin with, it doesn't take an extraordinary individual to be a killer. The most sane specimen will commit murder if compelled by the proper circumstances. But," he said, waving a finger at me, "to kill again and again with such commitment to style as Cain has, well, needless to say, he is a very special breed of cat.

"You see, there are three kinds of killers—psychotic, ego harmonious, and ego disharmonious. The psychotic has lost touch with reality, the ego disharmonious kills due to some inner unresolvable conflict, but the ego harmonious, ah, here is a man who has no qualms at all about killing his fellow man. He *revels* in it."

"And you figure Cain is the latter."

"Classically so. He is a social pioneer who does not merely commit forays across the bridge, he actually *lives* on the other side."

"The other side of what?"

"Conventional morality. He's taken all the cheap rules taught since birth and thrown them out the window."

"You mean a sociopath."

"I hate that word. Serial killers are not devoid of conscience—they have merely adopted their own set of rules. Heavens!" he said slapping the wheel, "what I would not give to sit down and talk with him for just a moment."

"Then maybe dinner and a little dancing, eh, Burt?"

He frowned at me. "Don't tell me you don't have the slightest desire to explore such a unique psyche."

"Shucks," I said, "I know it sounds crass, but all I'd like to do is shoot him."

"You hired guns are the worse sort of killer," Burt said, sliding me a mean glance. "You have no style, no substance, no redeeming qualities at all."

"We kill bad guys. That must count for something."

"Ha! It doesn't matter whom you kill, it's *how* you kill. Why, you're just a killing machine with nothing to say. Comparing you with Cain is like comparing Michelangelo with a common housepainter. All you do is shoot your victim and take the scanhand. It's like signing a blank canvas. But Cain, just look at the way he fashions his victims, with such deliberation, such *soul*. I mean, good heavens, it's pure art, that's what it is. He's really saying something."

"Good God," I fretted, "I'm not only a soulless killer, I'm a soulless killer without any *soul*."

Burt shrugged. "You're either born with it or you're not. Nothing to get upset about."

I regrouped what little self-esteem I had left and said, "So what exactly is Cain saying?"

"Well, it's hard to say, he speaks in such an exquisitely exotic language. Of course, the knaves at the SPF with their coarse number crunchers cannot fathom his depths—the very idea is ludicrous. Cain is much too deep and clever for their clumsy methods, or anyone else's for that matter."

"Just how then do you intend to catch Cain?"

Burt frowned for a moment, as if the idea hadn't occurred to him. "I really don't know."

"That's what I thought. Has Cain sexually molested any of his victims?"

"No."

"Don't most serial killers?"

"Yes."

"Maybe Cain's impotent."

"I hardly think so. Perhaps he is above such animal baseness."

"He strips them nude."

"Of course, clothes would only subvert his efforts. He strips them in the same way an artist prepares a canvas."

"I see. What do you make of the missing hands?"

"I think they represent his personal stamp of style, like Dali's clocks, a theme that carries through each work. On the other hand, there are mutilations particular to each victim—the carefully removed and displayed organs of Donald Basque, the divided body of Angela Romani, the vial in the mouth of Lindquist. I think they relate to something Cain feels specifically about each victim."

"He knows his victims?"

"I didn't say that. His feelings could be very generalized, how he perceives them from a distance. Or how he feels after he has shocked them unconscious, much as Donatello didn't know what he would sculpt until he touched the stone with which he would work."

"So he's not so much mutilating them as he's sculpting them."

"Bravo, Mr. Strait. You have surprised me. I did not think a creature of your ill nature could make such a leap of insight."

"I was being sarcastic."

"I should have guessed," he sighed. "The truth is, we will never understand the depth and magnitude of Cain's art unless we capture him alive and study him closely for many, many years. I cannot expound enough what a coup for criminal psychology it would be to capture Cain alive. Only the coarsest of philistines would shoot him outright."

"That must be why they brought me in."

"Such are my suspicions also."

I looked out the window. "You know, Burt, I can get you the addresses of Cain's fan clubs if you like."

"That's quite all right."

"Yeah," I sighed. "Those cretins wouldn't appreciate his art anyway. They only like him because he kills rich people."

"How base."

"Yes. Where do you think Cain hails from?"

Burt didn't seem to warm to the subject as much as he did the relative merits of mutilation. After a moment of off-putting silence he muttered, "The City seems to be the popular opinion."

"You really think the unrefined climes of the ghetto could produce such a refined artist as Cain?"

"It's possible. With proper schooling and dedication, one can imagine a boy of poor upbringing rising above his oppressive environment and attaining greatness."

"You sound like my high school gym coach."

"I frankly don't care what I sound like to you."

I nodded. "I think he's from the Hill."

"Why?"

"Makes more sense. I get the feeling Cain cases his victims thoroughly. A ghetto resident would have a tough time moving around the Hill without someone noticing him."

"With an extraordinary individual like Cain, anything is possible."

"Sure. Where'd Cain get his moniker, anyway?"

Burt smiled. "It just so happens yours truly coined the name. Rather good, isn't it?"

"Dandy. How'd the City rags pick up on it so fast?"

Burt shrugged. "Someone must have leaked it."

I leered at him. "Did you leak it, Burt? Are you the one spilling his guts to the ghetto tabloids?"

Burt opened his mouth, then clamped it shut. "Certainly not," he said between his teeth.

"What do you know about Newlife?"

Burt said nothing.

"Hiram Pennings?"

Burt kept his eyes on the road and his mouth shut. I spent the rest of the drive trying to pump him for information, but he didn't seem to think I deserved any. When he dropped me off in front of my office, I got in my car and drove ten blocks down Hayward to the office of Carlos Melendez.

5

The scion of a wealthy family, Carlos Melendez abandoned the family fortune to become a bogeyman for reasons he never bothered to explain. A Hayward bogeyman like myself, he moved his office up and down the boulevard like a crocodile hunter working a long-infested river, moving on whenever the local contracts dried up. Our paths crossed enough times to allow us to become friends and even co-workers when there was a particularly tough nut to crack.

Carlos presently lived in an office-apartment near the top of a pre-corporate-era ramshackle on the corner of Hayward and Goethe. I took the creaking elevator up to the fifth floor and knocked on an anonymous steel door that bore no title or explanation. Carlos didn't care much for client jobs, preferring warrant work.

"Who's there?" a muffled voice demanded from inside.

"Jake," I said.

"You alone?"

"Yeah, but don't rub it in."

The door opened and he let me in, holstering his pistol and smiling crookedly. "Jake! Come in. Bowlan called and said you were coming."

We shook hands vigorously. Carlos was tall and lanky with eyes and hair as shiny and black as hot tar. He

combed his hair straight back, defiantly exposing a cow-
ardly hairline and diabolic brow. He was a great raw-
boned son of Quixote, hopelessly deranged and, like
most shadows, larger than life.

He sat down on a fold-up metal chair behind a fold-up
metal desk. Except for a desktop computer, a canvas cot,
a tiny refrigerator and a tripod-mounted rifle leering out
the solitary window, the office was bare of personality or
ornament. The rifle and tripod bulged with electronic and
mechanical trappings, and thick cables trailed to the
computer. The only sound in the room was the hum and
click of the rifle shifting fitfully on the tripod.

"A better rat trap?" I said, nodding at the machine.

"My silent partner," Carlos explained. "So, how are
you, Jake? You look drawn."

"It's my new big-shot job," I said. "You recommended me, didn't you?"

He shrugged. "I figured you could use some easy
plastic. I'm always looking out for my buddies."

I started toward the fridge. "Any beer on hand?"

"Sure, help yourself."

I opened the fridge and immediately drew back. Like
pale tarantulas, a half-dozen human hands surrounded
a six-pack of vitabeer. I reached over them and gingerly
detached a beer from the ring. I closed the fridge and
opened the beer.

"There's a half-dozen hands in your refrigerator," I
said, moving to the desk.

"Oh, yeah," Carlos said. "I'm holding those for a
friend."

"Bogey friend?"

"Right."

I drained half the beer and sat on the edge of his desk.
"How'd you get involved with Bowlan?"

"Hiram recommended me."

"You know Hiram Pennings?"

"Our families are acquainted by the rude ties of conspicuous wealth. Hiram and my father were prep school roommates. I've been teaching his son the art of self-defense for the past three months."

"Christopher?"

"Yeah. It's all part of his renaissance education."

I nodded. "Bowlan said you've dug up some information on Cain."

"Nothing you want to hear."

"Try me."

The rifle at the window jerked and coughed, and Carlos hunched forward to stare into the face of the monitor.

"Quick, take a look at this," he said. I moved around the desk to see a digital image of a man with a bag of groceries drop to the sidewalk, his right shoulder blade gushing blood. He flailed his arms like a lizard with a broken back, trying to get up, and the cross hairs dividing the screen whipped around frantically, trying to reacquire the target. The wounded man struggled to his feet and began loping awkwardly down the sidewalk.

"That's right, run, you dumb bastard," Carlos whispered, grinning like a wolf. "Run!"

The cross hairs jerked down the sidewalk after the man, and the rifle coughed again. The top of the wounded man's head erupted like a volcano, and he collapsed to the concrete. The rifle coughed twice more, splitting the dead man's spine.

Data flashed on the bottom of the screen. "Yakov Vsevolod Ivanovich," it read, "Political Criminal. Death warrant. Reward Code: A-2. 4000 credits... Reclamation en route."

"Four grand!" Carlos cried. "Jackpot!"

"What the hell just happened?"

"Sheer genius, that's what. See, the whole thing is automated. The long-range scanner mounted on the rifle reads the ID chips of the passersby, runs them through the criminal want files of ART, then zaps any sap with a death warrant."

"They had something like that in Denver," I said.

"Denver? I thought you burned Denver down."

"I can't take all the credit. You're going to have to go down and get that hand if you want to collect."

Carlos grinned and shook his head. "No, I don't. See, that's the real beauty of it. With Bowlan's help I worked out a deal with reclamation and the SPF. The instant the machine executes a criminal, the computer contacts reclamation, relating the ID and location of the kill. Reclamation picks him up and confirms his ID before dropping him in the vat. They contact the SPF, and the SPF sends eighty percent of the bounty to my account and twenty percent to reclamation for their trouble."

"And you just sit back and watch the creds roll in."

"Without getting one drop of blood on my hands." He stood up and gazed out the window. "You know," he said dreamily, "some people look at Hayward and see a river of filth and decadence. I look down there and see a gold mine."

"Yeah. I'm surprised that thing isn't shooting nonstop."

Carlos laughed. "You should have been here when I first turned the mother on. I had it set up to execute all death warrants, regardless of the bounty. I figured even code-Ds would add up, you know?"

"What happened?"

"It went nuts! The second I turned it on, the thing opened up like a machine gun. It couldn't miss, the bastards were everywhere! It executed twenty-nine death warrants in two minutes and had as many pinned down when the neighborhood militia showed up. They thought I was the Rooftop Sniper, for crissakes. I had to drop down my private-enforcer license and a basketful of warrants before they'd stop shooting holes in my window. Reclamation showed up, and an hour later I had over twenty-three thousand credits in my account. *Twenty-three thousand!* Can you beat it?"

"You must be a big hit with the neighbors."

"Ah, fuck them. I have it set for A-2s and above now, no one cries over that kind of fiend."

"Code-As are generally political criminals."

"That's what I'm saying. Nobody likes those big-mouth rabble-rousers."

I checked the monitor. The machine had taken up its deadly vigil, leering at the crowd gathering around the dead man. "You're still going to have to move around a lot."

Carlos frowned slightly. "Yeah, that's going to be the biggest hassle. I figure I'll have to reposition every month or so, once they figure out why the local cretins are keeling over in the street. They'll either stop hanging around or somebody'll try and shoot me. Ungrateful bastards. If they'd just keep their noses clean, they wouldn't have to worry about getting waxed every time they cross the street."

"That thing ever miss?"

"It killed two saps with apprehension warrants during the initial onslaught. There's a split-second glitch in the loop between ID and shooting, so if the target moves fast enough he can get out the way and let some other poor bastard eat lead. I'll probably nail a couple nonwarrants a month, but—" he shrugged "—you know how that goes."

"It doesn't bother you?"

"Does what bother me?"

"Killing innocent people."

He stared at me. "Innocent people? Down there? You must be joking. There aren't any innocent people down there. If I went to the window and opened up with a speed gun I couldn't help but hit guilty people. Wise up, for crissakes." He lifted his jacket from the back of the chair and put it on. "C'mon, let's go get a drink, I'm suddenly loaded."

I hesitated for a moment, exploring the boundaries of my better judgment. It was a short walk. "Let me wash up first," I said, finishing the beer on the way to the tiny bathroom. "Cain's latest caper left me feeling slimy."

"Who'd he get?"

"Some pharmacist name Lindquist," I yelled above the rush of water. "Bowlan didn't tell you?"

"No. I'm taking a break from Cain. Sometimes it's best not to know too much. Knowledge can kill you just as quick as a bullet."

"Is that why they hired me?" I dried my hands on a paper towel and noticed that the mirror over the sink was painted black. "Because you quit?"

"Right."

"Why'd you paint the mirror?" I said when I came out.

"Mirrors represent the abyss," Carlos said, pulling on a black sweater. "It's like Nietzsche said. You stare into the abyss enough times and you become the abyss. Your brain starts editing you out. Familiarity breeds invisibility."

"I thought it bred contempt."

He laughed. "That's just the first stage. Let's go."

We hit the sidewalk the same moment a powder blue reclamation van pulled up beside the body. "Money in the bank," Carlos said, and a gang of winos swarmed us.

Carlos dug into his pocket and came out with a fistful of five-credit squares. "All right," he said, filling pawing hands with plastic. "Here's your share. Okay, goddamn it, here's some for you, don't be grabby, you'll get yours." A minute later Carlos had passed out the entire wad of bills, and the winos ran off to get a bottle.

"Jesus, where'd all those bastards come from?" I asked as we climbed into my car. "It was like they were lying in wait for you."

"They were. They understand my karmic payback system—they've tuned their ears to the cough of the rifle. Did you see all the plastic I laid on them? We're talking *serious* karma points."

"Makes up for taking a life?"

"It's better than stuffing bills in those confession machines down on Bukowski. Listen, I got all the conscience and karmic angles figured. As long as the guy you hit wasn't a goddamn saint, you gotta think feeding some winos cancels out the karmic debt. I mean, when you think about it, human life ain't that valuable, except to the individual, and fuck that egotistical bastard. Let's find a liquor store in Barridales, I'm not too popular around here."

As I climbed in I glanced over at the reclamation boys tossing the bullet-shattered body into the back of the van that would haul it to a reclamation plant. There the corpse would be processed into soy fertilizer or soy burger, depending upon whom you wanted to believe.

"Your silent partner likes to be sure," I said as I drove north up Hayward.

Carlos nodded. "A week ago it dropped a guy with a clean chest shot, except when the rec crew showed up the guy was still kicking. They wouldn't touch him until I came down with a pistol and head-shot the poor sap. Embarrassed the hell out of me. Now it's programmed to make sure the goner is gone. A mark can never be too dead, as the syndie shooters like to say."

As we passed my office building, Carlos peered around keenly. "This ain't a bad area," he said. "I could set up one of my machines in your office and make you some serious credit."

"I'll stick to the old-fashioned system," I said, turning right onto the Twelfth Street bridge.

Carlos shook his head sadly. "You reactionary bastard. You have to keep up with the meat grinder of technology or it'll chew you up. I know a bogeyman in Colfax who straps a scanner to his wrist so that whenever he shakes hands with somebody with a death warrant the thing starts playing taps. He pulls his gat, plugs the sap, then saws off the hand he's still shaking." Carlos shook his head in admiration. "Sheer efficiency."

"I'll bet he doesn't have many close friends," I said as we motored into the ghetto of Barridales. "At least none that will shake hands with him."

"Yeah, well, you know what they say about that."

"What?"

"Oh, I don't fucking know. I just thank the merciful Lord we're finally here."

I cut the engine in front of Spiva's Spirits and followed Carlos in. I went to the vitabeer section while Carlos went to the counter.

"Can I help you?" I heard the Pakistani clerk ask.

"I'll have a bottle of the devil," Carlos said.

I got in line behind Carlos, the clerk and I both giving him nervous looks. "A bottle of the devil, sir?" the clerk asked.

"That's right, you evil bastard," Carlos snapped. "A bottle of the goddamn devil."

"The devil? The devil?" the clerk said, frantically scanning the rows of bottles behind him. "What is this devil drink?"

"You know goddamn well who the devil is, you sneaky demon. Don't play dumb with me, I know *your* type. You probably got a big jug of it right under the counter for your own goddamn use." Carlos suddenly lunged over the counter and grabbed a bottle. "There it is, you conniving son of a bitch!"

The clerk spun quickly and they wrestled for a liter of cheap whiskey. "Thief!" the clerk shrieked. "Crazy thief!"

Carlos jerked the bottle from the clerk's grasp and loped out the door, laughing wickedly. I stepped in front of the clerk before he could take up pursuit, shoving plastic at him.

"Don't worry," I said, "I'll pay for it. And this liter of vitabeer."

"Is the whole world gone crazy?" the clerk gasped as he seized the plastic squares with trembling hands. "What is wrong with these crazy men?"

"That's what we'd all like to know," I said, and went outside. I found Carlos leaning against the Olds, slick with rain and sucking on the bottle.

"Aw," he said, after a long pull, "that's better. Now we're safe."

"Been drinking a lot, Carlos?"

"I go on a binge now and then, just to keep the gears oiled." He opened the passenger door and slid in. "Come on, let's motor."

"Where to?"

"Anywhere but Hayward," Carlos said. "There's only so much I can stomach."

We cruised deeper into Barridales, through run-down neighborhoods a short step above shantytowns. Youths, most wearing militia or gang rags, idled and ambled restlessly among the tired tenements and bombed-out buildings, trapped by their own small destinies, numbed and made dangerous by abject, brooding poverty.

"Jesus Christ, look at all these scumbags," Carlos said, "every one of them evil to the core. They haven't the smallest taint of morality."

"It's always been that way."

"Yeah, but each generation is twice as vicious and amoral as the last. The only way to stop the trend is to kill off all the adults and let machines raise the children, or jackals. They couldn't do much worse." He tipped the bottle and didn't stop until his eyes teared. "Goddamn," he gasped. "I wish I had a fusion bomb. I'd blow this whole son of a bitch of a City right up, wipe out the whole bad strain with one big ka-bang."

"You'd kill everyone?"

"Hell, yes. Kick the rotten barrel over and let all the bad apples roll right into hell. Pull over for godsakes, all this driving around is making me crazy."

I turned into the trash-strewn parking lot of a gutted Party food store, undoubtedly torched during one of Barridales's frequent riots. I sat on the hood and opened my bottle of vitabeer, letting the rain run down the back of my neck, watching Carlos prowl around the car, sniffing the air.

"I keep waiting for things to get better, Jake," he said, "I really do, but they don't. What the hell is so wrong with morality that it cannot endure?"

"It goes against human nature."

"Jesus, you're right. It was only a matter of time before we shook off that bullshit."

A garbage can clanged into the parking lot, immediately set upon by a gang of skinny street kids wearing strange and ragged clothing.

"Oh, Jesus Lord," Carlos groaned. "Newlifers."

"Newlifers?" I said, sliding off the hood. "How can you tell?"

"Are you kidding? Look at the way they move, man, they're on a different planet. One dose of that shit permanently rearranges your brain synapses. You're tripping for the rest of your miserable life. See how skinny they are? They're so wrapped up in their trip they forget they're supposed to eat. Three weeks and all those fuckers will die of malnutrition."

"There's something familiar about them," I said, watching them closely.

"They're all over the place. A guy down the hall from me is a Newlifer. He comes over at every odd hour and knocks on my door. I open the door, and he's just standing there in the hall, staring at me with this really weird smile. So I ask him, 'Can I help you, Mike, can I get you a cup of goddamn soy or something?' And all this bastard does is stare and smile at me. So I close the door, and an hour later I open it and he'd still be standing there with that crazy grin on his face. Thing is, he used to be a regular joe like you and me, a nine-to-five pickpocket."

I nodded slowly. "There was a vial of Newlife in Lindquist's mouth."

"It's spreading like a plague," Carlos said, and we watched the Newlifers play with the trash spilled from the garbage can. They made fine sport of stuffing it in their pants, but eventually the game became stale and they turned their attention to me and Carlos. They drifted our way, several picking up blunt instruments.

"Hiya," the foremost said. His smiling eyes were blank and shiny in a rabid animal sort of way, and I realized I'd seen the look before. The Russian in the subway.

Life, death, I wouldn't know the difference.

I reached inside my jacket.

"Let me handle this," Carlos said, taking a step toward the approaching pack. "You better beat it," he warned the Newlifers. "Or I'll turn into a giant rooster and peck your fucking eyes out."

The Newlifers halted, suddenly unsure.

"Cock-a-doodle-doo!" Carlos shouted, flapping his arms. With great howls of terror, the pack scattered across the lot.

"See that?" Carlos said. "They're tripping so hard they'll believe anything."

"Who's selling Newlife?" I asked.

Carlos shrugged. "Who else? The same people who sell all the other shit."

"The Pleasure Syndicate? I don't think so. The drug trade is based on repeat business. A one-dose permanent high is the last thing they'd want." I pointed my face at the rain. "Let's talk about Cain."

Carlos looked at his feet and smiled faintly. "Cain. Crazy ol' Cain. Sometimes I think he's the only one who makes any sense."

"How so?"

"He knows what he wants. If he sees something he doesn't like, he gets rid of it. That's the first rule of survival—stick them before they stick you. Do you remember Elijah Washington?''

''The Riverside bogeyman?''

''Yeah, the Murdering Moor, we used to call him. Always going after pimps, wouldn't work any contracts but pimps and chicken hawks, on account of what happened to his sister.''

''I remember. How's he doing?''

''He fell off the goddamn merry-go-round. He flipped out and took hostages at a reclamation plant. SPF commandos were about to move in when he tried to throw himself in a protein vat. They hauled him away from there, but an hour later he was right back in. Boiled to death. Ain't that funny?''

''I always figured he was endline. He brooded too much. Every time I ran into him he was screaming or crying.''

''And you know what they say,'' Carlos said, ''a killer who cries is about to die. There's nothing more temporary than a bogeyman with a conscience. It's like a big maggot in your belly—it eats and eats until you're hollow.'' He looked off to the left, and his voice became soft and distant. ''Sometimes I swear I feel that bastard gnawing at my insides, biting off little chunks, slowly eating me hollow.'' He held the bottle up. ''That's why I drink this. The maggot hates it.'' He finished the bottle, then let it fall to the ground. ''Someday I'll drink enough to kill the bastard.''

Endline, I thought, right to the core. He's just waiting for death to lead him away. I checked my chrono, suddenly uncomfortable. It was just past nine in the morning.

''Feel like grabbing breakfast?'' I asked.

Carlos leaned off the hood. "No, I think I'm going to walk around for a while, see how the pickings are around here."

"All right," I said. "I'll be in touch."

"Fine," Carlos said and wandered away.

6

I ate a large breakfast of soy strips and algae browns at the Silver Spoon Café on Hayward, then returned to my office to find a monstrous Cain file sitting in the belly of my computer. I mixed a pot of soy coffee, lit a vitacig and began the dissection of a serial killer.

I sifted through the victims' backgrounds first, looking for a common thread that would reveal how Cain selected his prey. Cain's first victim was Donald Basque, the forty-four-year-old overdog of Basco Technologies, a computer-manufacturing firm. Married, with two teenage children, he'd been murdered in his bedroom two weeks ago while the wife and kids were visiting out-of-town relatives. The rotating 3-D image next to his stats showed the strained, borderline-neurotic face of a life-long workaholic.

Cain killed Angela Romani in her bedroom nine days later. The thirty-two-year-old's occupation fell under the always-suspect actress-model-executive assistant category. She lived in an area of the Hill called Valley View, a group of elegant but modest town houses near the gate. I knew enough about the Hill to know that those who lived in Valley View were on the Hill purely out of favor, however temporary. Her 3-D image displayed a frail, doe-eyed, submissively pouting woman, the kind of helpless femme fatale that made power mongers tremble with lust.

Jordan Lindquist was described as a free-lance chemical engineer. He'd moved to the Hill a year earlier, after becoming engaged to a Hill debutante. His 3-D image was a vast improvement over the last time I'd seen him. He appeared fit, handsome and much younger than his forty-one years. His skin was tan, his grin sly, his eyes opportunistic, the classic caricature of a cruise-ship romeo.

Besides living on the Hill, the three appeared to have little in common. All were killed in their bedrooms, but that wasn't odd, considering the hour. Like most serial killers, Cain worked the night shift, striking between 1:00 and 3:00 a.m. Romani and Lindquist could both be described as social climbers, but there were enough of those on the Hill to invite coincidence.

I went over their stats again, added a splash of rum to my cup of soy coffee, lit another vitacig, then moved to the crime-scene photos.

Basque lay on his back, his nude body a pale island in a large pool of blood. Both arms were severed at the shoulder. The left arm was nailed horizontally above his head, the right horizontally below his feet. Nail heads also protruded from Basque's ankles and shoulders. The stomach was slashed vertically from sternum to groin, and horizontally under the ribs and over the pelvis, forming two large flaps. The flaps were pulled back, revealing a cleaned-out chest and stomach cavity that brought to mind an empty cupboard. The missing organs were separated into neat piles on both sides of the corpse. Basque's face was as deliberately wrecked as Lindquist's: mouth crushed, nose severed, eyes plucked and a nail through the forehead.

Miss Romani fared worse. After cutting her in half across the waistline, Cain propped the top half, minus the left arm and right hand, against the headboard of the bed. The bottom half lay next to the bed, the legs splayed open and the errant left arm bridging them at the knees.

Lindquist was much as I remembered him.

I went to the pathologist's reports, written in Burt's florid verbiage, and again searched for similarities. There were many, as Cain's method of mutilation was very ritualized. In each case he stunned his victim with an electric shock, nailed him or her down, removed tongue and eyes, then got down to the business of mutilation. The traumatized flesh around the steel nails confirmed that all three victims, with the help of smelling salts, became conscious before death, suggesting Cain was a sadist. The report also labeled Cain an exhibitionist. Not the sort to shyly bury his prey in a basement, he customized his corpses and left them for all the world to see.

Cain's motives were not larcenous. He apparently took nothing from the homes or persons of his victims, except for the victim's scanhand. He took it as a form of trophy, the report said, a memento to remind him of the deed. The only thing Cain left behind were nails, heavy-duty, eight-inch construction nails, available at any hardware store. The scoring on the nail heads identified the nail gun as a common Party model, portable and powered by small, disposable CO_2 canisters.

Microscopic examination and comparison of wounds narrowed Cain's cutting tool down to a miniature power saw the size of a steak knife. Primarily a geologist's tool for taking rock samples, it was equipped with a 1200 rpm titanium band that cut through marble like a knife through Jell-O, through human flesh as if it wasn't there.

ART's summary followed the forensic report. After collating every speck of data, it cross-referenced with past cases, then ran the results through its artificial-intelligence program, which churned out a mountain of speculation that meant next to nothing. After a grinding hour of statistics, probabilities studies and reports linking Cain's methodology to everything from the Aztec calendar to an obscure nineteenth-Century Dutch poet, I gave up. Cain was moving through their machines like a ghost, leaving nothing but conjecture and waterhead theories.

I dimmed the screen and closed my eyes. I understood that my conscious mind was analogous to a drunk and lazy librarian, unable and unwilling to cope with the huge volume of data I'd amassed. It was the subconscious mind that would assemble all the anonymous detail into truths, then float them up as hunches.

After five minutes of thinking about nothing, I added more rum to my soy coffee, then went back to the pathologist's report. I sensed there was a discrepancy somewhere, something that didn't fit. I skimmed lists of technical data again and again, and half an hour later I found my nugget. I switched to commo mode and called the HDS.

"Hillsdale Defence Society," an elderly receptionist snapped.

"Jake Strait here," I said. "Put me through to Burt."

"What do you want?" Burt said an instant later, appearing annoyed.

"Did you find the square of flesh cut from Lindquist's right biceps?"

Burt blinked at me. "No, we didn't."

"That makes it the only thing besides scanhands Cain ever took with him, right?"

"Hmm, yes."

"Now why would he do that?"

"Who knows? Cain's mind is so exquisitely complex that—"

"I think it was a tattoo," I interrupted. "Are there any tattoo shops on the Hill?"

"Certainly not."

"If I was a Hiller and wanted a tattoo, where would I go?"

"I wouldn't know."

"Ah, screw you, then," I said, then disconnected.

I went back to Lindquist's personal data. His debutante fiancée, Patricia Bonilla, lived at 2278 Goldenbrook Hill, Hillsdale. I read her number to the monitor and, identifying myself as Special Inspector Abel of the SPF, the butler put me through.

"What is it?" she snapped. At eleven in the morning the raven-haired, bitter-faced woman appeared mildly tanked.

"Miss Bonilla?" I asked.

"What do you want?"

"Special Inspector Abel of the SPF here."

She lit a stimstick and blew smoke at the camera. "I thought you assholes were done interrogating me."

"Just a few more questions, Miss Bonilla. Did Jordan Lindquist have any tattoos?"

"No," she said with a frown. "Why?"

"Are you certain? Nothing on his right arm?"

"Believe me, I knew every inch of his body, and he did not have any tattoos. Why do you ask?"

"Did he ever talk about getting a tattoo?"

"Not with me, he didn't. Are you—"

"When was the last time you saw Lindquist?"

"Six weeks ago. If you think—"

"Six weeks is a long time for fiancées to be apart."

"That is none of your business, spif."

"I'm afraid it is, Miss Bonilla. Did you break up?"

"I don't have to answer that." She stabbed out her stick and reached for the disconnect.

"*You* killed him!" I snarled. "Didn't you, Miss Bonilla?"

"I did not!" she cried, startled.

"I'm going to be straight with you, Miss Bonilla," I said, my voice authoritarian and cold. "Right now you are the SPF's *number one* suspect in Lindquist's death."

"*Me?* But Cain killed him!"

"Or someone pretending to be Cain. Unless you come clean, we're going to have to run you in for some heavy interrogation. Do you know what an infrared spectrometer is, Miss Bonilla?"

"Good heavens, no!"

"It's a very brutal and evil machine, Miss Bonilla. Normally we only use it on hard-core criminals and lawyers, but due to the obvious importance of this case, the Party says I can use it on whomever I damn well please. And do you know what? I *like* using it. It makes me feel *good* inside. Are you getting me?"

"I want to talk to my lawyer," she wailed. "He's a very prominent—"

"Oh, we know who *he* is," I said. "We've had our eye on that rat bastard for some time now. I sent a special interrogation team around Mr. Prominent Lawyer's office with a hundred-kilowatt genital clamp about an hour ago. I don't think he's up to defending your legal rights at the moment, Miss Bonilla. I think his biggest worry right now is getting out of intensive care."

"You can't do that," she sobbed.

"Oh, but I can. I can do whatever I damn well please and I have the papers to prove it. I have total power in this matter and, quite frankly, I'm just itching to snap the spine of anyone dumb enough to stand in my way. Am I clear, Miss Bonilla?''

"Yes," she sobbed. "Yes, yes, yes."

I fought down a premature surge of guilt and pressed on. "When was the last time you saw Lindquist nude?"

"What kind of question is that?" she wailed.

"Just answer, Miss Bonilla. And be truthful, I have you on the voice analyzer."

"A week before we broke up, seven weeks ago."

"Would you have noticed a tattoo on his right arm if he had one?"

"Yes."

"Was there a bandage on his right arm?"

"No."

"Why did you break up with Lindquist?"

"He was sleeping with someone else. He just used me to get on the Hill."

"Who was he sleeping with?"

"I don't know. Jordan was very secretive about it."

"How did you know he was cheating?"

"Believe me, Inspector, a woman knows when she's sharing a man." Her voice cracked, and she began to weep softly. "Jordan was in love, but not with me."

"I see. Thank you for your time, Miss Bonilla. I think we can take you off the suspect list."

"Oh, thank you, Inspector. Thank you so very much."

"Just doing my job. Good day, Miss Bonilla."

I disconnected and let the rum roll into the cup. "Just doing my job," I told the room, "that's all."

I emptied the cup then switched the screen to the City directory. When I told it to display all the tattoo shops in the City and burbs, forty-seven addresses popped up on the screen.

I called Degas.

"What?" he said, the screen blank.

"This is Strait. I need you to modem over Lindquist's scan record for the past two months."

"What for?"

"I'm trying to trace the missing tattoo."

"What tattoo?"

"The one Cain took with him."

"We're on it."

"I'll help you."

"We don't need any help."

"Listen, Degas," I said, "I don't want to have to go bawling to Bowlan every time I need support from you goons, but I will."

There was a brief silence. "When this is over, you and I are going to have a long talk in a parking lot."

"Whatever you say, champ. Standing by to receive." I disconnected, and ten spiteful minutes later it came over.

I pored over the list. It revealed that, as far as Party scanners knew, Lindquist had left the confines of Hillsdale just six times in two months. His chip popped up at a security checkpoint in the suburban borough of Southend on five of the occasions, returning to the Hill late in the evening each time. On his sixth and final excursion, a week prior to his death, he'd left the Hill just after 1:00 a.m. He'd made a small scan purchase at Taylor's Liquor Emporium in the borough of Barridales three hours later, then passed back through the gate forty minutes after that.

It seemed a long way to go for a bottle of hooch. I displayed the directory map of Barridales and found Taylor's on the corner of Broughton and Reinhart. I superimposed the locations of all the tattoo shops in Barridales and found the red dot of Kishintai Tattoos and

Life Readings three blocks away. I grabbed my jacket on the way out the door.

I took Twelfth Street across the river and turned right on Broughton, Barridales's main drag. Broughton wasn't quite as wicked as Hayward but not through any noticeable lack of effort. I turned left on Reinhart, drove three blocks, then parked in front of Kishintai Tattoos and Life Readings. The legend was painted in garish Manchu lettering on a glass storefront otherwise painted black.

Chimes announced my entrance, and a wizened Oriental wearing a black robe and extremely candid stare bounded in front of me.

"You want reading and tattoo," he assured.

"Maybe," I said, taking in the bamboo walls, Buddhist decor and jasmine incense. Two wooden chairs carved with dragons and tigers sat next to two low bamboo tables spread with diabolical-looking tattoo guns. "A friend of mine stopped by here a week ago. A Mr. Jordan Lindquist of Hillsdale. Muscular, good-looking blond chap. He got a tattoo on his right biceps. He showed it to me at a party but I forgot what it was. I was wondering if you could tell me."

"You want reading and tattoo."

"Right. When I saw Jordan's tattoo I decided I wanted one just like it. But I can't quite remember what it was, and Lindquist won't tell me because he's selfish. I was hoping you could help me." I took a hundred-credit square out of my pocket and showed it to him.

Seeming not to notice, he said, "You want reading and tattoo."

"Right. Right you are. The exact same as Jordan's. But I'd like you to remind me what the tattoo was before I actually get it."

"You want reading and tattoo."

I stared at the impenetrable mask. "Yes," I sighed. "I guess I do."

"Sit down," he said, pointing at one of the wooden chairs.

I took off my jacket and sat down. He selected a tattoo gun and whirred it once. "Right biceps?" he asked.

"Yes," I said, rolling up my shirt sleeve. "Just like my pal Jordan."

He seized my right hand with a tight grip and pointed his dead eyes at me. After a tense moment he let go and went to work with the gun. It was like being repeatedly stung by a foot-long hornet, and the Oriental had the disconcerting habit of staring at my face instead of my arm.

"I hope he didn't get anything too corny," I said.

"Who?"

"Lindquist," I said, distressed. "This will be the same as Jordan's, won't it?"

"I don't know," he said, his enunciation suddenly fluid. "I didn't do Jordan Lindquist's tattoo."

"Then what are you putting on me?"

"Your life sign."

"Fantastic. Did Lindquist even come in here?"

"A man came in seven days ago. He was from the Hill, but had not been there very long. A woman was with him."

"A woman? What did she look like?"

"I don't know. I've been blind since birth."

I stared at him. The gun was busy, but his eyes still pointed at me with the same unsettling stare. "A blind tattooist," I speculated. "That's about my luck. Who did Lindquist's tattoo?"

"Mr. Hito."

"Where's he?"

"In the desert."

"What's he doing there?"

"He is searching for his inner *ki.*"

"How long is it going to take him to find it?"

He shrugged. "One day, one week, one year, one life-time."

I sagged. "Sure, why not? I mean, what's a man without his *ki,* for crissakes?"

"I am finished," he said. He returned the gun to the table and went to a small sink. I examined my new tattoo—a black, superbly intricate black skull the size of a thumbnail.

"That's an endline tattoo," I said.

He shrugged, washing his hands in the sink. "It is your life sign."

"You mean death sign."

He turned his black-eyed stare to me. "Death is your life, is it not?"

"Let's not get into that," I said, shouldering my jacket. "What's the price?"

"Three hundred."

"That's some expensive ink."

"It's the reading that is expensive."

"Of course." I handed over the credit along with my card. "Tell Mr. Hito to call me when he comes back with his *ki.*"

He bowed. I started to leave, then turned around. "How do you know I didn't shortchange you?" I asked.

"Because I know your *ki.* More than you do."

I nodded and left.

I admired my new tattoo as I drove. Regardless of whatever dire fate it portended, it was an extremely fine piece of work. I wheeled to Bukowski Boulevard, the diseased heart of the City's corrupt soul. I parked in front of a small sidewalk shrine to St. Kerouac, patron saint of drunks, travelers and the criminally insane. I got out and strolled slowly among credit-hungry confession machines and street-corner prophets, past rescue missions ringing with songs of salvation sung by winos and junkies. I had only walked three blocks before I heard a sermon about Cain.

"Neither fallen angel nor risen demon is Cain!" the long-bearded whiskey evangelist railed from atop his wine-crate podium. "He is us! He kills in *our* name! He murders our misguided rich brothers on the Hill because they have left the fold. Just as the Almighty struck down the shinyhairs atop their Tower of Babel, Cain lays low those who would set themselves on yonder hill and call themselves *gods!*"

"Fuck you!" a wino called out. "Cain is a nihilist! Endline! He hates God! He hates you!" The wino reared back and hurled his empty bottle at the whiskey evangelist, smiting him across the forehead. The old man staggered back but maintained his balance on the crate.

"Look!" he cried, jabbing a finger at his bloodied brow. "Look carefully for the mark of Cain, for it is on us all. And as the good book says, those who would strike down Cain will be themselves struck down sevenfold." He leaped dramatically from the crate, then began fighting his way through the crowd. "And I'm gonna start with that son of a bitch who threw the bottle."

I moved on, stopping to witness more street-corner sermons as I went. Cain seemed to be the hot topic and all the ghetto prophets swore Cain was something more than a man with an appetite for gore; he was portent, prophet, punisher, pop star, all things vaunted to all the low men.

I bought a soy dog from a vendor and ate it on the hood of my car, watching winos light candles at the chipped feet of St. Kerouac. My attention eventually shifted to the bank of confession machines next to the shrine.

Why not? I thought, finishing the dog and slipping into one of the molded-plastic booths. The interior smelled of stale urine, and someone had done a bad job of wiping vomit from the plastic seat. Remaining on my feet, I pulled the black curtain shut and squared off with the monitor.

"Forgive me, for I have sinned," I said.

The video image of a smiling, gray-haired priest lit up the screen. "How long since your last confession?" the machine asked in a slightly choppy voice.

"Never."

The priest lost a little of his smile. "Please select your sins from the list," he said, vanishing beneath a monstrous roster of moral trespasses. I touched the Murder button.

"Justifiable or unjustifiable?" flashed onto the screen. I hesitated, then touched the former.

"How many justifiable murders have you committed since your last confession? More than one?"

I touched the Yes button.

"More than ten?"

I touched Yes again, climbing the pyramid. When I pressed Yes at "More than one hundred," the machine gave up and the priest returned to lay the verdict on me.

"Penance for one hundred or more justifiable murders is fifty-five thousand credits," the priest said gravely. "You may insert the required credit or place your right hand under the scanner for fund transfer."

"Good God!" I exclaimed. "My soul is in hock for fifty-five grand?"

The machine repeated its demand, and I slipped out of the booth. A flashing red strobe atop the booth announced my exit, along with a damning voice booming from hidden speakers: "Hell! Hell! Pay at once or your soul is condemned to eternal damnation!"

"Why don't you pay your penance?" said a short, dirty man kneeling in front of St. Kerouac.

"I didn't do anything," I told him, climbing into the Olds. "The damn thing is rigged."

I roared away, shoulders hunched, heart burning with regret. Well, I thought grimly, at least now I know how much. I found a parking space in front of my office building and was halfway across the lobby when I saw a familiar face.

"Hey, you," I said, cornering him against a vitacig machine.

"Me?" the human mop squealed. "I didn't do it!"

"Relax," I said, clamping a hand on his shoulder. "What's your name?"

"What for? I didn't do it, I swear!"

"Take it easy. I just want to ask you a question."

"I know who you are!" he cried, trying to break out of my grip. "I got the word on *you*. You're the bogeyman from upstairs!"

"No, no, that's not me. My office is *across* from his. I'm Jack the happy plumber, not Jake the soulless killer."

He stopped squirming. "You don't look like no plumber."

"Who does?" I said, then lowered my voice. "I need some Newlife."

"Christ!" he exclaimed, his voice cautious and low. "Keep it down. I don't deal that shit. Who sent you?"

"No one. I heard you had some to sell."

"Are you wacky? The Pleasure Syndicate has a bounty on anyone caught pushing that shit. I hear they got shooters dressed up like junkies going around with rotor pistols, gutting anyone who says they can score Newlife."

"All right," I said gruffly, slipping into what con men call the Tell-Me-Who-I-Am Sham, "you pass."

He squinted suspiciously at me. "Huh?"

"You pass. The Pleasure Syndicate hired me to check around for the stuff, and you played it just right."

"Goddamn, I *knew* it."

"You don't happen to know anyone pushing Newlife, do you? It could be worth a favor from the syndie if you come through."

"Yeah?" he said, rubbing his jaw. "What kind of favor?"

"We won't kill you."

"The only source I know about is the Reds, but you guys already know that."

"We sure do," I said. "And we're just about to knock them fuckers down."

He frowned. "I thought they had some kind of big-time protection."

"Bigger than the Pleasure Syndicate?"

"That's what I heard."

"Huh. I guess we won't be knocking them down, then. All right," I said, glancing around, "keep your ears open. If you hear anything about Newlife, let me know and I'll slide you another favor."

"What will this favor be? To not break my legs?"

"Bingo," I said, walking back to the Olds, wondering who in the City was bigger than the Pleasure Syndicate. No one came to mind, and there seemed only one way to find out. I would have to play a much more daring and dangerous game of Tell-Me-Who-I-Am.

7

The Pleasure Syndicate was originally an umbrella term for a small cooperative of drug dealers who had banded together during the dangerous days of the corporate wars. Over the years the group had grown into an intricately organized criminal reich, rivaled in the City only by the ever-eroding power of the SPF. It happened that I was primarily responsible for the destruction of one of the Pleasure Syndicate's major squeeze factories in months past, but I didn't believe they were aware of my guilt. I didn't think so because I happened to still be alive.

I parked in front of the Pleasure Syndicate's central office. I knew it was their central office because it said so on the front door of the boxy brick office building. Protected by a web of iron-clad treaties with every major gang, militia and syndicate in the City, the Pleasure Syndicate felt they had nothing to fear, and rightly so. They were as safe as the biggest, meanest tiger in the jungle.

As I walked up the concrete pathway to the front door I reviewed what I knew about Martin Mateaus, the present head of the Pleasure Syndicate. Street legend said he'd risen from humble beginnings, a man as practical and unpretentious as the building from which he ran his empire. He was known to speak his mind freely and was said to be ferociously evil but fair, which didn't make a hell of a lot of sense to me.

The thick Plexiglas door buzzed when I pushed it open, and a large, bullish man behind a spartan receptionist desk looked up. Two slack-eyed men lounging on a low-set sofa ignored me in a malevolent sort of way.

"Marty in?" I asked, stopping in front of the desk.

"Who's askin'?"

I looked over my shoulder to see if someone had followed me in. "Just me."

"Marty don't wanna see him," one of the men on the sofa drawled lethargically.

"How do you know?" I asked.

"I know 'cause I know, chump."

"Who are they?" I asked the receptionist. "The shoe-shine boys?"

I could tell I got them mad because they both half opened their eyes. "Don't make us get up," one warned.

"Oh, heck no."

"What do you wanna see Marty for?" the receptionist asked.

"It's about Newlife."

Our eyes locked and he leaned on an intercom button. "Boss?"

"What the hell now?" the boss responded.

"Some guy's here about the Newlife thing."

After a pause, Marty said, "Get his heat and show him in."

The receptionist stood up. "Give me your gun."

"What makes you think I have a gun?"

"By the look on your face."

I handed over the gyrapistol and the receptionist opened the door next to the desk.

Martin Mateaus sat behind a tidy desk deep in a tidy office. His features were strongly simian, and he had the nervous tic of curling his upper lip and baring his big canine teeth every few seconds. His hair was arranged into a pompadour, his sideburns into mutton chops, and he came off as some sort of psychotic, hairless, superintelligent, Elvis-obsessed gorilla.

Marty dismissed the receptionist with a wave. I began prowling the room, muttering to myself.

"What's your problem?" he said after watching me for a moment.

"I'm heated up, that's what."

"Heated up about what?"

I stopped prowling long enough to jab an accusing finger at him. "We told you not to lean on the Red Horde, *didn't we?*"

"What are you talking about? Who's 'we'?"

"All right, bust my balls," I said, stalking to the door. "*Fuck* with me. You'll be getting yours in about twenty minutes."

"Sit down," Marty said. I sulked at the door for a moment, purely out of drama, then sprawled on a cheap vinyl chair. He bared his teeth and stared at me for two full minutes without saying a word.

"I'm sitting," I said.

"You don't look right."

"My pirate outfit's at the cleaners."

"You dress like you was from the City."

Clue! I thought. "I'm incognito," I said.

After another long pause he said, "We ain't leaning on nobody."

"That's not what we hear."

"I don't care what those Russian monkeys told you. We ain't even spitting in their direction."

"Just can't be straight with me, huh? Well, let me tell you how it is. The Horde say you've been putting the mean grip on them: sidelong looks, soaped windows, swiped hubcaps, nasty letters, the whole bit."

"You a messenger or a comedian?" he snapped, but there was relief in his voice. "C'mon, you know how that Russian monkey is. He's been bawling about something or other ever since he took over those damn Commies."

"Is that what you want me to tell the man?"

"The man? Who's the man?"

"You know damn well who the man is. Damn well."

"No," he said, baring his teeth dangerously. "You tell me who the man is."

We stared at each other, and I became suddenly uncomfortable. "Chicken Little?" I ventured.

His face hardened, and I quickly reviewed my options. It didn't take me long to realize I didn't actually have any options. Leaning slightly forward, I tensed to lunge for Marty's throat the same instant the hard mask broke and Marty started to laugh. I laughed along.

"You better hope I don't tell him you said that," he said. "He'll have your balls."

"Yes," I sighed, standing up. "Anything you want me to tell him?"

"Yeah, you tell froggy everything is jake." He paused. "Strait."

I smiled uneasily. "You know me?"

"Of course," he said. "You're the son of a bitch who blew up my squeeze factory. Have a nice fucking day."

I exited without saying goodbye. Not because I wanted to be rude, but because my lungs and throat muscles had seized up. I picked up my pistol on the way out, and ten blocks later I still felt as if I'd left my guts lying back on the carpeted floor of Marty's office.

I drove home under dusky skies, mentally reviewing what I'd learned. First, whoever was protecting the Reds was not from the City. Second, Martin Mateaus, the vicious yet fair boss of the City's most powerful crime syndicate, was afraid of him. Third, he might possibly resemble a frog.

I stopped at a kabob shop for dinner, then drove home. I jogged the stairs to my fourth-floor Rood Avenue flat and immediately powered on Dr. Abuso, the high-tech workout machine occupying most of my living room.

"You wimp bastard!" the doctor roared as I changed into sweats. "It's been four days, twenty-one hours and thirty-nine minutes since your last workout!"

"Take it easy on me tonight," I said, sliding under the hydraulic bench press. "I'm a little tired."

A long, terrible wail blasted from stereo speakers. "Take it easy on you? I'll goddamn *croak* you, you simpering geek! I'll snap your will like a twig!"

I did three quick sets at each station, ignoring the doctor's rude cheerleading, trying to get a handle on Cain.

I was beginning to understand he was going to be one hard nut to crack. Even if I did manage to locate him, clipping him in the City would be akin to jumping the Pope on the steps of the Vatican. I'd be crucified and castrated before I could even think about cashing any bonus checks.

By the time I worked my way to the heavy punching bag, I came to know the two paths from which I had to choose. I could incur the wrath of my employers by following my leads to the Hill in hopes of solving the case, or I could remain in the City in hopes of bleeding Pennings for as much credit as possible.

I cooled down on the treadmill, took a long shower and still couldn't make up my mind. Wearing a bathrobe, I carried a vitabeer to the window overlooking Rood Avenue. A young couple under an umbrella walked arm in arm down the sidewalk below, and a gray loneliness crowded in the room with me. I finished the vitabeer and wandered to the bedroom, turning out lights as I went. I paused in the doorway to stare at a bed that, in the moonlight, looked much, much too large for me.

"Aw, I don't give a damn," I muttered, crawling under the sheets. I lay perfectly still, trying to ignore the sound of high female laughter from the apartment next door. Moments later I put my hands over my ears, squeezed my eyes shut and prayed for God to crush me flat.

THE MORNING SUN found me on the speedway, wearing my best suit and racing uphill. The Oldsmobile was as fast and headstrong as a rocket sled and handled nearly as well. I sometimes suspected the steering wheel was just for my amusement, having more in common with a suggestion box than a guidance device.

After scanning my chip and verifying my pass card, the SPF troopers at the gate gave me directions to the headquarters of the Hillsdale Defense Society.

I wasn't absolutely certain the architect who designed HDS headquarters was a phallic-obsessed fan of Albert Speer, but I figured it was a good bet. Huge, embarrassingly erect granite columns with rounded tops flanked the wide granite walkway, and you just knew the *men* were in control here. The mirror-glass entrance of the single-story granite monstrosity sat in the shadow of an immense granite statue of Thor. The Norse god faced the distant City and—judging by his expression and the way he held his hammer—every man, woman and child in the City had welshed on a large bet, laughed in his face, then called his entire family a pack of inbred curs.

I tried the door and found it locked. I stuck my Hill pass in the card slot next to the handle, but all it did was beep at me. I knocked on the glass. I banged, I kicked, I shouted obscenely. Yet the door would not open.

I leaned against the base of the statue and waited. Two vitacigs later an officious clerk with an armful of forms hurried up the walkway. His card made the door click, and he heaved it open. I crowded in close behind him, causing him to frown over his shoulder as he scurried through the reception room. He waved to the elderly receptionist behind a counter, then passed through a buzzing black steel door. I went to the counter.

I recognized the elderly receptionist from when I'd called Burt. She sat with her back to me, her fingers harrying a keyboard.

"Excuse me," I said.

"Yes?" she barked.

"I need to see Sir Henry Bowlan."

She turned around, took me in with a flickering glance, then turned away again. "You need an appointment," she said, going back to her typing.

"I have an appointment."

"Your name?" she barked, stabbing at the keyboard.

"Oh, it's on the list." I said, shifting to see the screen. She effectively blocked my view by shifting to the right.

"Your name, sir?"

"Jones-Smith," I gambled. "It could be under either."

Her neck tensed. "Just where in Hillsdale do you reside, Mr. *Jones-Smith?*"

"What makes you think I reside in Hillsdale?"

"Believe me, I don't."

"On Main Street."

"There is no Main Street in Hillsdale."

"No, I meant to say, on *the* main street."

"Which main street is that?"

"Whichever one I live on."

She turned around to show me her frown, then reached under the counter. "You can't see anyone until you've filled out a questionnaire," she said, holding out a bookish sheaf of papers.

"Certainly," I said, earnestly taking the questionnaire. I waited for her to turn around, then marched purposefully to the black door. I tried the handle. Locked.

"What are you doing?"

"Isn't this the bathroom?" I grunted, testing the lock's strength.

"The bathroom is back there," she said, pointing to an unmarked door beyond a collection of wicker furniture.

"Oh." I stopped tugging on the handle and returned to the counter. "Have you a pencil?"

She jabbed a short pencil with no eraser at me. I took the pencil and promptly dropped it behind the counter.

"I'll get it!" I said, gamely leaning over the counter to paw blindly, trying to locate the button that would activate the door's electronic lock.

"Here it is!" the secretary screeched, springing up from the floor with the errant pencil, stabbing viciously at my groping hands.

I seized the pencil and backed off, rubbing puncture wounds. I sat on a wicker sofa and waded into the thirty-odd pages of the HDS nonresident questionnaire. In no uncertain terms it demanded to know everything about me: what I'd done, where I'd been, who my friends were and just where did I get off thinking I deserved an appointment with the very busy Hillsdale Defense Society, anyway? I threw myself at the task and handed the questionnaire back forty-five minutes later.

"Leave it on the counter," she said without turning around.

"Do I get to go in now?"

"Sit down. I'll call you."

I sat down. Half an hour passed. The questionnaire remained on the counter, untouched.

"You should really take a look at it," I called from the sofa. "Especially pages fifteen and sixteen. It's about my trip to Europe. Quite racy. Go on, take a look, I don't mind."

"Be quiet," she said. "Sit still and be quiet."

I was still and quiet for fifteen minutes before I went to the counter and picked up the questionnaire.

"What do you think you're doing?"

"I thought I'd spice up the ending," I said. "It drags a bit."

"It'll delay your appointment."

"Yes, but I feel my artistic integrity may well be at stake here."

I walked the questionnaire back to the wicker sofa. Very quietly I crumpled the questionnaire into a head-sized ball. I stuffed the ball halfway down the cushion of the sofa and, taking out my lighter, lit it.

I scooted away from the spreading flames and watched the secretary.

Thirty seconds later the wicker itself had caught fire, and the secretary began sniffing at the air. She turned around.

"Hello," I said, smiling at her agreeably. "Rather hot in here, isn't it?"

"Fire!" she squawked.

"What's that you say?" I said, then looked to the fire devouring the sofa. "Yow!" I shouted, leaping up from the sofa and lunging for the counter. "This is an outrage! How do you expect me to fill out a questionnaire under these conditions?"

"The sofa's on fire!" she screamed.

"My point exactly! Open the door so I can get a fire extinguisher before flames engulf the entire building and you're held personally responsible for the entire tragedy!"

She clawed at a button beneath her desk, her mind completely unhinged, and the door buzzed. I pulled it open savagely and rushed down the hall, harried by the secretary's urgent screams. I found Bowlan's office and ducked in. An attractive young secretary smiled up from her desk.

"Hi," I smiled, closing the door with my back.

"Yes?"

"I'm here to see Sir Henry."

"What's your name?" she said, then cocked her head. "Are those alarm bells?"

"Oh," I said, waving a dismissive hand. "Some rude *urbanite* barged into the reception room and ran amok. He even had the temerity to set fire to the furniture!"

"What nerve! Has he been apprehended?"

"I'm afraid not. That sort of brute always seems to get away." I started for the door behind her desk. "Is Sir Henry in?"

"Yes," she said, half rising, "but he's in conference right now."

"Great," I said, dodging her clawing hands and pushing through the door. I locked it quickly behind me, my presence announced by the secretary's enthusiastic pounding.

"Hank, Roger," I said, nodding to each before sitting down in a padded oak chair. Bowlan sat behind a huge oak desk with the tacit authority of a pit boss manning a craps table. His second in command leaned on the desk with both hands and grinned as if he were about to try his luck with a pair of loaded dice. Both were in full HDS costume.

"What are you doing here?" Bowlan demanded.

I shrugged. "Oh, I just thought I'd come up here and pal around with you guys for a while, maybe pick up a few pointers."

"Well," Eliot said, "I've got to be going." On the way to the door he stopped to shake my hand. "Good seeing you again, Mr. Strait. Any leads down your way?"

"Yeah. The only problem is they all lead up here."

"Really? How odd. Be seeing you."

Eliot opened the door, stepped into the path of the secretary's blind charge, then ushered her out. The door clicked shut, and Bowlan and I had an impromptu staring contest.

"All right," I said meanly, "let's see it, you cagey bastard."

"Good heavens! See what?"

"The hooch, for crissakes."

Bowlan leaned back, interlacing his fingers across his chest and making a show of pitying me. "I don't imbibe," he said with the self-righteousness of a recently reformed alcoholic. "I'm afraid the strongest libation I enjoy these days is mineral water with a splash of lemon pulp." He lifted a glass of mineral water from his desk and sipped, just to prove he wasn't fibbing. I noted he drank his mineral water from a highball glass, as if to say it was the style of glassware rather than alcohol he'd been slave to.

"So what is it precisely that you require?" he asked, dabbing his lips with a handkerchief. "I thought we made it implicitly clear you are to investigate the City for leads. Not Hillsdale. The City. You are what we call our man in the gutter—or on the street, rather."

"The gutter isn't saying much," I reported. "So I came up here to see what your problem is."

"Problem? What makes you think we have a problem?"

"When someone like Cain is able to slay at will in a small, confined community like Hillsdale, the law-enforcement body involved is obviously screwing up. If I can find where you're screwing up, I'll know where to look for Cain."

Bowlan harrumphed, and it was like shaking hands with an old friend. "You young street hoodlum!" he raged. "How dare you come in here and accuse the HDS of incompetence! You'll return to the City at once or I'll have you fired!"

"Go ahead," I said. "Fire me. I dare you."

He eyed me, jaw agape. "What makes you think I won't?"

"Because you don't have the authority. I know your type. You're a trained monkey, a stuffed shirt full of bullshit. You don't give orders, you echo them like a parrot."

"Well, we'll just see what Mr. Pennings thinks about that!" he howled, picking up an old-fashioned telephone. "Yes, we certainly will!"

"Go ahead," I said. "Give Hiram a call. Lay it on him. Tell him I'll be right over with my report."

Bowlan froze, handset to his ear. "Report? What report?"

"My report to Mr. Pennings," I lied. "He called me yesterday and asked me why I thought the Cain investigation wasn't going anywhere. I told him I didn't know but I'd stop by when I found out."

"You're lying."

I smiled cruelly. "I might be. Why not call and ask? Tell him how you're impeding my investigation."

The handset returned to the cradle. "I am not impeding anything," Bowlan rumbled, shuffling papers busily. "You must understand, the Cain investigation is just one of many cases I dedicate my time and energy to. I therefore cannot be held responsible for any one case in particular." He nodded once, pleased with his logic.

"All right," I said. "I want to talk to whoever in the HDS *is* responsible for catching Cain. If such a person actually exists."

"Of course. I understand perfectly. Go down the hall two doors and turn right. Go into the first door on your left."

"All right," I said, standing up. "but if the sign on the door says Exit, I'm coming right back."

"Not to worry. It's the office of one of our top men working on the case. I'll tell him you're coming."

"I bet you will," I said. The secretary in the outer office did not leap on my back and claw out my eyes, but she looked as if she wanted to. I moved briskly to the hall and followed Bowlan's directions to an unmarked door. The door was unlocked, so I went in.

Inside was the kind of impeccable neatness achievable only through a severe case of anal retentiveness. I locked the door behind me and went to the gleaming stainless-steel desk in front of a wall crowded with framed degrees and certificates.

I really didn't have a reason to rifle through the desk, but I didn't have a reason not to, either. Polished wooden slats divided the top drawer into a grid of thirty-six boxes, labeled *A* to *Z* with tiny brass plaques. In the *A* box I found aspirin, in the *B* box bandages and a bottle opener and so forth. The three drawers on the left side of the desk accommodated stacks of various HDS forms. The single large drawer on the right side was locked. On a hunch I went to the top drawer, and in the *K* box I found a small desk key. I unlocked the large drawer.

"The dark underbelly," I murmured. The drawer was a devil's nest of hard-core pornography and gory crime-scene prints mixed with newspaper articles about Cain and the Iceman. Some of the photos were scissored and shredded, while others were defaced with a red ink marker. Buried beneath the vulgar jumble was a white handkerchief, stiff and musky with dried semen.

I heard a hand try the door. I quickly shut the drawer and fumbled to lock it. A keycard clicked in the door slot outside, and I jerked open the top drawer. The door opened as I dropped the key into its box.

Burt Swinburne, in full HDS regalia, froze in the doorway. "What are you doing?"

"Looking for a match," I said, lifting a matchbook from the *M* square. "Here it is."

Burt moved swiftly to the desk, and I got out of his way. He checked his grids, carefully closed the drawer, tugged on the handle of the large drawer, found it locked and, without further ceremony, sat down. He began minutely adjusting the positions of the desk's many accessories, making sure everything was in its proper place. "Please don't smoke," he said without looking up.

I sat in a stainless-steel chair and lit a vitacig.

He looked up hostilely, crossing his eyes at the vitacig. "I told you not to smoke."

"So?"

He kept his eyes on me for a full minute, giving me the kind of withering, unblinking glare that probably made his underlings wake up nights, screaming. "So *stop it,*" he hissed.

"Make me."

His eyes bulged with outrage, and his head began to tremble as he doubled the intensity of his stare. "You are infuriating me, Mr. Strait," he trebled, speaking as if he were reading from a script in which every other word was underlined. "*I* am *not* a *man* you *wish* to *infuriate.*"

"Yeah, I can tell by the tassels and shoulder boards."

His cheeks became even more florid, and he began straightening up the desk's accessories again, lifting each an inch off the desk then snapping it back down. "What do you want?"

"Information about Cain."

"We sent you everything we know about Cain."

"I already waded through that pile of crap. I came away with the feeling you're leaving things out. I don't think Cain's the sensitive artist you make him out to be. I think he's an executioner trying to pass himself off as a psycho killer."

"And what qualifies you to say that?"

"The mutilations are systematic, dispassionate, the work of a man doing a job, not a passionate psycho dedicated to his art. And no matter how obviously dead they are, he always puts an eight-inch nail through the brain."

"So?"

"So a mark can never be too dead. I think Cain is a hit man, and all the mutilation and gore is a smoke screen."

"A *smoke screen!*" Burt cackled. "And I suppose Michelangelo painted the roof of the Sistine Chapel to cover up water stains."

"Could be. I never knew the bastard."

Burt folded his hands on the desk, his eyes flickering among the accessories, making sure none had moved out of place. "You're groping at smoke," he said, "that's what you're doing. Your investigation isn't going anywhere, so you came up here to take it out on us."

"You ever hang out in the City, Burt?"

He hooded his eyes and squared up a pen holder with the forward edge of the desk. "I conduct field studies on occasion."

"You know anything about the Pleasure Syndicate?"

He covered his surprise with a mask of confusion. "The what?"

"The Pleasure Syndicate."

"Never heard of it."

"All those degrees in criminology, and you've never heard of the Pleasure Syndicate?"

"That's right. *Organized* crime is not my field of study."

"I see," I said, standing up.

"What? You're finished with your interrogation already? You haven't even tied me up and hit me with a rubber hose yet."

"I wouldn't do you the favor," I said, going to the door. "I came here looking for the key to Cain's success. I think I've found it."

"Really?" Burt trilled, resting his jowls on bridged fingers. "And what is your conclusion?"

"You," I said. "You're protecting him. And what's more, I think you know who Cain is. Good day, Burt."

8

I walked the hall, lost in thought. I didn't actually believe Burt knew Cain from his mother, but I did think he knew more than he was telling. Like a fanatical zoologist who had fallen in love with a rogue elephant, Burt would rather have it run amok for the sake of scientific study than kill it. I was betting my accusation would pressure him to cough up some of the facts he was holding on to.

I had to shove my way through the frantic mob of firemen and SPF troopers milling around in the lobby. They'd successfully extinguished the sofa but seemed to be having trouble with the receptionist. She had locked herself in one of the bathrooms and refused to come out, shouting incoherently about "outside saboteurs" and "not taking responsibility for anything." I kept my head down until I reached my car.

I got back on the main drag and continued uphill. I didn't know where Hiram Pennings lived but I did know that on the Hill altitude equated power. I followed the winding road up and up, passing consecutively grander estates until the road expired before a forbidding four-meter-high black granite wall breached by an arched entrance. The heavy arch was carved with a single word: Pennings.

There were no guards, no dogs, no posted threats, not so much as a camera. There was an arrogance in the flagrant lack of physical security, it spoke of rings of invisible protection more powerful than all the guards and Dobermans in the world.

I steered through the open gate and drove up to the castle occupying the very apex of the Hill. It was not a mansion pretending to be a castle; it was an actual castle with a moat and drawbridge and ramparts and places for archers to hide. I parked in a roundabout centered by a ten-meter-tall bronze statue of Atlas. This particular Atlas apparently didn't think much of carrying the world on his shoulders, preferring to carry it under his left arm like an overinflated beach ball. His right hand held a sword, his face held a venal sort of arrogance.

I caught myself trying to knead the wrinkles out of my suit as I crossed the drawbridge. I gave up at the front door, a three-meter-high oak slab with the Pennings crest bolted to its center; a two-headed imperial eagle with four legs, each claw crushing a smaller, visibly daunted creature.

As I reached for the heavy knocker, the door opened. An olive-skinned, craggy-faced man in a butler's uniform looked out at me. Slight of build and inscrutable of mien, he appeared to have all the personality and humor of a bullwhip. I smiled amiably, half expecting him to signal the men on the ramparts to pour the molten lead.

"May I help you, sir?" he asked in a voice completely bare of extravagance.

"I need to see Hiram Pennings," I said.

"May I ask why?"

"He hired me to kill someone."

He stared at me for a moment, his eyes black caves in a rocky cliff. "You are Mr. Strait."

"Yes."

"Come in, Mr. Strait." He moved aside, and I stepped into a high-ceilinged foyer. "I am Mr. Baily. May I have your jacket, sir?"

"I won't be here that long."

"May I have your armaments, then, sir?"

"I suppose it's the look on my face," I said, handing him the gyrapistol. He took the pistol in his left hand but otherwise didn't move.

"Well?" I said.

"You forgot the pistol in the back of your belt, sir."

I smiled and handed him the small automatic. "You've a good eye. Where'd you get it?"

"I served as a corporate raider prior to becoming Mr. Pennings's butler. And the knife in your right hip pocket, if you would, sir."

"Don't miss a trick, do you?" I said, passing him the flickblade.

"No, sir. This way, sir."

I followed Baily down the hall into a living room not much smaller than a bubble mall. Huge oak logs burned in the enormous fireplace, and a very drunk woman sprawled on a leather sofa.

"I will see if Mr. Pennings is available," Baily said, then disappeared.

"Would you like a drink?" the woman slurred, watching me from beneath lidded eyes.

"Sure."

"So would I. The bar's in the corner." She pointed vaguely over her head to a corner bar.

"What are you having?" I asked, moving to the bar.

"Oh, I'm not particular, just as long as it's strong."

I found red wine and vodka among the many crystal decanters and put together two Brutal Hammers. I added a handful of ice purely out of sarcasm and brought them over.

"'Bout time," she slurred, taking her drink. "Guess how young I am."

"What?"

"Guess how young I am."

I regarded her. Between the face-lifts, skin tucks and silicone injections, I could see enough to place her in her late forties. Of course, the gentleman's axiom was to make a rough estimate then subtract ten to thirty percent, depending upon how much of a gentleman you considered yourself to be.

"Fifty," I said.

"No, really."

"Fifty-five?"

She frowned. "Most men would say late twenties."

"Most men are liars."

She took a big swallow and squinched up her face. "Yes, they are, aren't they? What the hell is this?"

"A Brutal Hammer."

"It tastes like piss."

"You said you weren't particular."

She tossed the glass over her shoulder, missing the fireplace by a bare two meters. "Just who the hell are you, anyway?"

"I'm Prince Jacob of Hayward."

"Oh, *royalty*," she said, dropping the scowl for a sloppy salute. "I didn't realize ol' Hiram was having royalty over today. You sure don't dress like royalty."

"It's an elaborate disguise," I explained, sipping my Hammer. It did taste like piss, but that was the whole point. "Otherwise the nouveau bourgeois would mob me."

"Oh, *those* horrid people. I don't like them either. Make me another Hammer and leave out the grape juice this time."

"Maybe later," I said, and Christopher Pennings walked in from the foyer.

"Hello, Mr. Strait. What are you doing here?"

"I was in the neighborhood. I want to talk with you."

"Sure," he said, eyes flickering to the drunk woman. "Let's talk somewhere else."

I put my drink down out of her reach and followed him down a side hall into an airy sun room, all skylights, tropical plants and earthen pottery.

"You need to keep the maid out of the liquor cabinet," I said.

Chris glanced in the direction of the living room. "That's not the maid. That's my mother."

"I apologize."

"No need. I don't like her. I never have. She's been on the bottle since Liam died."

"Liam?"

"Her son."

"Your brother?"

"Yes." He turned to a lattice shelf, reached into an earthen cookie jar and came out with a fat wad of credits. "Do you want some money?" he said, holding out the plastic to me.

My hand starting reaching, then suspicion reined it in. Nothing, especially money, was ever for free. "What for?" I asked.

He looked at me, then at the money, his brow creased with mild confusion. "I don't know," he said vaguely. "There's a lot of it around here." He put the stack back in the jar, then wandered to a potted palm tree. "I don't even know where it comes from. Hey, do you want to smash the place up a bit?''

''Why would I want to do that?''

He shrugged. ''To vent your suppressed lower-class aggressions. All my ghetto friends get a big kick out of it.''

He appeared to be serious. ''Maybe later,'' I said. ''How do your ghetto friends get on the Hill?''

''I sponsor their passes,'' Chris said. ''Residents have the right to issue visitor passes to friends they have in the City. You need a pass?''

''I already have one. Your City friends come up here a lot?''

''Oh, just for parties and the like.''

''You have a lot of parties?''

''I guess so.''

''Where do you meet your City friends?''

''At the Hellfire Club, mostly.''

''Hellfire Club?''

''It's a nightclub on Regents Island. It's in the City, but it's a Hill joint, you know? But we invite a lot of streeters, as well.''

''Any criminal types?''

''Well, there's the Red Horde. But they're all right.''

''Red Horde, you say? When's this club open?''

''Fridays and Saturdays.''

''Can you get me an invitation for tonight?''

''Sure. Why?''

''To dance, of course. Why do you think they call us bogeymen?''

''Oh,'' he said, nodding absently. ''Are you going to talk to my father?''

''Yes.''

He nodded again and reached out to touch a palm frond. "You know, my father doesn't want Cain caught because he killed someone he loved. He wants him caught because Cain took away something that was his."

"You're talking about Miss Romani?"

He nodded, frowning. Then, without a word, he drifted out of the room through a side door. I went back to the living room.

Mrs. Pennings was still sprawled on the sofa. She slurred, "You over there, come over here."

When I got there, she handed me an empty glass and an insolent look. "You the new houseboy?"

"I'm the disguised prince, remember?"

"Oh, yeah. Another blue blood sucking ol' Hiram for money. Say, isn't it time you moved your dead ass and made me a drink?"

"Sure," I said. I took her glass, grinned at it, then hurled it at the fireplace. It hit the hearth dead center and shattered with a satisfying crash.

"Hey, what's the idea?" she said, trying to sit up.

"I was saving myself the trip."

"Get me another drink. Now."

"No."

"I'll have you fired."

"Go ahead."

She glowered, then put on an ugly little pout that probably worked wonders with the household staff. "Don't be mean to poor wittle Janice," she said in a childish voice. "All she wanted was—"

"I know what you wanted, Mrs. Pennings. You wanted to subjugate me. You wanted to push me around. You didn't want a drink, you wanted to put me in my place. I'm a prince, goddamn it. I won't stand for it."

She scowled for a moment, then went to work on an eye-fluttering cutesy look. With all the liquor mixed in, she came off looking as if she was trying to gnaw on her eyelashes. After a moment of sloppy failure, she exhaled heavily and said, "Will you *please* make me a drink, Mr. Prince?"

"All right," I said, and went to the bar. "What do you want?"

"Rye whiskey," she called. "Neat, sweet, and don't be stingy."

I put together a weak rye and soda. When I handed it to her, she took the glass and threw it at the fireplace where it shattered against the poker rack.

"There," she said, lying back and closing her eyes, "we're even."

She began to snore, and Baily appeared at the other end of the room. "Mr. Pennings will see you now," he announced.

I crossed the room and fell in behind him. "She always like that?"

"Mrs. Pennings is an unhappy coward," he explained as we marched down a long hall. "She cannot face what makes her unhappy so she makes herself blind."

"You're pretty sharp for a butler."

"Thank you, sir. You seem a particularly well-mannered representative of your profession, sir."

"Hired killers come around here a lot?"

"When needed."

Baily opened a large pair of doors at the end of the hall, and we went inside. He closed the doors behind us and said, "You may proceed, Mr. Strait."

It was impossible to tell how monstrously large the room was because the ceiling and eaves were lost in shadow. In the middle of the acres of greedy space glowed a single floor lamp. Under the lamp sat a large chair, and in the large chair sat a little man. A small, bloated, pale toad of a man wearing huge glasses and a cream white suit. I began walking toward him, my footsteps echoing off into the darkness like rocks skipped across a wide and lonely lake.

"Above all, I despise rudeness," Hiram Pennings lisped as I approached.

It was a simple statement of fact that didn't solicit a response, so I kept my mouth shut. I stopped three meters away, not far from a roll-away wet bar lurking just outside the circle of light. I regarded Hiram and thought, *froglike, definitely froglike.*

"All I ever tried to do was bring a little politeness into the world," he continued. "A little respect. There isn't much around anymore. But you must know that. You live down there."

He said "down there" with such vapid distaste that for a moment I thought he was speaking of hell. I started to say something inane, but he cut me off.

"I know the kind of things you do, Mr. Strait."

I opened my mouth again, and he said, "That is all." His eyes went out of focus, and it was obvious Hiram Pennings had said what he wanted to say and I was supposed to go on my merry way.

"There's more," I said.

His eyes refocused and widened as if I'd just bounded into the room naked and hooting. "What?"

"I want to talk some more."

"I didn't hire you to talk. I hired you to do a job. Go do it."

"It's not as easy as that. When someone hires me to do something, I expect him to cooperate in accomplishing that end."

"Haven't I put the combined resources of the HDS and the SPF at your disposal?"

I smirked. "The SPF treats me like a shit-eating dog, and I'm having trouble differentiating the HDS from one of Cain's more zealous fan clubs."

"All right, Mr. Strait," he sighed. "I see your game. I'll double your daily fee. Would that overcome your problems?"

"Some of them. But not the ones I'm talking about. I'm not bracing you for more credit, I'm trying to find out why Cain is after you. If I can find that out, I'll have a better chance of finding out who he is."

"You think Cain is after me?"

"You seem to think so. That's why you're so interested in having him stopped. That's why you brought me in."

"A list of enemies? Is that what you want?"

"That's a good start."

"All right, then. Mr. Baily?"

Baily appeared out of the darkness behind Hiram. He leaned close and Hiram whispered something in his ear. Baily nodded and disappeared. A moment later he returned with a fat book.

"Give it to Mr. Strait," Hiram said, and Baily unloaded the City residential directory into my arms. "There is my list of enemies, Mr. Strait. Every mother's son in the City. That's where you should look for Cain. If you find the task too overwhelming, I'll instruct Carlos to help you."

"Carlos is endline," I said. "He has no desire to find Cain."

"Endline?" He looked behind him. "Baily, what is this endline?"

"Endline psychosis, Mr. Pennings," Baily intoned. "A recent social phenomenon that has reached every stratum of society. A nihilist movement with no spokesmen, organization or goal, just a single shared belief—life on earth is the end of the line, there is no heaven or hell, no final reward or punishment. As far as an endliner is concerned, the entire universe dies with him, so there is no reason to be moral or kind or right."

"So," Hiram said, turning his strange fascination to me, "Carlos has become some breed of homicidal fiend?"

"More suicidal than homicidal."

"Suicidal?" he mused. "If they believe there is no afterlife, one would think them very afraid to die."

"They don't think enough of their lives to give much of a damn," I explained. "To them, the passage of life is equal to writing in the sand at low tide. Since the words will be forever wiped away when the tide comes in, what is written is ultimately of no intrinsic value."

"And you say Carlos has this condition?" Hiram said softly, lost in thought. "How fascinating. His father will be very disappointed."

"Yes," I said. "Why are you protecting the Red Horde?"

His eyes snapped at me like a whip. "Who says I am protecting the Red Horde?"

"The Pleasure Syndicate."

"Did they?"

"Yes."

"Did they say why?"

"No."

"I'll tell you, then," he said, leaning back in the big chair. "Two years ago the Red Horde saved my son's life."

"Chris?"

He frowned at the name. "No, Liam. Liam is dead now. When he was alive, he liked to go to the City with other Hillsdale youth for adventures they felt they could not find in Hillsdale. On one such occasion they became embroiled with a gang of ghetto toughs. The Red Horde intervened on behalf of the Cynics and saved my son's life. Since then I have put at their disposal whatever small influence I have in the City."

"I wouldn't call it small," I said. "The Pleasure Syndicate acts like you're holding a bloody sword over their head."

Hiram turned up a small white palm. "It is the way of things. There will always be men who hold the power of life and death over lesser men." He smiled dangerously. "You are aware of that, aren't you, Mr. Strait?"

"There isn't a man on earth more powerful than a single well-aimed bullet."

"Are you threatening me, Mr. Strait?"

"Do I appear that stupid?"

"Yes."

"I'm smarter than I look then. I'm just saying a man with this many enemies—" I waved the directory "—should start worrying about his personal security."

"I am very well protected, Mr. Strait. In fact, how do you know Mr. Baily is not at this very instant standing behind you, his gun aimed at your heart?"

"Because I would have heard him," I said, looking over my shoulder to find Baily standing directly behind me, the barrel of my gyrapistol a centimeter from my spine. "Or maybe not."

"You'll be returning to the ghetto now, Mr. Strait," Hiram said.

"I guess I will."

Baily followed me out.

"What the hell are you, some kind of goddamn phantom?" I muttered when we reached the foyer.

"I am whatever Mr. Pennings requires me to be," Baily said, taking the directory and returning my pistol.

"How long have you worked for Pennings?"

"Twenty-one years, sir."

"Have you killed for him?"

"Yes." He opened the door. "Good day, Mr. Strait."

"Not so far," I said, and went out.

As I drove back to the City I thought about something my father had told me when I was a boy. He told me that God, busy as he was, sometimes forgot to put souls in some of the people he sent down to earth. My father used this theory to explain mass murderers, slumlords, and lawyers, and I used it to explain the man I'd just met. Hiram Pennings struck me as a man born without a soul.

9

Forty minutes later I sat at my desk, smoking vitacigs and watching a popular underground news channel called City Watch on the monitor. Its twenty-four-hour, live-action footage was generated by a small army of news hounds wired with headcams, creeping around the black belly of the City like human weasels with a nose for tragedy and violence. The stories came and went at a dizzying pace, aired only until something more violent and sinister beamed into City Watch's control center.

The influx of gore and violence must have ebbed for a moment because the screen switched to the City serial-killer watch, a cartoon segment with colorful graphs showing each celebrated killer's body count to date, as if they were horses racing toward some discernible goal. The commentator noted that, as if in spite, the City's troupe of repeat murderers had redoubled their efforts since the rise of the publicity-hog Cain. The program accredited the ever-diligent Iceman with the latest kill, and footage just minutes old showed the view of a headcam peeping over the shoulders of a growing crowd. The victim, a young pimp, decorated the floor of a Barridales alley, his arms and legs severed and transposed, so that he had hands for feet and feet for hands and...

"Freeze frame!" I shouted, leaning forward to examine the frozen image. The dead pimp bore the ice-pick punctures and wild slashes of a typical Iceman slaying, but the severed and rearranged limbs were very Cain-esque. And what's more, there appeared to be something in the corpse's mouth.

"Close up here," I said, touching the face of the corpse. The screen closed in on the bulging cheeks, the gaping mouth, the plastic, bullet-shaped vial protruding from between the lips. I recognized it immediately as a squeeze injector, the big economy-sized version the Pleasure Syndicate manufactured by the tens of thousands.

"Save frame and go to news file," I said. "All articles about the murder of Jordan Lindquist."

I read each of the dozen articles thoroughly. There was evidence of leaked information, a lot of fabrication and absolutely no mention of the vial of Newlife found in Jordan's mouth.

A link, I thought. Either the Iceman had access to inside information or the two were communicating, to the point that the Iceman was beginning to imitate his Hills-dale peer.

The office door burst open, and a short, powerfully built young man filled the lower two-thirds of the doorway. He slammed the door with his heel and pointed a damning finger at me.

"You dirty bastard," he growled, glowering at me with murderous hate.

"You sure you got the right place?" I asked politely.

He rushed forward to lean his knuckles on my desk and grind his teeth until his meaty jowls trembled. "You dirty son of a bitch," he said between clamped teeth.

I glanced over both shoulders with mock surprise. "Is it *me,* you're talking to me?"

"Fucking right I'm talking to you. I'm talking now and shooting later. You know what I mean, *Jack Shitbag Strat?*"

"Jack Strat?" I laughed. "I see the problem now. You're looking for Jack *Sprat.* He's a fairy-tale character. He lives in Never-Never Land, very far from here. You see, I'm *Jake Strait,* a well-known innocent bystander."

He straightened up and stared at me with confusion. He reached into his breast pocket, pulled out a slip of paper, studied it closely, put it back, then leaned on the desk. "No, you're the shitbag, all right."

I leaned back in my chair and lit a vitacig. "Who sent you?" I said around the cigarette, feeling like a cheap actor. "The Pleasure Syndicate? Collection agency? Landlord? Mother Goose?"

"I'm declaring war on you!" he screamed hoarsely. "I'll kill you! I'll kill your family! I'll kill your dog! I strangle your mother and screw her corpse! So you gonna knock off or what?"

"You forgot to tell me what I'm supposed to knock off."

His eyes crossed slightly. "Oh, you know."

"Not until you tell me."

"Knock off whatever stupid shit you're doing."

"That wouldn't leave me much. Did Cain send you?"

"None of your business who sent me. What the hell are you doing?"

"Nothing," I said, passing the pocket scanner over his right hand. "Vladimir Fydor Rusitnov," it squawked. "Convicted in absentia by SPF judicial computer 2281. Three counts first-degree murder, six counts rape, twelve counts assault and battery, twenty-two counts grand larceny, one count canine molestation—"

"Canine molestation?" I repeated, looking at him wide-eyed.

"Turn that squawk box off," he said, clawing at the scanner.

I pulled it away and held it up next to my head. "Don't you want to know your rank?"

"Rank?"

"Sure. See how you measure up in the world of crime. Listen."

He cocked his head, and the scanner continued. "—sixteen counts burglary, six counts felony menacing, one count gang affiliation, six counts jaywalking. Code C-4 death warrant."

"Bingo," I said.

"Bingo what?"

"Bingo death warrant."

He seemed to revel in the knowledge. "That's *right*, motherfucker. I'm probably on the Party's top-ten wanted list!"

"Not according to judicial computer 2281. It says you're only worth four hundred creds."

"Fuck computer 2281! The street knows how down I am, you better believe it. Fuckers get in my way, and they end up just another statistic on my rap sheet, just another—what the hell are you staring at?"

"Didn't you read the sign on my door before you came in?"

He furrowed his great meaty brow and tried to remember. He leaned off the desk and went to the door. He threw it open, and together we read the gold-lettered legend on the outside.

Jake Strait, Private Enforcer
Wrongs Righted, Injustices Avenged

It took Vlad a tough moment to sound the words out and when he finished he turned around and looked at me dumbly. "Private enforcer?"

"Bogeyman," I translated.

"Oh," he said, reaching inside his jacket.

I drew my pistol and shot him between the eyes. His head snapped back and his body followed close behind. He dropped to the floor and thrashed in the doorway like a landed marlin.

I put in a call to reclamation, then waited until Vlad stopped thrashing. After a minute he played himself out, and I dragged him inside and closed the door.

"Who sent you?" I barked at the corpse. As rude dead as alive, Vlad completely ignored me. I searched his body systematically, starting from the top and working down. I found a slip of paper with my name and address on it in his breast pocket, a loaded 9 mm Killtech automatic sat in a shoulder holster and an adrenaline pack wrapped his left biceps. Three of the injector bubbles were crushed, explaining Vlad's excited manner and his fish-out-of-water impression.

Otherwise Vlad was completely bereft of any form of personal effects. Even more mysterious was Vlad's method of dissuasion. If he really wanted me off the case, he would have shot me the instant he walked in the door instead of wasting his breath with the big warm-up. Considering his record, I didn't think the speech was Vlad's idea. It was Vlad's master who was unwilling to kill me outright, for reasons I could not fathom. I deposited the 9 mm in my desk and came back with the minisaw.

"Just who did you think you were screwing with?" I asked Vlad, crouching beside him. "I'm a goddamn *professional*. You can't threaten professionals. You can't talk about their mothers like that. We love our mothers.'' I lifted his scanhand by the fingers, and the saw whirred to life. As I sawed, I thought.

Killing Vlad didn't actually solve anything. He was just a symptom, shooting him was tantamount to gobbling aspirin to combat a rampaging brain tumor. It made you feel better but it didn't do anything toward curing the disease. But the very fact someone had sent Vlad around proved I was ruffling feathers, making headway, whether it looked like it or not. I finished sawing and bagged the hand just as there was a knock at the door.

''Come in,'' I said, and two reclamation workers in powder blue uniforms came in with a stretcher. I sat on the edge of the desk, and the older of the two eyed Vlad's bloody stump, then the plastic bag in my hand.

''Got them coming to you now, huh?'' he said, stooping to roll Vlad onto the stretcher.

''Yeah,'' I said, dropping the bag into the bottom drawer of my desk. ''It's my new system. I send them nasty letters until they come around to slap me, then I shoot them. Saves me a lot of legwork.''

''I'll bet.'' He straightened up and unclipped a data board from his belt while his partner used a small sanivac to suck the blood from the carpet, filling the room with a mild odor of disinfectant.

''Donate the body bounty to the Homeless War Orphans Hooked on Whack Relief Fund,'' I told the older man. He made a note on the board, clipped it to his belt, and they hauled Vlad away to the protein vats.

I went to the bathroom, washed the blood off my hands, combed my hair and went out.

10

Regents Island sat in the middle of the river like a gigantic gravel-and-concrete crocodile. A single building rose from its long gray back, a bland four-story concrete building that had once served as one of the Party's more brutal "psyche-readjustment" centers. The only evidence that it was now a nightclub was the tall bloodred neon sign flashing from the rooftop like a monstrous beacon. *Hellfire* it said, and seemed to wink almost seductively against the night sky, or perhaps tauntingly.

The bridge linking Regents Island with the City was composed entirely of black steel. A bullet-scarred Plexiglas-and-concrete booth wedged between two powerful hydraulic gates guarded the City side of the bridge. Dire signs decorated the gates, warning of lethal voltage.

I steered the Olds to the end of the long line of cars idling in front of the entry gate. The line moved slowly, and most of the cars were turned back, the gate opening for only a select few.

The vehicle in front of me was a sunsplash-painted low rider full of loud, drunken ghetto youth. When it came their turn to shout into the booth's speaker grille, it was immediately evident by their howls they, too, would be turned back.

"We're on the guest list, *vatos!*" the driver protested.

"You're mistaken," the gate man's amplified voice said. "Turn your vehicle around and leave immediately."

"You lying *puta!*" the driver screamed. "Waste this *congolera cochino, camaradas!*"

A barrage of automatic fire exploded from the low rider, showering the booth with lead. The man behind the rattling Plexiglas didn't so much as blink. He leaned his mouth toward a microphone, spoke briefly, then stared at the low riders until their weapons ran out of ammunition. While they reloaded for another futile volley, a rotor appeared above them, caving in the top of the low rider with a dangling electromagnet the size of a small piano. The rotor lifted, and the cruiser went with it, its occupants shooting at the armored underside of the rotor while the driver inexplicably gunned the engine. When the spinning tires of the cruiser were ten meters from earth, the rotor turned fifteen degrees and headed downstream, gaining altitude as it went. Two hundred meters downstream and a hundred meters up, magnet and cargo separated and the low rider dropped like a rock into the river, sparking with gunfire until it hit the water and sank out of sight. There was a little clapping from the cars behind me, but not much.

I looked at the booth to find the gate man staring at me impatiently. I drove forward and rolled down the window.

"I'm on the guest list," I said with a big smile.

"Name?"

"Jake Strait."

He looked down at something I couldn't see, then looked back at me. "Turn your vehicle around and leave immediately."

"Hold on a minute," I said, improving my smile. "I know I'm on the list."

"I know you are, too. But you're dressed wrong."

"This is my best suit."

"That's the problem. You're dressed too formally. Guests from the City are expected to dress in strict ghetto fashion."

"Tell you what," I said. "I'll lose the tie and rub some dirt on my jacket when I reach the parking lot."

He leaned toward the microphone and stared at me, impassive as a reptile. "Turn around. Last chance."

I leaned my head out the window and looked up. Along with a faint whirring, I noted a black shape blocking out the stars directly above me. "Christopher Pennings sponsored me," I said, ducking back in.

"So? What's he going to do? Get me fired from this big-shot job?"

"He can tell me who you are."

"So?"

"I'm a bogeyman."

His expression changed a little. "You're *that* Jake Strait."

"That's right," I said, waiting for him to start howling into the microphone. I was mildly surprised when the gate hummed open. His eyes followed as I drove through.

The bridge creaked and clacked and emptied onto a nearly bare gravel parking lot. Most of the Hellfire's patrons appeared to be arriving by air, and I could hear the whir and flutter of rotors and skimmers landing on the roof. I parked near the entrance and got out.

"Leave all weapons and contraband in your vehicle," a mechanical voice blared from loudspeakers bolted to the outside of the building. "You will be thoroughly scanned and searched at the door."

I regarded the door. Four monstrous bouncers stood poised, watching me closely. They continued to watch as I removed the gyrapistol and three other weapons and locked them in the trunk.

"What were *you* planning?" one of them asked when I neared the door.

"Livening the place," I said, and they fell on me like a ravenous pack of jackals, yapping and slapping at me. After a thorough search they shoved me through a body scanner, then checked the guest list again. A long, solemn lecture followed, warning me not to even think about "screwing with or in any way offending the delicate sensibilities of our Hillsdale patrons."

"Can I talk to them?" I asked.

"Yeah, but watch your mouth."

"Can I make veiled insults about their avarice and greed?"

"You goddamn better not."

"So, if I use my mouth at all, it better be for kissing Hillsdale butt?"

"You got it, chump. We clear?"

"Clear as glass."

"All right, have a good time," he said, then grabbed my arm and looked me in the eye. "But not *too* good a time. You hear what I'm saying?"

"Clear as a bell," I assured him, and went in.

The stilted atmosphere of the security room lay in direct contrast with the exuberance inside. The cavernous and crowded club was decorated in the manner the rich imagined the inner-city ghetto to be: chipped and graffitied brick facades adorned the walls, manufactured trash was carefully spread on the gray shag and dim lighting shifted and flashed erratically. Ghetto rhythms boomed from the powerful sound system, the rich sported the garb of the poor, and the decadent children of Hillsdale were gearing up for an all-night bender.

I pushed my way through the sea of afro and mohawk wigs to the bar. Spread across its top was a junkie's dream: decanters of color-coded pills for every mood, vials of squeeze, whoosh and shoot, enough drugs to OD whole neighborhoods. I leaned on the bar's padded leather lip and waved down the barman. He wore a blue velour dress with high collar and billowing arms to hide Adam's apple and biceps. His red beehive wig was slightly askew, his makeup bordered on theatrical, but the biggest giveaway was the sheer immensity of his fraudulent bust line. If they were real, he would've needed a twenty-kilo counterweight strapped to his back.

"What are you having, flapperjack?" he asked in a practiced falsetto.

"Double highball. No offense."

"Us full-figured gals are used to that kind of tripe. You want some shoot or stim in that?"

"Just rum, and plenty of it."

"Sure thing. What's your name, toughie?"

"Robert Burns. I'm a poet."

"How lovely. My name is Annie and guess what I am?"

"Barmaid?"

"No, I'm *easy*," he giggled, overly shrill, then maneuvered my drink around the immense bosom.

"I see. What do I owe you?"

"Don't worry about it. No streeter pays at the Hellfire. It's the Hill's way of thanking you."

"Thanking me for what?"

"For being poor, silly boy."

"Aw," I said, collecting my drink.

"Say, that's a real mohawk, isn't it?"

I traced the question to the ruby red lips of a pixie-faced brunette suited up as an inner-city whore. Steadying herself against the bar with one hand, she reached out with the other to touch the shaved side of my head. "No, that's no wig. And those are real scars on your face."

"Childhood accident," I explained. "Got my head stuck in an infrared spectrometer."

"You're a ghetto boy," she cooed. "I can always tell." She moved closer and lowered her eyes. "You know, I like ghetto boys. I think your reckless poverty is very sexy."

"Sorry," I said. "But I'm just rich and decadent like you."

She took a step back and made a face. Without looking, she scooped a dozen red pills from a bowl on the bar, mouthed them all, then fixed me with defiant eyes that let me know the rich could be reckless, too. She pushed off the bar, and I watched her stagger into the crowd. She wandered for a minute, then beelined to one of the white-suited stomach-pump technicians stationed near the stairwell. She said something, and the tech smiled and led her to a back room where a machine would suck the recklessness right out of her.

I turned my attention to the crowd. On the dance floor pseudopunks and skinheads broke into an effete slam dance, trying not to spill their drinks. Across the room would-be gang bangers, half wearing blackface, practiced their ghetto slang and wrestled in mock combat. Cliques of pretend whores paraded about, loudly complaining how mean their pretend pimps were. Scattered around the farce were the invited poor, sporting upscale threads and carrying their egos like loaded guns, their faces twisted with chemicals and suspicion. The rich dressed down and the poor dressed up—nobody seemed happy with what they were.

I spotted the sole heir to the Pennings fortune sitting in a booth with a group of male Hillers and Slavic-looking ghetto thugs. The Hillers wore short bleached hair and black spider-silk jackets that ran about twenty thousand creds each and could stop a 7.62 mm round point-blank. Their inner-city peers wore their hair in familiar spiky neon red fashion. They all hid behind mirror shades and smoked stim joints with a conscious cool that made me want to bullwhip the lot of them.

"Man, just look at all these honky white-bread bastards."

I glanced at the spindly light-skinned black standing beside me. "Not a big fan of whitey, eh?"

"*Hell* no. These Hill fuckers think they got it all in the bag," he sneered, "but they can all kiss my African ass."

"Got them figured, eh?"

"Shit, yes, I do. Hell, I used to be white my own self. I used to be a white-bread Hiller just like them till I got tired of it."

"Race-change operation?"

"Straight up. I was going to go straight Bantu, but the doc turned me on to a Zulu-Thai mix that looked too good to pass up. What do you think?"

"Very stylish."

"Ain't it, though?" He began shaking his head. "But forget what my parents thought about it."

"Piss them off?"

He basked in the memory. "Boy, did it. Those vanilla-souled bourgeois crackers." He looked at me. "I can call them that now. Crackers."

"What do you know about those Hillers?" I said, nodding at Chris's booth.

"The Cynics Club? They're just a bunch of rich boys caught up in the glamor of gangs, the shine-ass posers."

I smiled at the utter lack of irony in his tone and studied the Cynics. They were posers, to be sure, but there was something about them that separated them from the rest of the costumed rich. In their manner I detected a base viciousness not relegated only to those brought up in housing projects.

"Who're the redheads hanging with them?" I asked.

He laughed. "That's the Red Horde, also known as the Red Whores. Rent a gang. It's sort of a Hill-City gang exchange program. The Cynics get them high-quality Hill drugs, and the Reds give the Cynics protection when they take their act to the City."

A Cynic looking our way said something, and the whole table enjoyed a good laugh. A chubby Red turned around to look, and I recognized him. The subway voyeur.

"Check out those mothers," my companion hissed, "laughing at us. I wouldn't let them get away with it, but those Russkie gangs are the worst, even us brothers don't throw down with them. They're all endline—just look at them funny and they'll rip your throat out."

"Aw," I said skeptically, "you just have to know how to communicate on their level, speak their tongue. Watch, I'll show you."

I picked up my drink and walked to the booth. They all paused to scowl when I stopped in front of them.

"I wanna fight the biggest pansy here," I announced.

Looks were exchanged, but no one volunteered. They were clearly daunted, and I pressed on. "Yeah, I guess it's hard to decide," I said, turning to the subway voyeur. "What about you, you appear a likely candidate."

He screwed on a smile and turned to Chris. "Who is this drek, little *chaka?*"

"Well, Louis," Chris began haltingly, "Jake is—"

"Louis knows me," I cut in. "I was in the subway when he set his new personal record for the thirty-meter sprint."

Louis slipped off his mirror shades with slow menace, showing me angry pig eyes. Hate flushed his face and made his voice a low croak. "I recognize you now, *kulan.*"

"No, it's Jake," I said. "Jake Strait. You know, the guy you sent Vlad to slap around."

Louis put his shades back on and yawned. "I don't know any Vlad."

"Aw, come on, you know *Vlad*. Short, stocky, poor reading skills, kind of slow on the draw. You know, the one who screws dogs."

A beefy Red shot to his feet, "Shut your hole, you *organi* bas—"

"Have a seat," I said, shoving him back down. He struggled to get back up until Louis calmed him with a short burst of Russian.

"Huh," I said. "Still the kid gloves. What is it you like about me, Louis? Who told you I bruise easy?"

"I don't know what you're—"

"You know!" I shouted. "You know damn well. And you're going to tell me the whole terrible story. Now!"

"No need for trouble!" Chris assured, holding up open hands. "A grave misunderstanding, that's what we have here! How about if I buy you all a drink? Or better yet, I'll buy a new sound system for the Horde clubhouse, how's that?"

I was shocked to see the antagonism I'd whipped up melt away like an August ice cube. Chris beamed in a motherly way and the Reds began jawing happily in Russian, probably discussing what sort of stereo they wanted. Red Whores is right, I thought.

"Well, what do *I* get?" I demanded. "Don't I get a good-behavior prize, too?"

Chris became nervous. "Well, sure, Jake, what exactly did you want?"

"Answers! Respect! My soul!"

The Reds and Cynics ignored me, Chris made a helpless gesture with his hands. I set my drink on the table and picked up a half-eaten soy burger. "This looks fresh," I said loudly, frowning at it. "Is that you, Vlad?"

The Horde leaped to its collective feet, and the Cynics weren't far behind. They appeared to be no longer daunted, and I took a step back, slipping a hand into my jacket. "C'mon," I sneered. "I'll drop the lot of you right here."

"You are still alive, Mr. Strait," Louis said, arms out, making a symbolic effort to hold back the troops. "You should leave while you remain so."

"Sure," I said, tossing the soy burger on the table. "Chris would have to buy you solid-gold crappers by the time you got through with me."

I walked back to the bar, and Chris, after apologizing profusely for my conduct, joined me.

"Are you crazy?" he whispered hoarsely. "You can't bully the Red Horde like that. They'll kill you!"

"Aw, I was just trying to piss them off, that's all." I ordered another highball from Annie. "I usually don't have such a hard time of it. I wonder who has them on the tight leash."

"I don't know, but you better lay off them. I know them pretty—"

"Yeah," I said, "how did you become their sugar daddy, anyway?"

Chris blushed, looking back at the table. "Through the Cynics. I grew up with most of them. The club has been around forever. My grandfather was a Cynic, as was my father and brother."

"Are you?"

"No. I'm the first Pennings not to belong." His expression sagged, and without another word he returned to his friends.

I was all ready to give up and call it a night when I spotted her out of the corner of my eye. She moved slowly through the crowd, her red sequin tube dress flashing like a many-hooked lure trolling the bottom of a murky lake. There was nothing frail about her; she radiated feminine strength, shoulders wide, breasts heroic, waist waspish, hips full and fluid. Most dangerous of all were her big brown eyes, shifting constantly above straight nose and full, insolent, bee-stung lips. She stopped in front of the Cynics and Reds and frowned, dropping a monstrous black velvet purse to her feet and wistfully clutching her hands behind her back. She wore her black heart like a merit badge and the Cynics made a big show of ignoring her. The Reds weren't so coy. She began speaking to Chris.

"Here's your drink, flapperjack," Annie said behind me.

I turned my head without taking my eyes off the woman. "I've a question for you, Ann."

"About time, sailor. I get off at three."

"Who's that?" I asked, pointing with my chin.

"Oh, *that* thing," Annie said, his voice climbing the scales. "That's Ellen, but we call her Goldy, if you know what I mean."

I glanced back. "As in gold digger?"

"More like strip miner, honey. She rolled with the Cynics until they got tired of passing her around. Now she's looking for a new angle. And it looks like she just found it."

I turned my head and dropped my jaw. Ellen's big dangerous eyes pointed directly at *me*. She hoisted her monstrous purse like a ship weighing anchor and started toward me, eyes steady and determined.

"What does she want?" I whispered as she bore down. "What can I give her?"

"Whatever you got," Annie answered. "She prefers wealth, but she'll sell you a glance for a slice of your ego. By the look in her eye, someone just told her you were a slumming billionaire with a powerful taste for floozies. Don't worry, though, once she finds out you're not from the Hill she'll leave you more than alone."

I nodded and she arrived, all exotic perfume and flashing sequins. I studied her from the corner of my eye, resisting the manifest urge to gawk, to feed my naked desire to the sharks of her ego heart.

"Champagne, Annie," Ellen said with a broad northern European accent.

I ached to say something, anything, before she walked away and left me wallowing in self-hate. She accepted her drink, and I was about to bark something completely ridiculous when she paused, dropping her purse on a bar stool and leaning back against the bar. I immediately became aware of the thick sensuality she emanated, eroding my self-control like waves crashing against a pillar of loose sand.

I have to be ready, I told myself. If she says something, I have to come right back with a snappy line, right off the cuff.

"Get your flint out, Hiller," she said.

"Huh?" I said.

"Spark some fire."

"Huh?"

"You got a match, professor?"

"Not since Superman," I said, slipping into gear. She turned my way, and I stared into eyes as cold, hard and murky as frozen puddles. Not actually brown, I thought, more a shade of beige, more cream than coffee.

"If I wanted funny lines," she said, "I'd hire a clown."

"Yeah, but I work for free," I said, lighting her cigarette. She inhaled deeply, blew out a stream of smoke, finished her champagne and didn't leave.

"Another champagne," I told Annie. "Put it on my tab."

"Sure, big shot," Annie said.

"Waiting for someone?" Ellen clipped, her manner that of a well-honed knife, all cutting and purpose.

"Seems like all my life," I said.

"Girl?"

"Yeah."

"What's her name?"

"Don't know, haven't met her yet."

She passed me a glance that said she might be able to help. "What's your altitude?"

"Six-two."

"You prick. Are you from the Hill or the City?"

"I owe fealty to no kingdom or crown."

She stood quietly for a moment, and I sweltered beneath her unspoken irritation. "You gonna tell me your altitude or what?"

"What if I was from the Hill?"

Her face softened, and the ice in her eyes melted to slush. She might have moved closer and her hand definitely touched my arm. "Are you?" she purred.

"Do I look it?"

"You come off as an arrogant-enough prick."

"Is that the only criteria?"

"That and a fat bank account. That's what I've learned. The more the money, the bigger the... jerk."

"So you figure I'm a billionaire."

"Yeah, but I don't hold it against you." She faced the crowd again, her wildly shifting eyes looking at everyone and no one. "You know, you'd be a very pretty man if you got rid of those scars on your face."

"My dance card's full as it is."

"Is it really?"

"No, but I don't give a damn."

"You don't?"

"All right, I do, but not as much as you think."

"That so?"

"Aw, why don't you leave me alone?"

"You want me to leave?"

I stared at her. "Where'd you learn to beat up on a guy like that?"

"I ain't doing a thing." She turned to pick the fresh glass of champagne off the bar. "I don't know if I love you yet. You just don't fall in love with a guy because he buys you a drink."

"Ah!" I said. "No one understands love like the working class."

She gave me a cutting glance. "Who says I'm working-class?"

"You sparkle with it."

"Well, I may not live on the Hill, but I'm no whore."

"I don't remember accusing you of being one."

"Good, as long as we're clear on that." She sipped her champagne. "If we screw tonight, I don't want you to think I'm there because you're rich. I'm there because I think you're attractive and funny."

"I'm glad to see I'm doing so well."

"Do you think I'm attractive?"

"Oh, you're attractive enough. It's just too bad about your eyes."

Her lips parted angrily. "What's wrong with my eyes?"

"Not a thing. Except your heart's full of ice."

"My heart? I thought we were talking about my eyes."

"That's where it shows the most."

She dropped her interest and attention like rocks down a shallow well and looked back at the crowd. "So, you think I'm a gold-digging whore. That's okay, you're a mean drunk."

"Yeah, but I'll sober up."

She shot me a hard look, stabbed her cigarette out in my highball, shouldered her purse and stalked away.

"I've never seen anyone fuck up as much as you." Annie giggled behind me.

"It's what I do best," I said, watching Ellen stop to pout next to the Reds and Cynics. "It's my *thing*. Man, that just eats me up."

"What's that, flapperjack?"

"That some things only money can buy."

"Especially when you don't have any, eh, flapperjack?"

Someone nudged my elbow, and I turned to find Carlos in a black stovepipe suit an undertaker would think morbid.

"We need to talk, Jake."

"I'm listening," I said, my eyes returning to Ellen.

"We need to talk in private. It's about Cain."

"Right behind you," I said, and followed Carlos to the stairs. On the way to the roof we passed three floors of dim art-deco romp rooms full of squealing Hillers. The roof itself was as big as a combatball field and completely unlit save for the intermittent flashes of the Hellfire sign. Every three seconds bloodred light flooded across expensive skimmers and rotors parked next to a vast forest of jutting metal shapes, some artist's vision of hell.

"What about Cain?" I asked as we strolled into the maze of twisted metal.

"He visited me last night."

I stopped walking. "What?"

"In a dream."

I started walking again, head down, uneasy. "A dream, you say."

"Yes. I dreamed I was sitting at my desk and he came to talk with me. He looked a lot like you."

"Me?"

"Yeah, you. But then he told me he wanted to give you a message, so I knew it wasn't you."

"What was the message?"

"He said to tell you he never killed his brother."

"You mean Abel?"

"I don't know. He kept saying it over and over again. Then he got up and went back to the bathroom."

"The bathroom?"

"Yeah. He comes out of the mirror."

"That's why you painted it black."

"One of the reasons." Carlos stopped in front of a tall slab of rusted metal and stared up at its jagged point. "Do you ever wonder if you're here, Jake?"

"Here on the roof?"

"No, *here*. Right here, right now." He turned around and stared at me. "I don't feel that I'm really *here*. I feel like a spectator watching the progression of my life on an out-of-focus movie screen." He laughed. "And I'm having a real hard time identifying with the main character."

Carlos's distraught face came and went in neon flashes, and I thought, he's a time bomb, won't last another week.

"The urban hustle makes us all feel a little disconnected sometimes," I said, knowing nothing I said would make any difference.

"Numb," Carlos said. "Totally numb and disconnected."

"Right. You just have to ride—"

A scream of terror carried from deep inside the maze. It's Cain, I thought with irrational certainty.

Carlos grabbed my arm. "Where are you going?"

"To see what's going on."

"What for?" he barked feverishly. "You save the damsel, and she stabs you in the back. You slay the dragon, and the villagers rise up and stone you to death. Terrible things are happening all over the world. You could be in a thousand places at once and you wouldn't make the tiniest of dents. So what's the point?"

"I think you're too wrapped up in the big picture," I said, jerking my arm free. I moved quickly, weaving through shadow and twisted steel bright red one second and pitch-black the next, guided by screams becoming increasingly desperate. I swung around a corner, and with a blaze of neon, there they were. Seven men in multicolored rags groping a screaming similarly dressed young woman.

"Let her go!" I shouted, clawing at a gyrapistol that wasn't there.

The girl stopped screaming, and they all looked my way. They were smiling. Madly.

"My hero!" the girl cried, breaking their hold and rushing me, arms wide. I didn't see the neurowand in her hand until she snapped it against the side of my neck. A powerful electric charge jolted my spine, short-circuiting my central nervous system and buckling my knees. Like a tangled puppet, I stumbled back against a slab of metal, and the pack rushed in.

The neon blinked, and I took a slow-motion swing at the mass of them. I crunched a nose, and the reply was immediate—a flurry of fists that knocked me away from the slab. I fought to keep my feet and in a flood of neon I saw them, their eyes huge with the hunt, circling me like snapping wolves. The light went out, and vicious punches and kicks rained in from all sides. I lowered my head and tried to charge out of the punishing circle, driving a handful of them to the ground before my skull collided with steel. In the passing light I saw my own blood on the slab as they hammered my back and kidneys. I twisted awkwardly, throwing out a sluggish flurry of jabs, trying to hold them off until my strength returned.

In the flash of red I saw the neurowand coming down again, striking my temple, filling my skull with rampant electricity. My brain became a ball of hot lava, and this time I sagged to the ground like a punctured bag of jelly.

A grinning circle of heads crowded the stars above me. A boy wearing a huge sun hat decorated with plastic fruit and hummingbirds hunkered down beside me.

"Brain trouble?" he asked, his breath fetid in my face, his lunatic eyes centimeters from mine. "Yes," he sighed,

"I see you got it bad. But fear not, for I'm a doctor and I have medicine. Nurse!"

The girl slapped a plastic vial full of blue fluid into his open hand.

"I'm afraid it's *bad* medicine," he sighed, "but medicine nevertheless." He opened the vial and moved it close to my lips. "Now, open your mouth and say *ahh.*"

I tried working my jaw. My tongue lay like lead, my lips were rubber, and there was the slightest ebb of feeling. Fingers pried my mouth open and I managed to mumble a single word.

"What?" he said, the tip of the vial centimeters from my lips, a fat drop of blue fluid beading on its rim.

"Snaynth," I slurred.

He looked quizzically at me, then leaned closer. "What's that?"

"Snaynkth!"

"Sneak?"

I shook my head slightly. "Snaynkes! Snaynkes!"

His eyes clouded and his smile uncurled. "Snakes?"

I nodded. "All. Over. *You.*"

I saw something shift in his eyes, and he began pawing at his neck with his free hand. "All over *me?*"

"Crawling...squirming...biting," I slurred, dragging out each word. "Poison!"

"Poison snakes! Poison snakes!" he screamed, dropping the vial to claw and flail at invisible serpents. He ran screaming into the night, and his friends wailed after him, ripping at their rags, investing in the new reality.

I lay still, counting neon flashes, staring up at the stars. They seemed particularly bright and lovely, and I couldn't remember the last time I'd taken the time to look at them. It took a good beating to make me look up out of the gutter and see an unassailable beauty that was always above me, pinpoints of distant purity that defied the horror below.

It's just us, I thought, the rest of the universe is safe and innocent. I hope to God we never develop interstellar travel, I hope the human virus never spreads.

"What's wrong?"

I shifted my eyes to see Ellen standing beside me, hands on hips.

"Have you ever looked at the stars?" I asked, my voice thick and alien. "I mean, really?"

She craned her neck and took a look. "They look the same as ever. What happened to you? Somebody go over you with a rubber mallet?"

"I paid them to do it. I needed more scars. How about a hand?"

She took my hand and with surprising ease pulled me to unsteady feet. I lost my balance and threw my arms around her just to stay up.

"Hey, watch where you put the tentacles, Mr. Octopus."

"But this is my best move," I complained, sensing the coiled strength of her body. "Just lean me against a slab until I get my legs back."

She maneuvered me to a hunk of metal, then stepped back. "Who jumped you? Was it streeters?"

"It was Snow White and her psychedelic dwarfs as far as I could tell. What are you doing up here?"

"I got tired of waiting for you to come back."

"I thought you hated me."

"I always give a Hiller a second chance."

I nodded. Feeling was slowly returning to my body and with it came agony. When my outer extremities began to tingle with pain, I noticed my left hand was sticky. I held it up to my face. A bluish fluid coated the skin. I looked to the ground, and my belly filled with dread.

The vial lay smashed, its contents spread into the shape of a hand.

"Help me to the bathroom," I said urgently. Ellen got under one arm, and we began moving across through the maze. With the first step, a throbbing itch awoke inside my skull.

"You're really drunk, aren't you?"

"I might be about to get much worse," I said. As we made the stairwell, I picked up the pace, lurching quickly down the stairs. Ellen guided me to a men's room on the third floor, where I lunged to a sink. As I scrubbed my left hand with soap, I checked the mirror. A bruise half closed my left eye, cuts crisscrossed my forehead and split my lips, and a mouse rose above each cheekbone.

"Look at you," Ellen said, leaning against the wall and smoking a cigarette. "You're beat up worse than a one-armed boxer, and all you're worried about is washing your hands."

"A gentleman's hands are always clean," I announced. I rinsed off the soap, and the stickiness and blue tinge were gone. "You're not supposed to be in here."

"Taboos are just cynical jokes to me. Psychiatrists say those who wash their hands obsessively are trying to wash away guilt."

"Not guilt," I said, toweling off. "Insanity. Thanks for the help."

She stepped in front of me. "Where you going?"

"Home. I think my fun meter has run out for the evening."

"I'm going with you."

"I'm not from the Hill."

She rolled her eyes. "Save it. I got the word on you, golden boy. How come none of you Hillers like to admit you got some altitude? It's nothing to be ashamed of."

I regarded her and, with the means of accessibility at hand, some of the aura of perfect, cruel beauty faded. Perhaps because of that I held out my arm. "All right," I said. "I won't argue."

She took my arm and I led her downstairs. On the way to the door I spotted Chris and Carlos talking near the bar. Carlos waved and Chris gave me a chummy sort of smile and wink.

When Ellen and I reached the Oldsmobile, she squinched her nose and said, "Boy, you like going seriously downhill, don't you?"

"All the way to the bottom," I said.

We climbed inside and she scooted so close I thought she wanted to drive.

"Take me to the Hill," she murmured sensually, her lips brushing my neck. "Show me your things."

"Sorry, baby," I said. "I lost the keys to the mansion."

Her body stiffened and she moved back to her side of the seat to light a cigarette. "Ashamed of being seen with me, is that it? My bloodline ain't pure enough for you, golden boy?"

For a brief instant I got the idea of telling her what my pedigree really was. The idea lasted about half a second and left with less fanfare then it lurched in with. "You know how it is," I said. "The neighbors do love to talk."

"We could use the back door."

"There are no back doors on the Hill," I solemnly assured her as I guided the Olds over the bridge. The exit gate opened, and we rolled into the City.

"Back in hell," she sighed bitterly. "How I hate it here."

"Where we going?" I asked.

"Third and Ginsberg."

"What's there?"

"My apartment."

"Great."

"You can help me pack."

"Moving?"

"Yes."

"Where to?"

"Your place."

"You haven't even seen it yet."

"I'm sure I'll like it." she said. "I'll check out your City digs for a while. Eventually you'll start missing your gold-plated toothbrush and you'll go back up. And I'm going with you."

"Not terribly confused about your personal goals, are you?"

"No. Park behind the Dumpster."

I cut the engine in front of a ramshackle six-story plastiplex with an outside stairwell that zigzagged up the front.

"Where in Europe are you from?" I asked on the way up the stairs.

"I'm not. I just have the accent."

"How'd you manage that?"

"I took a course. I can also speak in a French accent," she said, slipping into a husky French burr, "if you prefer, *mon ami.*"

"Why don't you speak in your real voice?"

"Oh, you don't want that," she said, switching back to the impertinent Nordic brogue, "it's very boring."

She unlocked a steel security door on the third-floor landing and went in, flipping a switch. A splash of light lit a room crowded with counterfeit totems from a bewildering mix of eras: flea-market Persian wall tapestries surrounded molded-plastic Queen Anne furniture sharing floor space with Grecian pseudomarble statues beneath a startlingly large 1920s cut-glass chandelier I had to duck to pass under. It seemed less a living room than a room full of props.

"Wow," I said.

"It's not much," she said, "but it reminds me where I'm going."

She passed through a door and I followed. The bedroom mirrored the same contrived opulence as the living room.

"Would you like tea?" Ellen asked, nodding toward a dented tea service set below what looked to be an authentic oil portrait of a mean-eyed tyrant.

"Sure," I said.

"Sorry. I'm out of tea. I just like to ask."

"Very polite of you. Who's the old fascist?" I pointed my chin at the oil portrait.

She spared a glance from her packing. "My father."

"Sorry."

"He *was* an old fascist. We were rich once, you know. Probably richer than you."

"I don't doubt it. What happened?"

"We lost everything to a hostile takeover during the corporate wars. Raiders executed my father in his own boardroom."

"Tough."

"Don't worry, I'll get it all back." She dragged a trunk to the dresser and began packing the sham icons of the wealthy crowding its top: a plastic miniature of a Big

Ben, a reproduction Victorian music box and many plaster busts.

I went to the connecting bathroom and found iodine in the medicine cabinet. A gang of cardboard mantras were taped to the cabinet's mirror. In language that minced no words, the mantras reminded the reader success was attainable only through profoundly cynical ruthlessness. I washed my face, painted my wounds and came out in time to help her carry the trunk and many suitcases down to the Olds.

"Have you ever thought about winning over a man's heart by being demure and coy?" I asked as we wheeled down the long boulevards separating our apartments.

"That crap takes too long," Ellen said, unlocking her monstrous purse with a key from around her neck. "My mother told me if you wanted something from a man you had to grab his dick with one hand and his throat with the other."

"Sounds like your mom knows the score."

"She's dead now. She died during an SPF air strike four months ago."

"Sorry."

"Don't be. I'm not." She dug in her purse for a moment, then got busy with a compact mirror and a tube of red lipstick. "I love you," she lied.

"About time," I said. "I was beginning to think I'd lost my touch. What finally won you over? My bank account or my scarred but pretty face?"

"Those are as good reasons as any to love someone. But I also love your, uh, rough laugh, yes, and your, uh, flippant nature." She adjusted her lipstick with a fingernail, folded the compact, dropped lipstick and compact into the maw of black velvet, dug around for a moment, then came out with a padded nail file. "Don't you believe me?"

"I'm egotistical enough to make that leap."

"Good. Do you love me?"

I glanced at her. She buffed her nails busily, blowing on them every few seconds. "I'm loveless and my soul is heavily in hock," I revealed. "Sometimes I lie in bed at night and shudder at what a terrible, bad person I am."

"That's okay." She blew on her nails a final time, then exchanged the padded stick for a tiny aerosol of fingernail polish. "I'll make you love me."

"You got a gun in that bag?"

She slid me impertinent eyes, finished spraying her nails the same deep red as her lips, dropped the aerosol back into the huge purse, locked the latch, lifted it to the floor, then scooted close to me. She wrapped her arms around my neck and touched my cheek with her lips. "I don't need a gun. All I need is time."

The Olds coasted to a stop in front of my apartment building, and Ellen peered up through the window.

"My God! What's this place?"

"Well, you know what they say, every octopus has a home."

"Yes, but how'd you let yourself sink *this* low?"

"It's the easiest thing in the world," I said, getting out. "You just let go and gravity drags you all the way to the bottom."

I enlisted the aid of two of the local kids hanging out in the lobby, and between the four of us we got all of Ellen's things on the elevator in one trip. I pushed the button for the fourth floor, and we started up.

"What are you staring at?" Ellen bluntly asked the youth whose name I thought to be Akmed.

He shrugged. "Jake doesn't usually do so well."

"He's joking," I said with a laugh.

Ellen frowned and said, "By the look of him I'm surprised he hasn't tried to run away with my suitcases."

"We wouldn't steal from Jake's friends," Akmed informed.

"The sign of a proper upbringing," I said.

"He pays you off," Ellen contended.

"We're afraid of him," Akmed explained.

"Afraid of him?"

"Afraid I'll call their parents," I said.

Akmed gave me a blank look. "No, we're afraid you'll kill—"

"Here's my floor," I snapped as the doors opened. "Let's get moving."

We unloaded the suitcases in the living room. I handed Akmed and his pal each a ten and ushered them out the door.

I turned around to find that Ellen had muscled the trunk to the unused fireplace. She transferred my mantel ornaments into the hearth and began setting up her icons in their place. She hung the mean-eyed portrait of her father last, after making kindling of my framed print of Lauren Bacall. She opened the music box, "Greensleeves" began to play, and she stepped back to take a look. After a minor adjustment of Big Ben she said, "There."

"Do you want me to start shoving my furniture out the window?" I asked.

"It'll do for now." She was absorbed in positioning other knickknacks around the room, bringing to mind a bear marking its territory.

"What the hell is that?" she said, confronting the monstrous sprawl of chrome and cable, clutching a pseudomarble statuette in either hand.

"That's Dr. Abuso," I said, "my workout partner."

"I knew you couldn't leave all your toys on the Hill."

"Let me introduce you," I said, laughing manically at the idea of bringing the doctor anywhere but a high cliff. "Hello, Doctor."

The red eye of the brain box winked on, and the doctor warmed up, hydraulics hissing and shifting.

"Good God," Ellen gasped, backing away. "It's *alive!*"

"Twenty-six hours and fifty-four minutes since your last workout, you wimp bastard!" Abuso howled. "I'll crush your goddamn soul, I'll—"

"Good night, Doctor," I said, and the red light blinked out. I looked at Ellen, who stared in horror at the machine. "Still think I brought him from the Hill?" I asked. "What's wrong?"

"For a minute I thought it was possessed by my mother," she said, visibly shaken. She hugged the statuettes and turned to offer a begging look. "Let's go to the Hill," she pleaded. "I feel a lot more passionate when I'm on the Hill, you know."

"It's just the opposite for me."

"You rich bastards are all the same," she snarled, slamming the statuettes down on the coffee table. "You don't appreciate what you have. You don't understand what money can do."

"It turns people into bastards, from what I've seen."

"Well, maybe I'd like to be a bastard for a while." She crossed her arms and pouted. "I'm sick to death of being poor."

"Poverty ain't all that bad."

"Oh, that's easy for you to say. You have that golden ladder to pull you out of the pit whenever this poor-boy routine wears a little thin. People like me have to wallow in it whether we like it or not. I hate poverty. It's boring. Poor people are boring. They can pose and act all they want, but in the end all they have is a big fat nothing."

She walked to the door of my bedroom and stuck her head in. Using her thumbnails, she slipped the straps of the tube dress from her shoulders and wiggled out of it. Thumbs moved to hips, and one leg at a time, she stepped out of black lace panties. She kicked off stiletto heels and looked impatiently over her shoulder. "Are you coming?"

A million credits, I thought, bounding into the bedroom after her. I have to get my hands on a million credits. She turned around at the bed, and I clawed off my jacket.

"Let me do it," she said, stepping up. She worked the buttons of my shirt slowly, deliberately, then leaned forward to pull the sleeves off my arms. Her nipples touched my skin like electric prods, and my pulse rate soared.

"I hope you tipped the surgeon that sold you that chest," she said, her hands dropping to my belt.

"Dr. Abuso doesn't accept tips. And quit stealing my lines."

My trousers dropped, and I pushed her back onto the bed. Starting with her forehead, I kissed, bit and caressed a path down to the tips of her toes then back up again, taking long, lingering detours, exploring, probing, pushing her breath rate into a rhythm of climbing passion.

She grabbed my hair and pulled me up, crushing her mouth against mine and immediately seizing the offensive, locking her ankles behind my back and thrusting up violently. I quickly rebelled against the furious pace she set, using my weight to slow her down. I already stood on the brink, and it took all my powers of concentration to crawl back from the sensual edge. I focused on the bruises waking up all over my body, directing attention away from the woman moving beneath me like an oily snake.

After ten minutes of biting my lip and breathing through my nose, brain seized control from groin and, workmanlike, I began the cruelest toil of all, sadistically crushing every rise of sexual pleasure. The muscles of my stomach and lower back coiled and curled with a relentless rolling motion, steady and firm, my lips and teeth bit and kissed her shoulders and neck, my hands worked her neck and buttocks, kneading, massaging, tuning the instrument, listening to the almost agonized strains of passion, the moans and cries that guided my efforts.

I labored as diligently and patiently as a piano tuner dedicated to his art and paid by the hour, and note by note her moaning reached higher and higher pitches until the sheets were soaked with sweat, the tuning was finished and only the delirious finale remained. I fell onto the keys like a madman, pounding, trying to play them all at once as I clawed desperately to hold on in the face of the rising crescendo of imminent and overwhelming ecstasy, I could not let go until the long duet reached the final note, the highest pitch of pleasure was struck, not until...

"*Yes!*" she screamed, her pelvis arching up, rigid as a tightly drawn bow, every muscle tense and trembling, eyes squeezed tight, mouth open wide, her face beatific and tortured. I leaped headlong over the edge, arcing higher and higher, suspended high above everything for that single, maddening moment...then falling, floating in perfect free-fall before slipping beneath the warm waves of a gently rolling sea, too happy to drown.

We kissed for a long, breathless moment, then collapsed to the sheets, drained, exhausted, at perfect ease with the world. For a long time nothing was said. It seemed enough just to breathe and float.

"You're different from them," she finally whispered. "You're the first Hiller that cared enough." She turned her head and looked at me. "Why?"

"Because I like you."

"You don't love me yet?"

"I'm still holding the line."

"A couple more days and I'll own you," she said, pillowing her head against my chest. "Mind, heart and soul." She reached between my legs and grabbed me. "I already own this."

I laughed. "Yes, you certainly do."

"Jake?"

"Yes?"

"Why did you let me come back with you?"

"Beauty does what beauty does best."

"That being?"

"Turning strong men into emotional cripples."

"Boo-hoo."

"That's my line."

"Do you want to make love to me again?"

"Again? No, I think I'm worn-out."

Her hand became insistent, demanding. "That's not what he says."

"He's never been on my side," I said, pulling her on top of me. "This time you do the work."

I held her firm hips, and she began moving above me, eyes closed, lips parted. Whatever it takes, I thought, watching her, I'll hang on.

11

I'd put six klicks on the treadmill before the doctor's howls of obscene encouragement woke Ellen up. I heard the shower come on, and half an hour later she came into the living room wearing my bathrobe, her head wrapped in a towel.

"Running from guilt?" she said, leaning against the wall in front of me.

"You might say that," I panted. "My God, you're beautiful."

She exhaled smoke and appeared genuinely embarrassed. "Thank you."

"You must hear that a lot."

"Not really."

"You better get used to it. We're not afraid to grovel and scrape in this household. Isn't that right, Doctor?"

"Just keep running, wimp," the doctor advised.

"It *is* my mother," Ellen said. "Why don't you get off that thing and make me breakfast."

"You mean lunch," I said. "Get dressed, and we'll grab something at a café around the corner."

"Can't we go somewhere nice?" Ellen pouted. "Have steaks and champagne at a place with some altitude?"

"While my ghetto brothers dine on beer and soy burger?" I shook my head. "No, that would just add to my already considerable debt of conscience."

"Oh, Christ," she said. "I wish you'd hurry and pay that freaking tab off so we can get uphill."

"Why do you want to be on the Hill so much? Besides the comfort and luxury, I mean."

She moved to the mantel to stare at the portrait of her father. "It's my mother's fault. When my father was executed we lost everything so we had to move down into the City. I was only six years old. As soon as we hit bottom, my mother began training me."

"For what?"

She turned around. "To get back what they took."

"By any means possible."

"Yes."

"I see," I said, leaping off the wheel. I put the doctor to sleep, then cornered Ellen near the door.

"Is this thing loaded?" she said, picking up the assault rifle leaning against the wall.

"Whoa," I said, freezing in my tracks. "Watch where you're pointing that."

"We going to the Hill for breakfast?"

"No, ma'am."

"Then you better go take a shower. A cold shower."

I laughed carefully, backing away. "I believe I will."

The shower started out tepid, then rapidly became cold as the hot water ran out. I toweled off briskly, taking account of all the bruises and cuts up and down my body.

I found the card while searching the medicine cabinet for disinfectant. Though mostly hidden by an aerosol of liquid bandage, its shiny surface caught my eye. I picked it up. The word "Hillsdale" was on one side, a magnetic strip on the other. It was a lot like the pass card Degas had given me, except there was no SPF insignia.

I wrapped a towel around my waist and found Ellen brushing her hair in front of a mirror in the bedroom.

I kissed her neck and showed her the card. "This yours?"

She frowned at gold rectangle. "A Hill pass? Are you joking? Do you actually think I'd be down here with you if that was keyed to my handchip?" She went back to brushing her hair. "No offense, but you're overrating yourself."

"Maybe I am," I said, pulling on a black jumpsuit. "You know much about the Reds?"

"Some," she said, putting down the brush and turning around to watch me lace my boots.

"You know where they hang out?"

"I know where they eat breakfast."

"Where?"

"A hangover haunt near Regents Bridge. Screaming Nietzsche's Café."

"We'll eat there."

"Whatever."

Moments later we exited the lobby to find the sidewalks bustling with the criminally employed. I instinctively put my arm around her waist and guided her to the Olds.

"Aren't you afraid of getting offed by one of these cutthroats?" Ellen asked as I pulled away from the curb.

"No more than anyone else."

"You should."

"Why?"

"You're a Hiller."

"So?"

"You have more to lose."

I laughed. "Personal wealth makes a life more valuable, is that it?"

"Sure. If you're not scared, why do you carry that big gun?"

"Which big gun?"

"That monster you strapped on when you thought I wasn't looking."

"Oh, that. That's just for signaling waiters. Where'd you say this place was?"

Ellen guided me to a small, shabby café a half block from Regents Bridge. The instant we walked through the door I understood that Screaming Nietzsche's Café was less a place to eat than to pose and brood. The windows were blacked out and the smoke was so thick I suspected a hidden machine was making it. Wide-brimmed lights hung low over individual booths, and there wasn't a lot of dining going on, which made me wonder how Nietzsche paid the rent.

We seated ourselves in a corner booth and ordered from a zombie-eyed junkie who claimed to be a waiter. I scanned the sparse crowd, and in the opposite corner I spotted three Reds and a Cynic wearing the requisite mirror shades. I recognized them from the Hellfire, and they seemed to have no trouble remembering me.

"Oh, look, there's Chip," Ellen said, waving at the Cynic. "I dated him a couple of times. He's a real wild boy."

"I don't want to hear about it."

"Oh, the jealous type," she said, unlocking her velvet bag. Most of her right arm disappeared into the maw as she dug around.

"I can determine a woman's personality by the contents of her purse," I announced.

"Can you?" she said, coming out with a nail file. She locked the bag and set it aside.

"Don't you want to know what kind of person you are?"

She smiled without looking at me and went to work on her nails. "I already know what kind of person I am."

I sighed and turned my attention to the Reds. By the time our food arrived, three different sets of obvious drug fiends, mostly teenagers, had paid the Reds' booth a visit. Items were exchanged, and the fiends scuttled away with the frantic vigor junkies reserved for only one occasion.

"What do the Reds deal?" I asked, digging into greasy algae browns.

"You kidding?" she said, chewing on a kelp salad. "They're the sole source of Hill fun drugs in the City. That's how the Cynics buy them off."

"Is that where they get Newlife? From the Cynics?"

She glanced at me. "You don't want to mess with that stuff."

"I'm just curious," I said, glancing at the Reds. I caught Chip making secret waving motions under his table. They seemed to be directed at Ellen.

"Be back in a minute," I said, getting up, "I think Chip wants to talk to me." I crossed the floor to the Reds' booth and slid into an empty space. "Hey, guys," I said brightly. "Where's Louis? Working on his sprints?"

"I don't think you know who you're up against," Chip said with lazy menace.

"Sure, I do. You're Goldilocks and—" I turned to the Reds "—these are the Three Bears. How about selling me some hot porridge, Papa Bear?"

"Porridge?" Papa Bear drawled, going into his I-no-speak-English-good routine. "What is this porridge?"

"You know," I said. "Newlife. That all-time high."

The Reds stiffened at the word, just enough to notice. "Who says we sell this Newlife?" Papa Bear said.

"You just sold some to those kids, didn't you? Your buddy Chip here supplies, you sell, and the kids spend the rest of their lives on Pluto. Isn't that how it works?"

"Maybe you should leave," Chip warned, his voice threateningly low, "before someone gets hurt."

"What for? It ain't gonna be me. Lindquist designed Newlife, didn't he, Chip? That's why Cain put it in his mouth, ain't it?"

A Red started to say something, and Chip cut him off with a look. A nasty silence gripped the booth.

"The cold-shoulder treatment?" I said. "Is that how it's going to be?"

Nobody said anything. I got up, then leaned a hand on Chip's shoulder, bowing to speak confidentially. "You know, Chip, you keep flapping your hand under the table like that and I'm going to get the idea you're trying to bird-dog me."

His eyes flashed petulantly. "I can do whatever the hell I want."

"Maybe up on the Hill or in that nightclub of yours you can. But down here you're just another bleeder, with or without your punk baby-sitters. Are you getting me, Chimp?"

He kept his mouth shut, but the animal fear in his eyes said he got me fine. I checked my hair in his shades, then went back to Ellen.

"What'd you talk about?" Ellen asked when I returned. "Chip seems upset."

"I kidded him about him being a hemophiliac and he got sore."

"He's a bleeder?"

"Oh, yeah. He just doesn't like to think so."

"That's too bad," she said with genuine concern. "Did he say anything about me?"

"Naw, he was too sore."

With a great rustle of coats they stood up. Instead of walking directly to the door, they took a long detour that passed by our table. The Reds dumped comically hard looks, and Chip dropped a napkin note like a short-fused stick of dynamite. I reached for the note and Chip, thinking I was reaching for him, tried to run up the back of the Red in front of him, causing a chain reaction that had them barreling out the door like a bullwhipped eight-legged buffalo.

I unfolded the note.

How'd you like us to tell that gold-digging whore what you really are, handchopper? How'd you like us to take her away from you and show her a real good time? Stay off our backs or else!

A drooling, fang-toothed skull and crossbones served as the signature.

"What's it say?" Ellen asked excitedly. "Is it about me?"

"He says we make a cute couple," I said, wadding up the note and stuffing it in my hip pocket. "He gives you his regards."

"That Chip," she said, chewing happily. "He's a real sweetheart."

"He's a real shitbag."

She stopped chewing. "How can you say that?"

"Because he's a Cynic. They're all shitbags."

"Oh, they're not so bad. It's just their philosophy to act that way."

"Philosophy is a dangerous drug." I started to eat my soy patty but found I wasn't hungry. "Did you ever hear of the Santa Fe Massacre?"

Her brow furrowed. "Just from history books. A Party unit went berserk during the mop-up and wiped out a suburb. Mass combat psychosis or something."

"Yes," I said. "A charismatic nihilist named Captain Whittaker commanded them. One morning he came to the conclusion life had no redeeming value, served no worthwhile purpose. He converted his key leaders, then went about putting his beliefs into action. Over a three-day period his company executed over two thousand civilians whose only crime was being alive. That's the danger of philosophy."

"He sounds like an endliner."

"He was a forerunner of the movement."

"How do you know so much about it?"

"I was in the Party unit that captured Whittaker."

"I thought you rich boys had ways of getting around the draft."

"I volunteered. It was my first taste of action. I was fresh out of the Ranger indoctrination program. We parachuted into Santa Fe and followed the trail of bodies. When we made contact, they surrendered without firing a shot."

"What happened to them?"

"The company was promptly refitted and dropped in the middle of the fighting in L.A., a suicide mission. All except Captain Whittaker. He was the bad seed, so he had to be executed. The Rangers had a tradition of giving all execution duties to the freshest face in the company. As a form of initiation."

"And you were the freshest face."

I nodded. "Captain Whittaker was the first man I ever killed. His hands were tied behind his back, and he was grinning like I was about to cut him loose." I looked away. "He said the strangest thing to me."

"What?"

"'Shadows are tallest just before they're eaten by the night.'"

She frowned. "What's that supposed to mean?"

"I don't know. He didn't bother to explain."

"Wars are such shit," Ellen said bitterly. "I'll be glad when there are no more wars. Won't you?"

"I don't know," I said after a moment of thought. "Sometimes I think we sacrifice in peacetime what we fight to keep in war. I think when we stop having wars we'll have given up on getting any better."

"No wonder you're down here. Can we go?"

"All right." I dropped credit on the table, and we got up. I put my hand on the butt of my gyrapistol on the way out the door in case Chip and the Reds had more than nasty notes in mind.

Ellen started for the car, but I hooked her arm. "Let's go for a walk," I told her. "I want to visit a friend who lives near here."

"Is he a Hiller?"

"Used to be."

We started down the sidewalk. "Another golden boy wallowing in the gutter of guilt, eh?"

"Oh, he's well beyond wallowing."

A tramp moved down the sidewalk toward us, parting passersby with his noise and odor. He pushed a squeaky shopping cart loaded with junk, mumbling and barking at a world that gave him no relief.

Ellen made a face as we passed. "How can people live like that?"

"Most are insane," I said. "Unrehabilitable."

"I don't think we should rehabilitate them. I think we should just get rid of them."

I glanced at Ellen's hard face, locked in a grimace of bitterness and contempt for the land of her exile. "I'll never end up like that," she snarled in a low voice, "I swear it."

I pulled opened the door of Carlos's building. "This is it."

We took the stairs, and Carlos let us in after I identified myself. Fatigue ringed his eyes, three days' growth shaded his face, and a bottle of whiskey dangled in his hand. He immediately went back to his desk to stare at a monitor buzzing with the chaos of City Watch.

"You any relation to the Hillsdale Melendezes?" Ellen asked after I'd introduced them.

"Jose Melendez is my father," Carlos replied without looking up from the monitor.

She studied him closely. "What are you doing down here?"

"Paying my karmic bill for living a frivolous and destructive life." He paused to take a hit from the bottle. "Unfortunately I've been disposed to commit more karma-damaging crimes during my stay and am thus stuck in an inescapably vicious circle spiraling down into the abyss. Old story, new face."

Ellen glared at him. "Another guilt freak. What the hell is wrong with you people?"

"The war made him that way," I explained.

"He fought for the Party, too?"

"No," I said, laughing. "Carlos was on the other side. He was an officer in a corporate militia."

"My father pressured me into it," Carlos said. "So I could protect his vault full of money."

"Doesn't it show you how silly war is?" Ellen said. "You two were once trying to kill each other and now you're friends. Doesn't it make you realize the soldiers on the other side were people just like you?''

"Are you kidding?" Carlos said. "Those guys were scumbags."

"How can you say that?"

"Because ninety-nine percent of the human race are scumbags, so it's a pretty good bet they were, too. I mean, look at Jake, *he* was on the other side."

Ellen made a face. "Is there a bathroom in this dump? I think I'm going to throw up."

Carlos pointed. "Right through that door."

She closed the door behind her, and Carlos asked, "She know what you are?"

"Not exactly."

"Don't tell her."

I frowned. "You think she'd care?"

"She'd leave you."

"You know her?"

"I know her type."

I jammed my hands in my pockets and stood silent for a moment, angry at the whole world.

"Don't take it so hard," Carlos said. "You can't help what you are."

"I'm not taking anything hard. What do you know about the Cynics Club?"

"A bunch of rich kids playing bad boy," Carlos said. "What's your interest?"

"I think they're the source of Newlife. The Reds sell it, and Hiram Pennings protects them."

"What does that have to do with anything?"

"I don't know. Since I took up the hunt for Cain, Newlife keeps popping up. In Lindquist's mouth, at the Hellfire Club. Newlifers attacked me on the roof last night."

"Is that what happened to your face?"

"Yeah." I went to the window and looked out over the humming rifle and tripod. "It was a setup. You don't know anything about it, do you?"

"Me? I'm the one that warned you *not* to play hero, remember?"

"I remember. How long have you known Christopher Pennings?"

"Why?"

"Just wondering."

"Since Hiram hired me to instruct him. Four months."

"Before Cain popped up."

"Yes. What are you getting at?"

"I don't know. I just keep getting the feeling the HDS and Hiram are protecting someone. I figure Chris might be a good guess."

Carlos laughed. "You don't know Chris very well."

"You don't think he's capable?"

"I think anyone is capable of anything. But I don't think he's capable of being in two places at once. He was with me at the Night Owl when Cain did his number on Lindquist."

"The Night Owl? The leather bar on Hayward?"

Carlos nodded. "I was teaching him how to spot social deviates. If you want to show someone what a hyena looks like, you take him to the zoo. Why would Hiram hire you to find Cain if he wanted Chris protected?"

"Maybe he's throwing up a smoke screen. Maybe he thinks I'm so incompetent I'll screw everything up."

"He doesn't know you *that* well. And there'd be easier ways for Hiram to screw up the investigation if he had a mind to."

"Yeah, like putting Bowlan and Swinburne on the job."

"Aw, what do you care? You're getting paid by the day, aren't you?"

"That's another thing I don't get. They lay all this plastic on me to hunt down Cain, then treat me like a pervert uncle they're bribing to keep away from their neighborhood. Go figure."

"Just take their money and forget about it," Carlos said absently, immersed in the buzz and flash of the monitor. I could hear a news hound babbling excitedly about a factory fire in the suburb of Southend.

"You'll data dose if you watch too much of that," I warned.

He rubbed his bloodshot eyes. "I was about to turn it off anyway." He reached for the keyboard, and a word stabbed into my head.

"Hold on!" I said, turning to the monitor. It displayed a massive factory complex engulfed by flame and smoke and surrounded by fire trucks and SPF troop carriers. "I thought I heard him say Basco Technologies."

"He did. So what?"

"Cain's first victim ran Basco Tech. Donald Basque. Listen."

"There are reports that the fire spread so rapidly not a single worker was able to escape with his life," the news hound reported excitedly. "Indeed, a great many human remains can be seen among the rubble thrown out by the tremendously lethal explosion." The camera zoomed in on what appeared to be a severed arm between the feet of two SPF troopers suited up in riot gear. "As you can see, there is a strong SPF presence here, for reasons unknown."

There was a pause, as if the hound were listening to something we could not hear. "The fuck if I will," he said, then another pause. "All right, goddamn it," he said bitterly. "City Watch control has requested I move forward and see if I can elicit some sort of explanation from the troopers as to why they are on-site in such significant numbers."

The camera bobbed toward the loose picket of riot-suited troopers. "Excuse me," the hound said, "but could you explain exactly why you fine troopers are here?"

By way of answer, a riot trooper took two quick steps forward, raised his shock baton and brought it down hard on the news hound's skull. The picture rolled, the baton came down again, and the screen went blank. After a buzzing delay, the monitor lit up with a distant view of a rooftop sniper pouring down fire on commuters at a bus stop.

"That'll teach that nosy little weasel," Carlos said, switching the screen to a computer menu. "A good clubbing is just what he needed."

Ellen came out of the bathroom, her makeup fresh. "What's with the mirror?"

"What's with you people?" Carlos muttered, pecking at the keyboard. "Why does everyone want to stare into the eyes of their most cruel and vicious enemy?"

Ellen looked at me sharply. "Can we leave?"

"All right," I said, opening the door. "Later, Carlos."

"Remember what I said about..." His eyes flickered to Ellen's back.

I nodded and followed Ellen out.

"What was he talking about?" she asked when we reached the sidewalk.

"Who knows what that wiggy bastard is ever talking about?" I replied, taking her arm in mine. "What the hell does he know, anyway?"

"Jeez, take it easy. And what's the rush?"

"A factory just blew up in the burbs. I want to take a look at it."

"Oh, God, you're not one of those gore freaks, are you? Is that why you like it down here so much?"

"You got me. You want to go?"

"No, thanks. I have to unpack the rest of my things."

I escorted her to the apartment door, giving her the keycard, a kiss and a promise to be back in a couple of hours.

I drove quickly out of the City, then jumped on the southbound speedway. I didn't have a map of Southend but I didn't need one; I just followed the column of black smoke rolling into the sky.

A crowd of thrill seekers already crowded the field of yellow grass surrounding the plant, held in check by the ring of SPF troopers. Most of the fire-fighting machines were inside the cordon, battling the blaze, but one beat-up and rusted machine idled outside the spectators. The markings on the side said it belonged to the south City borough of Kant. I approached one of the suited-up fire fighters leaning against the fire truck, a bearish black man impassively watching the blaze.

"A bit far from home, aren't you?" I said.

He glanced at me, then shrugged. "We're just containment."

"I don't blame you," I said. "The burb dings don't help us douse our fires, why should you risk your necks for them?"

"That's right. We wouldn't even be out here if the chief's house wasn't nearby."

I nodded, folded my arms and turned to the blaze. "I didn't know computer components burned so well."

"Huh?"

"That's what they manufactured. Computer components."

"Bullshit they did." He pointed a heavy gauntlet at the fire. "See the purplish red flame and all the black smoke? Do you smell that sweet odor, like calamine? That's liquid chemicals burning and a lot of it. But it wasn't the chemicals that set the thing off."

"What makes you say that?"

He pointed again. "Look at the debris around the base of the complex. It goes out a hundred meters past the security fence, and none of it is so much as scorched. A dry explosion leveled the place before the chemical fire started."

"Dry explosion?"

"Nonliquid explosives, like TNT or fusion even."

"I see. Think anyone inside the plant survived?"

"Not a chance."

I nodded. "Lot of spifs around."

"Restricted plant. Probably think people'll find something top secret in the debris."

"Maybe they think it was sabotage."

"I didn't say nothing about that." He glanced sideways at me. "You a reporter?"

"Just an innocent bystander."

"Well, you might want to bystand somewhere else. There could be secondary explosions."

I went back to my car, wheeled to the speedway ramp and shot north. I sped through the City and headed uphill. I had a strong hunch the destruction of Basque's plant had something to do with the whole Cain equation, and I thought there might be someone on the Hill who might know something about it.

I stopped at the gate, and a guard glanced the length of my car before stepping forward to point his subgun at me. "You got the wrong exit, buddy. Turn around and go home."

I laughed politely, then twisted on a big grin designed to overcome his professional aloofness. "I found this in my car the other day," I said, showing him the pass from the medicine cabinet. "Maybe you can tell me which of my friends it belongs to so I can return it."

"Gimme that," he said, snatching it out of my hand. He slid the magnetic strip through a reader attached to his wrist, then peered at the tiny screen. "It belongs to Jacob Wolfgang Strait," he said, then peered at me. "Where'd you say you found it?"

"Jake Strait?" I said. "Why, *I'm* Jake Strait."

"Oh, really?" he sneered. "Let's see your hand."

I held out my right hand, and he scanned it with a long-necked scanner from his belt. He listened to it squawk my name, then glared at me. "You trying to play games?"

"You sure it belongs to me?"

"You think I'm a moron?" he said, certain I was trying to provoke him by playing dumb. "You've used the thing four times in the past month."

"I have not."

"The computers don't lie, buddy."

I stared blankly at him a moment. Well, I wonder what that could mean, I thought.

"Well, give it back to me, then, dumbo," I snarled, grabbing at the card.

"It's been revoked," he snapped, jerking it out of reach.

"Revoked? By who?"

"By none of your goddamn business. Now get the hell out of here."

"I need to see someone on the Hill."

"Not without a valid pass."

"This one's good," I said, handing him the SPF pass.

He frowned at the SPF insignia, then ran it through. A moment later it joined the other pass in his pocket.

"Give it back," I warned.

"Revoked!" he shouted gleefully.

"Both of them?"

"That's right. Now turn around before I revoke your right to breathe."

I turned around. All the way back to my apartment I wondered how I could have used a pass I'd never seen before. I also wondered who wanted to keep me off the Hill. There seemed too many suspects to count.

I jogged the stairs and found the door unlocked. I stepped inside, then almost jumped back out, thinking I'd walked into the wrong apartment until I realized that Ellen had cleaned and rearranged the place. I sat on the sofa and read the number on Bowlan's business card to the monitor.

"You!" the elderly receptionist barked from the screen.

"Yes," I said. "Put me through to Sir Henry."

"I will not!"

"In that case, I'll be right up."

"No!" she moaned, and Bowlan's secretary popped on the screen. "You!" she said, not unfamiliarly.

"Quick!" I shouted. "I've a vital message from Hiram Pennings to Sir Henry!"

"Message?" she stuttered. "Pennings?"

"Life and death! Mayhem! Terror! Grievous injury! Murder most foul! *Move!*"

"Hold on!" The screen flashed to the HDS crest, and a moment later Bowlan appeared.

"What's this about, then?" Bowlan wailed, sagging at the sight of me.

"Who canceled my Hill pass?"

"Mr. Pennings did. He felt that your obsession with Hillsdale was distracting you from probing the City."

"That only leaves me half a deck to play with."

"Can it be said you ever played with a full deck?" Bowlan shot back, snickering in spite of himself.

"So that's the way it's going to be, eh? Why didn't you tell me Basco Tech belonged to Hiram?"

"You never asked," Bowlan sputtered. "And who says Basco is a Pennings factory?"

"He owns it, doesn't he? Just like he owned Miss Romani. Doesn't it strike you as strange that two out of three of Cain's victims had direct ties with Hiram Pennings?"

Bowlan took a moment to freshen his drink, and unless the Party had a new idea about packaging mineral water in whiskey bottles, the highball glass was no longer ironic.

"Most of the Hill has ties with Hiram Pennings," he said after a stiff belt. "That is the nature of things. We hired you to find a psychopathic killer, Mr. Strait. We did not hire you to invent wild conspiracies as a means of covering up your own investigative failures."

"Is that your line?"

"Yes, it most certainly is."

"Well, screw you, then," I said, and disconnected.

"Who was that?" Ellen said, walking into the room wearing cutoff shorts and halter top.

"Some lying drunk," I said distractedly. "Hiram Pennings is trying to keep me off the Hill."

"Hiram? Why?"

"I think there are things he doesn't want me to know."

Ellen sat down on my lap, her face serious. "Hiram Pennings is a lousy choice of enemies."

"You know something?"

"I know those who get in his way tend to die."

"Something you want to talk about?" I asked carefully.

"No," she said flatly.

I nodded and glanced around. "You've put a shine on the place."

"It was a mess. How long have you lived down here?"

"It feels like all my life."

She wrapped her arms around my neck and moved her lips close to mine. "Did you miss me?" she murmured.

"Every minute."

"Because you love me?"

"I don't know what I feel. I've forgotten what love feels like."

"It could be love, couldn't it?"

"I'm sap enough, if that's what you mean."

"I knew it," she said, melting against me. "Promise me, Jake."

"Promise you what?"

"Promise me you won't leave me down here. Promise me you won't leave me down here to die."

"I promise," I said, my insides twisting with guilt. "I promise."

12

I woke up in bed, lustily entwined with Ellen. The room was dark, and the phone on the bed stand was ringing. I groped the handset to my head.

"Hello?"

"Your boy was busy last night," Degas said.

"Oh, hell. What's the address?"

"You know where the Pennings mansion is?"

"Christ!" I said, sitting up. "Who?"

"Janice Pennings."

"All right," I said. "What time is it?"

"Six-fifteen."

"I'll be up in forty-five minutes. Make sure you tell the goddamn guards to let me through the gate."

"What happened to the pass I gave you?"

"Oh, I sold that for whiskey money."

"I told them you would," he said, then disconnected.

"Who was that?" Ellen mumbled.

"A business associate," I said, going to the closet and climbing into a black jumpsuit. "I have to go."

"What business are you in?"

"I'm a world-famous flimflam man."

"That's not hard to believe. Where you going?"

"The Hill." I finished lacing my boots and stood to find Ellen standing naked right next to me, her eyes disquiet.

"The Hill?" she echoed, seizing my arm. "Take me with you. I want to go."

"Not where I'm going, you don't." I moved to the door, and she came with me.

"You can't leave me down here," she said, her nails digging into my arm, "you *promised* me."

"I'm sorry, Ellen," I said, "but I can't take you."

She hit me. A hard, stinging slap that came out of nowhere. "Fuck you, then," she whispered, her face contorted into a mask of hate, "you and your money and your big house on the Hill. I don't want any of it. I don't want any of you. You can find someone else."

She started to turn away, but I grabbed her shoulders and leaned into her face. "It's time I made something clear to you," I said flatly. "I'm not from the Hill. I'm a bogeyman. A handchopper. Like Carlos, but without the pedigree. I don't have a mansion on the Hill or a billion in the bank. I don't even have a painted portrait of my father. My father was a goddamn wino, and I went one up on him and became a handchopper. They let me on the Hill to look at butchered bodies, then run me off like a carrion-eating jackal." I let her go, feeling vaguely relieved. "That's it. That's the whole story."

She stared at me a moment, lips parted, eyes wide. "You're making that up," she whispered desperately. "You're lying!"

"No," I said, "I wish I were, but I'm not."

She looked off sharply, mouth tight, cheeks flushed. "Why did you lie to me, then? Just so you could screw me?"

"I never told you I was rich."

"But you let me believe it. You used me like a whore, just like all the others." She covered her face and began to cry. "Just like all those other filthy liars."

I reached out for her and she flinched away.

"Keep your filthy hands off me!" she snapped.

"Maybe I did lie to you," I said, strapping on the gyra and covering it with a canvas jacket. "Maybe I did use you. Maybe I wanted something I wasn't supposed to have." I went to the door. "Maybe I'm just as bad as you are."

"I'll leave the keycard under the mat," she said.

Unable to think of any way I could screw things up worse, I nodded and left.

I socked myself in the stomach and begged God to kill me all the way to the Hill's gate. I wanted to beat the bejesus out of myself; I wanted to punish that mean, stupid bastard inside me who made a lifelong project of screwing up my life. Why did I tell her the truth? Wasn't there anything worth lying about? Wasn't it better to live the lie than live alone?

I'm really down this time, I swore grimly, I'm broken, wiped out, in the gutter, sprawled out at the very bottom of the abyss. No phoenix in these bitter ashes, no goddamn way I'll crawl out of this pit.

By the time I reached Pennings's vehicle-choked roundabout, my stomach was sore and I'd settled into a bitter fugue equal parts self-pity and self-hate. I parked outside the protective ring of vehicles, next to Carlos's electric buzzcar. Carlos leaned against the plastic fender, smoking a cigarette. Chris sat in the passenger seat, his head bowed. He might have been crying.

"Good morning," I snapped, getting out of the Olds.

Carlos nodded. "What's wrong with you?"

"Nothing."

"You told her."

"Get off my goddamn back, for crissakes."

"You're better off. She was trouble."

"Oh, God," I said staring at the morning sky. "Just get me through the day. I'll pay you back tomorrow, I swear I will."

"Always trying to con God," Carlos said. "Why don't you carry your own weight for once?"

"Yeah, why don't I?" I sighed. "You see Janice yet?"

"Chris and I found her."

"Tell me about it."

"We came back at 5:00 a.m., after I'd spent the night giving Chris the night tour of Hayward. Chris invited me in for a drink, and there she was."

"You didn't see anything?"

"No, she'd been dead for an hour or so. After I calmed Chris down, I checked out the house and grounds and came up empty."

"Where was Hiram and the servants?"

"Hiram skims to a spa down south every weekend. Baily goes with him, and the rest of the servants get Saturdays off."

"How convenient," I said, regarding Chris. "Looks like he's taking it rough."

"Yeah."

"I'll have a talk with him," I said, moving to the passenger window and leaning in. "Tough break, kid."

"She didn't deserve to die like that," he said in a small, broken voice. He started to sob and jerked his face away from me. "I know Jan was a drunk, but she deserved better."

I nodded, putting my hands in my pockets and looking around. Crying men made me uncomfortable. "Listen," I said brusquely. "We all go sooner or later. She just happened to get off the train a few stops early."

He looked up from under his tears and frowned at me. "What the hell kind of thing is that to say?"

I shrugged. "That's just the way I look at it."

"Oh, I'll bet you do," he snapped, wiping at the tears irritably, as if they belonged to someone else. "Why don't you go poke around my mother's guts, since you like it so much?"

"Yeah," I said, relieved the moment was over, "why don't I?" I waved to Carlos and moved past the flashing vehicles. A plastic-encased Degas met me on the draw-bridge with a plastic suit.

"Goddamn clown suit," I muttered, wrestling into the plastic.

"What were you saying to the kid?" Degas asked.

"I was consoling him."

"I hope you weren't rousting him."

"He has an alibi," I said, adjusting the mouth mask. "Let's get this over with."

I followed Degas through the crowded foyer and into the living room. I took one look at the carnage on the floor and immediately turned away.

"Son of a bitch," I said, moving along the wall, look-ing at anything but the body. I stopped at the fireplace. The fire was burning down, and there was a strong odor of burned soy burger. I wiped my sweating face with a handkerchief and recalled the one and only time I'd spo-ken with Janice Pennings.

"His pace is accelerating," Degas said from across the room. "Nine days between his first two kills, then four days, now two."

"The pendulum syndrome," Burt asserted.

"You mean the sick-bastard syndrome," I said.

"Ah," Burt chided, "a bogeyman with a sensitive stomach. What an unfortunate combination."

"I bet you have a raging hard-on," I snarled. "So, what's your opinion of this one, Burt, from the artistic point of view?"

"Why don't you turn around and see for yourself? It's really quite something."

I covered my mouth and nose with the handkerchief, took a deep breath and turned around. A wave of revulsion rolled over me, and I rode it out, forcing myself to stare, to take in every grisly detail.

Janice lay on her back. Her right leg and both arms were amputated. The stump of the left arm was buried in her hair, as if the limb were growing out the top of her head. The other two severed limbs were nowhere in sight. The still-attached left leg stuck out at a right angle, held in place by a nail. Nail heads also protruded from just below Janice's collarbones. A black leather pillow from the couch propped up her head, and she seemed to be gazing beyond her slashed cheekbones and breasts, to an empty crystal decanter of whiskey inserted neck first into a hole in her stomach. There was a strong odor of rye whiskey.

"He let her keep her eyes," I murmured, sick and angry to the very bottom of my soul. "And there's no nail in her head."

"Something scared him off before he could finish," Burt speculated.

"No," I said, wiping sweat from my eyes. "In the past he took the eyes before dismembering, remember? And look at the way he propped up her head. He wanted her to watch him. Does she still have her tongue?"

"Yes," Burt said.

I nodded. "What else is different?"

Burt looked to the cat-eyed blonde, who referred to a data board. "Cain didn't stun her with electricity," the blonde said.

"Unsurprising when you consider her blood-alcohol level," Burt said.

"What else?" I asked.

"The decanter inserted in her stomach."

"There's something inside the bottle," I said, staring harder.

"Her liver," Burt said. "He cut out her liver, squeezed it into the decanter, then inserted the decanter in the liver cavity. It seems our Cain is no stranger to irony."

"Anything else?" I asked the blonde.

"Cain cut out all her implants," she said.

"Implants?" Degas asked.

"Yes," she said. "Mrs. Pennings had extensive cosmetic surgery. Along with lifts, tucks and injections, she had cheek, breast and buttock implants put in. All were removed and are presently missing."

"How did Cain know she had implants?" I asked.

"It's obvious to the educated eye," Burt said.

"What else is different?" I asked the blonde.

"Her left arm and right leg are missing," she replied. "Took them with him, I guess."

I turned to the fireplace and stared into the hearth. Taking a poker from the rack, I jabbed at logs nearly burned to ash. Two oblong objects rolled from the embers, and the smell of charred soy burger became stronger. "They're in here," I said, replacing the poker. Techs converged and I backed away.

"All of a sudden he's changing his style," Degas remarked.

Burt smiled. "The mark of a true artist is an ability to adapt, to try new things." He sighed and his voice softened. "Every fresh example of his strange language makes me hunger for the day I'll get to study him."

"I hope his head will be enough," I said, "because that's all you'll be getting."

"More impotent breast-beating," Burt sighed. "You'll never catch him. It'll take more than a gutter brute to beat Cain."

"I'll get him, all right. If it's the last thing I do."

Degas began walking around the room, and Burt went back to directing the forensic team, more with the air of photographer capturing a piece of art for posterity than a pathologist gathering clues. Every now and then he paused to gaze down upon the butchered Mrs. Pennings and heave out a sigh.

I joined Degas near the wet bar. "Don't touch anything," he warned. "This is a crime scene."

I frowned at him, then said in a low voice, "He knew her."

"Who?"

"Cain."

"Why are you whispering?"

"I don't want Burt to hear me."

"Why not?"

"Are you kidding? He probably has Cain's hot line written on his hand."

He glanced at Burt, then lowered his voice. "What makes you think Cain knew her?"

"Lots of reasons. First, of all the decanters on this bar to replace her liver with, Cain chooses rye."

"So?"

"Rye was her favorite drink."

"She could have told him before he nailed her down."

"That's another thing. He didn't stun her. That proves she knew him."

"That proves how drunk she was."

"Well, what about the tongue? He left it in so she could scream. He knew no one was home to hear her scream."

"He could have cased the place."

"What about the implants, then? I don't buy that educated-eye bullshit. The cheek and breast implants maybe, but the buttocks?" I shook my head and mopped my brow. "He knew her. He knew about her drinking habits, he knew about her surgery, he knew Hiram and the servants would be gone."

"Cain could have got all that information from a scandal rag. The foibles of the rich are well documented by the yellow press." He made a face. "What's wrong with you? Are you on something?"

"What makes you say that?"

"You're sweating like a junkie, your eyes are all pupil, and your skin is flushed."

"Is it?" I said, and my left hand started to itch. "I must be sick."

"No kidding," Degas said, moving away to watch the techs tag and bag the limbs from the hearth.

I moved back toward the body. The blonde hunkered next to the body, taking a scalp sample. From where I stood, Jan's dead eyes pointed straight at me. I was about to move when one of the eyes winked.

"Good God!" I said, flinching back. "I didn't see that!"

"See what?" Degas said, looking over at me.

"She winked at me!"

"I did not!" the blonde protested.

"Not you," I said, putting my back to the corpse. "Janice did."

"What?" Burt said, laughing. "So good-looking even the corpses wink at you, eh, bogeyboy?"

"It's probably just nerves," Degas explained.

"Whose nerves is the question," Burt quipped. "Don't worry, handchopper. The human body can show movement days after death."

"Right, right," I sighed. I drew a deep breath, wiped the sweat from my eyes with the drenched handkerchief and heard someone whisper my name.

I looked over my shoulder at the blonde. "You say something?"

"I certainly did not."

"Jake," I heard again, and this time I recognized the voice. I turned around slowly. I watched the blonde tech run a humming machine over Jan's face, and saw Jan's lips curl into a smile.

"How about that drink, Jake?" she said.

"She's alive," I whispered.

The blonde turned to me and frowned. "What'd you say?"

"She's alive!" I howled, lunging back against the wall. Every head in the room whipped my way, and the blonde dropped the machine and lurched away from the body, not taking any chances.

"The rented fiend is wigging," Burt warned.

"What's wrong, Strait?" Degas asked with a warning tone.

"She's not dead," I said. I turned to lean both hands on the wall, eyes clenched tight. "First she winked at me, then she asked me to make her a goddamn drink. And don't try and tell me the human body can demand drinks days after death."

"Calm down," Degas said, moving up beside me, probably getting an angle on my kidneys. "You're ill. You're just seeing things."

"No," I said. "I *heard* her voice. I *saw* her lips move."

"She's dead!" Burt squawked. "All her blood is on the carpet!"

A hush gripped the room and I took deep breaths, trying to regain control. He's right, I told myself. She's stone dead, stiff as a board, an inanimate object. The stress is getting to me, that's all. With all the pressure I've been under, I have to expect this kind of crack-up.

I croaked out a little laugh. "Jesus, you're right," I said, rubbing my sweat-slick face. "I'm ill and stressed out and I lost my head for a minute, that's all. Now I'm going to a quiet bar to have a quiet drink and everything will be fine." Some of the buzzing tension left the room as I turned to leave.

Jan was sitting up now, her ripped and rendered face twisted into a big, wicked grin. "C'mon, Jake," she said, "a lady could die of thirst around here."

I looked with horror at Degas. "You don't see it?" I whispered.

Degas crouched, ready to jump me. "All right, bogeyman, what're you on?"

"I'm on my way out," I said, moving crablike toward the door, keeping close to the wall. "Modem over the package when you can."

"You're not leaving, are you, Jake?" Jan giggled, following me with her head.

"Yes, but don't get up!" I said, and rushed into the foyer. Shrill laughter followed me out, but it could have been Burt.

I ripped the plastic suit off as I scrambled across the drawbridge, startling the SPF troopers hanging around the statue of Atlas. I fell against the Olds and a voice called out, making me drop my keys.

"Jake!" Carlos said. "What the hell's wrong with you? You look like a nut."

I smiled and waved, then opened the door and tumbled in. I fumbled the keys into the ignition and got the engine going. Carlos started walking my way, but I floored the accelerator and roared up the drive. I charged onto the main road and powered downhill, sweating badly. My left palm burned and itched, and I looked to find it flushed a deep red.

Newlife hallucinations, I told myself. None of that was real, the dead do not demand drinks, it just doesn't happen. I accepted I was in the grips of a hallucinogenic episode that would soon pass, then realized I was no longer in control of my car. The steering wheel was moving beneath my hands of its own free will; I had no power over it. I became aware of a sound just under the roar of the engine, a distinct breathing sound.

"All right," I said, trying to get a grip. "So the fucking car is alive. I can deal with that, it's all right." I patted the dash. "Just take us home, baby. Once we get home, everything will be fine."

I smelled smoke. Of course! I thought. The treacherous machine was diverting the exhaust into the driver's compartment to kill me! I'm the resented master after all. The machine has bided its time and now, in my moment of weakness, it was moving in for the kill.

I pawed at the door handle, prepared to leap clear of the death machine, then realized it was cigarette smoke. Real tobacco, fragrant and heavy. Which was strange since I wasn't smoking.

"So, Jake." Jan giggled, her voice carrying from the passenger seat. "How old do I look now?"

The words hit me like multiple blows from a heavy sap, sagging me against the door. "I'm not going to look at you," I groaned, forcing my eyes to remain on the road. "You're not real. There's no way you're goddamn real."

"Will you believe me if I give you a kiss?" she said, her voice near my ear.

I flinched, then looked. "Oh, Jesus Christ!" I screamed. "Merciful mother of God!"

"Oh, you do carry on," Jan sighed. She sat in the passenger seat, right leg casually crossed over the left stump, a cigarette dangling from her mashed lips, no hand to hold it.

"What do you want?"

"A drink."

"Of course," I said. I reached across to the glove box and popped it open. I dug around for a fifth of whiskey and came out with a handful of eight-inch nails.

"Uh-uh," I said, powering down the window to toss them out. "Those aren't real, either." I snapped the glove box shut. "Sorry, nothing to drink."

I turned my attention back to the road. The lights of the checkpoint loomed ahead, and I began to fret that the car wouldn't feel like stopping at the gate.

"All right," I told the dash, "we have a stop coming up."

"Who in earth are you talking to?" Jan asked.

"The car," I said, laughing manically. "It's alive, you see, driving itself."

"How perfectly silly. Cars aren't alive."

"Oh, but corpses are, right?" I stroked the dashboard and firmly said, "All good cars stop at the gate."

"Oh, let it run the damn thing," Jan said.

"Don't listen to her!" I hissed. "We must stop! Must!"

"Quit being such a bore. Go ahead, car, run the gate. And kill the guards, too. They're always so rude anyway."

The Olds immediately accelerated. "No!" I shouted. "Don't listen to her! She's dead and has nothing to lose!"

"Go, go, go!" Jan encouraged. "I'll bet a big car like you can go *very* fast!"

"Chrome hubcaps!" I shouted. "I'll buy you chrome hubcaps if you stop!"

"Faster!" Jan cried excitedly, "faster, car, faster!"

"Fur dash!" I shouted. "Radial tires! Premium fuel!"

"Faster, faster!"

"Velvet headliner! Chrome valve stems!"

"All the way, you magnificent beast!"

We rushed the gate like a runaway juggernaut, and thirty meters away I could see the frantic expressions of guards waving submachine guns, their mouths wide with screams.

"Compound wax job!" I wailed, "a daily hand buff for the rest of your days!"

Rubber grabbed asphalt with a gruesome wail, and the Olds slid the remaining fifteen meters to the gate, the front bumper trembling to a stop bare centimeters from the steel barrier.

The first guard who rushed my window was unable to speak coherently, making do with a crude form of sign language that involved clawing at my eyes and jabbing the barrel of his subgun into my neck. A guard with a pistol in his fist shoved him out of the way and leaned in, speaking in a language I understood perfectly.

"You crazy asshole!" he screamed, spraying spittle. "Are you fucking nuts?"

"Inspector Degas sent me down to tell you something extremely urgent!" I shouted. "His com unit went out, and he said it's absolutely essential that you know, right this instant!"

The guard leaned back and gaped. "What," he gasped, "what *is* it?"

I opened my mouth, then stared off blankly. "You know, in all the excitement, I seem to have forgotten." I shrugged. "Oh, well. Let me through, and I'll call you from a combooth when I remember."

He stared at me for a moment, his entire body trembling with some terrible emotion. The other guard tried to shove his way forward to claw out my eyes, and his partner had to backhand repeatedly before he backed off, whimpering like a whipped dog.

The guard with the pistol took a com unit from his belt and asked for Inspector Degas.

"Tell him it's Jake," I advised.

"Inspector," the guard said, "this is Guard Post Alpha. Some lunatic just tried to ram the gate and he said...yes, sir... but...yes, sir, he does, but...I see, sir, I just—" He frowned at the com, then reattached it to his belt. "You can go," he said, signaling the other guard to activate the gate. "But you pull that kind of stunt again and I'll put a magazine of slugs through your windpipe."

"Oh, tell him to kiss off," Jan said.

"Keep quiet," I told Jan, then patted the dashboard. "To the office. Go to the office."

The guard crouched and peered in. "Who are you talking to?"

"Do you see the corpse of Janice Pennings sitting beside me?"

He squinted hard at Jan's dazzling smile, then frowned. "No."

"Then I must not be talking to anyone, am I?" The Olds started to move and a moment later we were barreling down the speedway. "See," I told Jan, "you're not real."

"Who are you talking to, then?"

"I'm talking to myself, that's who. I can prove you're not real. If I reach out and touch you, you'll disappear."

"Reach out and touch me, then, Jake," she said softly, smiling seductively. "Go ahead, I don't mind. Touch away."

I reached out a hand, then drew it back. "No, all I have to do is concentrate," I said, locking my eyes on the road. "I created you, I can get rid of you. I'll focus on something else. I'll think about Ellen. No, not her, I'll think about combatball scores, combatball, combatball..."

After a moment of intense concentration, the smell of cigarette smoke faded then vanished and I breathed a sigh of relief. "Thank the merciful Lord," I sighed, looking to the passenger seat.

"Do you have a cigarette?" Jan asked. "I can't seem to reach mine."

I started reaching in my jacket, then caught myself. "No, you don't," I cajoled, "I'm not going to waste cigarettes on imaginary dead people."

She pouted for a moment, her mashed lips pursed. "Aren't you at least curious who killed me?"

"Of course I am."

"Then why don't you ask me?"

I looked at her. "All right, Jan, I'm asking. Who's Cain?"

"I can't tell you."

"Why not?"

"The devil won't let me. He says you owe him money."

"Yes, it's true."

"A lot of money."

"Ah, fuck that greedy bastard." I looked at my eyes in the rearview. They looked crazy. "I'm going insane," I said.

"What makes you say that?" Jan giggled, "Just because your car drives itself and you're on speaking terms with the dead doesn't mean you're the tiniest bit insane."

"Of course not," I said, exiting onto Hayward. The Olds accelerated, zipping past liquor stores. A moment later the Olds parked itself in front of my office building.

"Good girl," I said, patting the dash. I opened the door and looked back at Jan. "You don't mind waiting in the car, do you?"

"I was hoping you'd invite me up for that long-awaited drink."

"We'll go somewhere later," I said. "You can hop over to the St. Chris in the meantime." My eyes went to the leg stump. "Sorry!"

"You mean bastard."

"Yes," I said, slamming the door and lurching into a familiar mop bopping down the sidewalk.

"I still ain't done nothin'," he assured me.

"Is there a cure for Newlife?" I demanded, seizing his lapels.

"Quit asking me 'bout that stuff," he shrieked, trying to get away. "I don't know nothing 'bout nothing 'bout Newlife!"

"What do you have for hallucinations, then?"

"Now you're talking, jonesy," he said, relaxing a little. I let go, and he opened his coat with trembling hands. "I got stuff here that'll make you see things you only dreamed—"

"No, no," I said. "What do you have that *stops* hallucinations?"

He stared at me a moment. "*Stops* hallucinations?"

"Yes!" I shouted, and I noticed his face was beginning to elongate, slanting his eyes and stretching his chin to a point. "Don't do it," I warned.

"Do what?"

"Turn into the devil. You know I don't have that kind of cash on hand."

"Be cool, man," he urged, backing away. "Be cool now." When he was out of lunging range, he scrambled away and I fought off the urge the race after him, howling and clawing at his neck.

I moved quickly through the lobby and up the stairs. By the time I reached the third floor, I was certain someone, some*thing* was following me. I crept down the hall, listening between steps. I could almost hear it, a lurching, one-legged demon hopping up the steps two at a time. I ran to my door, dropping my keys repeatedly, each time a new horror. I threw the door open, fell inside and bolted it behind me. Leaning against the door, I listened fearfully.

I heard the *clump! clump! clump!* of a slow, hopping step, closer and closer until it stopped just outside the door.

"Is that you, Mrs. Pennings?" I croaked. A brooding silence answered.

I shoved off from the door and stumbled through a room crowded with black shadows, afraid to turn on the lights, afraid of what I might see. I peeked through the shut blinds at the street below, rife with vice-hungry humanity. They either lurked or prowled, and I instinctively knew it was me they were looking for. Again and again I caught them looking up at my window with flashing devil eyes.

Janice hopped out of the lobby door and onto the sidewalk. Very agile for a one-limbed woman, I thought as she dodged traffic and pogoed into the St. Chris. Let Amal deal with her, I thought as a horrible buzzing filled the room. I went crazy with fear, lashing out at the monstrous wasp that had landed on my back to plunge its saber-sized stinger into my spine and pump my bloodstream full of deadly poison. I crashed into the file cabinet and fell to the floor, shrieking with agony. The buzzing continued, and after a moment of thrashing I realized it was the monitor.

"Hello?" I answered from the floor.

"Mr. Strait?" Baily's voice said from the blank monitor.

"Yes! That's *me!*"

"Mr. Pennings would like to speak with you, sir."

I got up slowly, staying out of sight of the monitor's evil eye. "Put him on."

"Mr. Strait," Hiram said heavily.

"Hello, Hiram," I said, moving to the rear of the monitor, squeezing its sides with my hands. "I offer you my—" I gritted my teeth to fight down the howling beast trying to crawl out of my belly and into my mouth "—sympathies."

"Accepted," he lisped. "I can't see you."

"I'm . . . indisposed."

"I see. I understand you've been up to the house, Mr. Strait."

"I have."

"What do you think?"

"I think Cain is . . . trying to frighten you."

"Not kill me?"

"No."

"You sound quite odd, Mr. Strait."

"I feel . . . quite odd."

"I was informed you behaved rather strangely at the scene of my wife's unfortunate circumstance."

"I'm . . . that way. I see you . . . are not."

"I am a man of few emotions, Mr. Strait, so I use them sparingly. But this incident has not left me unmoved. I'm upping the ante—as of this instant, Cain's bounty is now one hundred thousand credits."

"That's . . . very generous,"

"Yes. But with the new bounty comes a condition, Mr. Strait."

"What?"

"When you discover who this Cain is, you must tell me first. No one else. Just me."

"Why?"

Pennings's voice became faint and distant, like a whisper crossing a dark and empty room. "I have found this dish called vengeance filling only when eaten alone."

"All right," I said. "You'll . . . be first." I disconnected, then collapsed in the swivel chair behind the desk. "Computer on," I croaked. "The Cain file."

I skimmed through the file quickly, not allowing myself to focus on anything too long, sucking at the rotten plum that was Cain and hoping it wouldn't poison me.

I ended up on the crime-scene photos, Cain's grisly portfolio. I put them on loop, and the screen flashed from gory scene to gory scene until I lost track of time. Fresh data shot over the modem deep into the ordeal, Jan's corpse joined the loop, and I peered through four clear windows into hell.

I sensed there was a subtle language in each cut, each rendering of flesh. Cain nailed the bodies in place for a reason, he had something to say, a message he didn't want disturbed.

I speeded up the loop until the gore and mutilation became a flashing blur. Immediately I began to feel my subconscious bubble and percolate as the beast inside began to shift and stir, feasting on the gore and horror. Eventually he started to crawl his way out, and I didn't fight him. I cut him loose, and he rose out of my belly, a howling monster with different eyes. I whacked my head against the monitor, screaming, trying to break through the blurred wall of butchered bodies, then finally succeeding.

Late-afternoon sunlight was seeping through the blinds when I came to. My forehead was sore, and dried blood painted the monitor's flashing screen. I wiped the screen with my handkerchief and slowed the loop down, studying each frame closely, and it was plain to me.

Burt was right. Cain did speak in a language. The language was English.

I called SPF Central.

13

Degas's cubicle was ten-by-fifteen meters, most of it taken up by a slumped aluminum desk and shelves stuffed with books. Degas slouched behind the desk with the face of an insomniac resigned to never sleep again.

"Boot up Cain's photo banks," I said. "Display the overhead shot of Cain's first victim, Donald Basque."

"Why?"

"Just humor me."

Degas stared at me silently, then turned to his keyboard. A minute later we looked at Basque's splayed corpse.

"Now," I said, leaning on the desk, "look close and tell me what you see."

"I see a stiff."

"No, don't look at the body as a body. Look at it as a symbol. Now, what do you see?"

He stared harder. "Oh, right," he said. "Now I see a stiff symbolizing a stiff."

I sighed and pointed with a finger. "Stop looking at the details and draw out the major lines. Look at the way Cain arranged Basque, not only arranged, but nailed in place, like an insect pinned to a display board. Cain used nails because he wanted to make sure no one screwed with his message." I picked up a pencil out of a jar and used it as a pointer. "He nailed Basque's torso and legs in a straight vertical line, then nailed the severed arms horizontally, above and below the head and feet. What letter of the alphabet does that bring to mind?"

He stared for a minute then said, "An *I*."

"Bingo." I tapped the keyboard once. "Now, look at Miss Romani, Cain's second victim. Look at her bottom half. The way Cain laid the severed left arm across the splayed legs, forming an—"

"An *A*," Degas said.

"Right. Now look at Lindquist. He's on his side, legs and arm at opposite forty-five-degree angles."

"An *M*."

"No, the severed arm is too far from the body."

"An *N*."

"Right." I slapped the keyboard, and Jan popped up on the screen. "Now," I went on, voice tight, "look at Jan. Arm and torso vertical, the left leg stretched out at a right angle."

"An *L*," Degas said.

"And what have you got?"

"Ian L."

"Bingo!" I said, slapping the desk. "The bastard is spelling his name."

"How do you know it's his name?"

"Are you kidding? It's textbook. Deep down inside, most psycho killers hate themselves and want to be caught. That's why they leave subtle messages like this."

"A cry for help?"

"Either that or he's taunting us. He spells out his name, and we're too stupid to pick up on it."

"Or he could be trying to mislead us."

"I don't think so. If he wanted to mislead us, he wouldn't have to go through this much trouble."

Degas drummed his fingers for a moment, then went to the keyboard. He tapped keys, and data crowded the screen. "There are two hundred and twenty-six Ians in the City whose last name starts with *L*. That's just the ones we know about. If the *L* starts his middle name—" he tapped the keys "—add another hundred and eighty-five."

"How many Ian Ls are there on the Hill?"

He hit the keys. "None."

"You have a syndicate file, don't you?"

"Yeah."

"Cross-reference that."

"Why?"

"Just a hunch."

He did so. "Zero. Looks like we'll have to wait for the next letter."

"Maybe not," I said. "Doesn't the SPF keep a record of everyone who visits the Hill?"

He looked at me. "So that's why you let me in on your little discovery."

"Does it matter why?"

Degas clicked the keyboard, then looked at the screen. He sat up slightly. "An Ian Linski passed through Hill checkpoints fifteen times since Cain started." He ran a finger down a list of dates on the screen. "Holy shit! He was on the Hill during every Cain killing." He jabbed savagely at the keyboard, and a face jumped onto the screen. Slight of build, light brown hair, hunted hazel eyes, bookish, in his late twenties. A young white disaffected lower-class male.

"Jesus," I said, "how much more stereotypical can you get?"

Degas stabbed at a key, and the printer on his desk began cranking out hard copy. I scanned the data below the face for an address, only able to see the word *Riverside* before Degas switched to the commo mode and the duty sergeant popped on.

"Yes, sir?" he said.

"Scramble an inner-urban insertion team," Degas snapped. "ASAP."

"All teams are engaged, Inspector."

"Shit! Call in every available unit. I don't care if they're off duty or hot zone. As soon as one hits the pad, hold them until I get there."

The sergeant began shouting orders at someone, then blipped off the screen. Degas ripped copy from the printer and barked a new number at the monitor.

"You're still here?" he said without looking up.

"No need to thank me," I said. "I just like to help."

"Just stay the fuck out of my way." He paused to look up as the monitor began to buzz. "Maybe I should have you locked up for a while."

"Don't bother," I said, backing to the door. "Believe me, I just want to collect my check from Pennings and spend it. I'll leave the wet work to you dumb bastards." I opened the door, then hesitated. "Just out of curiosity, who sponsored Linski's passes?"

"The crown prince himself," Degas said, and the monitor stopped buzzing. "Put me through to Mr. Pennings," Degas told Baily's impassive face, and I went outside.

Less than two minutes later I stood in a combooth across the street from SPF central.

"Pennings residence," a voice said.

"Put Chris on," I said.

A moment later Chris said, "Hello?"

"Chris, this is Jake Strait."

"Oh, hi, Jake. Sorry about what I said—"

"Forget it. Do you know an Ian Linski?"

"Linski? Yeah, he's one of the Reds' whor—"

"Do you know where we can find him?"

"At the Reds' clubhouse, I guess. Why?"

"Never mind that now. Is the clubhouse in Riverside?"

"No, it's in Barridales."

"Good. I want you to jump into a skimmer and get down here as quickly as possible. I'll meet you on the City side of Regents Bridge. Okay?"

"Be right down," he said, and hung up.

I jogged to the Olds, made sure no one sat in the passenger seat, then jumped in. I hadn't seen Jan since I went up to my office, but that didn't mean she wouldn't pop in for another visit.

I drove quickly uptown, parking in front of Regents Bridge. I checked the load of the gyrapistol, then transferred an extra 30-jet magazine from glove box to coat pocket. Too jumpy to sit, I paced next the Olds, haunted by the flashing Hellfire sign across the water. Ten minutes later a skimmer touched down next to the Olds. I opened the passenger hatch and climbed in.

"Let's visit the Reds' clubhouse," I said.

Chris guided the luxuriously appointed skimmer off the ground and headed south, following the river.

"This about Cain?" Chris asked.

"Yes," I said.

"You think Ian Linski is Cain?"

"It's a fair bet."

"How do you know?"

I briefly explained it to him.

"It seems too simple," Chris said. "Too easy."

"That's just the way I like it, simple and easy. Where do you know Ian from?"

"He's at the Hellfire a lot. I don't really know him that well."

"Was he there Friday?"

He thought back. "I think he was."

"I don't remember seeing him."

He shrugged. "Maybe he wasn't."

"You sponsored his Hill pass, didn't you?"

He shrugged again. "I sponsor most of the Reds' passes, as a favor to the Cynics. The Pennings name carries a lot of weight with the Hillsdale Visitor Approval Board." He looked out the window. "My father said the SPF was going after Ian."

"That's right."

"Why don't you let them take care of it?"

"Because I'm not one hundred percent positive Ian is Cain. All the evidence is circumstantial. If I can talk to Ian, I'll know. But the SPF rubes won't be interested in talking. They'll shoot him on sight, or at least flush him into deep cover."

"Don't have a lot of faith in the SPF, do you?"

"I know their methods."

"You work with them a lot?"

"They've tried to kill me several times in the past."

"That bad, huh?"

"Right."

Chris nodded and rooftops slipped beneath us. "My father's bounty wouldn't have anything to do with this trip, would it?"

"Bogeymen have to eat, too."

He laughed. "I thought you ate your victims."

"Don't believe those lies. I for one haven't eaten a victim in a month."

His laugh became uneasy. "You're joking."

"All right, you got me. It's only been a week."

He labored out another laugh, then pointed down at a three-story warehouse. "There it is," he said, "the Reds' clubhouse."

I studied the rooftop as we hovered a hundred meters above. "What's the layout?" I asked.

"The second and third floors are living quarters. The ground floor is storage and firing range."

"How many Reds are usually around?"

Chris shrugged. "Might be a couple, might be a hundred."

"Maybe we'll get lucky. You have a gun?"

He shook his head.

I pulled Rasputin's 9 mm automatic from the back of my belt and handed it to Chris. "You know how these work?"

He stared balefully at the pistol in his hand. "Carlos has been teaching me."

"Good," I said. "Take us down."

The skimmer continued to hover. "We're not going to *shoot* anyone, are we?"

"Only if we have to. Probably."

"Can't we just talk to them?"

"Sure, but we can't tell them why we're there."

"Why not?"

"These gangs are a little funny about surrendering one of their own to the law, regardless of his personal failings. Now take us down before the SPF crashes the party."

"Maybe we should let them."

I turned in my seat to frown at him. "What are you afraid of? All they can do is kill us, for crissakes."

Chris goggled at me. "Yes! That's it. That's what I'm afraid of—them killing us."

I sighed and began the ritual of checking my pistol. "Oh, quit being so goddamn vain."

"Vain? I'm not vain. I just want to survive."

"Vanity, survival, it's the same damn thing—ruthless self-concern. He murdered and mutilated your mother, after all. I figured you'd be hot about offing him."

"I didn't like her! I never did!"

"Relax, for crissakes. I'll be doing all the shooting, you'll just be my guide. Now set this fucker down, you're making me jumpy."

Chris grudgingly lowered the skimmer onto the vacant rooftop. He cut the engine and, after a moment of feigning entrapment with the safety belt, joined me outside.

"Look," Chris said urgently, pointing at the sky. "SPF rotors. Let's scram."

"Those are pigeons," I said, taking his arm and hauling him to the door shed. Gyrapistol pointed, I silently pulled the door open. A dim stairwell littered with cigarette butts and beer cans beckoned.

"Which floor does Ian live on?" I asked.

"Second," Chris gasped, crowding in behind me, breathing heavily. "Or third."

I looked back at him. "Which is it?"

"Don't know."

I sighed and started slowly down the steps, careful not to kick any beer cans. Chris wasn't so careful.

I turned around to find him frozen in terror, staring at the can. "Sorry."

I turned back around and continued on. The door at the bottom of the steps was half-open, and I could see a dim hallway beyond. I slipped through, aiming down the trash-strewn hall. I heard a small shout, and Chris stumbled down the stairs, ramming the door with his head. I crouched and froze, prepared to cut down the horde of Reds that would surely flood out the many doorways. Except for the echoing boom of Chris's head butt, there was not another sound.

"I tripped," Chris whined, stopping beside me, rubbing a rising bruise on his forehead.

"You want to do that again?" I whispered. "I don't think they heard you downstairs."

"I think I have a concussion."

"It'll heal. Which room is Ian's?"

Chris peered down the hall, took a few steps forward, then back. "I haven't been here in a while, but I think his room was on the second floor."

"All right," I said, and we started down the next flight of stairs. The second floor was much as the third, ill kept and apparently unoccupied.

"Let's see," Chris said, holding his head and leading me down the hall. "I think it's, yes, it's this one." He pointed at a door with a ballerina poster shellacked to it. "Yes, I remember he likes ballet."

"Good work," I said. "Now open the door and see if he's home."

Chris shook his head and backed away. "I don't really want to know."

"Swell," I said, squatting low with my back to the wall. I turned the doorknob with my left hand and gave it a little push. The door opened with a tiny squeal, but no bullets rained out. I peeked around the corner, drawing my head back quickly. I stood up and went in.

Posters of ballerinas smothered the walls, and a double bed and bohemian mix of furniture crowded the carpet. I went through the dressers and closet and learned that Ian apparently kept a live-in girlfriend. The closet was divided along gender lines, and a woman's brush, makeup and perfume shared dresser space with a man's comb, electric razor and cologne. I also noticed that the faint odor of stim-stick hung in the air, fairly fresh.

"Could he be downstairs?" I asked Chris.

"I bet he isn't. I'll bet there's just a bunch of armed Reds down there."

"Don't worry, they *like* you," I said herding him out of the room. "You're little *chaka*, remember?"

Chris followed me down the stairwell as if I were towing him with an invisible three-meter rope. The high-ceilinged ground floor turned out to be much as Chris described. Stacked sandbags wearing bullet-riddled paper targets took up the wall nearest the stairs, and more bags were arranged into a firing line twenty meters away. Aside from miscellaneous junk, the rest of the room was stacked with huge plastiboard crates. Signaling Chris to remain at the foot of the stairs, I quietly circumnavigated the large room. I found it completely devoid of life, save for a small family of rats I was careful not to antagonize.

"What's in all the crates?" I asked when I'd returned to the stairwell.

"I don't know," Chris said. "I don't remember seeing them the last time I was here. Stolen stuff probably." Chris checked his chrono. "We better get out of here, Jake. This is the time of day they have their revolutionary council meeting."

"Just a second," I said, moving toward the crates. The gray lettering on the outside of the crates was too faint to read from a distance, but when I stood a meter away it was clear. Just two words, stamped on every crate. Basco Technologies.

"Bingo," I whispered.

"Do svidania," came the reply.

A chill froze my spine, and I turned around to see Louis strolling in the door across the room. Dozens of Reds boiled in after him and they kept coming. Some of them held firearms.

"Oh, I get it," I said. "The Red *Horde.*"

"What a pleasant surprise," Louis said. "And isn't it odd, just moments ago I was telling my comrades how much I hoped our paths would cross again."

"You mean you're not going to snub me this time?"

"Snub you? How could I snub the man solely responsible for my career advancement? This may be a surprise to you, but the first man you shot in the subway was the *khozyain* of the Horde. Now I am. So, you see, I owe you a large favor."

"Super," I said, backing casually toward the stairwell. "Just hand over Ian Linski, and we'll call it square."

"Oh, no" he said, stopping just meters away. "I had something else in mind. If you walk another step, I will have you shot."

I stopped and Chris stepped up from behind me, smiling savagely. "Hey, Louis! It's me, Chris."

Louis's eyes filled with contempt. "What are you doing here, rich fucker?"

"Hey, no, man, it's me. Little *chaka.* Remember?"

Laughter tittered through the Horde, and I said, "Why don't you tell Chris what *chaka* means, Louis?"

"What? And spoil our little joke?"

"It's Russian slang for shit-eater," I said. "They've been calling you little shit-eater all this time."

Chris's smile collapsed. "Say it isn't so, Louis."

"Say it isn't so, Louis!" Louis parroted in a high voice. "Oh, say it isn't *so!*" The Horde picked up the phrase and tone until the room filled with Chris's plea.

"I think we're in big trouble," Chris warned me in a low, tremulous voice.

"Are you kidding?" I said. "You're bowling them over."

"So, little shit-eater," Louis said after the mockery had run its course, "did you bring us our new sound system?"

Chris cleared his throat. "Well, no, we just came by looking for Ian."

"Ian, huh? If that skirt has been splitting on me, I'll cut his heart out."

"I better handle this," I told Chris, taking an aggressive step forward. "We need to talk to Ian Linski," I said in my dominant, daunting voice. "If he's not here, I want you to tell me where he is. If you won't, you will let us leave here alive."

I waited for effect, and it came a moment later. "Eat shit, handchopper," Louis said. He motioned significantly with his head, and what appeared to be a big muscle-bound guy riding some other big muscle-bound guy's shoulders moved up through the pack. It wasn't until he stopped beside Louis that I realized it was just one giant muscle-bound guy.

"This is my little brother Ivan," Louis said.

Ivan presented his hands. He held a red brick.

"Watch this, Ivan said, then smashed the brick to pieces against his forehead. He showed me the rubble in his hands. "What do you think of that?"

"I'll faint if you promise to catch me."

"Do you remember what you said to me in the subway," Louis said, trembling with malice.

"Sure. Apathy is the henchman of—"

"No! Not that! You asked me how fast I could run to the stairs, remember? I said fifteen seconds, and you the optimist, yes, you the great optimist, thought I was badly underestimating myself, that I could make it in ten. So now I ask you, bogeyman, how quickly do you think *you* can reach the stairs behind you?''

I looked over my shoulder at the stairway fifteen meters distant and depressingly proximate to the bullet-ripped sandbags. ''Does my life depend on it?''

''Oh, yes,'' he trebled, ''it most assuredly does.''

''Oh, about three seconds.''

Louis raised his eyebrows. ''Well! That's quite a boast! You are not a man who underestimates himself, are you, bogeyman?''

''I'm well aware of what I'm capable of,'' I said, my eyes moving from Red to Red.

''Are you looking for something?'' Louis said, glancing behind him.

''I'm counting you.'' I finished my tally, then smiled. ''Do you know there's sixty-four of you, four more than I have gyrajets? And that's counting the extra magazine in my pocket.''

''How very unfortunate for you!'' Louis shrieked.

''Maybe not,'' I said, looking to Chris. ''How good a shot are you?''

Chris's disbelieving eyes goggled at me. His face rolled with sweat, his jaw shook and his pistol clanged on the concrete floor.

I looked at the pistol. ''How very unfortunate.''

''Yes,'' Louis agreed, smiling.

''Well,'' I said resignedly, ''in that case I guess I'm going to have to whip the lot of you. Barefisted, as it were.''

Louis giggled manically. ''You have no shortage of optimism, I will concede you that, handchopper!''

"I myself prefer running for the stairs," Chris announced.

"Relax," I said. "You haven't seen me in action yet."

Louis laughed. "Well, this could be fine sport." He looked to his left. "Would you like to take him, Boris?"

A big Slav stepped forward, a little wild-eyed, making me deduce that my unbridled boasting had an unsettling effect upon him. "Sure, I guess," Boris said, and the grinning Reds spread into a wide circle. Boris stepped into the middle of it.

I turned to Chris and handed over the gyrapistol.

"You don't think you can really beat them all, do you?" he whispered.

"Oh, they'll shoot me long before then," I replied quietly. "Hopefully a window of opportunity will open prior to that eventuality. The pistol's set on automatic. When I give the word, pull the trigger and hose them down. Hose *them* down. Not *me*. Got it?"

He nodded. "What's the word?"

"It probably won't be a word. It'll probably be a long, horrible wail of pain." I passed him a hard look. "Don't drop it."

Chris nodded and I turned to Boris. I could feel my body going into the fight-or-flight mode: heart and breath rates skyrocketed, muscles gorged with blood, senses sharpened, blood-clotting ability increased, bowels and bladder shut down, and my liver dumped sugar, cholesterol and fatty acids into my blood stream for instant energy. I was primed for combat.

"What are you doing?" Boris asked.

"I always stretch out before I fight," I said, crouching to touch my toes. "To avoid painful injury."

Boris watched me for a moment, then began loosening up himself. The instant he bent over to stretch his thighs, I leaped forward like a frog and kicked the underside of his jaw. He flipped onto his back and went to sleep.

I smiled at the shocked audience. "Next?"

Some of the purists in the crowd began to mutter about my innovative technique as they dragged Boris out of the circle.

"I'll take you, you cheating bastard," a low-built ogre said. I spotted the dren pack wrapped around his bulging right biceps, and he immediately went to crushing five of the fat bubbles with his thumb, pumping diabolic amounts of artificial adrenaline into his bloodstream.

"Aaaarrrrrgggghhh!" he roared, dropping his arms to the chest-flex position favored by competitive bodybuilders.

"Don't you want to stretch first?" I asked.

"Aaaarrrrrgggghhh!" he replied, charging at me, veins and eyeballs popping.

I grabbed his collar with both hands and stuck a foot in his midsection, letting his weight and momentum carry me back onto my butt, then kicked him over my head with both feet. I held on to the collar and flipped over with him, ending up sitting on his chest, pounding the bridge of his nose with my fists. He howled and rolled left then right, rocking me off.

I somersaulted to my feet, and he sprang from the floor with an adrenaline surge, his chemical-crazed eyes glowing from his bloody face. He paused to flex and roar, and I sprang forward to drive a side-kick at his solar plexus. The edge of my foot thumped off blood-gorged muscle, and he charged again, flailing his arms like windmills. I crouched under the flurry and hooked him with three quick rights to the ribs before our masses collided. Shifting to the right, I slid him off my left forearm, stabbing the back of his neck with my right elbow as we went by. He stiffened under the blow and went down flat on his face. I spun for the quick knee-drop to the kidneys, but he popped up like a jack-in-the-box from hell, fueled by pure adrenaline.

I sprang back and began moving around him crablike, light on the balls of my feet. Patience, I told myself, the adrenaline would burn off in a few minutes and he'd be as limp as a wet rag.

He didn't seem to want to wait that long. He rushed at me again, and I sprang out of his way at the last moment, allowing him to collide with the crowd. They shoved him back in, shouting encouragements that would make Dr. Abuso blush.

"Stay still!" he demanded, rotating in place as I circled deftly around him.

"Make me," I said, and someone in the crowd tripped me.

I broke the fall with my right palm, but the bull was upon me, straddling my stomach, raining hammerlike blows on my head with both hands. The crowd roared as I covered up with my forearms, blocking only half the blows. I quickly came to know that if I didn't do something quick and clever, I was going to die.

I crossed my forearms over my face. When the next blows fell, I spread them quickly, knocking his arms apart. I did an explosive sit-up, crushing his nose with my forehead. I did it again, my brain jolting with agony, then once more. I felt the bridge of his nose give, and he stiffened then rolled off me, his nasal bone splintered into his brain.

I got up slowly, my head buzzing with pain. I looked into a sea of hostile faces, then lurched back to Chris.

"Is he dead?" Chris asked as they dragged the body from the ring.

"I sure as hell hope so," I said, leaning on my knees. "How do I look out there?"

"Carlos said you were a good fighter, but he didn't say you were so *vicious*."

"Fighting to the death is never pretty. How does my face look?"

"Like a crushed cabbage."

"Oh, an improvement, eh?"

"How can you joke?"

"Relax. I mean, there's only—what—sixty-two more of them?"

"Look out! Here the big honker comes!"

I looked up as the next pugilist came out, a towering, slat-muscled man who would have worried me except for two things: his eyes were blank and he giggled like a loon. It was a look with which I was acquainted.

"You're dead," he said doubtfully, then giggled. "Yeah, you're dead. Right?"

"Wrong," I said, sliding toward him, "you can't even hurt me."

He frowned. "I can't?"

"Heck, no. I *am* over three hundred meters tall, after all. And look at you, you're the size of a little mouse."

He looked down at himself. "I am?"

"Sure. Can't you see me towering above you?" I stood on my toes and cupped my hands around my mouth. "Hello, down there!"

He crouched down low and peered up at me. "Hellooo!" he called back.

"Watch out!" I warned, "I'm going to crush you with my thirty-meter foot." I lifted my foot high, "Run! Run! Here it comes!"

He broke, flailing back into the Reds, howling with terror. He was out the door before they could catch him.

"You prove to be a very resourceful opponent," Louis said. "I feel I must apologize at the embarrassingly poor challenge we've offered."

"Aw, I don't mind," I said. "Heck, I *like* poor challenges."

"You're just being polite. I think it's time we provided you with a real challenge. Aleksei?"

A grinning, handsome man stepped out of the crowd, moving with the menacing grace of a prizefighter. He was my height, with a slightly smaller but tighter build. His eyes were hard and clear, and there was a casual recklessness about him that went beyond being happy-go-lucky. He was endline, I could smell it on him. A suicidal Cyrano de Bergerac, too competent to die, and there was something very familiar about him.

"Would you believe I'm three hundred meters tall?" I hazarded.

He smiled warmly and said, *"Nyet."*

"Two hundred?"

He shook his head. "You're cheap," he said. "But good. Where'd you learn?"

"The Rangers."

"They forgot to teach you about honor."

"I was sick that day."

"Yes." He laughed, stopping two meters away. "It's like looking into a mirror, isn't it?"

"Don't know what you mean."

He turned over his right hand, and on the inner wrist was a small black skull. "Where's yours?" he asked.

"I don't go for those fly-by-night death fads," I answered, not wanting to explain the fresh tattoo on my right biceps.

"You might not wear the mark," he said, his voice low and personal, "but you're as far down the line as I am, maybe farther."

"Stop talking and fight!" Louis snapped.

"Time to ride," Aleksei said, and began his dance, moving from foot to foot, hands up high, palms down, neosavate style.

I shifted my stance, moving my weight forward a bit. If he was going to work with his legs, I'd have to get inside, where only his knees could hurt me. I immediately took the initiative, slipping in low, crouched, feinting a right hook then striking out with a front kick. He sprang back smiling, agile as a mongoose, countering with a balletic roundhouse kick that was a pleasure to witness, right up until it crunched my rib cage. I rode with the blow, sacrificing balance and position to lessen impact. I sidestepped to the right, and he came in, right foot raised high like a monster cobra poised to strike. I slipped in close, chopping at the raised leg with my left and driving in a stiff right cross, connecting with the point of his jaw, backing him up. I tried to stay with him, but he hopped to the left and back-kicked me in the gut. I stuck out a side-kick, which he deflected easily with a flashing knee that jackknifed into a front kick, numbing my right knee and sending me to the mean concrete. I immediately rolled left, escaping a hard heel that slapped the floor where my throat had been. I jumped to my feet and spun out a blind back-fist, no idea where he was. The back of my left hand glanced off his cheek, and I finished the violent whirl with a hooking right, smashing his mouth and driving him back.

We squared off again, fifteen seconds into the contest. He touched his bloody lips and grinned, hopping gracefully from foot to foot. I shuffled awkwardly, bent with the pain of my ribs, my right knee too weak to support my full weight, fists up high, elbows in, on the defense.

Time to get ruthless, I thought, and he danced in, telegraphing a right jab then dropping to the floor for a foot sweep. I leaped in the air, my lame right leg hanging back enough to be clipped. I lost balance and almost went down. I anchored my left leg behind me in time for an arriving blizzard of jabs. I kept my arms up, deflecting most of them, then counterattacked with a flurry of my own. I got him ducking, then straightened him up with a mean right uppercut that caught him flush in the jaw. I shuffled forward to finish him off with an overhand left and with perfect grace he executed a back flip. I lunged after him, he landed on his hands and kicked me in the groin with both feet.

A great malaise sped through my body. I backed up in an agonized crouch, trying to buy time. My hands were up, but my defense was a terrible sham, a great lie I didn't think Aleksei bought for a second.

"It's too bad," he said, closing in. "I was hoping you were my ticket to ride. But I think you want to take the trip more than I do. I see it in your eyes, like a beacon."

I stopped shuffling. I dropped my guard and sagged. "You're right," I sighed, my voice sounding almost relieved. "Time to get off this train."

"I'll make it quick and painless," he said, moving in for the kill. He moved to my side and set his feet. By his stance I could see he was going to raise his right foot high then drop it hard on the base of my bowed skull, breaking my neck with a single powerful blow. The foot swept up and held. "Goodbye, brother!" he said.

"Goodbye," I said, hopping inside the raised leg and chopping him in the throat with the extended fingers of my right hand. He lost all balance, and I cradled the back of his neck with my left hand, driving the palm of my right hand into his chin with a terrible shout, shoving his head back until I heard the sharp pop of his spinal cord breaking.

I held him up until the surprise left his eyes and a smile twitched onto his lips. He slid down my body to the concrete, trembling and dead.

I remained in the circle for a moment, doubled over, surrounded by silence, almost envious of the dead man at my feet. No soul, all right, I thought. If I had a soul, I'd feel relieved right now and I don't feel a thing. Just a big lousy blank.

Straightening up painfully, I dragged myself over to Chris like a broken machine with a drained battery.

"I was sure you were dead," Chris whispered. "I was sure you wanted to die."

"So did I," I said. "It's the beast inside me that wanted to live."

"He was very good," Chris said as we watched them drag Aleksei out of the circle.

"Yes."

"But you were better."

"No. Just less honorable."

"Well," Louis said loudly, "I think now the bogeyman is warmed up for Ivan."

A horrible roar filled the room as Ivan bounded into the circle, ripping his canvas shirt off his back as if it were packing paper. Great slabs of muscle rippled and rolled, and he held the rent shirt out to me as if I'd asked for it.

"We're *doomed,*" Chris moaned with consummate conviction.

"Don't be fooled," I said. "Canvas shirts are notoriously poor opponents."

Frantic hope sparked Chris's eyes. "You really think you can beat him?"

"Get ready to shoot."

I shuffled forward very slowly, buying time, for what purpose I wasn't certain. When I failed to move into striking distance, Ivan sprang forward and up, bringing down his monstrous fists from on high, as if he wanted to drive me into the floor like a spike. I recoiled and the fists flashed down in front of me, missing my nose by bare inches.

He stayed on the attack, throwing out an overhand right with the force of a slow-moving locomotive behind it. I ducked the fist and he left it out there like he wanted a receipt for it. Instead, I gave him an excellent left uppercut that seemed to hurt my hand more than his chin.

He roared and I got on my rickety bicycle. He marched after me like a machine, his hands clawing the air with uniform circular motions, chasing me around the ring like a demon-possessed wheat thresher. I snapped earnest jabs up at his face as I backpedaled, but he didn't seem to notice.

"You! You're dead!" he bellowed.

"Not yet," I snarled, setting my feet and committing myself with an arcing left hook timed to sneak over his right claw. I dropped my shoulder and rotated at the waist, locking my elbow and snapping my wrist, sacrificing the sum of my shoddy defense to pack in every ounce of weight and power.

The punch caught him square on the side of his jaw, snapping his head to the side. My heart exploded with joy as I bounced off his chest and staggered back to watch for effect.

Ivan's great head rotated slowly, the eyes going in and out of focus like a malfunctioning camera. He tottered slightly to the left, and the crowd drew its collective breath. Then the slack jaw clamped shut, the eyes focused, the crowd cheered, and Ivan was back with us.

"Now I'm dead," I said.

He roared with utter, murderous hate and sprang at me. I flopped onto my belly and shouted, "Now, Chris! Shoot! Now!"

My voice echoed around the room, and I heard a pistol rattle onto the floor. I looked up and Ivan towered above me, breathing heavily through his nose, his eyes lusty with hate. "Now, little man," he rumbled, lifting high his size-eighteen hobnailed boot. "You dic!"

I tried to roll, fully aware I'd never make it, and Ivan's head exploded dramatically, showering me with gore.

He fell on me, and the room erupted with a violent symphony of chattering machine guns, booming grenades and agonized screams. I surged from beneath Ivan and rolled for the sandbag firing line, knocking Chris down on the way. The storm of violence reached a crescendo seconds later, passing over us, then abating, except for the lonely pops of bullets being put through the skulls of the moaning wounded.

"I'm dead!" Chris croaked, curled up in a tight fetal position next to me.

I looked him over for wounds. "You're fine," I whispered.

He opened his eyes slowly, then blinked at me. "What happened?"

I peeked over the edge of the sandbags. "SPF commandos," I said. Chris started to get up, but I jerked him back down. "Wait," I ordered. "They'll shoot anything that moves."

Degas marched through the front door a moment later, barking over his shoulder at an explosives team, who fanned out among the maze of crates. Degas stopped ten meters away, and I called out.

"Degas!" I shouted, then ducked as the sandbags shuddered with a brutal interrogation of bullets, showering Chris and I with sand. When the volley abated, I called out again. "It's me! Jake Strait!"

An even more murderous fusillade chewed at the bags. While they reloaded, I played my last card.

"Christopher Pennings is with me."

There was a short, bitter silence, then Degas, his voice wrought with disappointment, muttered, "All right, hold your fire. Come on out."

I got up slowly, ensuring Chris was between me and the mob of tense commandos pointing speed guns. Their eyes flashed between us and Degas, hopeful he'd change his mind. Degas barked an order, and they rushed upstairs.

Degas began moving among the bodies, kicking them over where they were stacked on each other. He peered at each face closely.

"They wiped out the entire Horde," Chris whispered, aghast.

"Where's Linski?" Degas snarled.

"Not here," I said, finding my gyrapistol and holstering it. "The old soft touch, eh, Degas? I'm surprised you just didn't carpet bomb the whole fucking neighborhood."

"We still might do that. Where did Linski go? If you fucked this up—"

"He wasn't home," I said, watching the explosives team place satchel charges among the crates. "What's with the bomb squad?"

"Just repaying a favor. It turns out the Reds were responsible for a factory bombing."

"The Basco plant? Says who?"

"Says our evidence. What do you know about it?"

"Not a thing. The Reds have friends on the Hill, you know."

"Not anymore, they don't." The leader of the explosives team reported back and Degas looked to Chris. "You've five minutes to get out of here."

We started for the stairs, and Degas said, "Not you, Strait. You're coming with me."

I stopped and turned around. Degas had a pistol in his hand. It was pointed at me. "What for?" I asked.

"There's a few things I want to put to you."

"You mean questions?"

"Something like that." He glanced over his shoulder, and two commandos stepped forward, speed guns ready.

I stared into Degas's eyes, but there was no give at all, just cold contempt.

"Jake is giving me a lift," Chris said quietly.

"I'll call you a cab," Degas said. "Strait is coming with me."

"My father doesn't like me riding in cabs, Mr. Degas. I think my father would prefer I ride with Mr. Strait."

Degas stared at him, the hate crackling from his eyes. He turned his face to me, and his eyes followed a second later. "We're going to talk later, Strait. Count on it."

"Looking forward to it," I said. "Let's roll, Chris."

We lifted off the roof amid departing SPF troopships and shrieking jets executing fire-suppression rocket runs on the neighborhood below.

"Go up to one thousand meters and hold," I said.

Chris nodded, and we rapidly gained altitude. Tracers and minirockets arced up from scattered rooftops below as the local militias got their act together. A rapidly departing SPF transport sucked a rocket into its turbine and exploded in midair, its burning hulk dropping like a shot goose to the street below.

A small black box bolted to the floor between our seats buzzed urgently. "What the hell's that?" I asked.

"Code transmitter," Chris explained. "It's what keeps Hill skimmers from getting intercepted or shot down when they pass into Hillsdale airspace." He began peering around. "Someone's challenging us. There!"

I followed his finger to a monstrous black transport hovering a hundred meters away.

"Tarantula," I said as we rose above the machine.

"It looks like a cargo ship."

"It is. Crammed full of ordnance and jamming gear. During the mop-up it was a Ranger's best friend."

"Why?"

"You'll see," I said, pointing west. "Here comes the rabbit."

The lone rotor came in low and fast, its sleek armored body bristling with missile-jamming pods and antennae instead of ordnance. Antiaircraft and rocket fire erupted from a dozen rooftops as it streaked by.

"Now, keep your eye on the rooftops," I said.

The instant the rotor was clear, the Tarantula began to shudder and shake as rockets erupted from its belly, leaving the long, leglike smoke trails that gave the machine its name. The barrage lasted five seconds, and the dozen targeted rooftops became forests of flame, smoke and shrapnel. Its deadly work finished, the Tarantula hummed away. Chris leveled off at four thousand feet, and we gazed down at the growing conflagration.

"So much death for just one man," he said.

"There's more involved," I said.

He nodded absently. "I guess I kind of chickened out back there," he said. "Dropping the guns, I mean."

"Don't worry about it. You came through when it mattered."

He nodded again and peered down into the flames. "Where do you think Ian is?"

"Deep underground by now. He'll eventually be caught. They'll put a fat bounty on him, and one of his friends will shoot him in the back."

"Yes," Chris said, smiling sadly. "I thought the Reds were my friends. I guess you really don't know who your friends are until they try to kill you."

With the suddenness of a firecracker, the clubhouse exploded, flowering into a mushroom of smoke and debris. Two burning tenements next to the clubhouse collapsed in sympathy, spewing up more dust. The skimmer rocked slightly when the shock wave arrived an instant later.

"Wow!" Chris said. "Talk about overkill."

"That's how the SPF likes it," I said, watching the clubhouse. The dust began to settle, and a purplish red fire began to burn at the heart of the rubble, billowing up a thick column of black smoke.

"That's what I thought," I murmured.

"What?"

"Nothing," I said. "Let's go."

14

Chris dropped me off next to the Olds then skimmed away. I watched him go, then leaned against the grille of the car to listen to the distant sirens and watch the billowing columns of smoke rise from the southern horizon. I looked at a very odd piece of a very twisted puzzle and tried to guess where it fit, if it fit at all. After a moment of deep thought, I got a headache to go along with my body aches. I gimped to the driver's door, opened it, then froze. I turned and looked at the blinking Hellfire sign.

"A skirt, Louis called him," I remembered, realization hitting me like a bucket of ice water. I looked to the bridge with its threats of electrocution, then to the toxic, slow-moving river. I pulled off my jacket, locked it in the Olds, then slipped into the murky water.

I swam like a toad with a broken back, each stroke part agonized cringe, part desperate attempt to keep myself from drowning. By the time I reached midstream, I wished I'd thrown myself at the mercy of the high-voltage. When I finally crawled up the opposite bank, I was no longer a man, just a big hunk of pain shaped like a man. I lurched zombielike across the parking lot to the front entrance, stopping several times to vomit toxic slime. I tried the door and found it unlocked. I pulled it open and slipped inside, drawing the gyrapistol. I limped as quietly as possible through the dim reception area, then slipped into the main party room.

Annie sat on a bar stool, her back to me, wearing the same high-collared blue dress she'd worn the night she'd mixed me drinks. She cursed softly, trying to light a cigarette with a lighter that didn't seem to be working.

"Hello, Ian," I said.

Ian dropped cigarette and lighter and twisted around, almost falling off the bar stool, his mouth wide for a scream that got caught in his throat. Caked-on makeup couldn't hide two days' growth of beard, and thick black eyeliner failed to conceal the red rims around eyes crowded with doom. His jaw began to shake, and feeble words trickled out. "What are *you* doing here?"

"Looking for you," I said, moving toward him. I stopped two meters away and pointed the gyra at his falsies.

His rabbity eyes took in my muddy clothes. "Been beating the bushes for me, huh, flapperjack?" he said, and giggled hysterically.

"You could say that. Tell me why, Ian."

"Why *what?*"

"Why'd you kill them?"

Ian's face froze and his eyes glazed over. He began to weep, the tears running down his face in black mascara streams. "They deserved to die," he said through heavy sobs. "You know that as well as I do. Do you have a lighter? Mine's broken. Now, when I need it most."

I reached into my breast pocket with my left hand. I found my lighter and tossed it on the bar. Ian picked it up, shook a stim-stick from the pack on the bar and tried to light it. His hands shook so badly the lighter dropped into the immense cleavage of his falsies. A hand dived after it, and I immediately recognized his ploy. I shoved the gyra at him and pulled the trigger.

Instead of exploding his heart, the gyrajet fizzed and sparked without leaving the barrel. With nightmarish horror I realized the river's water had corrupted the chambered jet.

Ian's hand returned from his cleavage with a dainty machine pistol instead of my lighter. His hand wasn't shaking anymore.

"Give me the gun!" he screeched hysterically. "Now!"

"Catch!" I said, tossing the pistol. Ian fumbled with it, and I kicked the bar stool out from underneath him. I dived to the left, and the machine pistol erupted as Ian and bar stool crashed to the floor. A sharp pain shot through my leg, and I hit the floor rolling, bullets chewing up floor tiles behind me. I collided with a table, wrestled it down, and bullets thwacked into the thick plastiboard without passing through.

The shots stopped, replaced by running steps. I peeped around the table in time to see Ian's stiletto heels disappearing up the stairway. I picked up the gyrapistol on the go and lurched after him, my right thigh bleeding from a deep furrow. I jacked in a new jet and pulled the trigger at the floor. The jet buzzed out of the barrel like a drunk bumblebee. I jacked out three jets and tried again. The jet whooshed out with vigor, punching a fist-sized in the tile.

I made the stairwell, then lunged back to dodge a delirious flurry of bullets. I heard stilettos on stairs and started up after them, one agonizing, lurching step at a time. I paused and listened at every switchback, each time hearing a clatter of heels. When I reached the third floor, I heard the rooftop door banging open. I started up the

final flight of stairs, leaning sideways to haul my stiff-
ening right leg up each step.

The door was wide open, and I could hear the whir of
a departing skimmer. I hopped up the last half-dozen
steps with the help of the rail and charged into the early-
evening twilight.

I spun in each direction to find the rooftop bare of
skimmers and killers. I clubfooted to the nearest parapet
in hopes of spotting departing taillights, only to witness
nothing more than the rapidly decaying glory of a setting sun.

Cursing bitterly and heavy with despair, I sat down on
the parapet, letting my legs dangle over the edge. I pulled
off my shirt and wrapped it around my right thigh, more
or less stopping the bleeding. I took off my right boot, let
the blood drip out, then rolled off the blood-soaked sock.
I tried wringing it out, but it was too clotted with blood.
I dropped it over the edge and watched it fall. It seemed
to take a long time, tumbling end over end, and landed
not far from the dim shape of Ian's sprawled body.

I made the call from the bar, then hung around drinking screwdrivers until Degas and the goon battalion
showed up. I showed them the body, then limped across
the deactivated bridge to my car, nearly getting run down
by arriving news vans in the process.

It wasn't long before I stood before the door of my flat,
fearful of what lay under the mat. A plastic bag hung in
my hand, heavy with a crude contingency kit I'd put together on the way home: a diamond-and-gold necklace,
a very expensive bottle of champagne and a very inex-
pensive bottle of vodka. It was a very versatile combination. Versatile because if Ellen was still on the premises
I'd pop the bubbly, present the necklace and we'd celebrate my thwarting Cain. If she wasn't, I'd drink the en-

tire bottle of vodka and drop the jewelry and champagne out the window.

I lifted the mat, and the ugly little keycard lay there like a cruel indictment of my entire existence.

Forget dropping the champagne out the window, I thought as I unlocked the door. I'd power on Dr. Abuso and sit there drinking vodka until he pissed me off, then, why, then I'd whale the hell out of him with the bubbly. I'd crack the bottle right across his brain box. Then I'd hock the necklace to finance a week-long drunk.

A plan! I thought, reeling into the dark living room, I got a goddamn plan! I cracked my bad knee against one of the doctor's protrusions and nearly went down. "Oh, you'll be getting *yours*," I snarled at the machine, "just you wait!" I lurched to the sofa and asked the monitor for messages, hoping Ellen at least called to say good-bye.

"One message," the monitor said, and the stern face of an ex-girlfriend corrupted the screen, warning me to stop sending her anonymous poetry. She waved the offending letters at the camera, gave me the finger, then signed off with a suggestion on how I should spend my free time.

Jesus! I thought, screwing off the top of the vodka. I'm on a goddamn roll. What's next? Is the roof going to fall in? Is goddamn Lucifer gonna bound out of the closet with an IOU and a one-way ticket to hell? I tipped back the vodka, squeezing its plastic body, a long, masochistic guzzle. I came up gasping, my hcart wild with joy, feeling many times better. I put the vodka down and took the champagne bottle by the neck.

"Payback time," I sneered, advancing on the doctor. "It's all *your* fault. *You* scared her off, you filthy, treacherous—"

A sigh drifted into the room, and a paralysis gripped me. My eyes shifted to the closed door of the bedroom. Sure, a mean-spirited inner voice said. Go ahead, you goddamn masochist. Have a look. Why, she's probably in there trying on new outfits.

"No, not me," I told the door. I righted my grip on the bottle, raised it high and was about to smite the good doctor when another sigh slipped into the room.

I scuttled to the bedroom door, throwing it open. Ellen lay curled up on the bed, fully dressed, shifting and sighing like a sleeping princess with a bad conscience. Her trunk and suitcases surrounded the bed, but I found the strength to hurdle over them.

"You're still here!" I said, shaking her shoulders.

Ellen's eyes fluttered open. "Oh, god, I guess I am," she groaned. "I was hoping it was a nightmare." She blinked at me for a moment. "Good Lord, who beat you up this time?"

"The Reds. I challenged them to a fistfight."

She shook her head. "You're in deep trouble now."

"No, I'm not. They're all dead. So is Cain."

Her eyes opened wider. "Cain? You got him?"

"Yes. It was Annie the barmaid."

"Annie?" She looked off. "You know, he was always a bitch to me. I'd always be catching him spitting in my champagne."

"Not anymore, he won't. And speaking of champagne," I said, presenting the bottle, "we've three things to celebrate."

"Three?"

"Sure. The fall of Cain, all the loot coming my way and, most of all, you're still here."

"Loot?" Ellen said, sitting up. "What loot? How much?"

"A hundred-grand bonus from Hiram, and the twenty-grand bounty from the SPF."

All drowsiness left her eyes, and they began to shift around the room. "Say, that's not a bad roll of dough. What're you going to do with it?"

"Spend it on you."

"Me? Why?"

"Because you deserve it. It's time you had a taste of the good life. Look, I've already got you something." I went to the living room and returned with the necklace.

"Is it really real?" she gasped.

"Of course it is," I said, fixing it around her neck. "I bought it off a reliable fence. It was probably around the throat of a Hill debutante an hour ago."

She rolled off the bed and went to the dresser mirror to admire its sparkle. "Oh, Jake," she gushed, turning around, "it's just wonderful. I can't believe I have something so beautiful and real." She sat beside me and rested her head against my shoulder. "I don't know if I deserve it, the way I've acted."

"Don't worry about it. Besides, if I didn't spend it on you, I'd just squander it on trying to buy my soul back."

"I like the way you think, brother."

I started to kiss her, but she leaned away. "Not until you shower, darling. You smell like the river."

"You're right," I said, standing up. "Don't go anywhere."

"Just try to shake me."

A hot shower sapped some of the soreness away, but not much. I took account of myself in the mirror as I toweled off. I looked beat-up, tired and foolishly happy. Wrapping the towel around my waist, I opened the door to let the steam out. After digging through the medicine cabinet for supplies, I went to work spraying disinfectant and liquid bandage over my thigh and every other open wound I found.

"How did you find out Annie was Cain?" Ellen asked from the bed.

"Circumstantial evidence led me to him. But I wasn't really sure until he confessed."

"He confessed?"

"Yeah. I can't tell you what a huge relief it was."

"Why so?"

I laughed. "I was starting to think *I* was Cain."

"You?" She giggled.

"Crazy, huh? I thought I was subconsciously killing those Hillers."

She laughed. "You mean like a werewolf?"

"Right. The beast would crawl out of the abyss while I was sleeping to do terrible things, and in the morning I wouldn't remember any of it."

"That's crazy."

"Not really," I whispered so only I could hear, grinning at myself in the mirror. "I wouldn't put anything past this guy, not for a second." I sprayed the last of the liquid bandage on a cut on my forehead, then opened the cabinet beneath the sink and dropped the empty aerosol in the waste bin.

I was about to close the cabinet when the odor hit me. Sharp and coppery, there was only one thing in the world that smelled that way: *blood*.

A stone of dread settled in my gut. "You're not on your period, are you, Ellen?" I called back.

"No," she said. "Why?"

"No reason," I said, and an inner voice screamed, Close the fucking cabinet! Close it up and go drink champagne and celebrate because, believe me, chum, there is nothing you want to see down there, nothing at all.

As if in a dream, I gripped the forward edge of the sink, crouched, then peered into the cabinet beneath the sink.

Blood splattered the blue plastic bin. A lot of blood. Much more blood than you'd get from a nosebleed or even a bad cut. I picked up the bin with the tips of my fingers, careful not to touch the crimson, and dumped its contents into the sink.

Among the disposable razors and bare toilet-paper rolls was a head-sized ball of black rubber caked with gore. Using a disposable razor, I hooked the ball and shook it out. The ball expanded into a rubber bodysuit and mask, both splattered with dried blood.

Well, let's see, I thought, the blood looks to be about two days old, so that'd make it Jan's.

Ellen was saying something, but I couldn't hear a word through the rushing vacuum of horror I'd stepped into. "Did someone stop by here today?" I interrupted, my voice sounding as though I was talking through a garden hose.

"No. You don't think I'm cheating on you already, do you?"

"Of course not. Annie didn't pop in for a while?"

"Annie? What are you babbling about?" I heard her get up. "Are you okay, darling?"

I dropped the suit in the sink and slammed the door with my heel. She cried out, with pain or surprise, I wasn't sure. "Be out in a minute!" I yelled, locking the door, then spinning to face a wild-eyed reflection.

"Get a grip," I told it. "It's not what you think. Not at all." I hooked the gory suit and mask with the disposable razor, dropping both into the toilet. I flushed, and rubber whirled around and around but wouldn't go down the hole. I grabbed the plunger from beneath the sink and stabbed at the suit like a deranged whaler, forcing it down the porcelain maw. I flushed again, and the suit sucked down the hole to some distant, anonymous sea. I flushed again to speed it on its way, then quickly washed the dried blood off the bin. After I refilled it with the refuse from the sink, I put it and the plunger back in the cabinet.

I caught my breath and peered around the room, searching for other incriminating evidence. It looked clean. I checked myself in the mirror. I looked absolutely wild-eyed crazy. *Psycho killer* crazy.

"All gone!" I barked at my reflection. "No proof at all! We'll talk later!" I splashed cold water in my face, ran my fingers through my hair, put on my most ingratiating smile and opened the door.

Ellen stood just outside, holding her nose. "You jerk!" she nasaled angrily. "You almost broke my freaking nose!"

"Sorry!" I said, bounding forward to kiss her forehead. "Let's have champagne!" I rushed into the kitchen, rushed back with two glasses, popped the bottle and poured. Ellen watched me closely, frowning.

"What the hell is wrong with you?" she asked.

"Nothing! I haven't done a thing. Here's your champagne. Drink up."

By the time we finished the bottle, I was half-convinced I'd hallucinated the entire bathroom episode. There was certainly no physical proof it had happened, and I wasn't about to go looking for any. We eventually ended up in bed, and it was a lot like watching a bad porno movie.

"You seem distant tonight," Ellen said when we lay in the dark afterward. "Your mind is somewhere else."

"I'm always this way after killing someone," I said.

She got up on an elbow to look at me. "I don't think I've ever slept with a killer before."

"Don't be too sure. The world's full of them."

"I mean a professional killer. What's it like being a bogeyman?"

"It's like being a serial killer without a fan club."

"And you kill for money."

"No, I don't. If it was about money, I'd work for a syndicate."

"Do you like killing people?"

"Not particularly."

"Then why do you do it?"

"I used to know," I said. "When I first started out, I hated the gore but my ideals kept me going. Now my ideals are gone, and I don't mind the gore so much." I decided to change the subject. "Why did you put the keycard under the mat?"

She sighed. "I was on my way out. I'd packed all my things, I'd called a cab, I had those lobby hoodlums standing in the living room, ready to carry down my things and..."

"And what?"

"I don't know," she said irritably. "I stood in the doorway and froze. I didn't understand it then, and I don't understand it now, but I just couldn't walk out of this rattrap. Maybe I figured the Hill could wait a while, maybe..." She flopped onto her back angrily and glared at the ceiling. "Oh, what difference does it make? Isn't it enough that I'm still here?"

"You're right," I said, rolling to embrace her. "It's the here and now that matters. The past chases and the future runs away."

"I'll catch it someday," she whispered almost inaudibly. "I'll catch and kill it."

15

A ringing woke me. I pawed the phone off the bed stand, picked up the handset and mumbled hello at it.

"Congratulations," Carlos said. "The dark horse comes in first."

"It was a slow field," I said.

"Yeah, but you still get the prize. Baily called to say Hiram would like you to attend a party celebrating Cain's death. It's tonight in the carriage house behind the castle. I'll pick you up at seven."

"See you then."

I hung up and checked the clock on the bed stand. It was eight in the morning.

"Who was that?" Ellen asked sleepily.

"Carlos. How'd you like to go to the Hill tonight?"

She sat up. "The Hill? No kidding?"

"No kidding," I said. "They're throwing a big shindig at the Penningses' mansion."

"How'd we get invited?"

"I killed the guest of honor."

"Great!" she said, bouncing out of bed to throw open suitcases full of clothes. "Oh, no!" she cried, staring at me with horror. "I've nothing to wear!"

Ellen left soon after with my car keys and most of my money, off to buy a new outfit. I spent the day on the sofa, nursing my wounds and reading newspapers I ordered up with pizza and beer.

The previous night's events were splashed across the front pages of every City rag. Cain Is Dead! cried the *Barridales Vindicator,* Ghetto Avenger Murdered, accused the *Colfax Outcry,* Local Hero Mourned, grieved the *Riverside Rebel.* Photos of Ian graced every cover, retouched to make him appear either ruggedly handsome or beatifically angelic. The *Rebel* went so far as to airbrush a halo over his head.

The account of Ian's death varied wildly. Some had him holing up at the Reds' clubhouse for hours, single-handedly holding off a full brigade of SPF commandos before somehow escaping to the Hellfire Club to be shot off the roof by SPF snipers after disarming himself in accordance with a treacherous offer of clemency by Party negotiators. He was said to have shouted "Rise up, oppressed masses!" or "See you in hell!" as he tumbled over, depending upon which "highly reliable eyewitness" was being quoted. Another account had Ian shot in the back by a turncoat while alternately shooting down SPF rotors and dragging children from the clubhouse blaze. His dying words to a militia medic vainly trying to patch his terrible wounds were reported as being, "For godsakes, don't worry about me, save the children!"

Immediately following the announcement of his death, apparitions of Ian were witnessed in every corner of the City, and a delegation of Cain devotees were reportedly heading for Rome to lobby for Ian's sainthood and martyrdom.

The underground TV channels parroted the same dramatic ballyhoo and lies. One went so far as to claim to have bought the rights to Ian's life story from his mother and were even now assembling the cast of an upcoming miniseries entitled, "Heaven's Rage and Hell's Fury: The Strikingly Violent and Sensual Cain Story."

Nowhere in the papers or on the news was my name mentioned, and I thanked the powers that made it so.

CARLOS PARKED his buzzcar among the luxury cruisers in the Penningses' roundabout, and the three of us strolled the gaily lit walkway that circled the moat. The walkway led to a large pond behind the castle, bridged by a span of rosewood arching gracefully to the steps of a pavilion-sized carriage house. Ellen, gorgeous as a summer sunset in an orange-sequin evening gown, held tight to my arm. The full moon reflected brightly off the placid water, and I felt like a prince.

"Even the air smells rich," Ellen sighed dreamily.

"Underground atmospheric processing plants," Carlos explained soberly from behind us. "My father made a fortune on them after the mop-up."

"And look how clean the water is," Ellen continued. "It looks clean enough to drink!"

"I wouldn't," Carlos advised. "It's probably loaded with chemicals to counteract the acid rain."

"There's Chris and Chip!" Ellen cried excitedly, pointing at the open doors of the carriage house. Chris and three slouched Cynics worked the influx of guests, Chris grinning and greeting, the Cynics scowling and leering.

"Jake, Carlos!" Chris said happily. "Glad you both could make it."

"Hello, Chris," Ellen cooed, her hold on my arm slackening noticeably.

Chris looked blankly at her for a moment. "Oh, hi. Jake, I was just telling Chip, Walter and Sly here about how you handled the Reds."

The trio glared at me ferociously. "So," Chip sneered, "you think you're pretty tough, huh?"

I smiled. "Oh, don't be sore. I'm sure you can hire some new baby-sitters."

"You better watch your yap," Chip said, jabbing a finger in the direction of my chest. "You're on the Hill now, gutter boy. *Our* turf."

"Yeah, and I hear it's plenty rough up here," I said. "You get mouthy and the next thing you know somebody's chauffeur is slapping you around with a silk glove."

"You'll get a lot worse than that!"

"Sure, Chimp."

"It's *Chip!*" Chip cried, stepping up on his toes and puffing up like a frog. His two pals grabbed him by the elbows, apparently to keep him from floating off. "I'll be watching you very closely," he growled.

"Tell you what," I said. "If you see me getting too out of hand, just whip up another one of your scary notes. You better have the butler bring it by, though, because this time I'm likely to shove it down your throat." I nodded to Chris. "See you inside."

Ellen paused next to Chip, and I practically had to drag her into the greeting hall. Carlos remained outside.

"You're already ruining everything," Ellen said bitterly. "You promised you'd be civil."

"I'm just a bad apple, that's all," I said as we passed into the party room. The first thing I noticed about the place was the crucified man on the far wall. Alabaster white and larger than life, the statue dominated the room; all else revolved around it. It didn't take me long to realize it was Ian's face below the crown of thorns, sloe-eyed and beatific in his suffering. Flowers, gifts and what appeared to be a real roast pig crowded the cloth-draped table below Ian's feet and a long banner hung above his head reading: He Died For Our Sins.

"I guess this makes me Pontius Pilate," I remarked when we reached the bar occupying the entire west wall.

Ellen nodded absently, her eyes flickering surreptitiously through the crowd, like a recently tamed wolf eyeing a flock of fat sheep. She's hunting again, I thought, putting a glass of champagne in her hand and swallowing a double screwdriver. I tried to swallow my jealousy, too, but it got caught in my craw like a fist-sized ball of hot tar, making it hard to breathe.

"You also promised you weren't going to get drunk," she said without looking at me.

"Promises are cynical jokes to me," I said, ordering another screwdriver.

"Praise God, our savior has arrived!" a shrill voice carried from the milling humanity, followed immediately by Burt, obscene in a tight red rubber bodysuit. He wore the heavy rouge particular to fat drunks and cradled a bouquet of white roses in his arm. A tight gaggle of bulimic-thin models towered behind him, their eyes either dim with bovine stupidity or bright with feline cruelty.

"Hey, Burt," I said, securing my second screwdriver from the barman. "And to think I thought you wore those rubber suits for professional reasons."

"In a nasty mood, are we, *bogeyboy?*" Burt said in a voice loud enough to be heard halfway across the room. "Oh, and in case anyone is interested, this is the gutter brute that saved all our dear and precious skins from awful ol' Cain." Whispers rippled through the crowd like news of a proximate fire, and the full weight of their attention fell on me.

"Tell us, Mr. Working-Class Hero," Burt crooned, "how did the rich citizens of Hillsdale earn your favor and protection?"

"You're overestimating my fondness of you," I said cheerily. "Generally speaking, I wouldn't piss on your flame-engulfed head if my bladder were about to explode."

The crowd flinched and Burt beamed. "That's right!" he sang. "You kill for money! So how much, bogeyman, how much did they pay you to kill your brother?"

"I did it for free. Just to piss you off."

"I *am* pissed off! I think Cain's death takes all the excitement out of living on the Hill. Am I right, girls?"

The models responded with instant enthusiasm, laughing deliriously, their eyes slipping into the crowd to make certain everyone noticed just what an enviably good time they were having.

"Sure," I said. "Just as long as he didn't show up at your door, right, Burt?"

"Oh, no, Mr. Bogeyman," Burt whispered dramatically, moving closer to me. "You see, I have prayed nightly for Cain to visit my bedroom door. Oh, my, how we would have gotten on."

"Right up until he put a nail through your skull."

"Do you really think death frightens *me?*" he hissed. "I, who stares out death's lovely winter window and laughs joyously. Look!" He turned and peeled down his waistband to reveal an endline skull tattooed high on his buttocks. "That's right!" he whispered, "I'm *endline*. And I don't care who knows it." He let the waistband snap, then thrust the roses high. "I love death! Death is my mistress, my mysterious lover, my lovely master!"

He held the pose for a moment, then began shoving his way toward the effigy of Ian. "Out of my way, sheep," he barked. "I must lay these roses at the blessed feet of the *real* hero."

The models tittered after him, and for a moment the crowd's eyes remained on me, as if I was about to do a card trick or something. When I did none, they turned to take in Burt's act beneath the statue.

"You know Burt Swinburne?" Ellen whispered.

"Couldn't you tell?"

"Why didn't you introduce me?"

"I like you too much."

"Start hating me, then. Burt Swinburne's *the* hottest connection for Hill parties. Why do you think all those tall whores are sucking up to him? You think they're from the Hill?"

I looked across the room at the models, giggling as Burt made a big scene about licking Ian's feet. "Is that where you want to be?"

She frowned suddenly. "No, not exactly. I don't want to sell everything. Just enough to get in. Oh, you know what I mean."

"Sure. You just want your chance to be a bastard."

"Oh, get off your high horse, Jake. Not everyone shares your view that poverty is noble. All I want is enough money to cushion me from all the shit I have to put up with every day. Is that so freaking wrong?"

"No," I said, turning away from her rage. "Not at all."

"Glad to hear it. I'm going to mingle now." She shouldered her purse and, without a backward glance, melted into the crowd. A moment later I spotted her near the entrance, giggling with Chip and his two pals. Chip took his eyes off her breasts long enough to shoot me a smug sneer. I ordered another screwdriver and put my back to them. I leaned against the bar and slowly filled up with liquor and malice.

A son of the City pushed up to the bar, cursing the crowd and snarling orders at the bartenders. Kick Me Hard was painted across the back of his motorcycle jacket in big white letters. Below, in smaller but angrier script, it read And I'll Kill You. He continually threw apprehensive glances over his shoulder and after he'd received his beer, he caught me looking at him.

"Hey, what's the idea?" he demanded.

"Which idea was that?"

He squinted at me accusingly. "You were going to kick me, weren't you?"

"No."

"Yeah? Why not?"

"I see no point in it."

He relaxed a little. "Okay, chum. Just don't get any ideas. You downhill?"

"More and more."

He nodded and glared around. "Man, how I hate these rich scumbags."

"What are you doing here, then?"

"Where else am I gonna get free drugs and booze?"

"You could get a job."

"Oh, yeah," he jeered. "Lotta jobs if you wanna work, lotta girls if you wanna beg. What are you doing here?"

"Same as you."

"That's what I thought." He raised his drink to Ian's effigy. "Here's to Cain. Too bad he didn't gut all of these shit-heels."

I nodded, watching wealthy mourners stack tribute at Ian's feet. Everyone seem to have found their own reasons for canonizing Cain now that they believed him safely dead.

A commotion broke out near the entrance, and knowing whoops echoed through the crowd. A man wearing an oversize boar's head charged into the middle of the room, great tufts of narcotic smoke shooting from the mask's snout. Servants passed out black wands, and a chorus of "Kill the beast!" went up. The wand wielders swarmed after the boar-man, whipping him viciously, each blow punctuated by a short crack of electricity. The wildly charging boar-man writhed and bellowed with agony, parting his sea of tormentors with great blind rushes. He collided with a wall and collapsed, and the mob laid into him with their electric wands until he wailed for mercy. One of the hunters seized the boar's head, plopped it on, inhaled deeply, and the game began anew, the beast making his mad charges and the wands punishing him. The head changed hands again and again, and the chaotic frenzy of the hunt grew to a fever pitch as the charges became more desperate, the wands struck with escalating brutality.

With a last failure of strength, the boar-man tumbled out of the crowd and dropped at my feet. The wearer lifted the mask from his shoulders and shoved it up at me. It was Burt, sweating and red faced. "Take it!" he gasped as if bestowing a great honor I did not deserve. "Let's see the beast in you. Show us what you really are!"

The panting crowd pushed in close, wands twitching in their hands, eager to strike. Plumes of acrid smoke snaked up from the mask opening, fuel for the beast inside. Burt gestured with the head again, and the crowd began to whisper: "Look, this one's a real streeter, a ghetto boy, it'll be a vicious run...he's the bogeyman that killed Cain!...c'mon, handchopper, play with us."

Even Ellen joined the chorus, appearing beside me to whisper in my ear, "Go on, Jake. Show them what you got."

I took the head in my hands, and a surge of electricity ran through the pack. They gasped as one and half raised their wands.

I looked into the blind, idiot face of the boar, then into the shiny-eyed, rabid face of the mob. I searched and found the face of the beast again and again. I looked inside and discovered I wanted to become the beast, I wanted to run every last one of them mercilessly down, especially Burt. But that was also what *they* wanted.

I opened my hands, and the boar's head struck the floor. I raised a heel and stomped it, crushing the snout, cracking the plaster skull. I picked it up and handed it back to Burt. "There," I said. "I killed the beast. That's how easy it is."

The face of the mob twisted with hate, and for a charged moment theirs was the trembling mien of insulted rage, of a futility exposed. Then a narrow young man grabbed the fractured mask and lifted it high. "I'll do it! I'll be the beast!" He lowered it onto his shoulders, and for a silent moment the immense head sitting on such a narrow frame seemed absurd and ridiculous. But only for a moment.

"Be the beast, then," Burt snapped, viciously shoving him into the crowd. The beast fell to his knees, and the savage wail of the mob went up. He tried to find his feet, but the eager crowd pressed in too tightly for escape. He crawled on the floor and screamed as the wands rose and fell with renewed sadism. It was no longer a hunt but a public crucifixion. The boar became the Judas goat, and the mob beat their sins into him. When they finally tired, the mob dissolved into small, mean knots, many glaring at me, wands still twitching in their hands, eyes full of hate.

"Bravo!" Burt said, his face burning with humiliation. "You have once again saved us from our fun."

"Introduce me!" Ellen whispered urgently in my ear.

"The hell I will."

"Please!"

I stared at her begging eyes and gritted my teeth. "All right, fine." I turned to Burt. "Ellen, this is Burt. Burt, this is—"

"Oh, we know who *she* is," Burt said. "Don't we, girls?"

The ever-present models tittered to show that they did, and someone tapped my shoulder. I turned to find Chris standing behind me.

"My father wants to talk to you," he said.

"The floor show's getting a little ugly anyway," I said, turning to Ellen. "Let's go."

She shook her arm free. "Oh, Jake, I'm just starting to have fun. I want to stay."

"Let her stay," Burt said, smiling. "Maybe she's more interesting than the company she keeps."

The models tittered and Ellen joined in.

"Fine," I said. I wanted to march away without another word, but ended up adding, "I'll be back in a minute."

I followed Chris through the crowd and out the door.

"Why didn't you tell me Ian was Annie?" I asked as we crossed the bridge.

Chris started at the suddenness of the question. "I told you on the phone he was one of the Reds' whores."

I thought back. "I thought you meant he was one of the Red *Horde*."

"I guess it doesn't matter now," he said, and we stopped in the living room where Baily waited. "By the way," Chris said. "I'm glad you killed Ian. I mean, what he did was wrong. He deserved to die."

"Thanks, Chris," I said. "I'm glad someone thinks so."

Chris nodded and drifted back toward the party. I joined Baily, passed over my gyrapistol, then followed him down the hall. A moment later I stood in the same spot in the same dim room I'd stood before. Baily took up station behind Hiram's chair, his face lost in shadow.

"Thank you for coming, Mr. Strait," Hiram said, splendid in white cotton suit and furry slippers.

"Never miss a payday," I said.

"And thank you for bringing him, Mr. Baily."

"You are very welcome, sir," Baily said.

"Ah," Hiram sighed, "such sincere politeness. One cannot extol enough the vital importance of politeness. Did you know, Mr. Strait, that Mr. Baily is the politest man I know?"

"And look where it's gotten him," I said.

Hiram stared at me a moment, and I could sense his manner hardening like fast-drying cement. "I wish to congratulate you, Mr. Strait," he said curtly. "You, a single man, accomplished what the considerable resources of the HDS and SPF could not. You brought Cain to justice."

"Just dumb luck."

"I think not, Mr. Strait. You are an exceptional creature, that is why I hired you. You were able to catch Cain because you are so very much like Cain. Only a leopard knows the mind of another leopard."

"If you say so."

"Yes. Well, shall we get down to business, then? Mr. Baily?"

Baily reached into the shadows behind Hiram and came up holding a small silver tray. On the tray was a slip of paper.

"A certified check for one hundred thousand credits," Hiram informed. "Just as I promised." He studied me for a long moment. For my part, I stood and stared back at him. "A match, Mr. Baily," Hiram said, holding up his hand, still watching me.

Baily produced a single red-tipped wooden kitchen match from the watch pocket of his vest. He placed the match in Hiram's hand.

"Do you remember the small courtesy I requested, Mr. Strait? The condition on which you would receive your reward?" He picked up the check with the hand not holding the match. "Do you remember, hmm?"

I swallowed, then cleared my throat. "You wanted to eat your dish alone."

"That is correct," Hiram said, striking the match with a flick of his thumbnail. Hot white, then cool blue fire lit Hiram's face, and he stared into the flame, transfixed. "I did not get to eat my dish, Mr. Strait. I ate leftovers. You told Inspector Degas first. And Chris, and heaven knows who else."

"I needed their help to find Ian," I murmured, hypnotized by the destructive power of the tiny flame, so close was it to the check. "I wasn't positive Ian was Cain."

Hiram didn't appear to hear me. His eyes narrowed onto the flame and became vacant, his jaw slack. The flame burned low, and he did not let it go until it touched

258 Twist of Cain

his fingers. With a small cry he dropped the stubble of wood to the floor.

"It is something I've learned, Mr. Strait," he said, rubbing together the scorched digits. "Every tool, every weapon, every man will eventually betray you, given time. You just took less time than usual." He put the check back on the tray. "I forgive you, Mr. Strait."

"Very polite of you," I said in a small voice. Relief flushed through me, and I resented the emotion, despised the power he wielded over me with a piece of paper that meant nothing to him.

"In all things, politeness," he lisped, pleased with himself. "And if you are certain the Cain case is completely closed, the check is yours." He sat back and laced his fingers across his stomach. "The case is closed, isn't it, Mr. Strait?"

"What makes you think it isn't?"

"You, Mr. Strait. You tell me it is not over. Yours is not the face of the triumphant hunter. Yours is the mien of a man still chasing his prey. What are you still chasing, hunter?"

"Why did you flood the City with Newlife?"

He sat in tremulous silence for a moment, like a volcano about to blow. "I know nothing about Newlife."

"Sure you do. Your factory produced it, the Cynics smuggled it into the City, and the Reds, under your protection, distributed it."

"And why would I do something as insidious as that?"

"Yes, why?" I said, pacing in front of him. "Why destroy a generation of youth, why stir up the syndicates? There can't be that much profit involved, not for someone like you. But what else would motivate a man like you? There appears to be only one possible answer."

"And that is?"

"Revenge. That sweetest of dishes. Revenge for killing your son Liam."

"Liam," Hiram whispered, suddenly ashen and stiff. "My dear Liam."

"They lured your son away from you with their poisons," I said, "they lured him away and killed him."

"He wouldn't listen to me," Hiram said, his voice cracking. "His own father. I was going to give him everything, everything I have, and he turned his back on me. He was all I had."

"And you did everything a father could be expected to do. But it wasn't enough. They were too strong and too many, the users, the pushers, the syndicates, the entire drug culture. They conspired and they murdered him."

"Murderers!" Hiram shouted, angry tears brimming from his eyes. "They murdered my boy! My only son!"

"But they didn't know who they were screwing with, did they, Hiram? They couldn't even comprehend how much power you had. But they'd soon find out."

"They think themselves impolite gods down in their rude little ghettos," he muttered. "What good is all this power if I can't use it to avenge a good son's death? Good for nothing, that's what!"

"Yes," I said. "So you commissioned Lindquist to create a drug that would not only bankrupt the pushers, but destroy the very users who lured your son to his death. You'd plant the Newlife weed in their garden, and it would strangle everything. And vengeance, sweet, delicious vengeance, would be yours."

"A feast!" he cried. "A feast that would last the rest of my life!"

"But things didn't work out as you planned," I said.

Hiram looked at me, blinked once, then sagged back into his seat. "No," he whispered.

"The Reds started abusing the supply," I continued, "and the Pleasure Syndicate became upset about you poisoning their market. They leaned on the Reds, and when that didn't work, they leaned on you. First Donald Basque, because he ran the factory that made Newlife. Then Angela Romani, your mistress, as a personal warning. Then Lindquist, the designer. Then the factory itself." I stopped pacing. "And finally Janice, just to show you how easily they could kill you if they wanted to. Everyone thought a serial killer was loose, but you knew all along they were executions. You choked the investigation because if they caught the killer the Newlife plot would be exposed. That's why you hired me. You thought I might find out the who without finding out the why."

Hiram stared at me for a long time, his face a rock. "There's something wrong with your theory, Mr. Strait," he finally said. "Ian Linski. He was a member of the Red Horde, my alleged allies, not a syndicate hit man."

"He could have been a syndicate plant." I stuck my hands in my pockets. "Or maybe Ian wasn't Cain at all."

"Are you saying Cain might still be alive?"

"Yes."

"How unfortunate. Mr. Baily, a match."

Baily placed a wooden match in Hiram's hand, and Hiram picked up the check, watching me. "I ask you again, Mr. Strait. Is Cain alive?"

I swallowed, my throat dry as dust. "I don't know."

"What a shame," Hiram said, striking the match. He paused to watch the flame for an instant, then passed the check into it. The paper caught fire immediately, burning orange, curling black. "It's really too bad, Mr. Strait.

You could have bought a lot of things with a hundred thousand credits. Perhaps even the love of a woman."

An icy spike jabbed my gut. "What do you know about her?"

"I knew her father. He was like you, a rude and arrogant man, arrogant beyond his power." He dropped the check onto the tray, and together we watched a hundred grand with my name on it twist into a snake of black ash.

First I thought I was going to vomit cold mercury. Then I thought I was going to strangle the man in front of me. Then, strangely, I felt relieved, relieved of a burden greater than my ability to bear.

"Our business is complete, Mr. Strait," Hiram said. "You may leave."

"You capitulated, didn't you?" I snapped, my acquiescence gone with the check. "Things got a little too close to home when they nailed Janice to the living-room floor. The Pleasure Syndicate leaned and you bowed. That's why you're so eager to bury Cain. Why you had the Reds liquidated and their supply of Newlife destroyed. You worked a deal with the Pleasure Syndicate."

A silence played out. I stood, Hiram stared, and seconds ticked by.

"I am a very powerful man," Hiram said in a small but assured voice. "I hope you are extremely aware of that, Mr. Strait. Power is an ever-turning iron wheel, and it tends to crush those stupid enough to stand in its way."

"A truism for the times," I sneered.

"Men are born to die—that is the only truism, Mr. Strait. It would serve you well to consider that."

"Maybe we all better."

"Oh, but I do, Mr. Strait, it's all I think about." His eyes went out of focus. "To master a game, after all, is to lose all interest in it."

His chin sagged to his chest, and I took it as my cue to leave. I reached the door to find Baily holding it open for me. He escorted me as far as the back door of the castle.

"Any veiled threats to send me on my way with?" I asked, holstering my pistol.

"You seem informed enough to make your own choices, Mr.Strait. If I may be frank with you, sir, I hold you in rather high regard. I dearly hope I will not have to take your life."

"Yeah, me too," I said, starting across the bridge.

16

A meanness settled onto my shoulders by the time I made the door of the carriage house. I'd been made aware of how little personal power I possessed, and it put me in a sour mood.

I found the crowd formed into a tight doughnut, laughing at something in its center. The bar was bare of patrons except for a bartender and the ghetto son I'd spoken with earlier.

"What's all the excitement?" I asked after ordering a screwdriver.

"The Hillers are killing the beast again," the ghetto son said, swallowing his beer. "They never get tired of it."

He ordered another beer, and when the bartender turned his back to pour, the ghetto son dumped a bowl of pills into the already bulging pockets of his jacket. "Dumb fuckers," he continued. "They better hope I never get that damn thing on my head. I'll knock their guts out."

An individual wail of pain rose from the doughnut, quickly swallowed by a great laughing roar from the crowd. Burt's shrill voice cut through the laughter, and I suddenly got sick of the rich, the party, the Hill, everything. I pushed off from the bar and muscled into the crowd, looking for Ellen and Carlos.

The deeper I cut into the packed humanity, the more distinct and piercing became the wails of pain. A sick, miserable feeling got hold of me, and I began shoving in earnest, ignoring cries of outrage, working my way to the center until I reached the inner ring.

The surrogate beast ricocheted around the edges of the jeering circle like a rubber ball, shoves and kicks sending it reeling this way then that. Burt and the models stood in the center of the ring, sadistically whipping the beast with electric wands each time it stumbled past, every stroke eliciting a wail of pain from the beast and a cheer of pleasure from the crowd. The beast fell to the floor and crawled on bloody knees, and Burt laughed, reaching down to rip open the back of the orange-sequin dress, laying bare the skin for the sting of the wand. He lifted the wand high.

With a great violent heave I burst into the open, knocking screaming Hillers to the floor. Someone grabbed my shoulder, and I drove back an elbow, smashing teeth, knocking someone to the floor. I walked toward Burt, joints stiff, chest tight, head full of churning hate. One of the models stepped forward to strike me with the wand, giggling, her eyes dumb and cruel with the game. I swung without breaking stride, clipping her jaw with a mean right hook, dropping her like an icicle hit with a hammer. The other models scattered like crows, and Burt backed off a step.

"The gutter prince arrives to save his harlot maiden!" he cried, wand still held high. "How touching! How wonderful! I think I'm going to vomit!"

Burt continued his spiel, and Ellen blindly crawled into my path. I crouched beside her and pulled the beast off her head, dropping it to the floor. Ellen blinked at me, her face bathed in sweat, her eyes glazed.

"What's going on?" she mumbled as I helped her to her feet.

"You all right?" I asked.

"Of course I'm all right."

"Good," I said, then punched Burt in the mouth. I caught him in midsentence, mashing his lips against his teeth and knocking him back into the arms of the startled crowd.

Burt's tongue moved slowly around his grinning and bloody lips. "I'm starting to like you, bogeyman," he murmured. "May I have another bowl of that delicious pudding?"

"You can have the whole fucking pot," I said, starting toward him.

"Don't you dare hit Burt!" Ellen cried, jumping between us. "For heaven's sake, Jake, we were just playing a game, that's all."

"Swell," I whispered. "Now me and Burt are going to play."

"Don't make me leave you," she said suddenly, her manner dire. "Don't make me choose, Jake."

I stared at her, my heart turning to stone. "Is that the way it is?"

Her eyes flickered to the floor. "I'm afraid it is."

I nodded and turned away, stiff with anger. I stared at the head of the beast on the floor and wavered at the crossroads, wondering which path more horrible.

"Look at our hero sulk," Burt said behind me. "He's not mad because we had a little fun with his strumpet. He's mad because he knows I can take her away from him with a snap of my fingers." He snapped his fingers. "Just like *that!*"

The crowd snickered, and I picked up the head of the beast. I rolled it in my hands, feeling its weight. I smiled then laughed, and another great weight slipped off my shoulders.

"All right," I said, turning around. Ellen stood at Burt's side, where the models had stood. She didn't like the look in my eye.

"Don't hurt him, Jake," she warned. "I'll leave you if you hurt him. You'll never see me again. Ever."

"All right, all right," I said, smiling down at the mask in my hands, "it's a deal." I shoved Ellen out of the way, took a step forward, then cracked the boar's head over Burt's skull. The crown of his head punched through the beast's face, and he wore the mask on his way to the floor, the crowd melting out of his way.

Ellen clawed at my arm, screeching, "That's it! It's over! You've lost me!"

"I never had you," I said, pushing her away and catching up with Burt as struggled to his feet.

"Go ahead," he shrilled, peering out the bottom of the mask he couldn't seem to get off his head. "Hit me! I love it! Not a night goes by that I don't cry for the whip! Pain is my mistress!"

"I don't think you've ever really met pain," I said. "But let me introduce you."

I jabbed a punch through the bottom of the mask, breaking Burt's nose like a walnut. He staggered back as I worked his ribs with hard hooks, driving him toward Ian's effigy.

"How does it feel, Burt?" I asked when his back hit the table. "Can you appreciate the art of this beating?"

"Every bruise is a delicious treat to me!" he shrieked, clawing at the mask. "Every agony a sumptuous snack!"

"Let me show you the rest of the menu," I said, kicking him hard in his soft gut, doubling him over.

"I love it," he groaned at the floor as I went to work on his kidneys. "How delectable! How delicious! How scrump—Aarrggghhh! Help! Someone get this monster off of me!"

"But you haven't had dessert yet," I said, chopping him in the back of the neck. The mask fell off, and Burt sagged heavily against the table. I backed off a step to kick him in the head, but Burt lunged to the right, pulling two feet of carving knife from the ribs of the roast pig.

"Now, bogeyman," he said, moving the knife in front of him, "let's give *you* a taste."

He screamed and ran at me, the knife stretched in front of him like a lance. I leaned out of the way, seizing the knife hand with my left and chopping him in the teeth with my right. Burt fell back against the table, and my right hand joined my left, forcing the tip of the knife to Burt's trembling jowls. A drop of blood trickled down the shiny blade.

"Take a good, long look out the window of death for me," I whispered, our faces inches apart. "Are you looking?"

"Yes!" he screeched, his eyes huge and round.

"Good. Now tell me, Burt, how's the view? Is it lovely? Or is it lovely only when somebody else gets to die? Tell me!"

"It's horrible!" he wailed. "It's horrible and ugly! Don't kill me," he sobbed. "I don't want to go!"

"Uh-huh," I said, leaning off him and jerking the knife out of his hand. "I thought you were looking out the wrong window."

Burt slumped to the floor and began bawling in earnest. I turned to the crowd, and they gasped as one, eyes fixed on the large knife, certain I was about to run amok and exact the beast's terrible revenge.

The idea didn't lack a certain appeal. I jerked the blade high, and the mob drew its breath and fluttered, ready to bolt. I held my position for a moment, then let the blade clatter to the floor.

"Maybe some other time," I said, and the crowd opened up before me.

A man followed me out the door. I was about to hit him when I recognized Roger Eliot, Bowlan's second in command.

"I hope you're not going to try to arrest me," I said, squaring off.

Eliot raised his palms and smiled. "Not me. I'm one of those kooks who doesn't like pain. Swinburne has been asking for it for a long time, and I'm glad someone finally gave it to him. Here." He handed me a card, which read, "The Hillsdale Hunters' Club, Roger Eliot, Huntsman."

Below that was a com number.

"What's this?" I asked.

"It's a club I belong to. I'd like you to join. As a bushbeater."

"Bushbeater," I repeated, the name striking a chord. "What makes you think I'd be interested?"

He laughed. "Don't be coy. I saw you in there."

I wasn't sure what he meant but I didn't press it. "I don't have much time for hunting."

He enjoyed another laugh. "Yes, right. Give me a call." He went back inside.

I crossed the bridge and circled the castle, hands in pockets, muttering to myself, wishing I'd grabbed a bottle on the way out. As I reached the parking area, my name rang out behind me. I turned around, and Ellen ran to catch up.

"What are you doing here?" I said coldly. "Shouldn't you be inside tending to your new friend?"

She lowered her head and said nothing.

"I didn't get the hundred grand," I snarled, "if that's what you're after." I mouthed a vitacig, lit it and laughed. "I really have nothing to give you, I swear."

She continued to say nothing.

"You know what your problem is?" I asked, pointing a finger at her. "You're just not a very nice girl. Did you know that? You're not a very nice girl at all."

She nodded at the ground and wrapped her arms tightly around chest. "Sometimes," she said, "I lie in the dark and shudder at what a terrible, bad person I am."

I blinked at her. She looked up from under with those big brown eyes, and I thought my heart would burst. "You dirty bastard!" I shouted, shaking my fist at God. "You set me up!"

She started laughing. I looked at her sharply, then smiled, then laughed deliriously.

"Man," I said, "I'd have to be the dumbest bastard in the world to take you back."

She moved confidently forward and put her arms around me. "So I guess I'm in."

"Are you kidding? You're in like Flynn. Come on, let's blow this joint."

"I'll get Carlos."

"Don't worry about it," I said, moving toward a row of sleek motorcycles.

"But we don't have a ride."

"Sure we do." I stopped in front of the largest bike, all electric turbine and black rubber. Leaning back slightly,

I kicked off the keycard unit between the handlebars with my heel.

"You can't do that," Ellen said.

"Sure, I can. I just did." I straddled the bike and took out my car keys. I laid the metal ring across the bare ignition posts, and the electric turbine whined to life. I looked to Ellen. "You coming?"

"It's not yours," she said, face aghast. "It belongs to the Hill."

"It never belonged to them," I said. "Not really. You coming or not?"

She frowned, and I revved the engine louder, making Ellen jump. Looking around wildly, she got on.

"Hold on tight," I said, and she wrapped her arms tight around my waist. I dropped the bike into gear, twisted the throttle, and we ripped down the drive.

We hit the main road like a low-flying rocket and I opened it up, testing the limits of the machine. I powered into the first series of curves, quickly learning the bike was designed with straightaways in mind. The turbine was positioned a little high for tight corner work.

Lights appeared in the rearview mirror, close enough to hear the high-powered engine and the tires screeching on the corners. Under the full moon I could see it was a high-powered ghetto cruiser, moving fast, taking the corners headlong. It's the devil, I thought, he wants his money.

"It's the Cynics," Ellen screamed in my ear. "That's their City machine."

I twisted more juice out of the throttle, charging into blind corners, then easing off to muscle the big, top-heavy beast up from the blurred edge of the road, faster and faster, my eyes streaming from the rushing wind, forcing myself to remain relaxed and fluid. If I went rigid, we would die. Each successive corner became a new and lethal test of courage and machine, a wild leap of faith at ever-greater altitudes, blind jabs at the thin white line between controlled terror and tumbling end over end on the fatal asphalt.

What is the limit, I wondered, fighting huge G-forces and fear of death, how much can I get away with, what is the absolute edge?

The last corner vanished behind us, and the long, sloping, five-kilometer straightaway to the gate opened up. I screwed all the slack out of the throttle, and the bike took off like a bullet. Ten seconds later the cruiser shuddered out of the last turn, a full klick behind. I started feeling confident, then remembered we'd soon be pinned against a steel gate. I wanted to draw the gyrapistol but that meant taking my hand off the throttle.

"Reach into the left side of my jacket and grab my pistol," I shouted back at Ellen.

"Why?" she shouted back.

"So you can shoot at them."

"No! I won't do it."

"Please?"

"No!"

"Goddamn!" I screamed, and the bike abruptly lost power.

This *can't* be happening, I thought, my eyes glued to the instrumentation panel. The power gauge said there was plenty of juice, but a small warning light winked from the temperature gauge. The heat needle was buried in the red zone; the extra weight and excessive speeds had set off a safety governor. I toed the bike out of gear and we coasted down the slope, rapidly losing speed. I checked the rearview to find the cruiser coming up fast.

"What's wrong?" Ellen said in the relative quiet.

"Nightmare scenario," I said. "The bike over-heated."

"Well, pull over and we'll talk with them."

"I don't think they want to talk," I said, watching the headlights glow in the rearview as the cruiser voraciously devoured the distance I'd gained on the curves. The gate was two klicks down the road, and the temperature needle still lingered in the red zone. We slowed to a hundred kilometers per hour.

"Are we going to make it?" Ellen asked.

"I don't know," I said, my wildly shifting attention evenly divided between rearview, gate and needle. "It's gonna be close."

Our speed dropped to seventy, and the roar of the cruiser caught up with us, the deep and throaty voice of a big V-8. I drew the gyrapistol and thumbed the selector to automatic.

"When I shoot," I shouted above the noise of the cruiser, "be ready to crash."

She nodded against my back and squeezed tighter. I watched the headlights bloat in the rearview mirror, knowing I would have only one short burst to kill the driver and get out of the way of the hurtling machine. I waited until they were close enough for me to count the three Cynics inside, Chip at the wheel, laughing like a hyena.

"Get ready!" I shouted, and the blinking light on the temperature gauge went out. In the breadth of a second, I made my decision.

I holstered the gyra, dropped into gear and strangled the throttle. Turbine and tires shrieked in unison, and Ellen joined in, clawing at my stomach as the shuddering bike tried to take off without us. I worked through the gears quickly, charging the gate headlong, the rearview showing nothing but howling Cynics and cruiser grille.

The gate and screaming guards rushed to meet us, and ten meters away I braked savagely, laying the bike on its side, right knee braced against the hot turbine, right boot against the road, the cruel asphalt eating up the sole. We slid under the steel barrier wheels first and I kicked up from the road, righting the bike and sending it out of control, clawing and bucking at the road like a wild animal bent on total destruction. Squeezing the power pack with my knees, I let go of the throttle and drew the gyra-pistol.

The Cynic machine braked and began its short slide to the gate. Twisting around, I shot out the front left tire with a wild burst, sending the cruiser into a dizzy spin, swinging through the steel barrier and impacting with the guardhouse. The wrecked metal immediately burst into a ball of blue flame, flushing guards like rats from a burning shack. I got the bike under control and braked to a halt two hundred meters outside the gate.

We stared back at the flames consuming the guardhouse, licking at the night sky. A light rain began to fall.

"They're dead," Ellen said flatly.

"They deserved it."

"I wonder why they wanted to kill us."

"Men are born to die," I said, holstering the gyra. "And I think someone told them it was our turn."

"It's almost beautiful," Ellen said, staring into the flames.

"It is beautiful," I said. I dropped into gear and pointed the bike toward the distant lights of the City.

Later we lay in the dark of my bedroom, chilled by sweat that had turned cold. The rain rattled the windows, and Big Ben chimed in the living room.

"Listen," Ellen said softly, "it's four o'clock. The party will be starting to get wild now."

"Do you wish you were still there?" I asked.

"A little, I guess." She rolled over and laid her head on my chest. "Oh, Jake," she sighed, "why couldn't you be rich?"

"Rich men don't go to heaven."

"And you're not taking any chances."

"No, ma'am."

"Do bogeymen go to heaven?"

"I used to think so. I used to think I was carrying God's own banner, marching gloriously to heaven's gate on the backs of the evil dead."

"What made you stop believing?"

I shrugged. "Maybe I discovered I was as evil as the criminals I killed. Maybe I found out I didn't want to go to heaven as much as I thought."

"Everyone wants to go to heaven."

"Yeah, but it's a hard ticket to come by down here. When surrounded by evil company, it's not a glorious march to heaven. It's a slow, grueling crawl."

"What a terrible thing to say."

"Yes." I paused. "I won't be here when you get up."

"Going to go kill someone?"

"If I can find him."

"How hard that must be. To get up in the morning, knowing you have to kill someone."

I laughed. "That's just it."

"That's what?"

"That's how I know I'm not going to heaven."

"Because it's so hard?"

"No, because it's the easiest thing in the world."

17

The headquarters of the Pleasure Syndicate had taken on a markedly more martial air since my last visit. The morning light found sandbags in the windows, a surface-to-air rocket crew on the roof and armed men everywhere, many in the black-and-gray uniforms of the Atheist Front. A large truck was backed up to the front door, and it looked as if the Pleasure Syndicate was making a quick move.

I watched the building for another few minutes, weighing my courage. It appeared to be the kind of place a smart man wouldn't walk into, and I was feeling smarter than usual. I reached for the ignition.

"Freeze!" a voice hissed, and cold steel touched my neck. I shifted my eyes to see an armed atheist at the other end of the AK-47 poking in the window. "What are you doing here?" he demanded.

"I live down the street," I said. "I saw the moving truck and was wondering why Martin was moving."

"Down the street, eh? Quick, what's your address!"

I sputtered for a moment, then said, "Oh, come on, who really knows what their address is? I mean, *really?*"

"You wanna guess what your address is now, wise guy?"

"Up shit creek?"

"Give the man a prize," he said, stepping back. "Get out of the car."

I got out. Another armed atheist slung his rifle and shook me down, finding the gyrapistol. "What's this?" he asked.

"It's a novelty cigarette lighter," I explained. "Go ahead, try it."

He used it as a novelty bludgeon instead, cracking me across the temple. They let me lean against the car until I could walk straight, then marched me at gunpoint into the offices of the Pleasure Syndicate.

"We found this creep watching the place," an atheist reported to the heavy behind the desk. "I say we take him out back and shoot him."

The receptionist leaned back and stared. "I know you," he said. "What are you doing here?"

"I stopped by to help Martin pack, and these godless heathens jumped me," I explained.

The atheist pouted. "We don't get to execute him?"

"Maybe on the way out," the receptionist said.

They turned over the gyrapistol to the receptionist, then marched out scowling.

The receptionist leaned on the intercom. "Hey, Marty. Guess who's here?"

"Johnny Humungo," came the reply.

"No. It's the bogeyman that blew up our factory."

"You got to be kidding me. Send the dumb dead bastard in."

The receptionist got up and opened the door. "Go on in," he said.

I started for the exit instead. "Let me go feed the meter first. I'll be right back."

He pointed the gyrapistol at me. "Naw, go on in and talk to Marty."

I looked dolefully at the pistol for a moment, then went on in.

"You sure got a lotta nerve showing your scarface around here again," Marty said, packing books into a plastiboard box."What are ya? Endline?"

"Everybody thinks so," I said, sitting in a chair. "Finally making that big move to the burbs?"

He bared his teeth, smiling very slightly. "Naw, I was thinking of someplace a little safer. Like a reinforced bunker."

"Somebody put a brick through your window?"

"Yeah, and it had a nasty note tied to it. What the hell did you tell Hiram, anyway? That we were running around calling him a dickless faggot or something?"

"Not that I recall. Hiram's going after you?"

"Are you kidding? People's already talking about me in the past tense, like I was a corpse stinking up the place."

"I thought you and Hiram made a new deal."

He stopped packing to bare his teeth at me. "What are you talking about?"

"Nothing," I said, scrambling to rearrange the facts. "What more can Hiram do? The SPF has always been on your back."

"Yeah, but nothing like this. Our SPF plants tell us they're gearing up like Armageddon just popped up on the calendar. And that's just the half of it. I hear froggy's making massive cash and munitions donations to certain Christian and Muslim militias. Any minute now they'll announce a big fucking truce and tell the world they're going go after the Great Satan. And you know who that poor bastard's going to be."

"Won't the other syndies help out?"

"You shitting me? They're like sharks. Once the SPF draws blood, the syndies will rip my market share to pieces, the fucking cannibals." He moved a full box to the floor, then started emptying drawers into another. "All this hell and for what? Just because we whacked a couple of those chucklehead Reds pushing his dope."

"I think blowing up his factory is what really set him off," I said carefully.

He stopped packing. "What'd you say?"

"I said blowing up his factory is what really set him off."

"Blew up his factory? I thought that was more your line."

"He thinks you did it."

"What asshole told him that?"

"Beats the hell out of me."

He looked off and became thoughtful. "No wonder he's biting my ass. He thinks I blew up his fucking dope plant."

"And you didn't even do it. Did you?"

"Who you take me for? Wally the moron wonder?"

"And you didn't send Cain after him, either," I complained.

"Cain?" He stared incredulously at me. "What have you been telling that rotten bastard?"

"Not a thing. I'm just his shoe-shine boy. You didn't send a hit man disguised as a serial killer after his family and employees so he'd get Newlife off your back?"

He squinted at me. "Jesus! Is that what the crazy bastard thinks? He thinks I offed his two broads?"

"You hated him enough."

"Hate is one thing, suicide is another. I hated everything about the bastard before he decided to stomp me like a two-headed snake. But I knew Hiram had the SPF in his back pocket. I knew that if I leaned too heavy, the next thing I knew there'd be a SPF rotor rocket trying to nudge its way up my ass. Shit, I hate any bastard who holds a gun to my head. But that don't mean I'm going start spitting in his face and calling him a faggot.''

"You think the other syndicates feel the same way?''

"Are you kidding? Mention the word Pennings, and they shit their backbones. Hell, I wish Cain was still alive. I'd hire him to dissect that rotten frog bastard.'' He shook his head sadly while filling a box with data disks. "Things will never be the same again.''

"Sounds bad for you, all right,'' I said, distracted with thought.

"Yeah, well, don't write my obituary yet. I worked a deal with a couple militias, I'm going to use their bunkers until this thing blows over. I've pulled in all my favors and still got a few cards to play myself. If life hands you lemons, make hand grenades, right? Isn't that how it goes, bogeyman?''

"Something like that,'' I said, getting up. "Well, it looks like you've a lot to do. I'll get out of your way.''

"You know,'' he said before I could start for the door, "I let you walk out of here last time because I thought Hiram was protecting you.''

I studied him closely. "And now his protection doesn't matter.''

"More than that,'' he smiled, baring his canines. "I got a call late last night, before all hell broke loose. Someone told me you're persona non grata in the Pennings camp. You must not be putting too good a shine on his shoes.''

"Hiram called you?''

"Naw, it was that ghoul he calls a butler. How'd he put it? 'We would be extraordinarily pleased if Mr. Strait were to become deceased.'"

"And that," I said, hope rising in my chest, "is why you're going to let me walk out of here this time."

Our eyes locked tight for a long, terrible moment.

"Right," he said, then went back to his packing. "But you still owe me a factory."

"I'll see what I can scrounge up."

"Kill Hiram and we'll call it even."

"I'll see what I can do."

The receptionist seemed surprised to see me come out.

"I thought I was going to have to drag you out by your heels," he said, handing over the gyrapistol.

"So did I," I replied, and sirens went off. I bolted out the exit and charged across the lawn, dodging scurrying militiamen, certain Marty had changed his mind. I executed a running roll over the hood of the Olds and hunkered behind the engine block, pistol ready, waiting for the hail of militia bullets that I'd somehow outrun.

They never came. The militiamen seemed more interested in the western horizon. The radar and rocket crew on the roof seemed particularly excited, firing off a shrieking salvo of missiles.

I looked west. No rotors or jets were in sight, which could mean only one thing. I jumped in the Olds, started the engine and gunned down the street, heading west. Twenty seconds later a ragged group of slow-moving, low-flying SPF Skullcrusher surface-to-surface missiles buzzed overhead. Notoriously slow and inaccurate, they made up for their failings with sheer explosive punch. I floored the accelerator, steering around motorists sticking their heads out their windows, possessed of more curiosity than sense.

I made Hayward before the thump of heavy explosives reached my ears. I slowed down and wondered if Marty had got out in time. I didn't feel particularly bad about wrecking his career, even if he wasn't responsible for Cain. Despite his good graces and generous nature, he was a vicious thug and deserved whatever he got.

The real tragedy was, if the syndicates weren't responsible for Cain, and I strongly believed they weren't, I was back at square one. Only this time I'd be without the support, dubious as it was, of the SPF and HDS. If that weren't enough, my ex-employer, one of the most powerful and ruthless men on the face of the planet, would be extraordinarily pleased if I became deceased.

I parked three blocks from Carlos's office building and walked the difference, keeping my eyes open.

"You made quite an impression on the Hill yesterday," he said after letting me in. "I'm not sure if they'll put out a contract or make you a cult hero."

"They seem to go hand in hand," I said, sitting on the edge of his desk.

"Did you hear those explosions?" he asked, moving to the window.

"Yeah. The SPF's going after the Pleasure Syndicate with Skullcrushers."

"I knew their day would come," he said, nodding sagely.

"Only because Hiram says so."

"That's not all Hiram says."

"Yeah? What'd he tell you?"

"He asked me to kill you."

I remained quiet for a moment, watching him. "And?"

Carlos sat behind his desk and laughed. "I told him to get someone else to do it."

"Mighty good of you."

"What are friends for?"

"Indeed. You ever hear of the Hillsdale Hunters' Club?"

"The HHC? Sure," he said, eyes moving to the monitor. "I do some work for them sometimes."

"What kind of work?"

"Bushbeater."

"What's a bushbeater do?"

"It's a lot like bogeying except the pay's a lot better."

"Roger Eliot offered me a job as a bushbeater."

"Eliot? Yeah, I heard he was looking to stock his stable."

"What exactly do they hunt?"

"Animals. The ghosts of their consciences. That sort of thing."

"What kind of animals?"

"The two-legged variety. They're vigilantes. Why all the interest?"

"Something Ian said. After I got the drop on him, he asked me if I'd been beating the bushes for him."

"Yeah, the HHC was pretty hot after him."

"After Ian or after Cain?"

"Same thing, isn't it?" Carlos glanced up from the monitor and smiled. "You don't think Ian was Cain."

I began pacing in front of the desk. "It doesn't feel right. I can't believe every hunch I had about this case turned out wrong."

"I thought Ian confessed before he jumped off the roof."

"Yeah, that's the thing that keeps me from being certain Ian wasn't Cain. And he didn't jump. Someone pushed him."

"Not you?"

"No. I think someone tipped Ian off that the SPF was after him, told him to go to the Hellfire. That same someone was waiting on top of the building, waiting to kill him. To shut him up."

"You're right," Carlos said. "Ian wasn't Cain. Not entirely."

I stopped pacing. "You know something?"

"I know you can't kill Cain by shoving him off a roof."

"Of course not," I said snidely. "The real Cain would have flown off like a goddamn bat."

"I'm not saying that. You can kill Cain, but you'd have to wipe out the entire City to do it."

"The entire City? Why?"

"Because he's goddamn *everywhere,* Jake. Look around, and you'll see his face again and again. You can kill tiny pieces of him, like Ian, but you'll never get all of him unless you take everyone out." He sighed heavily. "There's a little twist of Cain in us all. More so every year."

"You should take your act down to Bukowski," I said. "Can I use the phone?"

"Go ahead."

I sat on the desk and dialed the Penningses' mansion. When a maid answered, I asked for Chris.

"Hello?" Chris said.

"Chris, this is Jake," I said. "What do you know about the Hillsdale Hunters' Club?"

"Are you kidding?" he slurred, and I realized he was drunk. Very drunk. "I know everything about those bastards."

"I want to come up and talk to you. Can you arrange a gate pass?"

"Sure, no problem. I need someone to drink with."

"Is Hiram or Baily around?"

"Naw. Mr. Manners and dear ol' Dad flew off to a Party meeting half an hour ago."

"Good. I'll be right over." I hung up and went to the door.

"You'll be sorry," Carlos said.

"Sorry about what?"

"You'll see."

18

Chris answered the door with a decanter of what smelled like rum in his hand. The liquor gave his cheeks a rosy flush and his eyes a blurry gleam; Chris appeared to be the happy sort of lush.

"Taking up where your mother left off?" I said.

"Sure." He laughed. "It runs in the family, a big ugly cycle. I guess that means I'm next to die, huh? Come on in and have a drink with me."

"No, thanks. I understand the HHC are vigilantes."

Chris laughed. "They're not even that. They hire people like you to do the dirty work."

"Bushbeaters?"

"That's what they call them."

"When's their next meeting?"

Chris brought his wrist up and stared blurrily at his chrono. "Started ten minutes ago."

"Can you get me in?"

"Sure, sure. But I warn you, they're terrible boors."

"That's all right. You ready?"

"Never readier. We'll take my skimmer."

"No, I better drive."

"Let's go, then." Chris followed me off the porch, swinging the decanter like a counterbalance. I started the motor while he struggled to overcome the complexity of the door latch. I eventually had to lean over and open the door so he could tumble in.

"What's the occasion anyway?" I asked as I steered down the long drive.

"Had a long talk with dear ol' Dad before he left," he slurred. "He laid down the law. Said it's time I started acting like a man. So the first thing I did was get stinking drunk!" He laughed himself silly, then sank into a somber mood. "He said it's time for me to shape up, assume big responsibilities. Because—" he waved the bottle in an all-encompassing gesture "—someday all this will be mine." His face became sad. "Mine, all mine."

"Where we heading?" I said as we started downhill.

"Just go to the HDS headquarters," Chris said. "The HHC clubhouse is in the basement."

I accelerated and Chris fell into a stupor, staring at something three inches in front of his eyes.

"Tell me about your brother, Liam."

"Liam," he said, hitting the bottle hard. "Dear ol' dead Liam."

"Hiram thought a lot of him, didn't he?"

"Liam was all he thought about. Dear ol' Dad didn't even know he had another son until Liam kicked. Liam, Liam, Liam. Best at everything. Top of his class, captain of the combatball team, leader of the Cynics." His voice quieted. "I was in the Cynics once, you know."

"Yeah?"

"For a whole month. Right up until initiation. Do you know what initiation is for the Cynics?"

"Lean against a wall and act bored for a whole hour?"

"Nope. You have to..." His eyes went out of focus, and his voice dropped to an incredulous whisper, as if he couldn't believe what he was saying. "You have to go to the ghetto and rape a City girl. I don't mean a prostitute or anything, just a regular neighborhood girl. The other Cynics and some Red guides find her and hold her down, then you have to..."

He looked up at me, tears clouding his eyes. "I couldn't do it. I just couldn't do it. I looked at her, and she was trying to scream, her eyes wide as anything. I just froze. Liam kept yelling at me, calling me queer, but I just couldn't do it." He looked away. "That's why they kicked me out. I couldn't do it. I couldn't even get it up."

"You did the right thing."

"Yeah. Did you know three Cynics died last night? They crashed into the gate house. Chip and—"

"I noticed the damage on the way up."

"I'm glad they're dead, I really am. Boy, you sure showed ol' fat Burt last night. You showed them all. Man, I've been getting calls about you all day."

"Yeah? Nobody bought a warrant, I hope."

"No, no. They all wanted me to invite you to their parties. They really got off on you last night. Now you're bigger than Burt on the party circuit."

"Maybe Burt and I can work up an act," I said. "Do a tour."

"Sure. Say, where's that girl of yours?"

"Back at my place."

"Man, Jake, she's something else. You know—" he leaned confidentially close "—I could arrange a place for both of you right here on the Hill, if you want. I could set you both up in Valley View."

"Yeah, I understand there's a vacancy."

"Sure! Man, that'd show the lot of them, wouldn't it?"

"It sure would," I said, turning into the HDS parking lot. Chris guided me to the back, where I parked next to a gaggle of sports cars and limos.

"No matter what," Chris said, crawling out of the Olds, "don't take any guff from these swine."

"Right," I said, following him to a heavy black door. After several failures, Chris managed to jab his keycard into the slot. "Why do you have access?" I asked.

Chris looked back at me as he muscled the heavy door open. "Are you kidding? My father owns the Hill. I have the key to everything."

I followed his unsteady gait through a cloakroom full of jackets and hats to another closed door. Above the door a large silver plaque read, Tradition Is The Cement Of History. Under the plaque was a thick man in a tuxedo.

"What are you doing here, Mr. Pennings?" he asked. His voice had the slow, alien inflection of a man long deaf.

"None of your business, you eunuch," Chris snarled. "Just get the hell out of our way."

"But I'm not supposed to let anyone—"

"You know who I am," Chris cut him off, grabbing the startled man's lapels. "You *know*."

The guard bowed his head and moved out of the way. Chris opened the door, and we went in.

"Well, well, the whole hooded gang is here," Chris snarled, staggering into a large room made crowded by a long mahogany table. "The great huntsmen, the murderous protectors of law and order, the great hypocrites of justice."

Fifteen huntsmen, anonymous in black robes and executioner's hoods, lined the table, seven to a side and one at the far end. The largest chair, at the near end, was empty. The room was as dim as a tomb and archaic weaponry and animal heads adorned the mahogany walls. None of the heads appeared to be human. Many of the huntsmen smoked pipes through mouth holes in their hoods, the fragrant smoke rising up to a languidly revolving ceiling fan that churned it to haze.

"What are you doing here, young Pennings?" the hooded man at the far end of the table said. I recognized the voice as Bowlan's.

"What do you mean?" Chris slurred, moving to lean on the high back of the empty chair. "This *is* dear ol' Dad's chair, isn't it?"

"That is so," Bowlan said, "but it doesn't give you the right to bring that fiend in here. You know these meetings are strictly secret."

"Fiend?" Chris said, looking back at me. "Jake's a goddamn saint compared to you bastards. He's a goddamn messiah."

"I know what he is," one of the hoods growled. "Chip told me what kind of bastard he is."

"Chip!" Chris said, reeling across the room to place his hands on the speaker's shoulders. "Your dear ol' dead brother Chip! Recently headed the Cynics, now headed for hell. But don't worry, gentlemen, the Cynic tradition carries on. In fact, guess where the Cynics are tonight? Guess what your sons and younger brothers are up to. No one wants to guess? I'll tell you, then. They're out in the City for a little rape and pillage. Your brother's getting initiated tonight, Roger, and yours, Bing, they're gonna put it to some poor City girl. But you all know about that, hell, everyone at this table used to be Cynics. You should call yourselves the Senior Cynics Club."

"Boys will be boys, after all," Bowlan said. "There's nothing wrong with a little rambunctiousness while young."

"Aw, but not if they're poor," Chris slurred. "Then they're killers and rapists and scum to be put down like rabid dogs. Animals to be marked for death by the fine upstanding Hillsdale Killers' Club."

"Yes, and we've all heard your drunken ravings before, haven't we?" a huntsman tapping a notebook computer said. Though deepened and disguised, the voice obviously belonged to Burt. "Now be on your way with your hired gun and leave us to our business."

"Fuck your business!" Chris roared. "Screw your fucking business!"

"Strong Spear, Tigerman," Bowlan said. "Please escort young Pennings home. Take the club limo and make sure he doesn't get away. In this state he's likely to hurt himself."

Two huntsmen rose from the table, and Chris recoiled back toward the door.

"Sit down, you bastards," Chris said. "We were leaving anyway. We can't stand the stink of the blood on your hands. Right, Jake?"

"I'm staying," I said.

Chris stared at me dumbly for a moment. "What?"

"I'm staying."

"Fine!" Chris said in a betrayed voice. "I'm going to find a bar." He reeled out the door.

"Good riddance," Burt said, and they all began clapping. When they finished, they turned their attention to me.

"Yes, and what are you still doing here?" Bowlan asked.

"I want to join the club," I said.

"Well," Bowlan said. "I'm pleased your attitude is separate from young Pennings's, but unfortunately your rather tragic station in life bars you from becoming a huntsman. You may become a bushbeater, but even then you must be sponsored and voted in.''

"I'm sponsoring him,'' a hooded man at Bowlan's elbow said in Roger Eliot's voice. "I invited him here. Hello, Mr. Strait.''

A current went around the table, and the huntsmen twisted in their chairs to get a good look at me. "Strait?'' an older voice said. "Why, he's the outside celebrity killer who smited old Cain. Good show, old chap.'' A spirited round of clapping ensued.

"Let's have a vote, then,'' Eliot said. "All those in favor of Mr. Strait assuming the station of bushbeater, raise your hands.''

Only Burt, Bowlan and Chip's brother kept their hands down.

"Twelve to three,'' Eliot said. "By majority vote, you are now a bushbeater, Mr. Strait, entitled to all privileges and courtesies that come with that honored title.''

"And none of those privileges allow him to attend a hunt council,'' Burt snapped. "He must leave at once.''

"I say we let him stay,'' Eliot said. "He may even be able to offer his unique killer's perspective on certain matters.''

"This is most irregular,'' Bowlan complained loudly. "You know these meetings are strictly secret.''

"I think we can trust Mr. Strait with our secrets,'' Eliot said, looking at me. "Let's put it to vote.''

They took another vote. This time I won only by one hand.

"You may stay, Mr. Strait,'' Eliot said, bowing his head slightly. "Please feel free to offer advice as you see fit.''

I imitated his gesture and leaned against the wall.

"Shall we continue?'' Eliot said.

"Right, then," Bowlan said gruffly, nodding to Burt. "What's next on the agenda, Beastmaster?"

I bit my tongue to keep from laughing. Burt, tapping furiously at the keyboard, squawked, "I'll continue but I am making note of my outrage at having an outsider overviewing these proceedings. I—"

"Outrage noted," Eliot said mildly. "Please continue."

I could hear Burt's teeth clamp together. A few deep breaths later he began reading from the computer screen, his voice tight.

"We were on the Ricardo Krakow file. According to our SPF sources, he certainly appears worthy of our attention."

"What was it he had done?" a hood asked.

"Among his more mundane offenses against decency and good manners, he's a virulent rapist and sometime mugger."

"But who isn't down there?" a bored-sounding hood sneered. "If we went after every stick-up man who has his way with ghetto tarts, we'd never—"

"He also," Burt cut in triumphantly, "snatched an expensive piece of jewelry from the very neck of a respected lady of Hillsdale."

"Why, that young ruffian!" the formerly bored hood shouted."How dare he!"

Cries of outrage and calls for immediate justice rose from every corner of the table, followed by a quick vote. The huntsmen unanimously decided that the offensive Mr. Krakow was to be dealt with, and dealt with harshly.

"Well, then," Bowlan said, "whose bushbeater shall do away with the unsavory Mr. Krakow?"

"My Beast of Barridales, I should think," one of the hoods volunteered quickly.

"You mean Bumbler of Barridales," another sniped. "Krakow will have ten changes of addresses before that suburban cowboy gets up the guts to go into the City. We need a ghetto mechanic for this bit of work, and I propose my own Rooftop Sniper."

"That nearsighted prima donna kills more bystanders than criminals," another argued. "I would think my Sidewalk Slasher more suited for—"

"How about my Iceman," Eliot said quietly, and the table hushed with a reverent silence. "It's his part of town, and he's always ready for a juicy kill, don't you think?"

Burt said, "I thought the Iceman was—"

"The Iceman is ready," Eliot assured, "I can assure you of that."

"The Iceman it is," Bowlan said. "Please note the selection, Beastmaster."

Four more cases rolled out, and the huntsmen followed the same procedure, deciding who would be killed by whom like boys trading combatball cards. It did not escape me that most of their bushbeaters shared the same monikers as the City's more notorious serial killers. I didn't think it was just coincidence.

"I saved the most-pressing matter for last," Burt announced. "Now that we no longer have to worry about Cain, we can turn our full attention back to the BBB matter." Burt paused to let troubled sighs run around the table then continued. "As we all know, the Butcher the Bourgeois Bastards organization, or the Killer Bees, as they sometimes call themselves, are devoted to the cause of liquidating any and everyone fortunate enough not to reside in the gutter. They have made as much clear in their rather unsavory underground newspaper and TV ads, in addition to various letter bombs sent to the HDS and other Hillsdale addresses. And, as you know, our bushbeaters have declined to go after such a well-organized force.''

''Why don't we just double their kill fees?'' a hood asked.

''We have. They seem to think no amount of money is worth taking up what they consider to be a suicide mission. Quite frankly the bees terrify our bushbeaters.''

''Those cowards!'' the bass voice roared. ''Can't we buy these bees off? Maybe they wouldn't be so mad at people with money if they had a little themselves.''

''We tried that. They just took our money and demanded more.''

''Well,'' another voice said, ''why don't we threaten massive and deadly retaliation?''

''We did that, too. Those rather terrible underground TV ads followed directly thereafter.''

More unlikely solutions were aired and shot down. After a moment they settled into a baffled silence.

Eliot broke the quiet. ''Perhaps the reason we cannot come up with a viable solution is because our perspective, shall we say, is slightly askew. I'd like to sound out our celebrated guest on this matter.'' He directed his eyes to me. ''How would you handle such a situation, Mr. Strait?''

''If a terrorist group was threatening to kill me?'' I asked.

''Yes.''

''I'd put a grenade through their window.''

The table tittered with laughter. ''It's not as simple as that,'' Burt trilled vindictively. ''They operate through a series of post-office boxes. Not even the SPF has been able to locate their hideout.''

"You don't need to. You people are making a fundamental mistake. You think the BBB is a terrorist organization."

"They do a pretty good job of passing themselves off as one, I'd say," Bowlan said.

"That's just effective PR. If the BBB put half the effort into killing you people as they put into fund-raising, they'd have stormed the gates of Hillsdale a month ago. The BBB are first and foremost a profit organization. Put them in the red, and they'll fold up like a wet cardboard box."

"And how would we accomplish that?" Burt snapped.

"Start sending them letter bombs. Get the SPF assassination bureau to make you up a batch, all sorts and sizes, with City postmarks and return addresses."

"Resort to their terror tactics?" Bowlan said. "I never—"

"Hey, I'm just telling you how I'd do it."

"It is immoral and dishonorable," a hood railed.

"Morality is like an expensive silk suit," I said. "It looks good and it's comfortable to wear, but don't expect it to stop a bullet."

"Say we took your advice," Eliot said. "We'd get perhaps a half dozen of them at the most. Then they'd simply stop opening their mail."

"Bingo. You stop them opening their mail, and you've cut off their primary source of revenue. They'll try changing their address a few times and you'll have to stay on top of them. When the creds dry up, so will their lust for Hiller blood. They'll find another devil to get worked up about."

"So simple it's brilliant," Eliot said. "Let's put to vote this ingenious plan."

Enough of the huntsmen managed to shed their coats of morality to deliver a comfortable majority.

"Splendid," Eliot said. "Burt, contact the SPF first thing in the morning and get them on it. Well, I guess we owe Bushbeater Strait a round of applause."

Everyone clapped except Burt, who pretended to be too busy entering data.

"I think that wraps up this week's meeting," Eliot said. "Any of you old ladies up for a running of the hounds?"

Most mumbled excuses and shuffled quickly out the door, pulling off mask and robes. Four huntsmen remained, Bowlan, Eliot, the bass-voiced man who introduced himself as Harvey, and a young ferret of a man named Stuart.

"We are taking an armored rotor, of course," Harvey announced..

"Don't be such a girl, Harv," Eliot said. "We'll take the limo and get a real street-level look." He turned to me. "Would you like to join us, Mr. Strait? As a tour guide of sorts?"

"Where you going?"

"The City," he said, his voice grim and foreboding.

"Why not," I said.

The four huntsmen and I took facing seats in the back of a long armored cruiser, and three bodyguards crowded in the front.

"I feel it essential we routinely check our progress in the City," Eliot explained as we pulled out of the parking lot. "We've been quite busy with our Abel Project, and I expect to see quite a dent."

"Abel Project?"

"Oh, yes. Every time Cain killed one of ours, we killed seven of them."

"Who's them?"

"Oh, you know, *them*." He waved his hand with a gesture that seemed to include the entire City.

"How long has the HHC been around?" I asked.

"Over seventy years," Bowlan announced. "Of course, our fathers hunted a rather different breed of animal. But," he sighed, "the times change, and we must change with them."

"Here, here," Harvey agreed. "What's the sense of gentlemen hunting innocent wildlife when there are much more deserving prey within our own species? Surely even you can agree with that, Mr. Strait."

"You forget whom you are talking to," Eliot interjected. "Mr. Strait here is one of the finest manhunters of our time."

"I was speaking from the standpoint of a gentleman hunter," Harvey grumbled.

"Killing human beings is not a very gentlemanly sport," Eliot said, smiling at me. "Is it, Mr. Strait?"

"Killing is as noble or evil as you want it to be."

"Here, here!" Harvey intoned.

"All depending on how much you like to lie to your conscience," I added.

They mulled that over as we cleared the gate and hit the speedway. The limo's wet bar opened for business, and the huntsmen were fairly plastered by the time we exited onto Broughton Avenue. The sun rested low on the horizon, and the sidewalk army of vice was on the march.

"Oh, just look at them!" Harvey hissed, peering out the tinted, inch-thick Plexiglas. "Heathens, murderers, thieves, rapists and sexmongers, every last godforsaken one of them."

"If they knew it was us in here they would drag us out and feast on our blood," Bowlan crowed fearfully.

"Our bodyguards wouldn't let them!" Stuart shrilled. "Our men would rather die horrible deaths fighting tooth and nail than let those cannibals drink a single drop of our blood. Wouldn't you, men?"

The increasingly nervous men in the front seat growled their fealty in voices I thought lacking true conviction.

"Look," Bowlan howled. "Look at that one. Examine his manner of dress. He's a killer pimp if I ever saw one."

"A morally corrupt cannibal!" Eliot croaked, getting caught up in the farce. "A rotten-souled child molester. My Iceman will gut you like a fish," he cried, shaking his fist. "Prepare for death!"

With each passing block their tirades became more rabid and comical until they were actually frothing at the mouth. I watched them closely, amazed at the amount of fear and hate bottled up inside them.

Midway down Broughton, traffic began to slow, then ground to halt. Car horns began to bleat, and a terrible fear gripped the huntsmen.

"What's wrong?" Bowlan shouted at the driver.

"I don't know," he cried over his shoulder. "Traffic just stopped."

"There are vehicles behind us!" Harvey wailed. "The dirty bastards have us sealed in."

"It's a traffic jam," I explained. "There's probably been a wreck up ahead."

"It's a trap," Stuart screeched, preferring to believe Harvey's interpretation of events. "The fiends know who we are, don't think they don't! Now that they have us trapped, they'll surely sodomize and disembowel the whole lot of us. We'll be forced to swallow our own severed testicles!"

"Good God!" Bowlan shouted. "I won't let them." He lunged over the seat to claw at the neck of the already unhinged driver. "Get us the hell out of here! Right now!"

The driver wailed and stomped on the accelerator. The cruiser travelled one-half meter and tail-ended the muscle car idling in front of us. A tall black and a stocky slav in matching factory work suits jumped out, slammed their doors and marched toward us.

"Intruders approaching!" Eliot shouted. "Twelve o'clock!"

"They're mobbing us!" Bowlan elucidated. "They've gone amok!"

"You just rammed their car," I said. "They'll want money for the damage."

"Rob, rape and kill us!" Stuart caterwauled.

"I'm calling for an SPF destroy-and-rescue team!" Eliot announced, clawing inside his jacket for his comunit.

"It's no use," Bowlan said grimly. "This is the heart of the ghetto. They wouldn't rescue their own mothers down here."

The black factory worker began rapping on the driver's window, and Stuart shrieked, "Security! Counterattack!"

"I'm not going out there," the driver reported. "They'll make me eat my balls."

"Mutiny!" Harvey wailed. "Full-scale mutiny. We're doomed. Do you hear me? Doomed!"

"Jake!" Eliot said breathlessly, turning to me. "You're one of *them*. What should we do?"

"Are you kidding?" Harvey screamed. "He's on *their* side! He'll help them pick our bones!"

"Just relax," I said, switching to a mock-solemn voice. "Let me talk to them. These are my people. I speak their tongue."

They seemed to relax slightly, apparently believing me. I traded places with Eliot and powered down the window a foot.

"Hey!" I said to the two men. "Back here."

They looked at each other, then moved to my window.

"You fucked up my ride," the black said in a growl.

"The driver had a seizure," I said, leaning out to survey the damage. It was minor. "Five hundred ought to fix it."

"Hell," the Slav said. "People driving a big expensive machine like this ought to be able to afford five thousand."

"Hold on," I said, powering up the window. I turned to the huntsmen. "How much cash do you have on hand?"

"We'll pay that scum nothing!" Bowlan railed.

"All right," I said, "but you're going to look awfully funny with your testicles hanging out of your mouth."

"No! No!" Bowlan said, digging out his pouch. The others followed suit, emptying their wallets on the seat.

I picked up the plastic and frowned. "There's only eight hundred and forty credits here."

"No one carries plastic on the Hill," Eliot explained. "Everyone scans."

"Perhaps you have some money?" Stuart said, eyeing me hopefully.

"I don't like you that much," I said, then powered down the window. "I just talked to Marty on the com," I told the factory workers. "He says five hundred is all you get."

"Marty?" the black said. "Who's this Marty?"

"Marty Mateaus. This is a Pleasure Syndicate staff car."

The Slav leaned down to peer at the huntsmen. "They don't look like syndicate staff to me."

"They're not," I said. "They're customers. We give our heaviest users a limo ride every month, as part of a new incentive program. I mean, look at their eyes, for crissakes."

"Squeezers?" the Slav asked, frowning.

"What else?"

"All right," the black said, talking the five bills I handed him. He paused to lean in and frowned disparagingly at the huntsmen. "Goddamn degenerates," he muttered, then returned to his car.

I powered up the window.

"Good show!" Bowlan congratulated. "You sent them off and saved us a bit of plastic in the bargain!" They all slapped me on the back with one hand and reached for the remaining credits with the other. I transferred the plastic to my hip pocket.

"But that's *our* money," Harvey complained.

"No, it's not," I said. "It's my parlay fee."

They whined until traffic started moving, then directed their energy toward exhorting the driver take the quickest possible route back to the Hill.

They hit the wet bar and cigar humidifier when we hit the speedway, and their courage seemed to swell in direct proportion to our proximity to the Hill's security gate. They began a cooperative and creative reconstruction of the traffic mishap, and by the time we reached the HDS parking lot the story was complete. The four huntsmen, waylaid by a diabolical gang by ghetto motorists, turned the tables on their would-be ambushers, bounding out of the stalled cruiser to beat off a whole horde of sex fiends and killer pimps with fists and bottles of Scotch while the bodyguards cringed and bawled for mercy in the front seat. The guards gritted their teeth and groaned with each new perversion of truth but were allowed to keep their jobs as payment for going along with the story.

The huntsmen staggered off to their respective vehicles, laughing drunkenly and congratulating each other's courage and prowess in the face of such incredible odds. Eliot followed me to the Olds, more than a little liquor showing in his walk.

"Your performance today was nothing short of brilliant," he said. "And I would like to take this opportunity to formally recruit you for my team."

"I'm still thinking it over."

"I pay extremely well."

"How well?"

"Five thousand credits per kill."

"That's well. How much does the Iceman get?"

"Nothing now. I have lost contact with him. I believe Burt stole him."

"Burt?"

"He is always coveting other huntsmen's stables. Burt is obsessed with killers, you understand, especially my Iceman."

"Who is the Iceman?"

Eliot laughed. "I don't know, I never met him. I would call a certain place at a certain time, and he would be there to take my message."

"What place?"

"What matter?"

I shrugged. "If I go to work for you, we could use the same system. Tradition is, after all, the cement of history."

"Agreed," he laughed. "I would call table six at the Night Owl Cabaret any weekday except Friday at midnight."

"He was always there?"

"Never stood me up."

"All right," I said. "Let me think it over. What would be my code name?"

"I'll think of something appropriate," he said and we shook hands. "Stay in touch."

I said I would, and he walked to his sports car and roared away. I got into the Olds and sat thinking. Many minutes later, I started up the car and headed home.

19

Ellen sat on the sofa, staring at the ferocious urban warfare booming and flashing from the monitor. A large infantry force with light mortars and shoulder rockets appeared to be conducting an all-out assault on a large fortified building.

"That's SPF Central," I said, dropping a bag of carryout Chinese food on the coffee table, then sitting down beside Ellen. "How long has this been going on?"

"Fifteen minutes or so."

Blurred figures scrambled, fought and died, swarming the smoke-and-fire-hazed silhouette of the SPF's last City stronghold. One of the half-dozen news hounds on the scene described the attackers as "an unholy alliance of Atheist Front militiamen, anarcho-terrorists and syndicate hit men."

The screen split, and an eye-witness interview near the scene alleged explosions had rocked the rooftop landing pad of SPF Central prior to the attack, inviting speculation of saboteurs and explaining the present lack of SPF air support.

"Looks like the local militias finally united to take the SPF completely out of the City," Ellen said.

I shook my head. "None of the attackers are local. SPF Central's in a Muslim sector. Martin's trying to knock the SPF off balance, test their resolve."

"Who's Martin?"

"Leader of the Pleasure Syndicate. Hiram and the SPF are going after him."

"What for?"

"Some nut told Hiram that Cain was working for Martin."

"And he wasn't?"

"No. Here comes the air support."

Rotors and jets from suburban bases filled the skies over SPF Central, but the attacking militiamen were too close to the fortress for the aircraft to be effective from a distance. They had to come in close, and the portable miniguns and SAMs of the attackers took a terrible toll on SPF fliers. After five minutes of heavy losses, the jets and rotors vanished.

The attackers redoubled their efforts, quickly fighting their way to the very walls of SPF central. Breaching charges shook the building, blowing holes through the thick concrete walls, and it appeared the fighting was about to move inside the fortress itself.

"The spifs are doomed," Ellen said with confidence. "They've finally lost the City."

"Don't be too sure. The troopers fell back inside too quickly. Something's up."

As if on cue, the streets and rubble surrounding the fortress suddenly rolled and rumbled with thunderous explosions, swallowing ten square blocks with fire and smoke.

"My God!" Ellen said.

"They must have a dozen Tarantulas up there," I said as one, another, a third, then a fourth news hound blipped out. They resorted to a rooftop view a kilometer from the fighting, the camera zooming in on a swarm of immense SPF transports landing on the yellow grass of

Allah Park, a half kilometer east of the besieged fortress.

"The Tarantulas are providing the covering fire for the transports to land," I explained. "In a moment the SPF will counterattack from Allah Park."

"The troopers will have to fight their way through the Muslims first." She pointed at the screen. "See, here they come."

The news hound zoomed in on a battalion-sized force of Muslim infantry supported by four APCs rushing headlong toward the light tanks and SPF troopers offloading in the park. The hound crowed excitedly about the imminent carnage, then an odd thing happened. Instead of attacking each other, the Muslims and spifs merged into a single force that immediately began marching on the rear of Marty's force.

"They joined up!" Ellen exclaimed.

"Money buys strange bedfellows," I said. "They're going to crush the attackers with a hammer-and-anvil maneuver."

Martin must have reached the same conclusion because his troops abruptly began to fall back, commandeering civilian vehicles, racing to escape the closing trap. SPF aircraft returned in force, mercilessly pounding the retreating invaders.

"Your pal Martin lost," Ellen sighed dejectedly.

"I don't think he expected to win," I replied. "I think he just wanted to test the strength of the Party's loyalty to Pennings. I think there's more cards to be played."

Ellen leaned her head against my arm. "You look tired."

"I am. I'd like to go to sleep for a thousand years."

"Why don't you? Let's both go to bed."

"I have to go somewhere in a little while. You like Chinese food?"

"Is it made from real Chinese?" she laughed, carrying the bag to the kitchen.

"You believe that line?" I asked.

"Not really. Do you?"

"Of course not," I lied.

She came out with a steaming plate of soy noodles. "Aren't you going to have some?"

"Naw. I'm not hungry."

She sat beside me. "What'd you do, kill someone?"

"No," I said defensively. "Why do you say that?"

"You're not hungry. And you're sweating like a squeeze freak."

"Am I?" I said, pulling out a handkerchief to mop my face. "It *is* hot in here."

"No, it's not. What's wrong with your neck?"

"What?"

"You keep rubbing the back of your neck."

"I don't know," I said. "It feels like some bastard is staring at me." I looked behind me. "It's your goddamn father."

"He's finally getting to you, huh? Imagine that thing looking over your shoulder every day of your life for the past thirteen years, silently screaming at you to take back what was his."

"Let's throw it away."

"Are you kidding? He's the only family I have left."

"I'll be your family."

"You?" She laughed. "You're just another orphan." She chewed her noodles. "So, you going to kill somebody tonight?"

"Maybe, maybe," I said, getting up. I moved around a room that suddenly seemed quite alien. "You really don't like my job, do you?"

"I think it stinks."

"Gotta make a living somehow."

"I think there's a lot of better ways to earn a living than murdering people."

"Sure, sure," I said. "I could go kiss Hillsdale ass and hope some debutante marries me."

"I'm down here with you now, aren't I?" she screeched, and I was suddenly wearing a plate of noodles on the front of my jacket. I stared down at them, intrigued by the patterns of noodle and sauce.

"What is *wrong* with you?" she said, walking toward me.

"With me?" I said, moving quickly to put the sofa between us. "What exactly do you mean?"

"You won't stay still," she said, prowling around the sofa.

"Werewolf!" I snapped, and, *yes,* she was taking on definite wolfish features. When she opened her mouth I could see her huge, bone-crushing canines. "I know what *you* want. I knew it all along. I've been waiting for you to make your move, I knew the whole time, you see."

"You're *mad!*" she laughed, but the big panting tongue rolling out of the side her mouth gave away her whole act. "Come on," she said, reaching out with long claws, "let's go to the bedroom."

I screamed and ran for the door. I fumbled badly with the dead bolts, looking over my shoulder to find she had taken on full werewolf form: long, slavering jaw with needle-sharp fangs, long pointed ears and huge yellow eyes glowing with hunger. She cleared the sofa with a great four-legged spring, and I lunged into the hall, slamming the door behind me and scuttling for the stairwell. A long, enraged howl chased me down the stairs, and I didn't stop running until I hit the sidewalk.

I walked quickly toward the Olds parked a block away. I kept my head and eyes down, afraid to look at those around me, afraid of what they might become.

I had ten steps to go when I heard the slow, heavy breathing. I glanced around, then froze in my tracks to gaze with horror at the Olds. The sound seemed to be coming from beneath under the hood, the doors expanding and retracting with each breath. I looked harder and, *yes,* I could see a shadowy, armless form lounging in the passenger seat, a lit cigarette dangling from grinning lips.

Out of the corner of my eye I saw the yellow flash of a cab, and I loped into traffic to head it off. The cabbie applied screeching brakes, and I jumped in the rear seat before he came to a complete halt.

"You wiggy nut!" the swarthy driver yelled back through the grille of the bulletproof shield. "I almost killed you!"

"Fine, fine," I said, trying to reassure him. "I have plenty of money and am a highly respected member of the community. Take me to my destination, and you will be rewarded handsomely, I can assure you of that! Yes, sir, I certainly can!"

"Oh, Great Allah," the cabbie groaned, "another nut. Where we going, nut?"

"The Night Owl and quickly! We must get there before midnight! Must!"

"Or what? You gonna turn into a goddamn pumpkin?"

"Could be! Could be!"

He swung the cab around and we headed west toward Hayward. "Night Owl's that transvestite bar on Hayward, ain't it?"

"Right!" I said, staring at my hands, refusing to look at the cabbie, fearful of his eyes in the rearview.

"This is it, bub," he said.

I looked up, then around. The cab idled in a gravel lot, and a big neon hoot owl winked outside. "Great God, that was fast. What time is it?"

He checked his chrono. "Eleven forty-five. Fare's fourteen-twenty."

Fifteen minutes had disappeared down the sinkhole without my noticing. I threw a twenty in the pass tray, then leaped out. Shoulders hunched, I scurried quickly in the door of the Night Owl.

Except for the brightly lit stage at the end of the room, the Night Owl was entirely lit by gas torches set into plaster walls sculpted and painted to resemble black rock. Dim caves were cut into the walls, each occupied by a rough-hewn table and benches. Atop each table sat a telephone.

Half the patrons looked like tall ugly sisters, the rest appeared to be extras for a gladiator movie. I went to the bar and ordered a triple vodka. I slammed the drink and gritted my teeth. A moment later the Newlife wave seemed to subside a bit and my head broke clear. I slammed another triple to be sure, then moved down the bar, trying to get oriented. Above each cave a crude number was carved into the black plaster. I prowled from cave to cave, keeping a safe distance, afraid of what might leap out. I stopped in front of cave number six and peered into the darkness.

A single creature sat in front of a dozen empty shot glasses, chin in hands, morose and lonely in black rubber jumpsuit and red rubber vest.

"Hello, Beastmaster," I said, sliding in across from him. "That's a swell outfit, but I like you better with the bag over your head."

After a long alcoholic lag, Burt recoiled sluggishly, squinching up his battered face. "What are you doing here?"

"Looking for answers," I said. "I suppose you're doing social research." I leaned forward. "Or are you reminiscing?"

"I don't know what you're talking about," he slurred, arranging the shot glasses into three tidy rows of four.

"This *is* where you and Ian used to hang out, isn't it?" I continued. "You the social scientist, Ian the up-and-coming young serial killer. What a pair you must have made, the fat Hill patron and his greasy little cheap ghetto cutthroat."

"He was an *artist!*" Burt snapped, eyes suddenly intense. "One of the best this filthy City ever saw!"

"Sure," I agreed. "Heck, with a little more time and tutelage, he could have become as good as Cain."

"Better!" he shouted, his face livid, half rising out of the booth. "A few more months and he—" Burt realized his mistake and sat down slowly.

"And he would have been better than Cain," I finished for him, lighting a vitacig. "They are not one and the same, are they? Cain and Ian? You know, it was Ian's confession that threw me off. It sounded too genuine to be fake, and I was right. But Ian wasn't confessing to Cain's crimes, he was confessing to the Iceman's."

Burt said nothing. In the dim light I could see that beneath the bruises and bandages Burt's face was pale and clammy with fear. He was afraid of something, but I didn't think it was me.

"Yeah," I sighed, "it must have burned you up that Ian took the fall for Cain when you knew he wasn't guilty, at least not of Cain's sins. But you had to keep your mouth shut and suck it up. They sacrificed your beloved protégé like a dumb sheep to—"

"Shut up!" he hissed, hunching forward. "Shut your dirty hole!"

"Like a dumb sheep," I continued, "to protect the same bastard you've been protecting since the Cain investigation started. I wonder who they'll sacrifice next? I wonder who knows too much to be allowed to live?"

Burt's jaw trembled, and I could sense levees breaking inside, overcome by a wave of alcohol and rage greater even than his hate for me. A tremor cut through him, he opened his mouth, and I leaned forward catch the name that would roll off his lips and...

A strangling fear tightened around Burt's neck like a noose, shutting his mouth.

"I won't tell you anything," he said between clamped teeth, getting to his feet. "You won't be around much longer, either, I can promise you that."

He staggered away, shoulders hunched, back bent. He wasn't just looking out death's window; he was hanging half-out. I thought about following him out to put the squeeze on him, but I'd learned long ago you couldn't squeeze anything out of a man who already considered himself dead.

I checked my chrono. Two till midnight. I lit a fresh vitacig, and the phone on the table rang.

I picked up the receiver. "Yeah?"

"Hello, sweetness," a male falsetto whispered. "I've had my eye on you since you walked in and—"

"Which table are you calling from?" I asked.

"Why, table twelve, if you must know. I—"

"Call me again and I'll rip your lungs out," I said, and hung up. Seconds trickled by, and I could feel the New-life tide rising again. The room began to crowd in around me, and the temperature seemed to go up a degree with each tick of the clock. Thirty seconds after midnight, the phone rang again.

"Hello!" I barked at the receiver.

"Hello, Iceman," Eliot said. "Are you ready?"

"Yes."

"Burt Swinburne," he said, and the line went dead.

20

The phone rang again. Except now the room was pitch-black and I appeared to be lying down. I searched out the ringing with my hands, then slapped the handset to my head.

"What?" I croaked.

"I knew that letter-spelling crap was a bunch of bullshit," Degas said. "I should have known you'd figure out a way to frame an innocent man to get that fat payoff."

"What are you talking about?"

"Cain's back."

"What? Are you sure?"

"It's trademark. Want a look?"

"Where you at?"

"I'm standing in the rain halfway up the Hill's main road."

"Who'd he get?"

"Your pal Burt. Is that poetic enough for you?"

"I'll be right up."

I hung up and peered around. I lay in bed, Ellen lay behind me. The clock next to the phone said 5:58 a.m., and I tried to remember how I got there.

"Who was that?" Ellen murmured.

"The SPF. Cain killed Burt."

"Cain?" she said, her voice suddenly alert. "Cain's dead."

"Not anymore, he isn't. The bastard had the chance to get off scot-free and he threw it away. He can't give it up. I have to stop him." I started to get up, and Ellen grabbed my arm.

"Why do *you* have to stop him?"

"Because no one else will. Because I have to."

"You have to make a choice," Ellen said, "that's what you have to do."

I swung my legs out of bed and looked back at her. "What's that supposed to mean?"

"I'm saying you have to choose between Cain and me," she said firmly, her eyes dead serious. "I'm sick of it, Jake. I'm sick of it right to my core. I can't stand to sleep with a killer anymore."

"But—"

"Choose, Jake," she snapped. "You have to choose right *now*."

"You're right," I said, reaching for her hand and staring deep into her eyes. "I will quit. I swear I will. I'll give up the whole bogey business once and for all. As soon as I nail Cain."

She pulled her hand free and rolled, putting her back to me. "No, you won't," she said meanly. "You'll never quit. There will always be a Cain for you."

"No, this is different." I turned inward and looked for words. "It's either him or me. It's not something I can ignore, I'm stuck in it, right up to my neck." I got to my feet and it was an effort. "Good God, I'm tired."

"That's what you get for dragging yourself in at 5 a.m."

"Five? I got in at five?"

"You're damn right you did. Crazy drunk and mumbling like a freaking wino."

"Sorry," I said, shuffling to the bathroom, trying to retrace the night's events. I'd left the Owl right after the call; I was sure of that. I vaguely remembered driving around for a while, no place in particular, then Degas woke me up.

I turned on the cold water and splashed my face in the sink, hoping to revive blurred memories. A moment later my face was numb and my brain remained so. I looked at myself in the mirror, and a familiar odor hit me. Copper.

"Screw you," I said to my reflection. "I didn't do anything." I jerked open the cabinet to find the plastic suit draped over the trash bin. I'm getting sloppy, I thought, picking up the suit. The blood was still tacky, and I knew from whose body it came. I tipped the bin, and a bloody ice pick rolled out. I picked it up and looked in the mirror.

"Oh, I suppose I'm the Iceman, too," I said, fear and anger blossoming inside me. "Bullshit. I didn't put these here and I did not come in at 5:00 a.m. I am not Cain. I am not Cain!"

I rushed headlong into the bedroom, carrying ice pick and suit, flushed with rage. I stopped beside the bed and shook Ellen's arm.

"Ellen," I said. "Wake up. We have to talk."

"What now?" she mumbled, her back to me.

I shook her shoulder again, and a dark, mean idea hit me.

"Of course," I whispered, "it's *you!* They *hired* you to live with me. You never thought I was rich. You were a *spy,* you and your big fat secret purse full of evidence.

All this stuff started popping up after *you* moved in! Good Christ, it's so obvious now!''

"What are you raving about?" she said angrily, rolling to face me. Her sleepy eyes immediately widened, flinching from bloody suit to ice pick. "Please don't kill me, Jake," she said, shrinking away.

"No, these aren't mine," I said, throwing down the suit and shaking the ice pick. "*You* planted them. They hired you to plant the doctored Hill pass and the bloody suits and the nails and this ice pick, so I'd think I was Cain and go crazy!"

With a flurry of motion she scrambled across the bed and ran for the door. Moving quickly, I bounced off the bed as if it was a trampoline and tackled her, pinning her to the floor.

"Don't kill me!" she begged. "I won't tell anyone, I swear it!"

"No!" I screamed. "You're not getting me! I'm *not* Cain!" I frowned at the bloody ice pick in my hand, then threw it across the room. "That's not mine!"

She stopped struggling to stare at me, eyes round with raw terror. "Let me go, Jake. Please. I won't tell a soul, I swear I won't."

"Stop it!" I shouted. "Stop pretending I'm Cain and tell me who put you up to this. Who told you to plant…" Out of the corner of my eye I suddenly became aware of her purse, sticking out from under the bed like a great black velvet toad. Her eyes followed mine, and we lunged simultaneously. We grappled for a moment before I succeeded in wrestling it away.

"Give it back!" she screamed, clawing at me.

"Not until I see what secrets are inside," I said, bounding out of her grasp. I smashed the purse's lock against a dresser and dumped its contents in the pool of light spilling from the bathroom, laughing wickedly. I kicked through the huge bounty, searching for nails, suits and bottles of blood among the compacts, makeup and hairbrushes.

I didn't find any. I found pictures, snapshots, dozens of them. I picked up a handful and shuffled through them, expecting to find gory butcher scenes. Instead, I found the kind of snapshots you'd find in an upper-class family album, pictures of mansions and limos and some rich family: a stern old man, a doting wife and a small pouting, black-haired child whose face I knew.

"Are you happy now?" Ellen sobbed, crawling to the scattered photos. She grabbed the purse out of my stilled hands and scooped the pictures up, jamming them back into the purse, tears streaming down her face. "You can never have so little that some bastard won't try and take it from you."

"I'm sorry," I whispered. "I really am." I tried to help pick up the pictures, but she screamed and slapped at my hands.

"Leave me alone!" she cried. "Just leave me alone."

I watched her for a moment, noticing with perfect clarity the curve of her trembling lips, the tears welling in wide-set eyes, the anguish of her brow. Ghosts, I thought, ghosts that will haunt me forever.

I pulled on pants, shirt, boots, packed my gun and left.

I found the small group of flashing SPF cruisers halfway up the Hill, parked on the shoulder of a wide curve about thirty meters uphill from the drive of the nearest estate. I parked behind them and walked to where Degas leaned against his beat-up sedan. He was watching three forensic spooks poking around the grass ten meters down a slight grade from the road. A bandage was wrapped around his head, and his suit was torn and filthy.

"These things don't draw the crowd they used to," I said, stopping next to him.

"We have a sudden manpower shortage," Degas said.

"Yeah, I caught your act on the monitor." I lifted the bottle of vodka hanging in my hand and took a good, long pull.

Degas frowned at the bottle. "What's that for? In case Burt asks you for a drink?"

"This? No, this is just an old friend I picked up on the way." I looked down the slight grade to the trio of spooks, now hunched over the corpse like sullen vultures. "Why am I up here?"

"You're supposed to be trying to catch Cain, remember?"

"Not officially. Hiram fired me."

"That's not what Bowlan told me this morning."

"What?"

"Sure. You don't think it was my bright idea to call you up here, do you?"

"Maybe Bowlan doesn't know Hiram dumped me," I thought out loud. "Pardon me while I go say hi to Burt."

I walked down the grassy slope and joined the spooks. I took a good, long look.

"He's laid out just like Basque," I said.

The cat-eyed blond spook nodded, her eyes flickering disdainfully toward the bottle I was trying to hide behind my leg. "There are a lot of similarities. And a lot of differences. Enough of each to make me suspicious."

I regarded her. "Copycat killing?"

"Maybe," she said. "The severed limbs are arranged just like Basque's, the eyes and tongue removed, the nails are the same make, he's nude, all very Cain-like, but the rest is very *un*-Cain-like. If you remember, Basque's chest cavity was neatly opened and his entrails carefully sorted and displayed. Here the stomach is wildly slashed with a razor and the chest repeatedly stabbed with an ice pick.''

"Ice pick?" I squawked. "He used an ice pick?"

"Yes," she said. "Which brings to mind another serial killer."

"No, it wasn't the Iceman," I said grimly. "The Iceman was Ian and Ian's dead. This is just Cain's way of expressing his knowledge of Burt's connection with Ian."

"Oh," Degas sneered, coming up behind me. "Ian's the Iceman now. What next are you going to pin on the poor dead bastard? The fucking corporate wars?"

"Well, look," I said, pointing at Burt. "Look at the way he's laid out. It's an *I*, just like Basque. He's still spelling Ian's name."

"Don't start that bullshit again," Degas warned.

I turned to the blonde. "How'd Burt get down here? Was he dragged?"

She shook her head. "No. Judging by the tracks, he was led."

I looked up the road. In front of the row of SPF machines was a canary yellow sports car. "That Burt's machine?"

"That's it," she said.

"Has it been moved?"

She shook her head.

I visited the sports car. I walked around it twice. There were no scratches or dents, and it was parked well off the road. I walked up and down the road twenty meters in either direction. There were no recent skid marks. I tried the door handles. Both were locked. I peered in the driver's window. A half-empty bottle of gin lay in the passenger seat, and a keycard stuck out of the ignition slot.

I joined Degas, who was leaning against his car again. "Any hot hunches on this one, bogeyman?" he asked.

"Nothing I didn't already know."

"Like what?"

"Burt knew Cain."

"What proof?"

"He wasn't run off the road. Somebody waved him over, someone he knew. Burt wouldn't stop for a stranger, not in the state he was in."

"That doesn't mean he knew this someone was Cain."

"He locked his keycard in the car. Burt was an order freak, he wouldn't goof like that unless he was frightened out of his head."

Degas's wristcom buzzed, and Bowlan's slurred voice came over, "Chief Bowlan to Inspector Degas! Urgent message! Come in, Inspector Degas!"

Degas touched the com and it went dead. "Drunk as a sot," he said. "I wonder who we can blame for that."

"It's the fine example I set," I said. I started for the Olds, then paused. "By the way, Degas," I called back. "I myself am glad you guys hung on to SPF central."

"Thanks a lot, Strait."

"No problem. I mean, there's a lot worse gangs than the SPF in the City."

"Thanks again."

I nodded and climbed inside. As I drove downhill I entertained no illusions I'd find Ellen curled up on the bed when I got back. I was drunk enough to recognize hope for the conniving little weasel it was and bedded down with grim and certain doom. I understood it was time to invest in a new reality, one without the gilded treachery of romantic love and frivolous bliss.

I threw open the door of my apartment, steeled to shout down the brooding emptiness within, and a tall brunette in a short negligee stepped into my arms. I kissed her as if it was my job, then she helped me out of my jacket and I dropped to the sofa, turning on the monitor.

"What's cooking?" I asked after a short tip from the bottle. "Smells like soy roast."

"It's the real thing," she said, following me to the sofa. "A thousand creds' worth. I thought I'd make tonight special."

"Swell," I said, voicing through the channels. "Who the hell are you, anyway?"

"A friend of a friend," she said, kneeling beside me. She took my hand and pressed it against her cheek, closing her eyes and purring like a cat.

"Tell me who it is so I can thank him."

"Now, now," she murmured, "a girl must have her secrets."

"Oh, I know about that." I glanced around the room. It was bare of anything belonging to Ellen. "Where's Ellen, anyway?"

"Who?"

"You know. The girl who used to live here."

"Oh, her. She left you. She said to tell you bye."

"Just 'bye'?"

"Yes. Let's don't talk about her anymore. Let's talk about me."

"All right. What's your name?"

Her sleepy eyes opened slightly. "My name is whatever you want it to be."

"How about Desiree? A mysterious name for a mysterious girl. Do you like that name? Desiree?"

She repeated the word slowly, sensually. "I love it."

"Good." I turned to the monitor. "Commo mode. Put me through to Taylor's Transpo."

Desiree's eyes opened completely. "What are you doing?"

"Calling you a cab," I said, and the monitor began to buzz.

"What for?" She let go of my hand and unbuckled my belt. "You don't like me? I like you."

"Yeah, but for all the wrong reasons," I said, removing her hands from my zipper.

A lovely, computer-generated image of a blond woman popped on the screen. "Where you at, bub?" the image said, lip-syncing a gruff male voice.

Desiree covered her face with her hands and started weeping. "Please don't throw me out," she sobbed theatrically. "They'll hurt me."

"I ain't got all day," the dispatcher said.

"Disconnect," I told the screen, then turned to Desiree. "Who'll hurt you?"

"I can't tell you."

"Fine," I said, getting up. I spotted her pseudoeelskin overnight bag on the kitchen table. I opened it and turned it over, dumping its contents on the table.

"What are you doing that for?" she asked, suddenly composed, taking my place on the sofa.

"I'm trying to determine your personality," I said, digging through clothes, cosmetics and tubes of exotically flavored body gels. Her negligees outnumbered her street garments by about four to one, making her an indoor person.

"Well, what kind of personality do I have?"

"I don't know," I said. "I was hoping to find rubber suits or a nail gun maybe."

"Oooh, kinky."

I stuffed the snare of clothing back into the bag, then turned to her. "I'm not a millionaire, you know."

Her eyes flickered around the room. "No kidding."

I watched her from the kitchen, trying to think around all the alcohol in my head. She smiled back, fingering the gold necklace around her neck.

"Where'd you get that necklace?" I demanded.

"I found it on the dresser in the bedroom. I didn't think you'd mind."

I crossed the room quickly and jerked the necklace from her throat. "Why are you here?" I barked harshly.

She drew back, startled at my sudden rage. "What's wrong with you?"

"I just want to know why the hell you're here. What do you want?"

Anger jumped in her eyes. "I just want the hundred creds a day they pay me to put up with your kind of shit," she blurted. "That's all I fucking want."

"All right," I said, "that's good, I can understand that." I opened my wallet and handed her a stack of plastic. "Here's five hundred. Go spend the rest of the week with someone you like." I gave her her bag, took her elbow and guided her to the door.

"What am I supposed to tell them?" she asked.

"Tell them I'm tired of brunettes," I said. "Tell them I didn't like your personality."

I locked the door behind her, and the monitor buzzed.

"Hello," I said.

A badly bruised oriental appeared on the screen. "Hello, Mr. Strait," he said through puffy lips. "I am Mr. Hito."

"The tattooist," I said. "What happened to you?"

"I found my inner *ki*."

"Beat the hell out of you, did it?"

"Yes."

I nodded. "I always thought it best to keep that bastard in its cage. You did a tattoo for a Mr. Lindquist six weeks ago."

"I did."

"What was the tattoo of?" I said, expecting him to brace me for credit.

"A name inside a heart."

"What name?"

"Angela."

A chill shuddered through me. "Was Angela the woman who came in with Lindquist?"

"That was my impression."

"Describe her for me."

He did. His description fit Miss Romani to the tee.

"Thanks for the information. Why didn't you brace me?"

"In my culture it is considered good for a person's *ki* to aid a dying man."

"Dying? Who says I'm dying?"

"Your *ki*. Good night, Mr. Strait." He bowed slightly, then blinked out.

I stared at the blank screen for a moment, playing a quick game of mental hopscotch.

Jordan Lindquist, Newlife designer, and Angela Romani, Hiram's mistress, were having an affair behind Hiram's back. The tattoo suggested something more permanent than your casual fling. A dangerous relationship that put in jeopardy not only their hard-won homes on the Hill, but their very lives. Like mice playing in the shadow of an owl, they were a couple willing to take risks, willing to...

"Oh, Jesus," I said, taking out my wallet. I found Eliot's card and read it to the monitor.

"Hello?" Eliot said. His voice was full of sleep, but his image was computer generated and chipper.

"It's Strait," I said.

"Jake!" he said, becoming excited. "Let me be the first to congratulate you. You work extremely quickly, I must say."

"Why did you want Burt Swinburne dead?" I asked.

"Oh, I just thought you'd enjoy killing him. And to get him back for stealing my original Iceman."

"Bullshit," I said. "You wouldn't kill a fellow huntsman for those reasons alone. Who put you up to it?"

His image remained chipper, but his voice became edgy. "Why, no one, Jake, I just thought—"

"It was Hiram," I said matter-of-factly.

"No! No! I, uh, just wanted you to—"

"Burt was a loose cannon, so Hiram told you to have your bushbeater clip him. Did Hiram know I joined your stable?"

"No, I never divulge—"

"That explains it. Who is Hiram's bushbeater?"

"He has three bushbeaters, Jake, why—"

"Just run down the list, I'll tell you when to stop."

"But—"

"Don't make me go up there for you, Eliot," I said, my voice a low growl. "Don't make me visit you tonight."

"Carron, Pullman and Melendez."

"Carlos Melendez?"

"Yes."

I disconnected, sagged onto the sofa, and all the slimy pieces slid into place.

Carlos was Cain and he killed for Hiram. Hiram's Newlife operation started falling apart just two months after the first vials hit the street. The syndicate started cracking down, the Reds were losing their nerve, and, worst of all, Lindquist and Romani decided to black-mail Hiram. How would it look, after all, if a hero of the revolution was caught trying to wipe out a generation of youth? With the whole operation falling apart, Hiram did what any smart businessman would do: he decided to cut his losses and every connection between himself and Newlife—Basque, Lindquist, Romani, the plant work-ers, Janice, whose only crime was being a mouthy drunk, the Reds and finally Burt, the man charged with cover-ing Carlos's tracks. Power crushed things that stood in its way, and the iron wheel had made the full circle.

But there was still one more man to die. Me, the scapegoat. They'd groomed me from the start as the fall guy, with Ellen planting the evidence for the eventual SPF raid that would nail me as Cain. I'd bought time when I'd fingered Ian, but now that Cain was loose again, I was back in line to take the fall.

I raced to the coatrack and retrieved my pocket hand-scanner. I plugged the scanner into the monitor's serial port and told the monitor the SPF's warrant update number. In a matter of seconds the scanner's data chip was updated. I unplugged the scanner, then passed it over my right hand.

"Jacob Wolfgang Strait," it squawked, "nine hun-dred and six counts first-degree murder, one count in-dustrial sabotage, six counts felony trespassing. A-1 death warrant with triple-bonus modifier."

"Yikes!" I said. I put on my jacket, pocketed the scanner and moved quickly to the door. I checked the peephole, then stuck my head into the hall.

"Say hello, Doctor, max volume," I yelled over my shoulder as I slipped into the empty hall. I heard the doctor begin to wail as I locked the door behind me and jogged to the elevator. It was one floor up and coming down.

Could be anyone, I thought, scuttling down the hall to the stairwell. The elevator dinged and opened. I closed the stairwell door behind me to a crack and peeked into the hall.

Twenty-odd SPF commandos bounded out of the elevator, brandishing speed guns and rotor rifles, led by Inspector Degas and the scantily clad Desiree. Without hesitation, they rumbled down the hall to my door, following Desiree's damning finger. She and Degas consulted quietly, then she backed off and Degas ordered the sweating troopers into position. They put their backs to the walls flanking my door, and Degas knocked.

"Strait," he called, drawing his own pistol. "It's me. Degas. I want to talk with you about something."

Oh, I'll bet you do, I thought, and a huge, megaphone barrage of meanness erupted from inside my flat.

"Mount the fucking rowing apparatus, you weak-willed pansy son of a bitch!" the doctor roared. "Move, goddamn it, or I'll crush your simpering soul like a handful of squirming, fat maggots!"

The troopers flinched back, and a speed gun went off, chopping up the ceiling with a wild 10-round burst. Degas paused to tip plaster chips off his hat and glare at the red-faced trooper, then spoke again. "C'mon, Jake," he said in a reasonable voice. "I just want to talk with you for a minute."

"Talk? *Talk?* You candy-ass bastard! I'll have you crawling on your goddamn *knees* before I'm through with you! Get on the goddamn lat pull, or I'll croak you! Move, goddamn it, *move!*"

"Endline!" the trigger-happy trooper wailed. "Let's blow a hole in the door and shove grenades in. It's the only thing that kind of monster understands."

With that note I let the door close quietly and began creeping down the stairs. Let the doctor deal with them, I thought. I never liked that rude bastard anyway.

I turned right on the sidewalk and immediately spotted the unmarked spif cruiser parked behind the Olds. I kept my face to the sidewalk and bopped by like a frantic junkie looking for a connection. When I was two blocks from Carlos's office building I cut right and then left onto the back alley that ran between Hayward and Marshall. I went up the fire escape quietly, stopping to peer in Carlos's rear window.

Carlos sat at his desk, staring at the monitor, appearing mesmerized. I rapped on the window and he leaped up, eyes and pistol interrogating every corner. I rapped again, ducking low, and Carlos shot a hole in the window.

"It's Jake!" I shouted. After a moment the window opened and Carlos stuck his head out.

"Sorry about that," he said as I crawled in. "I thought my goddamn reflection had finally come to get me. Why the back-door routine?"

"I dumbly thought it was your silent partner that would take the shot at me."

"Yeah, I heard about that," he sighed, closing the window and returning to the desk. I waited until he put the pistol down, then crept toward the center of the room.

"What did you hear?" I asked.

"Degas called twenty minutes ago. He said to watch out for you, that you'd gone amok, completely endline." Carlos smiled. "He said you were Cain."

"Why'd you let me in, then?"

Carlos laughed. "We're *all* Cain, Jake. You know that."

"Yes, that's right," I said, turning to the fridge humming in the corner. "May I have a beer?"

"Help yourself."

I walked to the fridge, palming the pocket scanner on the way. I opened the door, and the smell of putrid flesh hit my nostrils. There were now five hands on the rack. Thumbing down the volume, I crouched and reached in with the scanner, passing it over each hand.

"Angela Carmen Romani," it whispered. "Donald Hartford Basque. Jordan Andrew Lindquist. Janice Jillian Pennings. Burton Raoul Swinburne."

I straightened up and returned the scanner to my jacket pocket. I closed the fridge and drew my gyrapistol.

"What's that for?" Carlos said when I stopped in front of the desk.

"The gig is up," I said.

Carlos smiled. "Which gig is that?"

"You know which gig. I like you, Carlos, but I'm not taking the rap for your ugly crimes. You're going to tell them the truth. You're going to tell them I'm not Cain."

"I told you, Jake. We're *all* Cain."

"Yeah, but some more than others, right?" I took out my handkerchief and mopped my face. I felt a spell coming on, the first rolling waves of insanity, each stronger than the last.

"Now, Carlos," I said, gritting my teeth to stay afloat, "you have to call Degas right now...and tell him...I am *not* Cain.... I'll stall them as long as you can...I'll give you a head start."

Carlos began to laugh. He got up and laughed his way to the window. "Head start? What, so I can go hide down *there?*" He turned to laugh, and with a start I realized that, no doubt about it, Carlos had in fact been the devil all along. Glistening white fangs sprouted in his wide, laughing mouth, horns jutted out of his forehead, and yellow slits split his pupils. "I'm not going down there," he said, his voice deep and timorous. "It's not safe. Not even for *me*. Now," he said, leaning back against the sill, "where's my goddamn money!"

I flailed back shrieking and I heard a shot and a body hitting the floor as the last terrible wave struck, knocking me screaming into the abyss.

21

I surfaced standing in the middle of the room, swaying forward and back, gyrapistol in hand, staring with mounting horror at Carlos, who lay on the floor next to the tripod, bleeding from a terrible stomach wound.

I broke through the paralysis and stumbled forward, crouching beside him. "Jesus Christ, Carlos, who did it?"

"You did!" he croaked painfully. "You goddamn gut-shot me, you dirty bastard!"

"I did?"

"You see anyone else in the room?"

I holstered the gyra and took off my jacket, bunching it into a ball. "Press this against the wound," I said, pushing the ball against the gushing hole.

"Ah, screw it, Jake, it's all over for me, I'm a goner. Jesus, what a carnival ride this life has been, all blur and nausea."

"Quit talking like that," I said. Carlos took the ball, and I grabbed the phone, dialing quickly. "Just hang on, buddy. I'll get an ambulance."

"Don't let the reclamation vultures get me, Jake, promise me that. I don't want to end up as a case of protein paddies. Take me out into the country. Lay me down in the deep rich soil and plant roses over my head. You gotta promise me."

"Shut the hell up. You're not going to die."

"Emergency assistance," an androgynous voice at the other end of the line said.

"I need an ambulance at 1902 Hayward at once."

"I'm sorry, sir, but the Party hospital does not operate an ambulance service in that sector."

"What? Who does?"

"There are several independent firms that sometimes—"

"Put me through to one of them."

"Which one would you like, sir?"

"Anyone goddamn one you like."

"I'm sorry, sir, but Party policy forbids my recommend—"

"Jesus! Give me the one that starts with an *S,* then!"

After a hellish pause, the voice said, "I'm sorry, sir, but none of them start—"

"*T!*"

"Thank you, sir." There was a click, then a buzz.

"Trueblue Ambulance and Organ Salvage," a listless voice said.

"I need an ambulance for 1902 Hayward, Suite 32. A man with a gunshot wound in the stomach."

"He got insurance?"

I covered the mouthpiece. "Carlos, you got insurance?"

"Oh, hell no."

"Yes, he does," I said into the phone.

"What's his number?"

"I don't know, he's unconscious for crissakes."

"No number, no pickup."

"I'll pay you when get here."

There was a brief silence. "How much?"

I looked in my wallet. I had twelve credits. "Twelve hundred credits," I said.

There was a brief discussion on the other end. "Okay, but if he croaks, we get his organs."

"You sure that won't affect your level of care?"

"I resent that insinuation. You want pickup or not?"

"All right, goddamn it. How long?"

"Fifteen minutes. We don't touch him till you give us the credit."

"You'll get it, all right." I hung up, then looked to Carlos. "Ellen was part of the plot," I said.

"Yeah," Carlos said. "I warned you about her."

"Yes, you did," I said. "What'd she get out of it?"

"A place in Valley View when she finished the job."

"I should have guessed." I hunkered down beside Carlos. Blood was beginning to pool under his back, and his color was leaning toward pallid. "You have to hold the ball tighter against the wound," I told him.

"I am," he said. "It's coming out my back, I can feel it."

I reached around his back, and Carlos flinched when I touched the exit wound. I pulled a sheet off the cot, balled it up and shoved it tight under his back. I drew the gyrapistol and sniffed the barrel. It smelled of propellant, but it wasn't fresh.

"I didn't do it," I said hopefully. "A gyrajet would've blown your spine out your back. A bullet made that wound." My eyes went to the open window. "A sniper! A sniper got you!"

"Sure, whatever you say, Jake. Hey, you know what? I think you got that bastard."

"Got who?"

"The maggot in my belly." He shifted a little. "Yes, I can feel it, it's dying, you cut it right in half. You croaked the bastard."

"I didn't shoot you *or* the maggot," I stated, duck-walking to the window and peered out. Considering the downward angle between entrance and exit wounds, the shot would have to come from the roof of the opposite four-story building. I scanned the roof, but it was too dark to make out anything.

"I'll be right back," I told Carlos as I rushed to the door.

"I'm not going anywhere," Carlos said. "Jake?"

I stopped half out the door. "Yeah?"

"I don't care if you shot me. Even in the gut. I know you have your reasons."

"I didn't do it!"

"I'm just saying if you did, I don't hold it against you."

"Thanks, pal," I said, then started down the hall. I leaped down the stairs and sprinted out the lobby door to collide with a gang of winos. They clawed and howled, but I fought my way through them, shoving, cuffing and cursing. I dodged through Hayward's heavy traffic, waving my pistol like a stop sign, reached the opposite sidewalk and remembered something.

The sweat on my back chilled, and I crouched as I spun around. A few of the winos shook their fists at me, but most seemed more interested in the front door of Carlos's building. They stood with an expectant air, tilting their heads upward every few seconds. My eyes moved up three stories, to the mechanical silhouette in the window.

How forgetful of me, I thought, dropping to the sidewalk as high-velocity bullets cut the air above me, chipping at the wall behind me like a jackhammer. I somersaulted into the front wheel of a parked envirocar, and the sniper machine went to work on it, shattering the glass bubble and showering me with fragments. The envirocar's alcohol tank exploded, igniting my back. A door behind me opened and I charged across the sidewalk, knocking down a curious patron and diving inside what appeared to be a bar. Customers screamed and bullets pounded the door behind me as I rolled across the carpet, extinguishing the flames devouring my shirt. I got up and took account of myself. The alcohol fire had singed the back of my mohawk to the skull, ate up most of my shirt and peeled several layers of skin off my back. I eased off the shoulder holster and scorched rag, realizing the gyrapistol was nowhere on my person.

I went to the window and peeked outside. The gyra lay on the sidewalk next to the burning envirocar. I crouched a little and above the booing winos I could see the sniper machine in the window, shifting back and forth patiently.

A reclamation van pulled up beside the envirocar, and two crewmen got out with a stretcher. They peered around the burning vehicle, then crossed the street. They went into Carlos's office building the same instant a flashing ambulance skimmer landed on the roof. I waited, hope against hope, and two minutes later the rec boys came out. They carried the stretcher between them, and it was not empty.

I leaned against the wall and thought hard. Carlos's silent partner had not only shot him, but had also called the reclamation boys to haul him away. Someone had put a death warrant on Carlos, and I had an idea who.

But it didn't make any sense. Why would Hiram go through all the trouble of covering up for Carlos, protecting him at every turn, only to put a death warrant on him when things were wrapping up? Hiram had even put Chris up to providing alibis for Carlos . . . and then it hit me.

"Uglier and uglier," I murmured at the departing reclamation van. I turned around to find that five minutes after my spectacular entrance, I was still the center of attention. I started for the bar.

"No shirt, no service!" the bartender blurted. I nodded, jumped the bar, cut through a storage room, then went out the back door. I walked the alley to Paradise Boulevard, made a call from a combooth, then caught a cab.

22

Half an hour later I stood on the roof of the Hellfire Club. My hand was cut from climbing in a ground-floor window, my skin was caked with river muck, and my insides were numb, right to the core. I stared up at the pristine and pure stars shining through the rain and mist and waited.

One of the stars moved closer until it became a humming skimmer. It set down not far from me, its wash chilling my bare skin. The engine died, and the lone occupant stepped out.

"I know why you called me here," Chris said as he walked toward me, smiling.

"Do you?" I said.

"Uh-huh," he said, stopping three meters away, his eyes searching my body for weapons, his hands jammed deep in the pockets of his heavy jacket. "You're going to tell me who Cain is."

"Am I?" I said.

"Yes," he said, walking around me to the edge of the roof. He stared at the lights of the City as I stared at his face, a face smiling and innocent in the moonlight, then leering and demonic in flashes of neon red. "You're going to tell me Cain's right here on this roof."

"Is that right?" I said, slowly shifting back from the edge.

"Oh, come on!" Chris laughed. "Don't be ashamed! You were brilliant! You didn't do anything wrong, you just moved your bogeyman act to a better part of town."

"Did I?"

"Don't think I'm condemning you, Jake," he soothed. "They were all whores and pushers and perverts and blackmailers, protected from justice by money and status. They all deserved what they got."

"Me?" I said. "I'm Cain?"

"Of course! You probably won't believe this, but I kind of knew from the moment I met you. I just had this feeling."

"It's all so blurry," I said, taking another step back. "I can't remember much." I screwed up my face. "I guess I'm in big trouble, huh?"

"Not if I can help it, brother. You saved my skin once, and a Pennings never forgets a debt. We'll get in the skimmer and go up and see Dad. We'll put it all on Carlos. We'll change your face and hide you somewhere—we have property all over the world. You can start a new life as a wealthy man in a protected community."

He held out a brotherly hand the same instant he took a smooth sidestep away from the edge, foiling my plan of shoving him off the roof. "I'll take care of you, Jake," he said. "C'mon, brother, let's shake on it."

I looked at the offered hand, then the other hand in the pocket of his jacket. "You mean like the way you took care of Liam?"

His eyes clouded over, but he held on to the smile. "What?" he whispered.

"The way you took care of your brother, Liam," I repeated. "The way you let him overdose. Hiram told you to watch over Liam and you failed. You murdered your own brother."

The smile began to twitch. "No, you don't understand," he said in a reasonable voice. "You see, it wasn't my fault. Liam was out of control, he killed himself."

"No," I said, shaking my head. "*You* killed him. You and the City. Hiram punished the City with Newlife and punished you by making you clean up the mess when the Newlife plot began to unravel. Carlos showed you how, and you went out and did it. You even brought their hands back to Carlos as proof of your fine work, the star pupil bringing his teacher rotten apples."

He shook his head slowly. "I don't know what you're talking about."

"Sure you do. You figured the only way Hiram would ever love you as much as Liam was if you got rid of all the thorns in his side. That's why you couldn't stop killing, even after Ian took the rap. Hiram told you to stop, but he didn't understand what you were doing, that you couldn't make up for murdering Liam until you *became* Liam. That's what you were spelling out. 'I am Liam.'" I laughed cruelly. "And you even screwed that up. The maid surprised you at Lindquist's, and the *M* came out as an *N*."

His eyes glazed over and his jaw hung dumbly, and I could see that nothing I said was getting through. "I didn't kill my brother," he whispered, and a gun came out of his pocket. A small .25 revolver. "Say it wasn't my fault," he said, "Say I didn't kill him."

I stared at the pistol. "All right, Chris. You didn't kill him."

"You're darn right, I didn't. I—"

I dived at his legs, hitting him just below the knees and knocking him over. The gun went off once as we rolled across the rooftop. I scratched and clawed blindly for the revolver as we rolled, finding the barrel with my right hand. I rolled on top and hooked him twice in the jaw, and he groaned and let go of the pistol. I got up and he followed a moment later.

"Tell me you killed them," I said, pointing the pistol at his chest.

He rubbed his jaw and stared at the gun. "Killed who?"

"Them. Basque, Romani, Lindquist, your mother, Swinburne."

"Who told you that? My father?"

"Yes," I said, lying.

"Well, he's wrong. I told him I didn't do it, but he just couldn't believe me." His insane eyes went to mine. "You. You killed Liam. You killed them. You're Cain. It's always been you. You've been killing your brother all your life."

"There's only one thing wrong with that story," I said.

He frowned. "What's that?"

"I'm holding the gun." I shot him once, twice, again, then again, each bullet thunking into his chest and driving him back to the edge of the roof. Four bullets in him, and he was still able to stand up and speak.

"Where's thy brother, Cain?" he whispered.

"I'm an only child," I said, putting the last bullet in his head. He threw up his arms as if he were going to flap off, then tumbled over the parapet.

I walked to the edge and looked down at his body, not far from where Ian had hit. I dropped the empty pistol after him and walked to the skimmer.

23

Baily answered the door. "Come in, Mr. Strait," he said.

I stepped inside, and he shut the door behind me. When he turned around he had a machine pistol in his hand and an embarrassed look on his face.

"A relic from your raider days?" I asked.

He bowed apologetically. "I am afraid times have changed, sir. Mr. Pennings is waiting for you in the study."

"You ever work with explosives?" I asked as I led Baily down now-familiar halls.

"It was my field of experience while serving as a raider, sir."

"You do fine work."

"Thank you, sir."

We arrived at the study door. I waited for Baily to open it, but the gun seemed to have removed a measure of his courtesy. I opened the door, and he followed me in.

Hiram sat in the same chair under the same lamp, wearing the same tone of suit. Yet the room seemed colder, gloomier. When I stopped in front of him, I noted he appeared haggard, defeated.

"You killed Christopher," he said.

"Yes."

"I was afraid it was he doing those terrible things." He shook his head at the floor angrily. "I tried to save the boy, I told him to stop, but he wouldn't listen to me." He suddenly choked up and began weeping, head bent to his lap. "It's my fault. I paid you to kill Cain, and that's what you did."

"Knock off the act," I said. "You knew Chris was Cain all along."

He looked up suddenly. "No! The bushbeaters were supposed to kill them, not Christopher!"

"You admit your guilt, then."

Hiram sighed and the grief fell off his face like a slipped mask. "Does it really matter, Mr. Strait? The SPF will not move against me. It is not a matter of guilt or innocence, right or wrong. It's about power. I have enormous power, and you have none. In fact, how do you know Mr. Baily is not at this very moment standing behind you, about to shoot you dead?"

"I don't know that at all," I said, going to the bar. I selected a crystal decanter, sniffed its top and smelled vodka. I splashed two fingers into a glass and swallowed it. "Do you remember what I said about power, Hiram?"

He sighed and smiled then, like a tired traveler catching sight of a long-awaited train. "Yes," he whispered, "I do."

"Good," I said, putting down the glass and picking up the crystal decanter. I took three quick steps, swung the decanter in a high overhead arc and brought it down on Hiram's head. His skull cracked like an egg, and Hiram rolled out his chair, dead. I stood still for a moment, waiting for the shot from the shadows, the bullet that would knock me dead to the floor. When none came, I dropped the bloody decanter beside Hiram and walked to the door.

"Mr. Strait."

I let go of the doorknob and turned around. Baily stood in front of me, machine pistol pointed at my stomach.

"You're a little late," I said, completely indifferent.

After a moment his eyes softened, and the gun dropped to his side. "Yes, it would appear so."

"You could have shot me before I hit him," I said.

"Mr. Pennings told me not to interfere, no matter what happened. And to report his death as an accident."

"He said that before I came here?"

"Yes."

"That was very polite of him."

Baily bowed his head, and I noticed his shoulders were shaking, that he was crying. "Mr. Pennings was a very polite man."

I remained at the door for a moment, feeling bad for the man in front of me. "What's next for you, Baily?" I asked.

"I believe that, as Mr. Pennings, I am about to reach the end of my line." He took the knob and opened the door. "Goodbye, Mr. Strait."

"Goodbye, Mr. Baily," I said, and left him there, a small, bowed man alone in a very large room.

EPILOGUE

"What are you doing here?" Ellen asked, opening the door of her apartment.

"My place is a little hot," I said, slipping past her. "What are you doing here?"

She closed the door. "I live here, remember?"

"I heard you moved up to the Hill."

"I found out I couldn't afford the rent. I thought you'd be dead by now."

"So did I." I turned to face her. "I found out I had one more reason to live than to die."

"And what's that?"

"I'm looking at it."

She lowered her eyes and moved close to me. "You just came from the Hill."

"Yes."

"You killed Hiram."

"Yes. He was endline. He wanted to die."

She nodded at the floor. "And Chris?"

"Yes."

She lifted her head, smiled, then kissed me on the lips. "Good," she said, moving to the fireplace.

I sat on the Queen Anne sofa. "Your father's in the fireplace," I observed.

"Yes, I'm finally going to cremate him." She struck a match, smiled back at me, then lit the pyre of ripped-up photographs beneath the portrait. She watched the flames grow for a moment, then joined me on the sofa.

"Gave up on getting it all back?" I asked.

"You got it back for me," she sighed, laying her head in my lap.

We watched the flames for a moment, and a creeping sensation began traveling up my spine. "Hiram killed your father," I said.

"His raiders did," she murmured. "I was in the boardroom when they did it. They were going to kill me, too, but the leader intervened."

"Baily."

"Yes." The flames moved up the painting until the angry eyes were consumed by blue flame. "You can rest easy now, Dad."

"What's your last name, Ellen?"

"Carron." She turned her head slightly and caught me staring at her. "Relax, Jake," she said with a lovely smile. "Cain's gone now. I promise."

I nodded and we stared back into the dying flames. "I guess Carlos was right," I said.

"How's that?" she murmured.

"There's a little twist of Cain in us all."

TAKE 'EM FREE
4 action-packed novels plus a mystery bonus
NO RISK
NO OBLIGATION TO BUY

Don't miss out on the action in these titles featuring
THE EXECUTIONER, ABLE TEAM and PHOENIX FORCE!

The Freedom Trilogy

Features Mack Bolan along with ABLE TEAM and
PHOENIX FORCE as they face off against a communist
dictator who is trying to gain control of the troubled
Baltic State and whose ultimate goal is world supremacy.

The Executioner #61174	BATTLE PLAN	$3.50	☐
The Executioner #61175	BATTLE GROUND	$3.50	☐
SuperBolan #61432	BATTLE FORCE	$4.99	☐

The Executioner ®

With nonstop action, Mack Bolan represents ultimate
justice, within or beyond the law.

#61178	BLACK HAND	$3.50	☐
#61179	WAR HAMMER	$3.50	☐

(limited quantities available on certain titles)

TOTAL AMOUNT	$
POSTAGE & HANDLING	$
($1.00 for one book, 50¢ for each additional)	
APPLICABLE TAXES*	$ _____
TOTAL PAYABLE	$ _____
(check or money order—please do not send cash)	

To order, complete this form and send it, along with a check or money order for the
total above, payable to Gold Eagle Books, to: **In the U.S.:** 3010 Walden Avenue,
P.O. Box 9077, Buffalo, NY 14269-9077; **In Canada:** P.O. Box 636, Fort Erie, Ontario,
L2A 5X3.

Name: _____
Address: _____ City: _____
State/Prov.: _____ Zip/Postal Code: _____

*New York residents remit applicable sales taxes.
 Canadian residents remit applicable GST and provincial taxes.

GEBACK5

Don't miss out on the action in these titles featuring
THE EXECUTIONER, ABLE TEAM and PHOENIX FORCE!